# Do Not Disturb

CLAIRE DOUGLAS

PENGUIN BOOKS

PENGUIN BOOKS

UK | USA | Canada | Ireland | Australia
India | New Zealand | South Africa

Penguin Books is part of the Penguin Random House group of companies
whose addresses can be found at global.penguinrandomhouse.com

First published 2018
001

Set in 12.5/14.75 pt Garamond MT Std
Typeset by Jouve (UK), Milton Keynes
Printed and bound in Great Britain by Clays Ltd, Elcograf S.p.A.

A CIP catalogue record for this book is available from the British Library

ISBN: 978-0-718-18790-3

www.greenpenguin.co.uk

'Oh, What a tangled web we weave
When first we practise to deceive!'

Sir Walter Scott

# Wednesday, 25 October 2017

I'm awoken by a shrill scream. *Something's happened to the girls.* I sit up in bed, my heart racing. The air is still. Silent. Did I dream it? My eyes dart to Adrian's side of the bed. It's empty, the sheet creased and slightly damp, the duvet thrown back as though he left in a hurry. Where is he? My alarm clock shows 5.37 a.m. and, through a crack in the curtains, the sky is still dark, the tips of the mountains disappearing into early-morning mist.

I fumble for my dressing-gown, which I'd thrown across the foot of the bed the night before. I pull it on as I hurry from the room. Across the landing, the door to the girls' room is closed. I'm just about to go to it when I hear the scream again.

There's no mistaking it this time. It sounds like my mother.

I race down the first flight of stairs, trying to quell my rising panic. My mother isn't the type of woman to scream. I think about the guests ensconced in their rooms, knowing she must have woken them, too, and, despite the circumstances, I worry about upsetting them.

When I reach the top of the second flight I stop in my tracks. I blink, hoping my eyes are playing tricks on me, but the image remains. The hallway below is shrouded in darkness but it looks as though Mum is crouched over a body, its limbs spread-eagled on the refurbished Victorian tiles. I can see the flash of a pale calf, a slim wrist. I can hear Mum groaning.

It doesn't look like a child. The legs are too long.

*It's not one of the girls. Thank God.*

'Mum?'

Her head shoots up at the sound of my voice, her eyes wide with anguish and something else – fear. She holds up her hands, as though she's about to pray. They're coated with blood.

# PART ONE
# Before

# I

*August 2017 – two months before*

The girls are unusually quiet in the back seat. From the rear-view mirror I see them gazing out of the window as the scenery unfolds before them: the built-up suburbs with graffiti-stained high-rises and cluttered roads transforming into rolling hills, valleys and mountains. Amelia's expression is morose, as though she's harbouring thoughts of murdering both me and her father for taking her away from her friends. Evie, on the other hand, is more serene, dreamy as she takes in the road signs in English and Welsh. My six-year-old has always had a vivid imagination. She'll see this as an adventure, try to seek out the magic in it. She believes in fairies, Father Christmas and the Easter bunny. She sees animal shapes in the clouds, four-leaf clovers that aren't there, a face in the moon.

Amelia, five years older, is more sceptical. Her sensitivity announces itself in different ways. As soon as you enter a room she'll feel your mood and behave accordingly. At least, she used to. Not so much now that the hormones have kicked in. She's no longer so eager to please. Adrian and I have tried to hide how badly the last eighteen months have affected us, but she's more astute than Evie. She won't have failed to notice the strain we've been under. But, even so, she can't really understand why we've decided to leave London. There have been occasions, in the preceding weeks, when I've had the same thought.

We hadn't planned to move back to Wales. Not yet, anyhow. Buying a guesthouse in the Brecon Beacons had been a long-held ambition of mine. Something to daydream about while I toiled at my dead-end job in marketing, or when I was on maternity leave, surrounded by nappies and wet wipes. The Brecons held fond memories for me, of picnics in the foothills, of family days out, my brother, Nathan, and I bickering in the car, our dad barking at us good-naturedly. Of home-made egg sandwiches and milky tea from a flask. Of Frisbees. Of those hills and mountains that seemed to go on for ever. When I was a kid they always reminded me of the drawings in the *Mr Men* books, they were so perfect – they seemed worlds away from where we lived in Cardiff.

Moving to Wales and running a guesthouse was something we imagined we'd do in the future, when both girls were at university, when we were in our late forties or early fifties and had had enough of our cramped terraced house and frantic city living. Then, suddenly, the idea of fresh air and peace became more appealing, more urgent. A gentler pace of life, a quiet spot for Adrian to write – which he's always wanted to do – and a safe haven for the girls, away from all the distractions and temptations of London.

In the distance I can see the glint of sunshine beneath the clouds, beckoning us. I reach over and squeeze Adrian's hand. He returns the gesture and I flick a glance in his direction. He looks happy and relaxed. He's grown a beard and his hair is longer, now touching the collar of his blue polo shirt. There is nothing left of his City persona. He shed the smart suits and the clean-shaven look as soon as he walked out of his job. But there are other changes too. The old Adrian would be trying to coax excitement out of Amelia right now. He'd be fiddling with the radio and singing along to Absolute 90s or playing I Spy with Evie, rolling his eyes when she pretended to spot a unicorn or a pixie. Instead he's staring at the road ahead, the radio switched off. He's calm and content in his own way. Just . . . *different*.

But at least he's here.

I want him to reassure me that we've made the right decision in leaving. That Amelia won't hate me for ever. That it will all turn out for the best.

Anxiety curdles in the pit of my stomach. In all my fantasies of running a business in the place I love the most, I never envisaged I'd have to do it with my mother.

'Kirsty?' I'm jolted out of my thoughts by Adrian's voice. 'When is Carol expected to turn up?' It's as though he's read my mind. We used to joke about that. *Before.* How we always seemed to know what the other was thinking.

'Um, next month, I think.' I change gear as we head into the national park, the SUV juddering over the cattle grid. I notice Evie sit up straighter, and I know she's hoping to see wild ponies clustered at the side of the road, as we did the last time we visited.

'Next month?' he says incredulously.

'She said something about waiting until the house is more habitable.'

'So, not until the renovations are done, then.' He's laughing as he says it, to take the sting out of his words.

'She did up plenty of houses with my dad before he died.'

'Yeah. Over twenty years ago.'

'Her DIY is a lot better than mine.' I'm nettled that he's so easily putting her down. I'm allowed to say what I want about her, but he isn't. Despite her faults my mother is one of the most capable, practical people I know.

'Great. Then what's she waiting for?' He laughs. 'Tell her to get here pronto! We'll need all the help we can get.'

*Hasn't she done enough?* I want to ask, but I don't. I'm trying not to feel resentful that we were forced to eat into our savings after Adrian left his job. It wasn't his fault. And it was kind of Mum to agree to come in with us. Her money means we could buy the house and carry out the restoration. Going into business with her wouldn't have been my first choice, but now we have, we must make it work.

*

8

We first saw the Old Rectory six months ago.

We'd been on a family holiday in Brecon, driving through those mountains I had so admired as a child. Adrian was shrivelled up in the passenger seat, still shell-shocked from all that had happened, as if he were a war veteran or disaster survivor. We were still tentative with each other, like lovers who had been apart for many years and were getting to know each other again. The mist was like dry ice, nudging the hills and draping itself over the mountains in the distance. The land was spread out in front of us in varying shades of green, our road zigzagging through it. There wasn't another soul for miles.

It was when we were on the edge of a little village called Hywelphilly that we saw it: a double-fronted Victorian detached house, almost Gothic, with its pointed roof gables and arched windows. Set back from the road, next to a beautiful old church, and framed by mountains in the distance, it had a 'For Sale' sign propped up in the driveway. The tiles were falling off the roof, the paint was flaking and some windows were boarded up, but I could see the beauty in it even then. With a bit of TLC it could be magnificent, I thought.

I pulled on to the kerb, blocking the driveway with its rusty iron gates, to get a better look. Weeds protruded through the cracked tarmac and a large oak almost obscured one of the windows. Adrian must have been thinking along similar lines because when

9

he turned to me, his eyes were bright. For the first time in ages he looked excited.

We arranged a viewing for the next day, and as the four of us followed the estate agent through the crumbling, neglected house, the anticipation hummed between us.

'It's a bit creepy,' Evie said, as we stood on the threadbare landing carpet. She stared up at the ceiling as if expecting a ghoul to descend from the attic.

'And it has a weird smell,' offered Amelia.

But I was convinced it was what we needed. A project. A change of direction for Adrian. A distraction. For all of us.

Now we stand in the front driveway and look up at the house, horror dawning. It's going to need a lot more work than I remember. Not for the first time the weight of what we've undertaken threatens to crush me.

'Are we really going to be living in that?' Amelia asks, wrinkling her nose as she surveys the holes in the roof, the boarded-up windows, the ivy that spreads up the walls, like unruly facial hair. The builders have already begun on the roof and scaffolding has been erected, although there's no sign of any workers.

'Not yet,' I assure her. 'We're going to be staying in the flat we've rented at the other end of the village. Remember?'

'Great,' she mutters, folding her arms across her skinny chest. 'Cramped in some dumb flat for the summer.'

'It'll be fun,' pipes up Evie. 'We get to share a room.'

'And the thrills keep coming,' Amelia deadpans.

I ignore her cheek, deciding to cut her some slack today of all days. Instead I enthuse about the huge garden, reminding Amelia that I'd agreed to buy them a trampoline – they've been pestering me about one for the last year but there wasn't the space at our old house. 'And we can get those rabbits you've always wanted, Evie,' I promise. She jumps up and down with glee.

Adrian throws an arm around me. Although it's August, there's a chill in the air and I move closer to him, glad of the embrace. Before it happened, Adrian was very affectionate. I secretly thought – somewhat guiltily – too much so. Always wanting to hold my hand, touch the back of my head, or my knee when I was driving. I used to feel embarrassed in front of the girls or our friends if he nuzzled the side of my neck when I was cooking. I'd come from an undemonstrative family – the most I ever got from my mother was a perfunctory kiss on the cheek. And then the touching had stopped and I missed it. Now I reach around his waist and pull him closer to me, resting my head on his shoulder.

'I'm never going to get used to the pronunciation of this place.' Adrian laughs.

'What – "the Old Rectory"?' scoffs Amelia.

'Don't be facetious. You know what your dad means,' I say.

'Stupid Welsh words,' mumbles Amelia, prodding the ground with the toe of her lilac Supagas.

'It's easy – Hywelphilly. Pronounced *Howell Filly*,' I say, rolling the Ls, liking the way the language feels in my mouth. When we first met, Adrian delighted in my accent. He'd make me pronounce long Welsh words over and over again, and stared at me in awe as I said them with ease. He'd try to copy but they sounded like bizarre tongue-twisters coming from his lips.

'Can you speak Welsh, Mummy?' asks Evie, looking at me with her wide blue eyes.

'Of course.'

'Will we learn to speak Welsh?' Evie asks. 'I want to talk like you.'

Amelia looks as though she can't think of anything worse.

I move away from Adrian and cuddle Evie, kissing her soft blonde hair. She looks kooky in her clashing colours: a red-and-yellow-spotted tunic with pink leggings and green frog wellies. Over her head I notice that Amelia moves away before I can coax her into a group hug.

'Come on, then,' says Adrian, heading back to the car. 'We'd better get the keys for the flat.'

We troop behind him, my gaze following Amelia. Her head is bent and her arms are folded around herself. She's shivering slightly in her thin hoody. I want to grab her and hold her close, reassure her that everything will be okay, that I love her. But she gets into the car before I can catch up with her. She'll cheer up once she gets used to living here.

We drive through the village in silence, each of us taking in the ornate arched bridge, the hills and mountains of the Brecons in the distance, the green parks and fields of sheep, the cobbled high street with its shops, and the only pub, the Seven Stars, which overlooks the River Usk.

Although I've never lived here before, I feel as if I've come home.

## 2

### *A month before*

My mother turns up on a Saturday at the end of September, less than four weeks before we're due to open. I spot her from the living-room window climbing out of a taxi, smart in black trousers and heeled boots. She always dresses as if she's about to go into an office, even though she retired eight years ago. She still has a good figure, trim and tidy, as my dad would have said, with auburn hair and bright blue eyes that are occasionally twinkly, regularly disapproving and often judgemental. I glance down at my own baggy cardigan and shapeless T-shirt, and brush the dust from my faded jeans. It fogs the air in front of me, causing me to cough. Mum once observed, disparagingly, that I like to 'dress for comfort'.

I reach for my inhaler and take a few puffs, then return it to my pocket. I always have one on me. Without it I panic: as a teenager, a severe asthma attack had kept me in hospital for days. I'm relieved that, so far, I haven't spotted any symptoms in my daughters.

I can feel Adrian's disapproving gaze on me even though I can't see him. He's behind me, painting the living-room door satin white. He's said before that I'm too reliant on the inhaler, that overuse isn't good for me because it contains steroids.

'Mum's arrived,' I announce, mainly to distract him. I move away from the window, resisting the urge to flick a duster around the room.

I want to laugh at the alarm on Adrian's face. I know he's also worrying that she'll be disappointed with our progress. We've been in Hywelphilly for more than a month but only moved into the Old Rectory yesterday. We've done so much, though – knocking some rooms into others to make them bigger, incorporating en-suites, fixing the roof, restoring the geometric black-and-white Victorian tiles in the hallway, and we've divided the attic space into three bedrooms and a bath-room for us to live in so that we're separate from the guests. But there's still so much to do before we open to the public: painting, sanding, waxing and sourcing furniture. At the thought, my stress levels rise.

The doorbell rings and I realize that Adrian and I have been staring at each other in mild panic. He has paint on his clothes, in his beard and on his cheek. I laugh nervously. 'Brace yourself.'

'The Wicked Witch of the West,' jokes Adrian, the name Nathan and I gave Mum as kids after watching *The Wizard of Oz*. He steps off the ladder, paintbrush in hand, and follows me into the hallway.

'We only ever called her that when she was in one of her moods,' I say, feeling disloyal. I throw open the door to see her standing on the step, a suitcase at her feet.

'Kirsty. Adrian.' She nods at us in turn. And then, 'This door needs sanding and painting. It's not exactly welcoming, is it? I think we need to buy a new one.'

I bite back my irritation. The door is beautiful, Victorian with stained-glass inserts of pink roses. I've already decided I'm going to paint it Hicks Blue by Little Greene. There's no way I'd change it. 'Hello to you, too,' I say.

She gives me one of her trademark looks and steps over the threshold.

'We haven't got round to painting it yet. But we will,' I add. 'I have just the colour in mind.'

'And I hope it's green,' she says, much to my dismay. 'It needs doing before we open. Kerb appeal, Kirsty, kerb appeal.' Like I didn't know! She bustles past me, leaving Adrian to pick up her suitcase. We exchange glances over the top of her perfectly coiffed bob.

'Lovely to see you, Carol,' says Adrian, bending to kiss her cheek.

She winces. 'This facial hair,' she says, reaching up to touch his beard. He's a good head and shoulders taller than her. 'When's it going?'

He turns to me, clearly bemused, and raises an eyebrow. I stifle a giggle.

She steps into the hallway, taking in the newly refurbished tiles and the recently painted walls. 'What colour is this?' She indicates the walls. She already has a fine layer of dust on the shoulders of her smart wool coat. What was she thinking, wearing it to come to a house undergoing renovation?

'French Gray. It's Farrow and Ball.'

'It's matt.'

'That was the intention.'

She nods. I think that means she approves.

'Who did the tiles?'

'We had to get a guy in.'

'Was it expensive?'

I clear my throat. 'Um . . . not too bad,' I lie, thinking of the fortune we ended up paying him.

'Are you going to give me the tour, then?' she asks, and I feel a fresh wave of shame that this is the first time she's viewing the house she co-owns. We'd asked her at the time, of course, but she'd seen the estate agent's details and said she was content enough with that, which was a bit of a shock: usually she's so controlling. She looks as out of place in our hallway as she would if she'd wandered into a nightclub. Not for the first time I imagine what it would have been like to do this without her.

Adrian resumes painting while I escort Mum along the hallway to the only bedroom downstairs. We've called it Apple Tree because of the view of the apple trees in the garden. It's one of the first bedrooms we completed and still my favourite: pale green walls and French windows that lead on to the patio. She glances around but doesn't say anything. Then I show her the dining room opposite. It overlooks the churchyard, with its centuries-old gravestones, and still needs painting.

'It's a bit gloomy,' she observes, frowning. She pushes the strap of her handbag further up her shoulder.

'It *is* a dark room,' I concede. 'But look.' I open the internal double doors that we installed to separate it from the kitchen. 'When these are pulled back it's much lighter in here. See?'

'Hmm. If you'd put glass in the doors you could have kept them closed.' Mum wanders through the double doors to the large kitchen, with its cream flagstone tiles, pale grey Shaker-style units and the bi-fold doors that lead into the garden.

'Only family allowed in here,' I explain, from behind her.

'So you can lock these doors?'

'Yes. To keep the kitchen private.'

'Looks expensive,' she observes. 'Those worktops don't look like laminate.'

'They're stone. More hardwearing.'

She mutters something under her breath that I can't hear and I feel a surge of annoyance. It wasn't as if she was here to help us make these decisions. She was still in Cardiff, selling her own house.

I show her to a small room off the hallway and next to the dining room. 'This will be the playroom for the girls. Somewhere separate from the living room so they have a place of their own that's away from guests.'

She turns to me. 'Where *are* the girls?'

I suppress a sigh. 'School, Mum.' I look at my watch. It's gone two o'clock, not long before I have to pick them up. One of the main benefits of moving to a village is the little local school, which has small classes and is only a short walk away.

'Are they enjoying it?' she asks, and her face brightens as it always does when we talk about her granddaughters.

'Ye-esss . . .' It comes out as a hiss because the truth is that, while Evie seems to be revelling in making new friends and being the exotic new girl from London, Amelia hates it. They've only been going there since the new term started a few weeks ago, but Amelia constantly moans about the boys, the girls, the teachers, the building, the smell of manure, the fields of 'depressed sheep', the rubbish facilities. I try to take it all with a pinch of salt. It's early days, I remind myself.

'That's good,' says Mum, but she would have picked up on my tone. Nothing gets past her. She wraps the navy wool coat closer around her. 'What's going on with the heating? It's extremely cold in here.'

'Radiators still need to be fitted in some of the rooms. But our bedrooms have them. And the living room.'

'Right. Well, you'd better show me the rest. And then we must have a cup of tea. I'm parched.'

I show her the living room. We've installed leather sofas and found a Welsh dresser in an antiques shop to put the TV on. I've added fluffy cushions to soften the look.

Mum wanders over to the open fireplace. 'I like this.'

'We wanted to keep it.' I'd fallen in love with the wrought-iron Victorian fireplace when we viewed the house.

Her eyes go to the photographs on the mantelpiece. There is a picture of me on a 1970s brown-patterned sofa holding baby Natasha on my lap. I must have been about three. I usually keep it in our room, but until it's decorated I've put it here. I notice a fleeting wave of emotion cross Mum's face, but then, just as quickly, it's gone.

I go to it and touch the silver frame, almost apologetically. 'It won't stay here. There'll be nothing personal in this room,' I say.

Mum pushes her glasses up her nose and seems to collect herself. 'No. No, that wouldn't be wise. This isn't your home, remember. It's a business.'

'I know.'

She turns to me, her blue eyes penetrating. 'Do you?'

I swallow. 'Of course. But we still have to live here.'

After that there's a weird tension between us. I show her the other five rooms on the first floor, then take her up to the attic. It has a decent-sized square landing with beams overhead. Her bedroom is a small single room next to ours and opposite the girls'.

'When's your furniture arriving?' I ask.

'I haven't got much. Just my bedroom things.

20

Everything else I've put in storage. You don't want my old stuff cluttering the place, do you?' She meets my gaze, and I find myself squirming.

'Well, it's not that. It's just . . . you know . . . we have to be careful. Fire regulations and suchlike.'

She tuts. 'I'm having you on, Kirsty. Goodness, have you always been so serious?' She comes closer and peers at me through her bifocals. 'It's changed you, hasn't it? All this business with Adrian.'

*All this business.* As though what's happened to him – to us – is so trivial it can be dismissed.

*Of course it's changed me*, I want to say. *Just like losing Natasha changed you.* Aren't we all shaped by the events that take place during the course of our lives? As though our souls – if they exist – are made of Plasticine to be remoulded over and over again. But, as usual, I keep my mouth shut, not wanting to offend her. She's been so kind to us, I remind myself. All of this wouldn't be possible without her. And she's had so much grief in her life.

It will be okay, I tell myself, as we head down to the kitchen for the tea she's requested. It will take a bit of getting used to, us all living and working under one roof, but we can do it. I make an effort to push away any doubt.

## 3

Evie's face lights up when she comes out of school to see Mum standing beside me. I'm wearing a coat over my tatty decorating clothes even though Mum had tried to insist I change. It brought back memories of being a teenager and how she used to try to feminize me, disgusted by my rock-band T-shirts and DM boots. Evie barrels into her stomach, wrapping her arms around her waist. 'Nana!'

Mum bends over and kisses the top of Evie's unruly hair. Thankfully, she's much more affectionate with her granddaughters than she ever was with me.

'Do you like my school? It's like a castle, isn't it?'

I watch Mum's expression as she follows Evie's pointing finger and I can tell she's struggling to see the comparison in the Victorian stone building. 'Ye-es. All those peaked roofs. Like somewhere a princess would live . . .'

'Yes! Like Rapunzel. And it has a tower round the back.'

'A tower? Really?' Mum meets my eye questioningly and I shake my head without Evie noticing.

Mum chuckles and stands up straighter. 'Always so fanciful,' she says to me. 'She reminds me of Selena when she was little.'

I stiffen, and Mum's cheeks colour. She hardly ever mentions my cousin. It's like an unspoken rule between us. 'She's nothing like Selena,' I say, more harshly than I intend to.

'No,' Mum concedes. 'I suppose not.'

I've tried not to think about Selena over the years, but returning to Wales has brought back the memories. She was practically a sister to me. Our dads were brothers and we were always in and out of each other's houses, living just streets away from one another in Cardiff. But we haven't spoken since we were eighteen. I never ask about her – and Mum doesn't venture any information. I'm not even sure if they keep in touch, although I suspect they do. Mum was always so fond of her.

After a couple of minutes of Evie gabbling away about her day, and who she played with, Amelia comes trailing out, looking small and skinny under the weight of her backpack. Despite the drizzly weather she refuses to wear a coat and she looks cold in her fern-green jumper and grey skirt, her long dark hair whipped by the wind. At least she's wearing tights. Every day I hope she'll bounce out of school in the way she did in Twickenham, usually with a couple of other girls. But she's always alone, her face sad. I've tried to make eye contact with a few of the other mothers at the school gates, hoping that if I make some friends Amelia will too, but although they're polite to me, they cluster together in their impenetrable groups, chatting, while I stand awkwardly alone. The only other mother I've got talking to is called Sian, who has a daughter, Orla, in Amelia's class. A few days ago, we exchanged numbers but Sian isn't always at pick-up: more often than not, Orla walks home on her own – which I won't allow Amelia to do yet.

'Hi, Moo,' I say, when she reaches us. It was the nickname Evie had for her when she was little. 'Good day?'

'Fine,' she replies, in a tone that implies it was anything but. Her face brightens slightly when she spots Mum. 'Hi, Nana.'

'Hello, my darling,' says Mum, wrapping Amelia in her arms and hugging her close. 'Ooh, you feel cold. Haven't you got a coat?'

She gives a half-giggle that lifts my spirits. 'Coats aren't cool.'

'No, they're warm,' Mum jokes, linking one arm through Amelia's and the other through Evie's. And, for the first time since she arrived, I'm glad she's here.

We amble along the high street, the girls and Mum in front. It's one of the busiest times of the day, with families walking home from school, and there's a lovely atmosphere in the village, with the sounds of laughter, chatter and the occasional bark of a dog. I wonder if Mum is taking in her surroundings. The hills and mountains that envelop the village are so beautiful that I can't help but be wowed by them every time I see them. I take deep breaths, savouring the fresh air in my lungs and thinking, once again, how lucky we are to be away from the grime of London. There are some drawbacks, of course: the convenience of late-night shops, of having a Starbucks or Costa on every corner. But, so far, I'm enjoying the gentler pace of life.

Sometimes, on the way home from school, we'll pop into the one and only café for a hot chocolate (Evie was most upset when we first arrived to find that they didn't do a Babychino) or the local chemist to see grumpy Mrs Gummage (Amelia loves all the hairclips) but today we go straight back to the guesthouse.

'What are the locals like?' asks Mum, when we get back.

The girls have dumped their bags and shoes in the hallway and gone straight upstairs to their room.

'I've not met many. There's old Mr Collins next door. He's a widower and about eighty. He walks with a stick,' I say, as I shake off my coat and dump it in the little room off the hallway that will, eventually, be the office. It's the only room we haven't re-plastered and it's very 1980s, with yellow striped wallpaper and cornflower-blue borders. 'And I've met a young couple who live in one of the cottages opposite. Kath and Derek from the Seven Stars have been brilliant, passing on a few bookings because they were already full, and giving advice.' I'd liked Kath immediately. Big, blonde and brassy, with a hearty laugh, she'd warmed to me too when she'd realized I was from Wales originally, and we talked about the Cardiff haunts of our youth. I don't tell Mum about the locals who have been less than friendly, like Mrs Gummage in the chemist, and

Lydia with mauve hair, who lives two doors down and scowls when she sees us.

'Hmm,' says Mum, as though she's not listening. She's surveying the hallway. 'You need to get some kind of cupboard or coat rack. There's nowhere to put coats and shoes.'

'Yes, that's true . . .'

'And should we get some tourist brochures? I've seen other bed-and-breakfasts have them. It might be helpful for the guests to know what's going on, details of local attractions, walks, that kind of thing. People come here for the hiking.'

I hadn't thought of that. 'It's a great idea.'

She rewards me with a smile. Then she brushes against the living-room door and tuts when paint comes off on the elbow of her coat. 'I thought you'd be further along than this,' she snaps, taking off her coat and examining the paint stain. 'We open in a few weeks.'

I swallow a retort. 'Then it's good you've arrived. We need as much help as we can get. And don't say anything to Adrian. He doesn't need to feel the pressure.' She opens her mouth to speak but I continue: 'I mean it, Mum. This is supposed to be a fresh start for us.'

She scowls but says no more. I leave her to it and run up the stairs to find Adrian.

The bedroom door is closed. I take a deep breath as I turn the handle. I still hate doors being closed. The memories are too fresh. I never know what I'm going to find behind them.

Adrian is lying on the bed with an arm flung over his face. For a moment – a half-second – I have the insane thought that he's dead. I hurry over but he moves his arm and his eyes snap open when he senses me looming over his prostrate form.

He sits up, resting on his elbows. 'Sorry. I'm knackered. I must have fallen asleep.' He rubs his eyes. They're red, and one is blood-shot. He still has white paint on his beard and hair. I feel a rush of love for him. He's been working so hard on this renovation . . . too hard, considering.

I perch on the bed beside him. 'Mum and I can take over the painting.'

'I'll be all right. But it's good that she can help.'

We sit in silence for a while, and then I say, 'It feels weird, doesn't it, having this huge old house to ourselves?'

'It won't feel so big when guests start arriving.'

'I hope Evie sleeps through tonight.' She woke up at two this morning, screaming because of a nightmare.

'She'll get used to being here.'

'She said the room was "creepy". She doesn't like having a churchyard next door. She's worried the house is haunted.'

'We'll decorate her room soon and then she'll feel more at home. It's only been one night.'

I bite the nail of my little finger and tear a piece off.

Adrian reaches over and takes my wrist. 'Are you okay? You seem tense?'

27

I sigh and get to my feet. 'It's nothing. I need to go and check on the girls.'

Adrian stands up too. 'They're fine.' He pulls me close to him. 'Look, I know it's a bit overwhelming. I get it, Kirst. I feel the same.' He kisses me softly. His beard tickles my chin. 'But we'll get through it. We've got through worse.'

The sound of Evie screaming makes us spring apart and Amelia runs into the room. 'Evie's bleeding!' she cries.

I dart past her to find Evie standing in the middle of their bedroom, cradling her hand. At her feet is a doll I don't recognize, its china head at an odd angle, its one glassy eye staring up at me. The hair is long and black, in two messy plaits, and it's wearing a filthy Victorian-style dress. One leg is missing, amputated at the knee, a jutting edge of porcelain where the calf should be.

'Let me see,' I say, taking Evie's hand gently. Blood is oozing from a cut across her palm. Evie is crying silently, her little body juddering with each sob. 'It's okay,' I say soothingly, trying not to panic. I lead her to the bathroom across the landing. Amelia and Adrian follow and we all crowd around the sink. I wash the cut under the tap, then wrap her hand in a towel. If it's still bleeding we'll have to take her to A and E.

'I . . . need . . . a . . . plaster,' she stutters, between sobs.

Adrian disappears to get one. It makes me smile that Evie thinks a plaster will fix any ailment. Amelia used to be the same.

I sit on the loo lid with Evie on my lap. 'Look, the bleeding's stopping,' I say, after a while. Adrian reappears with a *Ben and Holly* plaster and I cover the cut with it. Evie examines it and promptly stops crying.

'What happened?' I ask Amelia, as we lead Evie back into their bedroom.

'She found that,' says Amelia, pointing to the china doll, 'under the floorboards.'

'Under the floorboards?'

'Yeah. We saw that one was a bit loose so we looked under it and Evie saw the doll, but when she picked it up it cut her hand.' Amelia shudders. She hates dolls. Especially the china variety. She's always thought them sinister.

'You're okay now?' Adrian asks, kissing Evie's forehead.

She nods, chewing her lip and laying her hand gingerly on her lap.

'Then we can get rid of this,' I say, bending down to pick up the doll by the arm.

'No!' she cries. 'We can't get rid of her! She's special.'

'It's hideous,' interjects Amelia.

Evie sits up and stretches out her hands, her injury forgotten. 'No, I want to keep her. She's magic.'

'It's dangerous,' I say, examining the jagged edge. 'Look, it's broken and it might cut you again.'

'Let me have a look,' says Adrian, taking it from me. 'I'll try to mend the leg.' He flashes a smile at his younger daughter and she beams back at him. 'Come on.' He takes her uninjured hand. 'Let's see what we can find downstairs.'

I watch them go, smiling to myself, pleased to see them connecting again.

Amelia sighs heavily and I spin around. 'What's up, Moo?'

'This house is jinxed.'

'Don't be silly. And don't say things like that in front of Evie. You'll scare her.'

'She's already scared,' shoots back Amelia, crossing her arms defensively. 'You might love it here, but nobody else does.' She stalks off before I can reprimand her for backchat.

I'm woken in the night by footsteps outside our door. I sit up, blinking in the darkness as my eyes adjust. I'm expecting to see Evie creeping into our room, like last night. I wait, but nothing. I turn to Adrian, who is fast sleep, his mouth open, breathing deeply. Just as I begin to think I'm imagining it, I hear it again. A hushed, pleading voice now and creaking floorboards. I reach for my phone. It's 3 a.m.

'What's going on?' Adrian grunts, as I get out of bed.

'I'm not sure but I think it's Evie.' I grab my dressing-gown and leave the room. Across the landing the girls' bedroom door is wide open. They're not in bed.

Then I hear a voice from the landing below. 'Evie, wake up!' It sounds like Amelia.

I head down the first flight of stairs. The girls are illuminated by the moonlight flooding in from the picture window and they look small in their pyjamas.

'What's going on?' I hiss, when I reach them. 'Why aren't you both in bed?'

Amelia turns to me, her face stricken. 'It's Evie. She just started walking out of the room and down the stairs.'

Evie is standing outside one of the guest bedrooms, a strange look on her face. Her eyes are open, but they're glassy, unseeing. I approach her carefully as though she's a pony about to bolt. Gently I take her hand. 'I think she's sleepwalking,' I whisper to Amelia. 'I'm going to take her back to bed.'

Amelia looks as though she's about to cry, but nods. Evie is trance-like and there's something unsettling about seeing my usually animated little girl like this.

I lead Evie into our bed, hoping there will be no more sleepwalking if she's with us. She slips beneath the duvet, turns over and closes her eyes with a sigh. Adrian is oblivious. He grunts something indecipherable, then carries on snoring gently.

I accompany Amelia to the girls' room and tuck the duvet around her. 'What happened, Moo?'

She shakes her head. She's pale in the half-light, and clearly scared. 'It was so weird. I woke up to see Evie opening the bedroom door. I thought she was just going into your room, you know, like she does. Then I heard creaking and knew she was going downstairs. So

I followed her. But she just stood there, on the next landing, looking freaky, and then I remembered that stupid doll she found and . . .' She lets out a sob.

'Ssh. It's okay, sweets. She was sleepwalking, that's all.'

'I tried to wake her up.'

'You mustn't wake her up if it happens again. Okay? Just lead her back to bed. Then come and tell me.'

Amelia sniffs. 'She's never done it before.'

'I know.' I lie down next to her, expecting her to turf me out of her bed, but instead she huddles against me. I hold her trembling body close and stay with her until she falls asleep.

# 4

*Six days before*

Mum has been jittery all morning, as though she has something on her mind. Three times I had to ask her if the carpet fitters had called, and when I tried to talk to her about the girls – usually a favourite topic – I could tell she wasn't listening. At first I wondered if it was nerves because we're opening this weekend. We're both anxious, wondering about making small-talk with the guests and if they'll be difficult or demanding. When I found her glasses in the fridge, though, I guessed it was something more – or the beginning of dementia.

Then I discover her hoovering the leaves on the front porch with the Dust Buster.

'Mum? We have a leaf blower for that.'

She looks up at me and then at the Dust Buster, as though she's seeing it for the first time. There's a pile of orange and red leaves at her feet.

She runs a hand through her hair. 'Ah . . . of course. Just trying to get everything sorted.'

'Everything is sorted, Mum. You know that.' In desperation, we'd hired a painter and decorator to help us finish because we were running out of time, which eased the pressure but cost money we could ill afford. At least we're up to speed. Mum's been living with us for three weeks now and it's not been easy – especially as Adrian's been retreating more and more to our bedroom. He's started writing a novel, which he's wanted to do since he was a teenager.

I help Mum over the threshold. 'What's going on?' I ask.

She steps into the hallway and shuts the front door on the wind that has started to pick up, scattering autumn leaves across the driveway.

She swallows. She's not usually afraid to speak her mind.

I have a sudden, awful thought. 'Are you ill?'

She glares at me. '*Ill?* Do I look ill to you?'

'Then what's wrong? You've been acting strange all day.'

She sighs. 'I've been trying to find the right time to broach something with you.'

'O-*kaaay*.' I don't like the sound of this.

'It's Selena. And before you pull that face you need to hear me out,' she says.

I pull *that* face anyway. I always pull it when Mum mentions Selena – which, thankfully, isn't that often. At first, it seemed to be every time I visited her. But eventually she resigned herself to the fact that Selena and I were no longer in touch and stopped pestering me. I often hoped that she had lost touch with her too.

'What about her?' Dread swills in my stomach.

'She rang me in a bit of a state. She's leaving her husband. He sounds a nasty piece of work. She asked if she could stay here for a few days.'

'What . . . what did you tell her?'

'That I'd speak to you.'

I feel a surge of anger. How dare Selena try to wheedle her way back into my life after all these years, just when Adrian and I are starting afresh?

'I haven't seen her for almost seventeen years,' I say, my jaw clenched. 'She's not going to want to come here.'

'She has nowhere else to go. We're the only family she's got.' She looks at me pleadingly. Her eyes are huge behind the thick frames of her glasses.

This is so typical of the Selena I remember, leaning on Mum for everything, getting herself into trouble. Mum's never been able to say no to her. And I know why. After Natasha died and Mum and Dad adopted Nathan, Selena's family fell apart so Selena spent most of her time at our house. She filled the gaping hole Natasha had left and, I'm not going to deny it, we were close. Once. But that was a long time ago. Before Selena's lies destroyed our relationship.

'What about Aunt Bess? Or Uncle Owen?'

My mum whistles through her teeth. 'Bess is a waste of space.' She's an alcoholic. I often wondered if Selena had turned out the same way. 'And Selena lost touch with her dad after he walked out. I don't think she ever forgave him.'

Or maybe he never forgave *her*.

I clear my throat. I can't have Selena here. I just can't. 'I'm sorry, Mum, but I don't want her here. It's been too long. It would be awkward. And this is a guesthouse not a women's refuge.' I've gone too far. I didn't mean it – but, knowing Selena, she's probably embellished the story. I bet she just wants to have a nose round the Old Rectory.

'That's a terrible thing to say.' Mum looks appalled. 'She'd be a paying guest. She has money, by all accounts. She's not a scrounger.'

I look down at my hands, feeling guilty. How do I tell Mum that I can't have Selena back in my life? That she's dangerous.

Before the secrets, the lies and the anger, we were inseparable. I put it down to there being only nine months between us but, really, we just got on. We had the same sense of humour and, although I was the elder, I looked up to her. She had courage, which I lacked back then. She threw herself into everything. She had no inhibitions and no fears, while I was shyer, more cautious. She brought me out of myself. She made me do things I'd never have done otherwise, like smoke my first cigarette, drink cider in the park when we were underage, and get chucked out of a shop for putting knickers on my head. At heart, though, I was a good girl. I didn't like to break rules. She relished it.

Mum watches me, waiting for an answer. 'You know,' she says slowly, 'she's got a little girl not much older than Evie.'

My head shoots up. 'Really?'

'And her little girl isn't well. She's in a wheelchair, poor child.'

I glare at her. I know what she's doing.

Mum smiles triumphantly and stalks off to the office. She leans over the desk and opens an A4 leather-bound diary with gold-edged pages. The diary I'd bought with such excitement only a few weeks ago from a little shop in the next town, thinking of all the potential guests' names that would fill it.

Mum flicks through it now, with a tight smile. 'Okay,' she says, when she finds the right date. She picks up a scratchy blue biro and taps it against her teeth. My heart sinks. I'd bought a fountain pen to write the names of forthcoming guests neatly, so that we can look back in years to come and remember our first customers, as well as the excitement, the nerves. Adrian had tried to convince me to use an online booking system, but I'd much rather have something tangible. Something we can keep. And I told him computer software was an expense too far right now. Adrian calls me a perfectionist, a high achiever. And it's a good job I am because he is disorganized and messy. He was a lawyer for years, great at his job, but he had a secretary to sort him out. 'I'll stick Selena and Ruby in here then, shall I? It's the day before the first guest arrives so you'll have a chance to catch up. Apple Tree will be best because of the wheelchair.' She doesn't wait for an answer as she scribbles on the page.

'I don't want Selena here!' I cry, shocked by the strength of my anger and resentment even after all this time. I sound like a toddler and I despise myself. But I'm desperate. My mother still brings out the child in me.

Mum breathes in sharply, holding her chest theatrically. 'Kirsty! There's no need for that. It's my home too, and I think we should let her stay.'

Already she's taking over, just as I knew she would. I hold up my hands in surrender and walk out of the room, before I say something I'll regret.

To clear my head I decide to find the girls. They're in the garden playing with the lop-eared rabbits and my heart lifts. I stand at the back door and watch them as they sit on the grass, not caring that it's damp, chattering away to each other. Evie has hung a crown that belongs to one of her Barbies from the ear of her rabbit, which she's aptly named Princess. All this space, I think, surveying the vast garden, with the trampoline and a swing set. Even Amelia has seemed happier over the past few days. She's had a playdate with Orla and, although she still insists she hates it here, her new friend has definitely cheered her up. And half-term is approaching.

I leave them to join Adrian. He's tapping away at his laptop on the table in a corner of our bedroom. He's concentrating so deeply that he doesn't hear me. I watch him for ages, taking in the line of his long neck, the nodules of his spine, the sharp peaks of his shoulder blades. I think of his heart, beneath his grey T-shirt, pumping away. And I remember how he was eighteen months ago, his mind eaten away by self-destructive thoughts.

When he came home from work that day, unshaven, his tie askew, his face grey, and told me he'd walked out of the job I thought he loved, I'd been shocked. When he took to his bed and wouldn't get up, when he snapped at me and the girls, when the Adrian I knew and loved seeped out of him to be replaced by a stranger, I rang my brother's wife, a GP, in a panic.

I'll never forget Julia's words: 'Get him to the doctor,' she'd said urgently. 'It sounds like he's depressed.'

Depression had never affected my life before. Even when Natasha died Mum hadn't experienced depression. She was in deep grief, and over-protective of me, but there was no sign of the fog in which Adrian was lost.

I'd taken Julia's advice and frog-marched my husband to the next available appointment. It's been a long road since but it has brought us here.

And now Selena is to be back in my life. This was supposed to be our getaway from the stress of city life, our new start. And I can't let Selena swan in with her lies, messing it up for us. My family has been through too much and I'll do anything to protect them.

## 5

*Four days before*

The day Selena arrives, so do the dead flowers.

It's a Friday, the day before we open officially. The house is quiet, the girls are still in bed and Mum hasn't surfaced yet. I'd hardly slept last night after Evie came into our room at one o'clock saying she was scared. I was so worried she might sleepwalk again (it hasn't happened since the first time) that I let her into our bed, where she proceeded to fidget. She took up all the room, her body spread out, like a starfish, so Adrian and I were forced to sleep on opposite edges of the mattress. I woke up feeling sick. At first, I couldn't attribute it to anything in particular, until it hit me that today I'd have to face Selena again.

I sit in the dark in an armchair in the front room, drinking tea and waiting for the sun to come up. When the sky whitens, I start dusting. I'm a doer. My hands need to be busy. I can't sit for too long without the nagging sense that I have to get on with something. Mum is exactly the same. When I was a kid I could never relax if she was around. She was always on the go, cooking, organizing, tidying and chivvying – although I've noticed since she's moved in that she hasn't contributed as much as I'd hoped. Maybe that will change now that we're due to open.

I'm sweeping a cloth across the TV screen even though I did it yesterday (why is there always so much dust?) when I hear the crunch of footsteps on gravel. I rush to the window expecting to see Selena, surprised she's arrived so early, but the driveway is empty, apart from our beaten-up Honda parked in the corner, under the yew tree that overhangs the churchyard wall. We hardly use it now that I walk the girls to school. In the distance I can see the ring of mountains that forms part of the Brecons, their tops disappearing into cloud. Evie jokes that there's another world up there, as though the mountains are like the Faraway Tree in her favourite Enid Blyton story. They feel like a safe haven, worlds away from crime-ridden London.

I notice something on the steps. I squint, but the view is obscured by the wall of the house. Perhaps the postman made a delivery but didn't ring the bell, not wanting to wake us. I can just make out some stems poking out of a plastic covering. Intrigued, I open the front door, letting in a whoosh of cold air. I'm expecting to see a fresh bouquet, maybe from friends in London or from a local wishing us luck on our opening weekend. Instead I'm faced with a mass of dead roses, their once peachy petals wilting and edged with brown. The scent of death and decay drifts up to me.

Dismayed, I step back – and jump when arms go round me.

'What are you doing?' Adrian peers over my shoulder. He smells of toothpaste and sleep. He's still wearing the T-shirt he slept in. Usually he tries to go for a run in the morning. He must have overslept, thanks to Evie. He frowns at the dead roses on the doorstep. 'Where did they come from?'

'They were just left there.' I'm not superstitious but this feels like a bad omen. Adrian steps forward, feet bare, and bends down to gather them up. Brown water drips down the stems and along his arm. Wordlessly he holds them out in front of him as he walks to the green garden bin we keep by the garage and shoves them into it. As he comes back he winces as the gravel digs into his feet, swearing under his breath.

'It's bloody cold out there,' he says. He leans against the closed door, his dark eyes fixed on me. 'Are you okay? You look freaked out.'

'Wasn't expecting a delivery of dead flowers.' I try to keep my voice light. 'I wonder who put them there.'

Adrian stretches his arms over his head and yawns. His T-shirt rides up to reveal his belly, once soft but taut since he started running. His antidepressants make him put on weight so he's taken to exercise. 'Oh, I expect it was just kids messing about. I bet they came from the churchyard next door.'

I turn and watch his retreating back, familiar in the old T-shirt and checked pyjama bottoms, as he climbs the stairs. It's lovely to see him more relaxed. If Selena wasn't arriving today I wouldn't think anything of the flowers. I'd agree with Adrian. And, okay, some of the locals have eyed us with suspicion, particularly Mrs Gummage. Her face had set rigid with disapproval when we revealed we had bought the Old Rectory and turned it into a guesthouse, as though we'd defaced the walls of the church with foul language and sworn at the mild-mannered rector, Mr Somers.

And Stan something, who'd been in the Seven Stars, had commented to Adrian about Londoners coming in and bumping up house prices. I was outraged. 'I hope you told him I'm Welsh!' I'd cried.

Adrian's right. It's just a prank. A coincidence. Nothing to do with Selena.

When she arrives I'm on the first floor, in Tulip, straightening the duvet for the umpteenth time, plumping the pillows, moving around the items on the dressing-table. Each one needs to be exactly positioned: the tea tray, the vase of fresh flowers, the vintage-style jug and bowl. Everything must be perfect for the opening tomorrow, even the rooms that aren't booked in case we attract passers-by. Sian, Orla's mum, warned me that could happen. She grew up in a guesthouse in Abergavenny and has given me some tips. She told me the village sees a lot of hikers looking for beds for the night.

I hear the thrum of an engine, then the grinding of gravel, as a midnight blue SUV pulls into our driveway. The dread I've felt all morning intensifies. The passenger door opens and I hold my breath as I wait for Selena to step out. The last time I saw her she was a teenager, drunk, wearing too much make-up and swearing in a short skirt, her breasts practically hanging out of her strappy dress. Now her hair, once bleached and halfway down her back, hangs in a soft blonde bob. It hasn't frizzed in the drizzle, like mine does. She's wearing heeled boots that sink into the gravel, dark jeans and a grey poncho that looks like cashmere. She's still whippet thin. She stands by her car, looking up at the house, ignoring the fine rain falling on her clothes and hair. I dart back behind the curtains, my heart racing. *Has she seen me?* When I'm brave enough to peep out again, she's helping a little girl into a wheelchair. The child, Ruby, looks younger than Evie. She's skinny with pale brown hair and a white, drawn face. I picture my own daughters, with their plump cheeks and glossy hair. The little girl untangles her arms from around Selena's neck and Selena kisses her tenderly. My eyes smart with tears.

'Selena!' I hear Mum call, as she darts over the gravel in a way that belies her years. She grasps Selena's hands in hers.

I hear Selena cry, 'Aunty Carol!' but their next words are snatched by the wind. There is something in the way they hug that makes me think they've seen each other over the years, although Mum has denied it.

I grip the windowsill, inhaling deeply, preparing myself. I have to put on a polite façade and it's going to be bloody exhausting. *You can do this*, I tell myself. I still can't believe she's here, that I'm letting her into my life again, that she's going to meet my husband, my children, that she'll draw me back in then leave me broken, like she did before.

I plaster a smile on to my face. I'd made an effort to tame my unruly curls with serum so they didn't resemble a frizzy halo, but my reflection in the mirror on the upstairs landing shows me it hasn't worked. My cheeks are too ruddy and the liner I'd applied earlier has disappeared into the folds of my eyelids. I want her to think I've aged well, even when I know I haven't.

I hold the banister to steady myself as I descend the stairs. Selena is standing in the hallway, calm and graceful. She's already surrounded by people. She's like a magnet. Always has been, especially with men. And my husband, it seems, is not immune. He's shaking Selena's hand in both of his, saying how lovely it is finally to meet her, as though he's heard all about her, even though I've barely mentioned her. He doesn't know the ins and outs. He doesn't know why we lost touch.

Mum looks on with a proud smile. Ruby is sitting in her wheelchair, fiddling with a Jellycat mouse in her lap and avoiding eye contact, My girls are gawping at her in such a way that I long to go down there and tell them to stop.

Then Selena looks up and meets my eye. For a brief moment panic registers on her face, but it's fleeting, unnoticeable to anyone else. Adrian glances at me and frowns, I realize I must be wearing a manic smile.

'Kirsty!' Her face is warm, open. 'It's so lovely to see

you – it's been *too* long.' She moves away from the others and takes a few steps towards me. I hope her stilettos aren't marking the floor tiles. Her last words to me had been nasty. Cruel. I wonder if she remembers them as clearly as I do.

By now I've reached the bottom of the stairs so that we're on the same level. We were always a similar height but with her heels she's a good three inches taller than I am, and I feel at a disadvantage. She air-kisses the space beside my head. She is wearing too much perfume, although it smells expensive.

I stand back, resisting the urge to cough. 'Selena. Lovely to see you too.' But my words sound fake.

She totters over to the wheelchair and crouches beside it. 'And this is my daughter, my precious Ruby.'

'Lovely to meet you, Ruby,' I say, sounding more genuine now. 'And these are Amelia and Evie. They've been looking forward to seeing you.' Ruby continues to study the toy in her lap. 'They'd love to show you around . . .' I falter. The chair will make that difficult. I almost sense Selena stiffening, her smile wavering. She's resting her hand on her daughter's denim-clad knee. Ruby's jeans have embroidered butterflies on them and Evie is eyeing them enviously.

'I think you're a bit tired, aren't you, Rubes? The journey was long. If it's okay we'd love to go to our room.' She flashes me a bright smile but I can see the shadows under her eyes that she's done her best to conceal. She looks small and frail crouched over her daughter and I feel an unexpected burst of tenderness towards her – towards both of them. She must sense it because she gets up, her chin jutting defiantly. Her body language reminds me of the day she stood up for me against the bully who lived down her road. Leighton Jones. Big and butch with crooked teeth, he was always teasing me. I can tell the fight is still in her. And I wonder what her life has been like, with the doctors' appointments, the tests and the constant worry. It's my biggest fear that something will happen to my daughters but Selena lives with the reality. I find it hard to reconcile the flighty, irresponsible Selena of my youth with this grown-up responsible version.

Amelia and Evie's disappointment at not being able to play with Ruby is evident, but Mum hurries over, taking charge, urging Adrian to help with Selena's bags. Without another word to me, Selena pushes Ruby's chair down the corridor as my mum leads her towards Apple Tree, near the kitchen. I stare after them, my daughters next to me.

'I wanted to show her the rabbits,' says Evie, her voice full of disappointment.

Amelia wrinkles her freckled nose. 'What's wrong with Ruby? Why does she need a wheelchair? Do her legs not work?'

'I don't know,' I say honestly, looping an arm around Amelia's shoulders. She's grown so tall, she's not far off my height. 'I think she was born with some kind of condition. Genetic, I think.' I have no idea. I haven't talked to Selena since 2001 and Mum seemed to be aware only that Ruby needed a wheelchair. Now, seeing her with Selena, I'm wondering if she knows more than she let on.

Evie considers this. 'Aren't we family with Ruby?'

'You mean we're *related* to her, you weirdo,' says Amelia. I prod her side. 'Ow, what did you do that for?'

'Don't be mean to your sister.'

'I'm just *saying.*'

'Well, don't.'

Amelia shuffles away grumpily. Evie looks up at me. 'Is Ruby our cousin?'

'Selena's my cousin, so I think that makes Ruby your second cousin,' I explain. 'And no,' I add, when I see where Evie is going with this line of questioning. 'You and Amelia haven't any kind of illness. So don't worry.'

Evie twirls her hair around her finger. 'Poor Ruby,' she says seriously. And then she runs upstairs, her pink stripy T-shirt clashing with her flowery skirt.

Amelia says petulantly, 'Can I watch some TV?'

'Haven't you got any homework?'

She shrugs. 'Mum, it's Insect Day!' It's a standing joke between us since Evie had asked me, very seriously, why they had a day off to celebrate insects but not cats and rabbits. She'd confused 'inset' with 'insect'. 'And, anyway,' she adds, 'they hardly give us any homework.' I feel a flicker of anxiety. Her school in London was too pushy but here I worry that they're too laid back. Adrian prefers the ethos at their new school. He doesn't believe in pressuring kids because his parents were so strict. They made him do extra maths tuition and piano and violin practice every night – he hasn't touched a musical instrument since he met me.

Amelia wanders off in the direction of the playroom. I watch her leave. How will she cope when the guests arrive tomorrow and the rambling house she's had to herself since September will no longer be just ours? She'll have to share the TV, the garden, the living room with strangers. I'd had this romantic notion of what running a guesthouse would be like and I'm already realizing it will be nothing like I imagined – and we haven't even opened.

I'm still standing in the hallway when Adrian reappears. I haven't seen much of him since we found the dead flowers this morning. He went for a run and since then has been up in the bedroom, hunched over his laptop. He's powering on with his novel. It's a thriller, although he refuses to let me read any of it yet. All I know is that it's about a psychopath who loses his job, gets depressed and goes on a killing spree. He actually laughed about it in bed last night, joking it definitely wasn't autobiographical.

'Selena loved the room,' he says, as he walks towards me. 'Your mother's still in there, acting as if she's her prodigal daughter.'

I think of Apple Tree. It has two beds that can either be zipped together to make a double, or separated as two singles. I've kept them separate, thinking that

Selena and Ruby would rather not share. 'I'm not surprised she likes it. It's one of our best rooms.'

He lowers his voice and steers me into the living room by my elbow. 'Is she paying to stay here?'

'Mum said so. That's the only reason she's here.' I stop when I notice his expression. 'What?'

'Bit harsh, isn't it? She's your cousin whom you haven't seen in nearly seventeen years. She was telling me how close the two of you used to be. Like sisters, apparently. She said she was always at your house.'

I stiffen. 'What else did she say?'

He runs a hand over his beard. 'She said your mum basically saved her.'

I frown. 'From what?'

He shrugs. 'I don't know. Only that her own mum was a waste of space. I have to say, it sounds like she's got a lot on her plate. She said she'd left her husband.'

'Did she say why?'

'He couldn't handle the stress of Ruby's illness and had become argumentative. Sounds like a nice bloke.' He smiles wryly.

'So she's told you her life story.'

He laughs. 'She does like to chat.' Then his expression darkens. 'Do you think it's right that she's paying? Shouldn't we offer to put her up for free as she's family?'

'We're not a charity. This business needs to work.'

He folds his arms across his chest. One of the buttons on his shirt is missing. If Mum notices, I'll get a lecture about not looking after my husband, even though I'm always telling her we're not living in the 1950s. 'It will work,' he says. 'Stop being negative. This was all supposed to happen. Everything was meant to lead us here.'

Since Adrian was discharged from hospital nearly a year ago, he's been seeing a therapist in London – he's now been transferred to someone in Cardiff – and, as a result, he's trying to be very Zen, lots of meditation and positive thinking. That's all well and good but it doesn't pay the bills. I've shielded him from so much since his breakdown but I can't tell him I'm worrying for both of us without hurting his feelings or setting him back in his recovery.

I go to the window and stare out at the row of terraced cottages opposite and the mountains. The sky is grey, heavy with rain and I wonder what living here in winter will be like. It was beautiful during the summer: clear skies. fresh air and birdsong. But now, since the nights have drawn in and a permanent dank mist hangs over the mountains, it's very different.

'There's a lot you don't know about her,' I say. The muscles in my shoulders are tense and I rub the back of my neck.

'You mean Selena?'

I nod. 'She's dangerous.'

'Dangerous?' He barks a laugh of disbelief. 'Bit melodramatic.'

I bite my lip to stop myself saying more. He doesn't know her, I remind myself. He doesn't know what she's capable of.

'Can you do me a favour?' I say, spinning round to face him. 'Try not to find yourself alone with her too often.'

He steps back, horrified. 'You think I'm so weak I can't be trusted with an attractive female?'

'It's not that. It's for . . .' I want to tell him it's for his own protection, but he's right: it does sound melodramatic. And I sound jealous.

My head pounds. I turn away, then I feel his warm hands on my neck. He starts massaging my shoulders. 'I don't know what's going on with you and Selena, but I hope you trust me.'

'Of course I do. I didn't mean it like that.' *It's her I don't trust.*

'Is that better?' His voice is low, gravelly. 'You're all knotted up. You should go for a massage.'

'When have I got time for one, Ade?' I say, moving away.

He looks like I've kicked him. 'I'm only trying to help.'

The hurt in his voice makes me feel guilty. 'I'm sorry. I know you are. I just feel stressed, that's all.'

For a moment he seems to want to say more, but instead he leaves the room in silence. Why do I feel so threatened by Selena being here? She took a grenade to my life once before, blowing it apart, and I'm terrified she'll do it again.

# 6

It's not until the evening that I talk to Selena. All afternoon I've been dreading it, knowing there will come a time when it'll be just the two of us, alone. Will I acknowledge what happened when we were eighteen? Or should I just avoid it, which was easier to do when I could avoid *her*?

Evie is tucked up in bed and Adrian is lying with her until she falls asleep or Amelia comes up. He does it every night. She says she's scared to fall asleep on her own. When we moved in, Amelia wasn't happy that she still had to share with Evie (Evie was overjoyed). And we had to compromise by painting the walls pale green rather than the pink Evie wanted, although she's put some flamingo stickers on the wall by her bed to make it look more girly. Evie won't go to sleep until Amelia is in bed and even then, she cries out in the night until one of us scoops her up and brings her into our bed so that she doesn't wake her sister. Adrian and I tell each other it's just a phase, that she's only six and will grow out of it soon.

Amelia is in the TV room with Mum, watching a programme about polar bears.

'Do you want a cup of tea, Mum?' I ask, poking my

nose around the door. Amelia's only half watching the TV while scribbling in her diary. 'It's bedtime soon, honey,' I say to her. She grunts but doesn't turn, and Mum says she'd love a brew.

I'm heading into the kitchen at the back of the house when I see Selena coming out of her room. It's the first time I've seen her since she arrived. She looks tired, as though she's just woken from a nap. There is a faint crease down the left side of her face. Without her heels she's my height again but much slimmer. She looks small and vulnerable standing there. She pulls the sleeves of her jumper over her hands and it jolts a memory – of us at Barry Island when we were fourteen and meeting those lads off the waltzers. One was called Levi, which had sounded so exotic. She'd kissed him, a proper open-mouth snog, and I'd watched with a mixture of jealousy and awe. Afterwards she'd behaved as though she did that kind of thing every day, although I knew she didn't. She'd worn black jeans and DM boots with a baggy jumper, the sleeves of which were too long and hung over her fingers. That day I'd looked at her differently: nine months younger than me yet she had kissed someone and I hadn't.

'It's weird, huh?' she says now, as though reading my mind. 'Seeing each other again after all this time. You've hardly changed.'

I think of the frumpy, overweight teenager I used to be and inwardly wince. And it wasn't as if Selena had been beautiful. We both had the Hughes nose, long and angular, but she'd exuded confidence, and her style had made her a head-turner. My mum always said Selena would look good in a bin bag, while I'd make an expensive dress look like it had come from a charity shop. To this day I'm more comfortable in jeans and a jumper.

I'd had boyfriends before Adrian came along: at Durham there had been a few serious, intelligent young men, who admired my independence, my feminist ideals. Selena was intelligent too: she just used it differently. While I was the over-achiever, she was the flaky, creative one. She had such a vivid imagination that I always thought she'd be a writer one day, but she was a rebel too. That was the problem.

She folds her arms across her chest. 'Still the solid, dependable one by the sound of it. And I'm still the emotional fuck-up.' She gives a bitter laugh.

I ignore it, refusing to be drawn. That was always her excuse for acting irresponsibly as a kid. As though having an alcoholic mother sanctioned it. I couldn't understand why it didn't have the reverse effect. But maybe it has now. She seems to have done well for herself, although I have no clue as to how she earns a living. And she's hardly a fuck-up, I think, as I remember how she was with Ruby earlier. Commanding, responsible, caring. 'I'm making a cup of tea,' I say, trying to keep my tone light. 'Do you want one? Or something stronger? I could open a bottle of wine?' I don't know why I say that. It implies I want us to have a cosy chat and I don't.

'I don't drink any more.' She shrugs. 'My mum. It can be hereditary.'

'Tea it is, then,' I say, bustling towards the kitchen. She follows me.

'Lovely place you've got here,' she says, glancing around. I see the kitchen through her eyes – cream flagstone tiles, painted wooden units in soft greys, a marble-topped work-surface and bi-fold doors leading on to the garden – and wonder if it gives her the wrong impression that we're financially well off.

'It was a wreck when we bought it,' I say, remembering the 1970s units we ripped out. 'We couldn't live here at first. We had to do everything. This room used to have hideous wallpaper and foam tiles on the ceiling.' I laugh at the memory. It had taken ages to scrape off that paper. I remembered my annoyance when half the plaster came with it.

'It must be hard work, running a guesthouse. All that cleaning and making beds.' She laughs softly. 'Although you were always the neat freak.'

'We've hired a local woman to help out with the cleaning. Changing the sheets, hoovering, that kind of thing.' I click the kettle on and turn to face her while it boils. She's standing by the island, running her hands along the worktops.

I remember what Mum said about Selena marrying a wealthy older man and wonder what happened. There is so much about her that I no longer know and I find it strange. For the first sixteen years of our lives we knew everything about each other – I knew what her favourite colour was, which albums she loved, whom she fancied. I knew her neck went red and rashy when she was stressed, that when she heard bad news her first instinct was to laugh, that she had a birthmark the texture of porridge behind her left knee. Then she'd met Dean Hargreaves and begun to change: she'd become more secretive, pulling away from me. And now here she is again, the new adult Selena.

I want to ask her so many questions but I'm terrified of getting too close – and of hearing something I wish I could un-hear. Like before.

'So . . .' She hesitates and brushes her hair off her face. She's not wearing her poncho now, just a silk shirt tucked into her jeans.

'So . . .' I say at the same time. We burst out laughing, and in that instant she's the girl I grew up with, the girl who got the giggles at every little thing, who hated silences, who talked non-stop, who couldn't watch a film all the way through without asking endless questions, who always wanted to know what happened next, after the story had ended.

'It's so lovely to see you again. I've missed you.' Her face crumples and I'm shocked to see that her eyes have filled with tears.

'Selena . . .' I move towards her.

She shakes her head, as though she's trying to make the tears disappear, and holds out a hand. 'I'm sorry.' She sniffs. 'I'm trying so hard to keep it together.' She reaches inside her sleeve for a tissue and blows her nose. 'It's just been so hard, you know. The last few years. With Ruby. And now with Nigel.'

'Nigel?'

'My husband.' She dabs at her nose. 'We've been rowing so badly. Such awful rows.'

'Has he – has he hit you?' I remember what Mum said about a violent husband.

She hesitates, and I wonder if she's going to clam up, which would be understandable, considering we aren't used to confiding in each other any more. But eventually she nods. 'His temper . . .' Her voice is hoarse. 'I've left him. I had to. For me and for Rubes.' She meets my gaze head on. She doesn't flinch, or look away. Is this another of her 'stories'? Then I remind myself that she's not that silly, eighteen-year-old fantasist any longer.

I break eye contact and move towards the kettle to make the tea. When I turn, she's perched herself on one of the wooden bar stools at the island. 'So, you've definitely left him? No going back?' I ask, as I hand her a mug.

She takes it with thanks and sips the tea, not speaking for a few moments. Then she says, 'Yes. We had an enormous row. The worst, probably. He doesn't know where we are. I – I just took Ruby and ran.'

'Oh, Selena.' Part of me, the selfish part, inwardly curses her, this woman who seems to leave destruction in her wake. Why does she have to choose now to come and see me? Now, when Adrian and I are still delicately putting our lives back together, as though our relationship is like the china doll the girls found: broken, now glued back together. When we're just about to open for business. Why does she have to involve us in the messiness of her life?

'He won't find me here,' she says, over the rim of the mug. 'He knows I hardly keep in touch with my mother. I haven't told him about you or Aunty Carol. No, he won't find me.'

I wonder if she's trying to convince me or herself. 'So what have you been doing all these years?'

She sighs. 'After Dad walked out I decided to leave Wales. I travelled for a bit and ended up in Manchester. Chasing some man. Isn't there always a man?'

*For you*, I want to say but don't. Instead I smile, encouraging her to continue.

'I ended up blagging my way into advertising. Did quite well. Then my mum became ill. Liver damage.' She rolls her eyes. 'It didn't kill her, or make her give up the drink. She still lives in the house I grew up in. Anyway, I know it's not very daughterly of me, but I couldn't stay with her.' She gives a derisive laugh. 'But she was never much of a mother, was she?'

I say nothing, although it's true.

'When I returned to Manchester I was looking for something. Someone. And then I met Nigel. He's quite a bit older than me and he made me feel safe, I suppose, after everything.'

And there it is. The lie. It hovers between us, a

spectre from our past. Does she still maintain it actually took place? I thought – hoped – that it was just another of her inventions. She was famous for them back then. She always enjoyed telling a story. Embellishing things so that the truth was buried, like a hazelnut in chocolate. What had been a little quirk in her personality – Nathan and I rolled our eyes in mock frustration when she wasn't looking – suddenly became a lot more damaging. Defamatory. Dangerous, even. Maybe she doesn't remember exactly what she said that night. Maybe she was just too drunk, too immature, to grasp the impact her latest 'story' would have. Maybe she was angry with me and wanted to shock. To frighten.

Or maybe – and this is the part I've struggled with over the years – I didn't *want* to believe her. And if that's the truth, what does it say about me?

# 7

## August 1989

*The first time I realized that Selena liked to tell 'stories' we were eight.*

*It was the summer holidays and we were bored, waiting on a bench outside Woolworths in Cardiff town centre while Mum was inside, hunting for a bargain. We often went shopping with her in the hope that she might be in a good mood and buy us sweets. Today was a good day. She'd let us have bubble gum. Pink and smelling of strawberries. Mum was also shopping for Aunty Bess, who often seemed to forget that her family had to eat. Uncle Owen was the same. He was a maths teacher, softly spoken and academic – so different in personality, if not in looks, from my larger-than-life, fun-loving dad – drifting around the house in his beige cardigan with the oversized chestnut-brown buttons that reminded me of conkers, head in the clouds, thinking of sums. But he was kind, and he adored Selena and me. Mum didn't approve of Aunty Bess. She never said so, but every time her name was mentioned Mum's lips would go thin in a way I knew meant she was annoyed. When we went over to their house – which was nearly every day – Mum's gaze would sweep around their small, square kitchen, taking in the empty vodka bottles on the sideboard and the newspapers stacked in the corner. Even at eight I could see that our house was nicer, more cared for. Homely.*

'You'll never guess what I found out?' Selena said, out of the blue. We'd been talking about how we wanted a pet, even though she kept stopping to blow bubbles. She did it now, and I waited, holding my breath. The gum popped against her face and she peeled it off, rolling it back into a ball and slipping it into her mouth again. 'I'm adopted.' Her face was serious as she picked at a scab on her knee. I stared at her legs, bruised at the shins – she was always falling over, spraining her wrists and ankles – then glanced at mine, which were much chubbier.

I fidgeted, suddenly feeling uncomfortable. 'What do you mean? That your mum and dad aren't your real parents?'

She nodded. 'Yep. I was helping Dad clear out the loft and I found it.'

'Found what?'

'This box. It was beautiful – pink and shiny. I looked inside and there was a birth certificate. Other names instead of my parents'. Lovely-sounding, they were. Greta . . .' She rolled the name around her mouth with the gum. 'Dad told me that he and Mum couldn't have kids of their own. That's why there's just me. And somewhere,' she threw her arms open, 'in this country, I have lots of brothers and sisters. More than you. More than just a brother.'

I thought of Nathan. Two years younger, always getting into trouble at school and taking up all of Mum's attention. Being an only child definitely had its advantages, I thought. Nathan had been this frightened two-year-old when he came to us. His real mother had been very young. She'd tried to look after him but couldn't cope. Mum said he hadn't been hurt, just neglected.

Mum couldn't have loved him more.

I frowned. 'But if you're adopted that means we're not related. We're not cousins after all.'

She tilted her chin defensively. 'Oh, we are. Of course we are. Maybe you're my sister. You could be adopted too and we were sent to different mums and dads when we were babies.'

I liked the thought of this. 'But if I was adopted they'd tell me. They told Nathan.'

She didn't have an answer to this. She just sat there, staring into space, chewing her gum.

But as we walked back, each carrying a shopping bag for Mum, I felt more and more despondent. Selena stayed for tea — she often did. I heard Dad say once we had to keep an eye on her, make sure she was being fed properly. But when she had gone home and Dad was sitting in front of the TV with Nathan, watching The Wonder Years, I asked Mum about it.

'Selena says she's adopted,' I burst out, while Mum bustled around our newly fitted kitchen, wiping down the glossy laminate worktops even though there wasn't a speck on them.

She turned to me and laughed, cloth in hand. 'Adopted? She's saying that because of Nathan. You only have to look at her and Owen to see they're father and daughter. You can't mistake that Hughes nose. You've both got it.' I touched my nose self-consciously. Mum hadn't made it sound like a good thing.

Selena never mentioned again that she was adopted. When I asked her about it — the next time I saw her — she pulled a face and said we must never talk of it because it was a secret.

That was the first of many.

# 8

I wake up with a start, my heart knocking against my chest, my throat dry. I lie here for a few seconds, wondering what woke me, then sit up, reaching blindly for the glass on my bedside table and taking quick gulps of water. I fumble for my phone, pressing the button and creating a white flash of light in the otherwise dark room. It's two a.m. I pick up my inhaler and have a few puffs, then fall back against the pillow, my breathing regulating.

Adrian is on his back, one arm slung across his eyes, snoring gently, his naked chest rising and falling, the duvet pulled up to his waist. I turn on to my side, but my mind is racing with thoughts of Selena and the conversation we'd had earlier.

After she told me she'd left Nigel I tried to press her on her plans, but she clammed up, proclaiming exhaustion, stepped daintily down from her stool and returned to her room. Now all I can think is that she's not going to leave. That she has no other plans and will stay with us for the foreseeable future.

I try to reassure myself as I turn on to my other side, my back to Adrian. I know she's family but she can't stay with us indefinitely even if she is paying. And what about all the money she's supposed to have? Does it all belong to her husband? If they get divorced, she'll be eligible for a pay-off, won't she? She could move into her own place. She's got Ruby to think about. My heart is racing again at the thought that she and Ruby have nowhere else to go. This is what Selena is like: a hose on a vacuum cleaner, sucking everyone around her into her life.

And what happens when the other guests arrive? Mum and I will be busy. We won't have time to worry about Selena. I keep thinking of the strangers who will descend on us tomorrow, filling some of the five bedrooms on the floor below. They could be anyone, paedophiles, murderers, psychopaths. Not for the first time since we embarked on this venture, I'm seized by anxiety. I want to wake Adrian, to share my worries with him. I always thought he was so strong. *Before.* An over-achiever, like me. I'd admired him. I'm no psychiatrist but I know I was attracted to Adrian because he shared the same qualities as the father I adored. Losing Dad when I was fourteen devastated me. I still miss him. I always will.

Before his breakdown, Adrian would have reassured me that everything was going to be okay. That we would sort it out together. As a team. But now everything is left up to me. Before Selena turned up, like an ex at a wedding, the only thing I feared was something happening to my girls. There are other niggles, of course – lack of money, living and working with my critical mother – but I can shrug them off because there's nothing I can do about them.

I stiffen. There's a noise coming from below. I sit bolt upright, straining my ears, heart thumping. Is Evie sleepwalking again? But it goes quiet, just the rhythmic sounds of Adrian's breathing. I'm about to lie down when I hear it again. A thud and a bang. I spring out of bed. I pull a cardigan from the chair by the door and wrap it around me. I dart into the girls' bedroom, exhaling with relief when I see they're both tucked up, fast asleep. Amelia's a messy sleeper – she's kicked off the duvet, is muttering as she dreams. Evie is in the same position as she was when I checked on her earlier, the duvet up to her chin, her smooth, plump cheek on her pillow. I can't resist going over to them both and planting kisses on their foreheads. I should get a lock on their door. All the guest bedrooms have keys, but up here we're vulnerable without some kind of security device. It doesn't seem right. Yet it seems equally wrong to ask the girls to lock themselves into their room at night. Why didn't I think of this before? Why didn't I consider the reality of having strangers living with us in our house?

I'm on the landing when I hear something else. Footsteps, I'm sure of it. The creak of a door, perhaps. It's coming from below. It must be Selena. It has to be. No one else is downstairs, apart from Ruby. Maybe she's ill. I need to check. I creep down the first flight, fumbling for the handrail so that I don't fall. There is more light on the next landing, thanks to the picture window. I can see the dark swell of the mountains behind a field of sheep. It's no longer raining and the night is clear, with a half-moon in the sky.

When I glance down I have a view of the front: I can see our Honda and Selena's SUV. And something else. Something moving across our driveway, nippy and animalistic. It looks like a man on all fours. My heart picks up speed again and I press my nose to the glass. There is definitely a man on our driveway. He's bending down behind the bonnet of Selena's car and keeps peering around it to look at the house. Should I ring the police? I'm frozen with fear. His features are in shadow and he's wearing a dark baseball cap pulled down over his face. His lean frame is swamped in a black Puffa jacket. From his clothes I would say he's youngish, but without seeing his face I can't tell.

Cold air brushes my ankles. I move away from the window and peer over the banister. The front door is open, knocking slightly in the wind. What the hell is going on? Just as I'm about to flee back to the attic to wake Adrian and call the police, I notice a flash of white outside. An angel in a long gown is walking towards the man. I take a closer look. It's Selena.

What is she doing outside? She's putting herself in danger. She looks like she's confronting this man. He stands up from his crouched position and rushes towards her, grabbing her arms almost aggressively. She's being attacked! I need to call the police. But then, to my surprise, she reaches up and touches his face tenderly. She knows him. This is so typical of Selena. I knew she wouldn't have changed that much. She's here, meeting men in the middle of the night. Some secret rendezvous. She'd better not invite him in.

And then she turns back to the house, her face worried, a perfect pale oval in the light of the moon. She pauses, swivels round so her back is to me again and starts gesticulating. Is she telling him to go? He pulls his cap further down over his face, thrusts his hands into his pockets and strides off. There is something familiar about his gait. She watches as he walks away, her back rigid. She's shivering. She must be freezing standing out there at this time of night in just a thin nightdress. Who was he and how did he get here?

I lean over the banister again, wondering if I should confront her, but she closes the door with a click – I'm gratified to see that she's turned the lock – and then she scuttles across the tiles. She looks like she's floating in her long nightdress. The moonlight catches her face, and I'm shocked to see that it's filled with fear.

# 9

*Three days before*

When I open my eyes the next morning, Evie is curled up next to me, her little body warm against mine. I didn't even notice her come in during the night. Adrian is still in the T-shirt and checked pyjama bottoms he slept in, bent over his table in the corner, his hands flying over the keyboard. He usually starts the day at six to go for a run or do some writing before the rest of us wake.

I sit up carefully, so I don't rouse Evie, and slide out of bed. Saturday. There is a lot to do before the first guests arrive, and Nancy can't start until tomorrow.

I glance at Adrian. He has his back to me but I can tell from his posture, and the constant tapping of his fingers on the keyboard, that he's concentrating. The noise goes right through me, setting my nerves on edge. I can't tell him about last night. Not yet. But it reinforces why I don't want Selena back in my life.

Selena is sitting at one of the oak dining tables next to Ruby. We've managed to cram eight into the reasonably sized room. I'm pleased we installed the doors in the dining room so that the kitchen can be sectioned off. I wish we'd done something to separate the attic from the rest of the house. I've been mulling it over in my mind since I woke up.

Mum is fussing around them, an apron with cartoon cats on the front tied around her middle. She's holding a frying-pan in front of her, trying to coax another egg on to Selena's plate. Selena barely looks up when I enter the room. Does she know I saw her last night? She looks fresher this morning, more colour in her cheeks. She's groomed and seems well-dressed, even though she's wearing jeans and a jumper, the same as me. Hers look more stylish, more feminine, the jumper thin with a large keyhole shape at the back that shows off her tanned neck and shoulders. I'd be cold in it.

Ruby is picking at her food in silence. I notice the absence of her wheelchair and wonder if Selena carried her in. I want to ask about her condition but I don't want to appear nosy or insensitive. Mum disappears into the kitchen with the frying-pan before I can ask for the remaining egg.

'Morning, Selena, Ruby,' I say brightly. Ruby looks up, a ghost of a smile on her lips. I sit opposite her. She's so pale and thin, with large grey eyes like Selena's. And mine. They are the Hughes eyes. In front of her there is a bowl of what looks like very runny porridge, mostly untouched. 'Would you like something else to eat? Toast? We have jam.'

As soon as I've spoken I see panic flash across Ruby's

features. She looks at her mother, but Selena shakes her head. 'I'm sorry, sweetheart. You know you can't have wheat.' She turns to me. 'Ruby is allergic to everything. We've spent years getting her diet just right. It's been . . .' She gives a heavy sigh and I see the pain in her eyes. I imagine all the years she has spent getting Ruby tested, worrying over her health, her diet, persuading doctors that she isn't just another neurotic new mother, that there really is something wrong with her child. I remember my own sister, Natasha, who did not live beyond eighteen months. I was four at the time but I'll never forget Mum's fury that the doctors had missed the vital signs in her of pneumonia. After the funeral, she'd stormed into the surgery, dragging me with her, and screamed at Dr Saunders that it was his fault, she was going to file a complaint, then collapsed in a sobbing heap on a chair while we both looked on in horror. That was the one and only time I ever saw my mum give in to her emotions. Usually she's so *stoic*.

'It's been very stressful.' Selena puts her head into her hands, suddenly looking older than her thirty-five years.

Mum, who has quietly appeared behind me, is galvanized into action. 'Shall I take Ruby outside to see the rabbits? The girls will be up in a minute. Although I expect Evie woke in the night.' The last words are aimed at me and there is a judgemental tone to her voice.

I bite back a retort. What does she think we should do? Leave Evie to cry in her room so that she wakes her sister and everyone else? Yes, the nightmares concern me, but I know it's just a reaction to the move, to the new business. Everything has changed for her: it's only natural that she's a bit unsettled. It doesn't help that she insists on keeping the hideous china doll she found. It sits on one of her shelves and she calls it Lucinda. That would be enough to give *me* nightmares. Mum had sewn some fabric around the doll's broken leg but it's a grubby thing. I hope Evie will get bored with it soon so that I can throw it away.

Selena turns to Ruby and asks gently, 'Do you want to go and see the rabbits with Aunty Carol?'

Ruby's eyes light up and she nods enthusiastically. 'Yes, please,' she says, and I'm surprised to hear her voice. It's soft, well-modulated, with no trace of the Welsh accent that Selena and I still possess. I'm stunned to see her pushing back her chair and walking tentatively towards my mum. It's then I notice the leg braces.

Selena meets my questioning gaze. 'Growth problems,' she whispers, when Ruby is out of earshot. 'She's small and skinny for a seven-year-old.' Seven? I had mistakenly taken her for five, maybe six at the most. She appears younger than Evie. I look behind me to see Mum helping Ruby through the kitchen towards the bi-folds that lead to the garden. My heart contracts and I'm embarrassed when my eyes sting with tears.

How could I have been such a bitch, resenting Selena and Ruby for coming to stay? I was so callous, worrying about my bloody business when I have two healthy daughters. In the end, that's the only thing that matters. I reach out and squeeze Selena's hand. 'Oh, God, Selena, I'm so sorry.'

She raises her eyebrow. 'What for?'

'For Ruby.'

She places her other hand on top of mine. 'It's not your fault.'

'No, I know that. It's just . . . it's so shitty. And I haven't been there for you . . .' I swallow the lump in my throat '. . . over the years.'

'I've missed you,' she says, in a small voice. 'And Ruby, she could get better, you know. I'm still hopeful. There are issues, a lot of issues, but we've come a long way and she might grow out of them.'

'What is she suffering from, exactly?'

Her shoulders sag. 'We don't know. She's still being tested. But what we do know is that she has Crohn's disease. Growth problems. Lots of physical issues . . . I think she has ME too, but the doctors, they're not sure about that. Trying to get nutrients into her – that's the main challenge when she's allergic to dairy.'

I eye the porridge she'd been eating. Selena, following my gaze, adds, 'She has to have porridge with water.'

'And, um, how is she mentally?'

Selena smiles weakly. 'She's fine. A little behind, with having to miss so much school. We had a tutor for a while. But she gets so tired. That's why we have the wheelchair. By the end of the day she finds it difficult to walk. Lack of energy. In the end I decided to home-school her, but there are definite gaps in her education.'

I think of her husband, Nigel. And of the man I saw her with last night. I'm tempted to ask her about it, but I feel we've reached some kind of understanding and I don't want to ruin that.

I haven't forgotten about the past, the lie. Of course I haven't. But we were different people back then. Just kids. We're adults now.

I find myself telling her that she and Ruby must stay, of course they must, for as long as they need to.

Evie's out of bed, her nose pressed to the attic window, when I return upstairs. I stand behind her, wondering what's holding her interest, and see Mum in the garden, placing Amelia's rabbit in Ruby's arms. There is mist in the air, obscuring the mountains and giving the garden an ethereal look.

When Evie senses me, she whisks round, her eyes bright. 'Ruby can walk!' she says, as though she's Colin from *The Secret Garden* – her favourite book at the moment. 'But what are those funny things on her legs?'

'They're leg braces.'

She chews her lip while watching Ruby cradle the black rabbit with Mum's help. 'Why does she have to wear them?'

'Because her bones haven't grown properly so she needs them to help her walk.'

74

'Why haven't her bones grown properly?' She turns to me, one of her fine eyebrows raised.

'Because of her illness.'

She frowns and opens her mouth to ask more questions.

'Why don't you get dressed and then you can play with them too?' I suggest, trying to change the subject. It will be good for Evie to have another child to play with, someone nearer in age. Since we moved here Amelia has pulled away from her. She's pulled away from me too. Everything I do or say is an embarrassment. I've seen her rolling her eyes at the school gates when I've waved goodbye. I try not to feel offended. I remember what it was like being on the cusp of puberty and embarrassed by your parents. Evie, on the other hand, still waves excitedly when I go to pick her up, rushing into my arms for a hug. And although Amelia has brightened since making friends with Orla, she still says she wants to move back to London. It's been a stressful year for her, first with Adrian's breakdown, then moving away from her friends. I've managed to shield Evie from Adrian's illness but Amelia, five years older, notices more. I just hope that, in time, Amelia will start to see Hywelphilly as her home.

Evie darts from my room and across the landing to hers. I can hear her wrestling with her wardrobe door – we bought it from an antiques shop in town, sanded and painted it, and the door always makes a sucking sound when it's opened. I'm still watching as, a few minutes later, she bounds out of the doors into the garden. I'm too far up to hear what they're saying but Mum turns round, her face breaking into a grin at the sight of Evie. I smile inwardly when I see what she's wearing: a summer dress and leggings. The fabrics and patterns all clash – floral prints with spots and stripes. Amelia would be appalled. Evie dresses with such abandon – she does everything that way – and I love it.

Evie pushes herself between Ruby and Mum and takes Princess from the hutch. The rabbit is so heavy she nearly drops it and laughs. Ruby steps back, looking a little unsure with Mrs Whiskerson in her arms. It looks cold outside. The children should be wearing coats.

I'm just about to move away from the window, my mind already flicking to the other guests' arrival, when I see Selena has wandered into the garden. She's standing to the side of the others. She has her arms wrapped around herself and is obviously unaware that she is being watched. I can see only the side of her face but her eyes are fixed on Evie. Something in her expression unnerves me. If I didn't know better, I'd think it was hatred.

## 10

Janice Lowly is a big, busty woman resplendent in a flow-ered caftan, carrying a fawn-and-black pug under one arm. She stands on the doorstep wearing a huge smile on her ruddy face. I notice a red gerbera entwined in her white frizzy hair. I like her immediately, even though my heart sinks at the sight of the dog. We have a no-pets rule.

Evie, behind me, squeals in delight.

'His name is Horace,' says Janice, stepping into the hallway. Immediately, Evie is stroking him and cooing. He wiggles and squirms, his tongue poking out of his mouth. Janice beams. 'Oh, he likes you, my dear,' she says. She has a trace of a Welsh accent. Then she turns to me. 'And you must be Kirsty. I think I spoke to you on the phone.'

'That's right. I hope you had a good journey.'

She nods beaming. 'Yes, I don't live too far away. Warwick. But I'm visiting my sister and she hasn't the space to put me up.' She turns to Evie. 'And what's your name, my dear?'

Evie blushes and buries her face in Horace's fur, muffling her reply.

Janice bends down so that her face is close to Evie's. 'Evie, well, that's a beautiful name.'

I don't have the heart to tell her we don't allow pets. I should have made it clear on the website. I have a sudden unpleasant vision of a Noah's Ark of pets descending on us this week. It's not that I don't like animals, it's just easier to say no from a hygiene and allergies point of view. Is Ruby allergic to dogs? I'll check with Selena.

'Well, Mrs Lowly, you're in Honeysuckle.'

She stands up, putting a hand to her back. I'd probably put her at sixty-five, seventy at a push. I'm not very good with ages. 'Call me Janice, please. Mrs Lowly will always be my mother-in-law!' She chuckles. Perhaps she'll be a recurring guest, with a sister in the village. I like the thought of getting to know her better.

'Great. Well, Janice, your room is just up the stairs, second on the left. I'll show you.' She has one small suitcase and a large shoulder bag. I offer to take the case but she waves me away.

'It's not heavy.' She follows me up the stairs, Evie close at our heels. 'Lovely place you've got here,' she says, taking in the pale grey walls, the biscuit-coloured carpet, the gilt-edged mirrors and French-style furniture.

'Thank you. We refurbished it. You're our first guest,' I say, discounting Selena.

'But you're from around here, aren't you? I detect a Welsh accent. Although it's not as broad as the locals'. My sister's is especially thick.'

I laugh. 'Years of living in London watered it down.

Although my friends there don't think so. They think I'm proper Welsh.'

She stops at the top of the stairs, panting, her gaze going to the arched window at the opposite end of the landing, which overlooks the mountains. 'Beautiful view.'

'Yes. We were very lucky to find this house.'

She turns to me. Her eyes are a startling bright blue. Spanish blue, I think it's called. 'Something bad happened here,' she says.

'Pardon?' I couldn't have heard right. My eyes flicker to Evie, my sensitive worrier, but she's still enraptured by Horace, who is squatting by Janice's large feet.

'This house has a bad energy.'

*She's one of those.* Adrian's mum is too. She's into anything mystical: angels, auras, energies, spirits. I have no time for it. 'Are you saying you don't want to stay here?' I'm trying to keep my voice even but there is an edge to it. I won't let her spook Evie. 'Have you changed your mind?'

Her face relaxes again. 'I'm sorry, my dear. I can pick up on energies, that's all. Do you know the history of the house?'

I shake my head. 'It was built in the late nineteenth century, 1875, I think the deeds say. It was standing empty for a long time before we bought it.'

'Get it for a steal, did you?'

I blanch at the forthright question. 'Well, um, I suppose. Although we had to spend a lot doing it up.'

'Hmm.' Her eyes dart around the landing and she runs her hand along the wooden balustrade. 'My sister will know more. She's lived here for the last forty years. I couldn't wait to move away. I left at eighteen when I married Roy. Although I remember the rumours . . .' She shoots a glance at Evie. 'I'll tell you another time. When there're no little ears flapping.'

I stand outside Honeysuckle, key in hand. When I turn Evie has legged it downstairs and Horace is in Janice's arms again. She's standing behind me but looking towards the staircase that leads to the attic where we sleep. 'I heard it happened up there,' she says, her face contorted. How do I tell her I don't want to listen to idle gossip without sounding rude? She's a paying guest, and we need to keep her happy.

'What happened?' I say, in an effort to be polite.

'Someone died . . .'

I turn the key and push open the door. 'Here we are then,' I say pointedly, relieved that Evie is out of earshot. I hope Janice isn't going to say this room has a bad vibe too, especially as it overlooks part of the churchyard. If I'd known, I would have put her in Freesia on the other side of the house. She breezes past me, Horace jumping out of her arms to land on the small double bed.

'Ooh, this is nice,' she says, all talk of energies and death seemingly forgotten. Horace is making snuffling sounds as he pushes at the duvet with his nose. Janice strides to the window and pulls back the curtains to get a better view. It's started to rain. Over her shoulder I can see the church's spire and the weather-beaten, ornate tombs jutting out of the ground, many cracked and leaning at odd angles.

'I know it overlooks the graveyard . . .' I wonder if I should offer her a different room.

She swivels round to face me, her expression serious. 'Oh, my dear. I'm not worried about that.' She narrows her eyes. 'Believe me, the dead can't hurt you. It's only the living who can.'

Later, after I've vacuumed the stairs, dusted the large French cabinet in the hallway, and dabbed away a smear on the rectangular mirror, the next guests arrive. I can't wait for Nancy to start tomorrow.

I hear voices and the crunch of gravel before the bell rings, reverberating through the house. My mother appears from nowhere to answer the door, wrestling it back with force on to the dark night. Somebody nearby must have started a bonfire as smoke drifts in with the guests. They announce themselves as Peter and Susie Greyson. I've put them in Hyacinth, a family room with a view of the garden. I shove the duster into the back pocket of my jeans and go to join them.

They look to be in their late forties. Susie is small and squat with a round, attractive face and dark hair piled on top of her head. Peter stands behind her, tall and thin, pink scalp showing through white candyfloss hair. He resembles a sergeant major. Two boys hang about by the front door. The older one – maybe fifteen – seems sulky, as if he'd rather be anywhere else, but the younger boy smiles, his freckled face lighting up when he notices something behind me. I turn to see what's caught his attention. Amelia is standing at the other end of the hallway, near the playroom. She's swamped in a lilac hoody and is twisting a strand of hair, scowling in the boy's direction. She turns away abruptly and disappears into the playroom.

The boy thrusts his hands into his pockets, appearing bemused.

'I'm Kirsty,' I say, stepping forward so that I'm standing beside Mum.

Susie Greyson smiles. She has a grey streak through her dark hair and is strangely glamorous, like Mrs Robinson in *The Graduate*. 'Are you the owner?'

I can feel Mum pulling herself up to her full five foot three. 'We are both the landladies here,' she says, and I swear she takes a step forward so that she is ever so slightly in front of me. I try not to let my irritation show as she offers to show them to their room. They trudge after her with their bags, Peter Greyson hauling his suitcase up each step with a huff, beads of sweat on his wide forehead. I hope he's not scuffing the wool carpet with his wheels. I wonder where Adrian is and if I should fetch him to help. Mum is wittering about the local area, as though she's been living here for years instead of weeks. I stare at their retreating backs with dismay, suddenly feeling redundant.

'Don't let it bother you.' Selena is standing in the living-room doorway, her arms folded. 'Aunty Carol means well.'

I consider saying I don't know what she's talking about. But she's family: she knows all our dynamics, our oddities and idiosyncrasies. Even after all these years apart.

'You know what she's like. Always trying to take over. To be in charge.'

I remember running to Selena's house after a row with Mum over homework and she'd listened as I ranted about how controlling and selfish she was, how she wanted to ruin my life. Selena had said, a little sadly, that her behaviour showed she cared. That it was better to have a mother who was interested enough in you to be controlling than one who sat in front of *Neighbours* drinking vodka and didn't give a shit about what you got up to.

I take the duster out of my pocket and move towards her. She steps aside so that I can get into the living room. It's empty – I wonder if any of them will use it later. Perhaps they'll sit on our sofas and watch TV while we hover in the kitchen feeling like intruders in our own home.

Selena follows me. Her eyes are sad. 'She's a strong woman. The way she coped with what happened to your sister, and then when Uncle Derren died . . .'

I flinch. 'I'm sorry to bring up your dad,' she says.

'It's fine.' But it's not. Losing Dad was the worst thing

that ever happened to me, even worse than losing Natasha. One day she was there and then she wasn't. I can't remember her being ill, just the void she left behind. But Dad was my world. He made me feel safe. He wrapped us all in his protective embrace, even Mum, so that we felt as though we could do anything. *Be* anything. Their marriage didn't crack when Natasha died: they seemed to grow stronger, crying together, talking about her, visiting her grave on birthdays and at Christmas. Her death wasn't a subject everyone was scared to bring up in case it turned Mum into a quivering wreck. No, Natasha was talked about. She continued to be one of the family. It was only after Dad died that Mum became the emotionally cut-off person she is today.

It wasn't until I held my own baby for the first time, all those years later, that it hit me. I loved Amelia. I'd do anything for her. I'd kill for her if anybody ever tried to hurt her. And then I thought of Mum and her little girl, who didn't make it past her second birthday, and cried as though my heart would break. Having my own daughter had given me an insight into what Mum had been through and how much she had lost. It frightened me. Looking back, I realize I could never enjoy my children when they were babies: I was too wrapped up in the responsibility of trying to keep them alive. Dad had died by falling off a building at the site he was working on, and Natasha died of pneumonia. How easily the people you love can be snatched from you. Suddenly. Without warning.

'Kirsty?' Selena is staring at me, an eyebrow raised. She must have been speaking to me. 'Are you okay?'

I nod and sit heavily on the sofa, swallowing the golf ball in my throat. 'Sorry, it's Dad. It's been over twenty years but I still miss him. Every day.'

She perches next to me, touching my hand lightly. 'I know,' she says. 'Your dad was the best . . . better than mine.'

I move my hand away and push back my hair from my face, suddenly feeling uncomfortable. 'Uncle Owen was great too. He tried, he really did. It couldn't have been easy for him, with your mum the way she was. And losing Dad was hard on him too. They were close, as you know.'

The air between us has changed. It's become charged, dangerous. Anything said out of turn could lead to a row like we had all those years ago. I need to tread carefully yet I'm compelled to continue, to clear the air once and for all so that we can truly move forward, now she's back in my life. 'I still can't believe he walked out the way he did. You were his life, but then he just disappeared.'

It was after her eighteenth birthday – after our row and her accusation. I wonder if he found out and left in disgust. Or were the wheels already in motion long before that? Was he waiting to leave his toxic marriage until his only child was old enough?

Selena stares at me, her face drained. Is she going to admit that she lied all those years ago? I return her stare, willing her to say something about the night of her eighteenth birthday, to admit she shouldn't have said it. That it was one story too far. But she doesn't.

She juts out her chin. 'Do you know what I think?' she says. 'I think you idolized my dad because of what happened to yours. But he wasn't perfect.'

I swallow. 'I know he wasn't. Nobody is. But he loved you, Selena. You have to admit that.'

'True. He did. But his love suffocated me.'

'Is that why you lied?'

Something changes in her expression and I can almost see her conflicting emotions rippling across her face. This is a pivotal point in our relationship. If she admits that she lied, we can move on. We can continue to be in one another's lives. But if she doesn't, well, our relationship is irretrievable, the damage too great.

She holds my gaze. 'Yes,' she says eventually. 'That's why I made it up. I made it all up. I was young and I was stupid. And I blamed Dad for Mum. For being weak. I'm sorry, okay? I should never have said those things to you. It ruined everything.' Her words tumble out, fast and furious.

She'd lied. Of course. I'd always known it deep down. Kind, soft Uncle Owen – *my dad's brother* – would never have been capable of the disgusting things she'd accused him of doing.

'Oh, Selena,' I say, sad that seventeen years have been wasted.

'I was messed up,' she mumbles, looking into her lap. 'I had an overactive imagination.'

An understatement.

'But I shouldn't have lied,' she continues. 'I lied about so many things.'

I take her hand this time, grasping it firmly. Her fingers feel thin under mine, like spindly twigs that would snap easily. 'I know. But, like you say, you were a messed-up kid. I'm sorry for running away. I didn't want to face it. I was shocked you'd make up something like that. Appalled, even. It made me question everything – our family. Us.'

She shuffles and the leather sofa creaks. I'd never have leather normally, preferring something cosier. But I needed something functional. Another reminder that this is a house for guests, not just for us. 'I'm sorry,' she mutters, not meeting my eye. 'I was jealous of you. You were always such a goody-goody, clever, off to university. And I didn't get the grades I needed. You were starting a new life and I was stuck in mine. I was a stupid little fool. I wanted to hurt you. I'm sorry.'

'Oh, Selena.'

She stands up abruptly and brushes down her jeans. 'I'd better get back to Ruby. She's asleep.'

I glance at the clock on the mantelpiece. It's a few minutes to seven. 'Wow, she goes to bed early.' I'm lucky to get Evie to bed by eight on a school night.

She plays with the ring on her wedding finger. A huge diamond. I wonder why she hasn't taken it off. She's still not looking at me. 'She gets over-tired . . . Being here, it's all very exciting for her.'

87

I stand up too. 'I'd better sort out my girls. I think they're in the playroom and the last guest should be arriving tonight.'

We walk towards the door. She stops and turns to me, looking me straight in the eye. 'I'm glad we had this chat. Can we forget about the past now, Kirsty? Can we move on?'

I nod. 'There's nothing I'd like more.'

She gives me an awkward hug. 'Great,' she says, as she pulls away. 'See you in the morning.'

My mouth twists into a smile. 'Maybe.'

She laughs then. The first genuine laugh I've heard since she arrived. 'Oh, my God! You remembered!'

I laugh too. 'Of course.'

'You were such a bitch.' She's wiping her eyes with mirth.

Adrian walks in. 'What's so funny?' he asks, bemused.

'Your wife. Tell him, Kirsty!'

I smile. 'Selena used to have this fear as a kid that she'd die in her sleep,' I say. 'She told me when she was staying the night at our house and after that I used to wind her up. When she said, "See you in the morning," I used to reply, "Maybe!" in this spooky voice. It became a standing joke.'

Adrian smiles blandly but I can see he doesn't really get it. 'Right. I just came in to ask if you want me to run Evie a bath.'

I lift my head in surprise. I usually have to ask him to sort the kids out – either that or I end up doing it

88

myself. 'Yes, if you don't mind. She's been rolling around outside with the rabbits again.'

He nods good-naturedly and wanders out of the room.

'You've got a good 'un there,' says Selena. 'Nigel never helped me with Rubes. He left everything to me.'

I feel a bit disloyal admitting to Selena that I usually have to nag Adrian into doing anything. Before, he was too busy working fifty-hour weeks and since his breakdown he's been distracted. Mum probably sent him in to ask.

I watch as Selena saunters down the hallway towards Apple Tree, a feeling I can't quite place tugging at my insides. I should be happy that she's admitted it was all a lie and relieved that we can put it behind us. But I'm not.

# 11

## 29 June 2001

*Aunty Bess and Uncle Owen's small terraced house was crammed with bodies. They were everywhere – clustered around the kitchen sink necking home-made cocktails, gyrating to Groove Armada in the living room, snogging on the sofas, puking in the toilet. I wandered through the rooms, bewildered and slightly panicky. What would Uncle Owen say if he could see the state of his house? He and Aunt Bess weren't exactly house-proud but this was something else. Why was Selena letting everyone run amok over his things? His lovely old books and his model train set in the spare room. He was very particular, Uncle Owen. The rest of the house might be in a muddle, with piles of newspapers littering the coffee-table and empty wine bottles lined up along the mela-mine worktops in the kitchen, but Uncle Owen liked his own things in their place. Fastidious, I heard my mum say once but I thought it was his little bit of control.*

*Uncle Owen was the complete opposite to my dad, who had been like a whirlwind. Everyone knew he was there when he entered a room. Big, loud and fun. He'd bought our 1930s semi from an old lady who'd lived in it for fifty years and he'd done it up single-handed. Uncle Owen was quieter. My granny always said he was 'the thinker' of the family. And he tried his best, he really did. As I'd grown older and more aware, I could see how hard it was for him to hold down his job and look after Aunt Bess and Selena. That was why Selena was always at our house. Uncle Owen could do only so much.*

*And since Dad had died Uncle Owen was like a surrogate father. Not that he could ever replace my dad, but I loved him. He was there for me and Mum, popping over to make sure we were okay with his half-hearted offers of DIY, even though he couldn't have put up a shelf. And my mum was more than capable: Dad had taught her well. She always knew how to put furniture together and could change a plug. But I think it was his way of keeping in touch, to make sure we were all still family, I suppose. Since Selena had got together with Dean Hargreaves six months before, I'd hardly seen her and I was worried that we were growing apart. In two months' time, we would be off to different universities. Different worlds.*

*Selena had been so excited when she'd told me her parents were allowing her to have the house to herself so she could celebrate her eighteenth birthday. It was obviously Uncle Owen's idea. He'd agreed to take Aunt Bess away for the weekend to Blackpool so that Selena could enjoy herself. Not that she'd seemed grateful when she was telling me about it, the week before. She'd alluded to a row she'd had with him but didn't elaborate. And I wasn't the best listener when she tried to slag off her dad. Only four years since my own father died, I thought she was lucky to have a dad. And anyone could see that Uncle Owen tried his best. Aunt Bess hadn't been sober in years.*

*I was becoming increasingly concerned as I wove my way through the throng of gyrating bodies. I hadn't seen Selena for* hours, and I was terrified that the police would be called and I'd get into trouble as the eldest.

'Have you seen Selena?' I asked one of Dean's mates, who was huddled in a corner with what looked like a crudely put-together bong. I'd tried to convince her not to invite Dean, or any of his crowd, but she'd just laughed and said she had to invite her boyfriend. I was worried Dean would cause trouble. He was always getting picked up by the police for something – petty theft, vandalism, drugs. I wished Selena would stay away from him. He walked around his estate like he owned it and most people were scared of him.

'Upstairs,' he muttered, before inhaling again. I pushed past the couples in the doorways, stepped over bodies on the stairs and found Selena in her bedroom. She was slumped on her bed. On the wall over her head was a black-and-white poster of Robert Smith. An empty pint glass was on its side on the faded pink carpet. She was alone.

'Selena?' I ran over to her, shaking her shoulder. Her leg was bent under her and her eyes were ringed with mascara, her dress riding up to show her bare legs. I wondered if she was drunk. Or, worse, on drugs. 'Selena!' I cried again, louder this time. Her eyes blinked open. They were puffy, as though she'd been crying.

'What?' She sat up, rubbing her eyes.

'What are you doing up here on your own?' I cried. 'The party's getting out of control. Do you know that Dean's friend has a bong? You need to tell everyone to go. They're wrecking the place.'

She sat up straighter and pushed the hair off her face. Her lips looked unusually pale. 'I think you should go home,' she said, her voice deadpan. She blinked at me.

'What?'

'You heard me. I think you should just fuck off home. You're a party pooper. A square. Face it, Kirsty.' Her words were slurred, spittle flying out of her mouth and wetting her lips.

Blood pounded in my ears. 'Why? Because I don't want you to trash your parents' house? Uncle Owen—'

She jumped off the bed, her face red. 'Shut up about Uncle fucking Owen! Do you know why I'm up here on my own? At my own party?'

'You're drunk,' I said, turning away in distaste.

She grabbed my arm and spun me around so that I was facing her. 'I'm up here because of Dean.'

'Dean?' I wondered if they'd had another row. I couldn't understand the attraction, especially as they didn't seem to like each other much.

'Yes, Dean. Another person you disapprove of because you're so fucking perfect, aren't you? With your Durham University place and your perfect grades. And me? What's going to happen to me?'

I frowned. 'What are you talking about? You've got a place at Glamorgan.'

'I'm not going anywhere. But I think you knew that, didn't you? No. I'm staying here. With my fucking perfect dad and my bitch of a mother.'

She was ranting, talking nonsense, slurring her words.

'Have you had a row with Dean?' I said, trying to stay calm.

'Yes, I've had a row with Dean!' she cried. 'And do you want to know why?' She didn't wait for me to reply. 'Because he wanted me to sleep with him. And I said no.'

'Well . . . that's great,' I said, thrown. 'You've done the right thing. If you don't feel ready . . .'

*She stared at me for the longest time, then laughed. It sounded cruel. Mocking. I couldn't understand why she was behaving like that. I assumed it was the drink.*

*'Oh, but I'm not a virgin.'*

*This conversation was making me uncomfortable. There was a time when we shared everything but she had changed since she'd met Dean.*

*'Look, Selena. Whatever. I don't want to be having this conversation with you.'*

*'Why?' she said. Her fists were clenched by her sides. Her eyes were wild, the pupils huge. Was she on something?*

*'Because.' I was stone-cold sober. I'd had a half of lager hours ago. I sighed. 'Because I never know what to believe, okay? One minute you're a virgin. Then you're not. Then you are again. Whatever, Selena. I don't care.'*

*Her expression changed, her lips turning up so that it looked like she was snarling. 'You don't care? Well, that's pretty obvious. Do you want to hear who did take my virginity, eh? Your precious Uncle Owen.'*

*I staggered backwards. What was she talking about?*

*'Yes, that's right.' She laughed, setting my nerves on edge. 'Are you jealous about that? Did you want my dad for yourself?'*

*'You're disgusting!' I said, my voice shaking. 'You're a bullshitter. You always have been.'*

*She laughed cruelly.*

*'You lie about everything!' I cried. 'About being adopted. About getting into university — because I imagine that's a lie too. I don't know who you are any more.'*

*The door opened then and Dean staggered in. He had the*

kind of grey complexion that looked unhealthy. He was holding a can of lager.

'All right, Kirsty,' he said, winking at me.

I tried to keep my face impassive but I wanted to recoil.

He wagged a finger at me. He was clearly off his head. 'The trouble with you is that you're a snob,' he slurred. 'Ain't she, babe? She thinks she's better than us.' He went over to Selena and threw an arm around her neck. She leaned into him, while shooting an evil stare in my direction.

They were ganging up on me. I felt bullied. Selena, who was always on my side, had turned against me. Because of him.

Why had she said that thing about Uncle Owen?

She was bound to apologize. We'd never rowed like that before. She opened her mouth, her eyes narrowed. Flashing. 'Yeah, why don't you fuck off?' she spat, snaking her arm around his waist. 'Fuck off back to your perfect little life.'

I stared at her, hurt that she could be so poisonous to me after everything we'd been through. Then I turned and ran from the room.

# 12

The last guests turn up late, gone eight o'clock. They step into the hallway in macs and wellies and I try not to show surprise at how young they are. They can't be more than about eighteen. The boy is tall and gangly with mousy hair and freckles. The girl is pretty, with curly dark hair and big blue eyes. She blushes and steps behind him slightly.

'Um, we, um, booked a room. Under Toby Wilson,' the boy says, his face turning so red that his freckles are obscured.

'Of course,' I say, trying to remain professional when, really, I want to ask them if their parents know where they are. I ask him to fill in a registration form, then show them to the bedroom we've named Tulip.

'Please let me know if you need anything,' I say, and they both nod eagerly but I can tell they want me to leave.

I'm glad that everyone has checked in, although I can't relax. Each guest has a key to the front door as well as their room in case they want to go out, but the thought of people coming and going until God knows when does worry me.

I long to lounge in front of the television in my dressing-gown but I can hear that the Greyson family are in the living room, *Strictly Come Dancing* blaring. I love that programme but haven't had the chance to get into it this year. Will I ever get used to strangers using this house as though it's their own?

Adrian is perched at the kitchen island with a newspaper spread in front of him, the ceiling lights shining on the hair that is thinning at the back of his head. He has dark circles around his eyes, one of which is still bloodshot. The girls are next to him, with freshly washed hair, smelling of fruity shampoo and bath bombs. They're sipping hot chocolate, huddled in their dressing-gowns, Evie's legs, still too short to reach the bar of the stool, swinging. Looking at them, the people I love more than anything in the world, I can almost forget we have strangers in the house. Mum has gone up to bed and I try not to feel irritated that she's thought nothing of leaving me to see to everything. I know we need to discuss the ground rules, because I go from thinking she's taking over at one minute and not doing enough the next.

There are two vacant rooms ready for last-minute bookings. I need to speak to Adrian about locks for our bedrooms in the attic, but I don't want to bring it up now in front of the girls. I won't give Evie another reason to have nightmares.

'Do you think I need to go in and speak to them?' I say to Adrian, as I hover by the kettle.

'Just leave them,' says Adrian, without looking up from the newspaper.

I'd never expected to feel like this. I'd made the mistake of using this house as a home and now I feel that my space has been invaded. We'd usually sit in the playroom but felt uncomfortable as soon as Janice wandered in with a wet Horace, saying she'd been caught in the rain giving him his last walk of the evening. We had planned to use it just for the girls, but I hadn't the heart to tell Janice it was out of bounds. Maybe that needs a lock too.

'I want to watch TV before bed,' says Evie, putting her cup down and looking at me beseechingly. She has a chocolate moustache.

'Yes,' hisses Amelia. 'It's not fair that we're stuck in here and everyone else is in our living space.' I smile to myself. Living space. It's the sort of thing my mum would say. 'And they have TVs in their bedrooms. Why are they down here too?'

'Be quiet. They'll hear you,' I say, putting a finger to my lips. 'We're just trying to work it all out. Okay? This is the first weekend with guests. Maybe we can do something about the playroom. Make it off limits?' I look towards Adrian. He's still immersed in the newspaper. 'Ade?' He looks up. 'Locks. On the playroom maybe. Then the girls can have somewhere private to go.'

'What's wrong with their bedrooms?' He looks up, rubbing his beard, his eyes searching out the newspaper again.

'We don't have a TV upstairs,' points out Amelia, 'because you won't let us have one.'

This last statement is aimed at me. I'm about to retaliate when Selena wafts into the kitchen in a cloud of perfume. I haven't seen her since our conversation earlier. She's wearing the long white nightdress she had on last night. It shows off her tanned arms, and as she walks towards me I can see the outline of her underwear. Adrian looks up from his newspaper.

'Everything okay?' I ask. It's only eight thirty but I'm exhausted and want to go to bed, which I can't until the Greysons have retired.

'Do you have a thermometer? I think Ruby's running a bit of a temperature. I left in such a hurry I forgot to pack mine. I could kick myself.'

She looks distressed and I tell her not to worry while I ferret in one of the high cupboards where we keep all the medicines. 'Here we are.' I hand it to her. 'Is Ruby feeling okay?'

Her face crumples. 'God, Kirsty, I hate this. I hate this *fear*. Every temperature. Every pain and ache. Every time she says she's tired or feeling sick . . .'

Adrian hops down from his stool and comes to stand beside her. 'She'll be okay,' he says reassuringly. He's so good at putting on a brave face. Even during his breakdown he tried not to make a fuss. I sometimes wonder if it would all have happened as it did if only he'd admitted how he really felt, how desperate he'd been. But he'd put a brave face on it for as long as he could. He's so much better at that than I am. 'You're doing a great job, Selena. You're keeping her safe.'

99

'Am I?' she says, anguish in her voice. 'I've taken her away from her father and her lovely home, from everything she's familiar with. And I have no plans. I don't know what to do, where to go . . .' Her voice is rising and Evie is looking at us in alarm.

I move away from Selena and go to the girls. 'Amelia, will you take Evie up to bed, please? It's way past her bedtime as it is. Clean your teeth and I'll be up in a minute.'

For once Amelia does as she's told. She takes Evie's hand and leads her into the hallway and up the stairs. 'Don't be long, Mummy!' Evie wails, her eyes darting to me and then to Selena.

Selena does look a bit unhinged with her usual pristine bob awry, her eyes wild, cheeks flushed. I can see she's scaring Evie. 'Don't worry, honey. I'll be up in a minute.'

Adrian is murmuring comforting words to Selena. I can't hear what he's saying but he's obviously talking her down. He's almost like he was before his breakdown. I remember how many times he had to talk me down when the girls were little and I'd be fretting about their health, or their safety.

'I'm sorry,' she says, moving away from him. 'I just don't know if I've done the right thing, leaving Nigel.'

'You can't stay with him if he's violent,' I begin.

'Violent?' interjects Adrian. 'I didn't realize he was violent. Then you've definitely done the right thing, getting away from him.'

She sighs and smoothes down her hair with one hand. I feel uncomfortable with her in that nightdress. Not that I'm a prude but it's quite revealing. Adrian must have noticed.

She holds up the thermometer. 'Thanks for this. And for being so kind.' Her eyes go to Adrian and she smiles. I can see him blushing and feel a stab of jealousy, like the jab of a sword to my gut. Adrian hasn't looked at me like that for ages.

'I've got Calpol, if you need it,' I call, as she heads to her room. But she doesn't hear me.

I'm lying next to Evie in her bed, my arms wrapped around her, listening to her gentle snores, when I hear it. Footsteps on the stairs. I glance at Amelia in the next bed, the scant moonlight from the half-opened curtains highlighting her face, serene in sleep. Tomorrow I'll be sending Adrian out for locks to put on these doors. I was so worried about the girls being in an unlocked room above strangers that I had no choice but to sleep with them. I could tell Adrian thought I was being over-protective, and he's probably right. But I can't risk their lives. I'd never forgive myself if Peter Greyson ended up being a psycho, or Janice a child-thief.

I strain my ears, my heart pounding. But there's nothing. I'm just about to settle down again when I hear another creak and the bang of a door. Is Selena going out to meet another mystery man?

Gently, so as not to wake Evie, I swing my legs out of bed and carefully open the bedroom door. Across the hallway I can see a figure outside my bedroom. I gasp. My first foolish thought is that it's a ghost, that Janice was right, but then my eyes adjust to the dark. It's Selena in her floating nightdress. Her hand is on the doorknob. Why is she sneaking into my bedroom?

'Selena?'

She spins around, her face nearly as pale as her nightie. 'Kirsty. I was coming to wake you. I need to call an ambulance and I can't find my phone charger. It's Ruby. Please hurry.'

'What's happened? What's wrong?'

'She's had a seizure. It hasn't happened for a long time so I'm worried. Please, call an ambulance!'

I dash past her into my bedroom and retrieve my phone from my bedside table. Adrian wakes with a grunt. 'What's going on?'

'It's Ruby,' I say. 'I'm calling an ambulance. Keep an eye on the girls.' I run from the room again to join Selena. She's pacing the landing. 'Ambulance, please.' I reel off the address to the operator while Selena looks on, chewing her thumbnail. I wonder why she hasn't gone back downstairs to be with Ruby. I wouldn't want to leave my child alone if she'd had a fit.

Mum emerges from her bedroom in her pyjamas. 'What's going on?' she whispers.

I fill her in, while steering Selena towards the stairs.

'Ruby?' Mum's face crumples. 'Is she okay?'

'I don't know, Mum.' As I pass my bedroom door I see Adrian getting out of bed to check on the girls. I don't have to turn to know that my mother is following us.

Selena's words are coming out in gasps and I have to jog to keep up with her. 'She woke up screaming and then she started thrashing and jerking. It was terrifying – it's been such a long time since she fitted.' Her voice wobbles. 'And my phone was dead. And I forgot to pack my charger.' She gives a muffled sob. 'And I had to leave her to get help.' She's actually running now.

'It's okay,' I say, even though I have no idea if that's true.

She reaches Apple Tree first and pushes the door open. Ruby is lying on one of the twin beds in her vest and pants, her sheets twisted beneath her, a sheen to her skin. 'Ruby.' Selena runs over to her and pushes back her hair. It's wet with sweat. 'It's okay, darling. I'm here. I'm here now. We're just going to take a little trip in the ambulance.' By the bed I see a wet towel crumpled on the floor.

'Not the hospital again,' Ruby wails.

'It's okay, they'll just check you over. Make sure there's nothing to worry about.' She sinks to her knees, gripping Ruby's hand in both of hers. Ruby looks resigned to what's about to happen. Selena glances across Ruby's prostrate body to me. 'She's still very hot. I gave her Calpol . . .' She notices me frowning and adds, quickly, 'I forgot to take it from you earlier but I

103

remembered you had some in your cupboard. It hasn't brought her temperature down.'

'Could it have been a febrile convulsion?' I offer.

'She might be a little too old for them,' says Selena. She's standing up now and is pulling on jeans and a jumper.

Mum bursts through the door, her hair elegant even at two in the morning. 'The ambulance has arrived. Do you need any help carrying Ruby?' she asks Selena.

'It's fine. We'll be fine. Thanks, though, Aunty Carol.' She helps Ruby into a pink dressing-gown, then scoops her up as though she weighs no more than a doll and carries her out of the room.

Adrian has let in the paramedics, who are waiting in the hallway, the front door wide open. The blue lights of the ambulance are flashing, reflecting in the windows of the cottages opposite. My next-door neighbour, Mr Collins, has his face pressed to an upstairs window. The paramedics strap Ruby to a chair and Mum rushes back to Selena's room to get her coat and shoes.

'Do you want one of us to come with you?' I ask.

Selena shakes her head. 'No, thanks. Go back to bed. I'll ring you from the hospital.' She throws me a wan smile. 'You'd think I'd be used to this by now, wouldn't you? But it doesn't get any easier.'

I go into the office and snatch up a spare phone I have in my drawer. It's only pay-as-you-go and I'd planned to give it to Amelia when she starts senior school next year. I punch my number into it. 'Here, have this,' I say, pressing it into Selena's hand as she won't have hers. 'Please let me know how she is.'

I watch as they carry Ruby to the ambulance, Selena trotting behind them. My heart is heavy as I close the door on them.

'She'll be okay, love,' says Mum, rubbing my arm in a rare show of affection. I should be the one comforting her. It must make her think of Natasha.

As we climb the stairs I see Janice on the landing outside her room in a hot-pink velour dressing-gown, cradling her pug. She's wearing a hair net.

'I'm sorry if we woke you,' I say.

She shakes her head and I think she's going to tell me not to worry, or ask who the ambulance was for, but instead she mumbles something about bad energy, then goes back to her room.

# 13

*Two days before*

It's torture getting up early the next morning to make breakfast. Even though it's Mum's turn (we set up a rota so that one of us would get a Sunday lie-in once every three weeks), I feel, as it's our first proper morning, I should be on hand to help.

As I shower and get dressed I think wistfully of all those Sundays in the past when we got up late and mooched around the house, the girls playing together, Adrian watching football, me pottering in the garden or kitchen. Would we ever have another lazy Sunday?

Mum and I creep down the stairs, hoping not to wake anyone. It's still dark outside and the wind is howling down the chimney and rattling the windows. I hardly slept after Ruby was taken to the hospital and now I feel sick with tiredness. I don't know how I'm going to face cooking bacon and eggs.

As I pass the front door I pause. I can see a dark shadow through the glass as though something has been tied to the door knocker. I think of the dead flowers we received two mornings ago. I hadn't mentioned them to Mum, or Selena, not wanting to worry them and not even sure if it was anything to worry about. Mum hasn't noticed that I've stopped and continues on to the kitchen. But I open the front door, wanting to make sure there isn't anything untoward hanging there for Selena to find when she returns home with Ruby.

I look down at the empty doorstep. Then I turn to the door. I was right. Something has been attached to the knocker: a bouquet of dead flowers tied with twine and hanging almost upside-down, obscuring the glass panel in the door.

Even though I'd been half expecting them, I still gasp in shock, the cold air hitting my lungs. Calla lilies this time. I love them. I had them in my wedding bouquet. But most people think of them as funeral flowers. I reach out and touch a petal, once creamy white but now yellow. Who is leaving them here – and why?

My hands tremble as I untie the flowers. I dispose of them quickly, shoving them into the designated gardening bin on top of the dead roses we'd received the other day. Despite how unsettled I feel, I'll only tell Adrian if he finds them and asks.

Mum and I are cooking and making tea when we hear the bed creaking in the room above us. It's Room Five – Tulip. It must be the teenage lovebirds. Mum turns to me in shock and I clamp my hand over my mouth to stop myself giggling.

'Didn't you say they were only about eighteen?' says Mum.

I nod, unable to speak.

'Well, they're obviously here for a dirty weekend.' She sounds disapproving and I shush her, knowing they'll be mortified if they think we can hear them. They looked like they wanted to shrivel up with embarrassment just being in the hallway with me yesterday.

'I'll put the radio on,' I say eventually, when the creaking speeds up.

'Good idea,' Mum replies, not looking at me but at the sausages she's prodding with a spatula. I can see a flush on her cheeks. Soon Radio 1 obliterates the creaking – once it would have been Adrian and me, when we first met. If Adrian had been here with me now we would have been in hysterics and, in that moment, I miss him. I miss the way things used to be between us.

The teenagers come down first for breakfast, about nine o'clock. They barely make eye contact with me as they slink into their seats, and when they talk to each other it's in very low voices. They're staying for two nights, and I try not to feel uneasy that we've had no more bookings even though it's half-term week. I remind myself that the house was practically derelict before we bought it and had been standing empty for over a year. It had been a type of boarding-house once, but that was decades ago. When we'd first met Kath and Derek at the Seven Stars, they'd told us how busy they always were and how they'd wondered why nobody had thought about turning this place into a guesthouse again. It had given us hope that it would be a good business venture, not something that could potentially bankrupt us, but now, as I glance around the empty dining room, I feel a twinge of anxiety.

Mum must notice because when we return to the kitchen to put more sausages on, she says, 'I know bookings are a bit sporadic at the moment, but I think it will be quite slow until the Easter holidays.'

'We should advertise on those Brecon Beacons websites,' I say, throwing another sausage into a pan.

'You might be right,' she agrees, running her hands down her apron, then going to put the kettle on. 'You look like you need a cup of tea.'

'It's a pretty village,' I muse. 'There's the little café and the gift shop, the church, great walks, and it's only a few miles from that lovely market town, Crickhowell.'

She clicks her tongue. 'Stop panicking. We have quite a few people booked in on the weekends leading up to Christmas. And we still need to decide if we're going to have paying guests over the Christmas period itself.'

My heart sinks. I hadn't wanted to but we don't have much choice. Not if we want to start breaking even. 'Maybe.' I think of the girls. It can still be special for them, even if we are open to the public.

'Have you heard from Selena?' I move away from the sausages to get a plate. I can see Janice and her dog settling themselves at a table next to the teenagers.

My mum shakes her head. 'She rang me earlier in a bit of a state. Poor child.' I'm not sure if she's referring to Ruby or Selena. 'She said she'll ring back when she knows more. Here, drink this.' She hands me a mug. 'You look exhausted. You could take those bags under your eyes on holiday they're so big. I'll just go and see what Janice wants for breakfast.' She bustles off.

At least Janice is staying for the week, as are the Greysons.

It suddenly gets busy as the Greysons also come down for breakfast, disrupting the peace and quiet. Janice frowns at the two boys as they shove and jostle for a place at the table. I'm dashing around, plonking eggs, sausage and bacon on plates, when Amelia and Evie come in, still in their pyjamas. They look cute but out of place among the other guests, who are all dressed and ready to go out for the day. Mrs Greyson is even wearing dark red lipstick along with her hiking boots. I smile to myself, wishing I could look glamorous in hiking gear, when I turn to see Evie by my side. 'I'm starving,' she moans.

'Me too,' says Amelia. Her pretty face is dour as she examines her fingernails, and I know it's for the benefit of the younger Greyson boy, whom she can see through the open dining-room doors.

'Can you just get out from under my feet for two minutes while I finish serving the guests? Sit at the breakfast bar,' I say, rushing out into the dining room with two plates of food. Mum follows me with a tray of tea and toast.

'This is more exhausting than I imagined,' I say to Mum, when we're back in the kitchen. 'And we haven't even got a full house. Right, girls, what can I get you?'

They both want Shreddies so I reach into the cupboard to retrieve the box and shake them into bowls.

'About that,' begins Mum, at my elbow.

'About what?' I hand the girls their cereal and Amelia hops off of the bar stool to get milk.

'About the fact we have rooms unoccupied this week . . .'

I have a bad feeling about this. We already have Selena staying here uninvited, who else does she want? 'Yes?'

'Well, Nathan called yesterday. He wondered if he and Julia could come and stay. They'll pay. I haven't told him Selena's here. It will be a nice surprise.'

I'm sure he'd love to see Selena again. He had a huge crush on her when he was about fifteen. This week really is turning into a family affair. I sigh. 'I can't really expect them to pay. He's my brother.'

'He knows we're running a business.'

I laugh. 'You know Selena's not paid yet, right?'

She frowns. 'That's different. She's going through a hard time right now but I know she'll pay her way.'

I hold my hands up. Mum is like a bulldog where Selena's concerned, always has been. I don't voice it, but I'm surprised Nathan wants to come. We've hardly seen him since Adrian's breakdown although I've missed them, particularly Julia, whom I adore. 'Whatever, Mum. If you want Nathan to come, it's fine by me.'

She flashes me a victory smile. 'He'll be here about five.'

'Five! He's coming tonight? Why so soon?'

Mum stands up straighter and purses her lips. 'You've forgotten, haven't you?'

My mind whirls. What have I forgotten?

'My birthday. I know – at my age there isn't much to celebrate but Nathan likes to come and see me.'

I feel like the worst daughter in the world. Because she's right, I had forgotten. 'Oh, Mum, I'm so sorry. I've had so much on my plate, what with opening and Selena coming and . . .'

She waves a hand dismissively. 'It's fine,' she says, in a voice that clearly means it's not. She picks up a jug of orange juice and stalks out.

Nancy turns up at ten thirty, as she'd promised when I met her last week, her dyed black hair scraped up in a topknot. She has on too much liquid eyeliner, and her dark leggings are stretched so thin in places you can see glimpses of her flesh. She's older than me – I'd put her at mid-forties – but dresses much younger.

'Hi,' she says, as she breezes into the hallway and takes off her padded coat. She looks around and then, not finding an obvious place to hang it, hands it to me. 'Where shall I start?'

She's never been here before as I'd hired her in the Seven Stars after Kath and Derek recommended her, and I'm surprised she doesn't make any comment about the house. Kath said Nancy lives in the village, so she would have seen how rundown the place was. 'Well, the guests in Tulip have just gone out so there's the bed to make, hoovering, dusting, the en-suite needs cleaning, and there's the tea tray to deal with.'

'What about the other rooms? Are they all named after flowers?' She laughs as though the idea is ridiculous.

I ignore the question. 'The same, apart from the two unoccupied rooms, but I'll also be helping.'

'Cool.' She's chewing gum. 'I'd better get a wriggle on as I've got to go to the Seven Stars after to do their rooms.'

'Okay.' I hand her a plastic box of cleaning equipment. 'I'll bring the vacuum up.' I dart into the office, throw her coat over the back of the chair and retrieve the key to Tulip. 'Here we go.'

'Great. Thanks.' She takes the key and wanders up the stairs, looking around her as she goes, taking in everything.

'Third on the left,' I call up after her but she doesn't answer.

I follow her up the stairs with the vacuum and knock on Janice's door before entering, even though I'm fairly sure I saw her go out with Horace earlier. Her bed is unmade and there is a dog-shaped indentation on the chair where Horace must have slept. I straighten the bed and run the vacuum cleaner over the carpet, amazed by the amount of dog hair. As I'm replacing her tea tray I notice a stack of tarot cards by her bed. Intrigued, I pick them up. They are loose and the one on top is Death. I flinch at the sight of the armoured skeleton on horseback and replace it quickly.

When I'm outside the room I take out my inhaler, closing my eyes as I puff and breathe in, feeling my airways open.

'Are you okay?'

I open my eyes to see Nancy standing in front of me.

I return the inhaler to my back pocket. 'Just the dust. Gets to my chest at times.'

'It's all the building work you've had done,' she says, still chewing gum. 'It unsettles things.'

I think of the tarot cards in Janice's room, the broken doll Evie found under the floorboards, and repress a shiver.

After I've left Nancy vacuuming, I let myself into Selena's room. It's just as it was in the middle of the night. Beds unmade, clothes spewing out of a suitcase. As a kid she was always untidy. I notice her mobile phone on the pine dressing-table and, remembering what she said last night, I pick it up so that I can look at the model to see if it will fit my charger. The battery sign to the right of the screen indicates that she has 27 per cent charge. Puzzled, I replace it where I'd found it.

I straighten the beds and make up her tea tray with fresh cups, coffee, teabags and biscuits, all the while thinking about her phone. Maybe she'd panicked. It was dark, she was worried about Ruby. Maybe she'd assumed it had died. That must be it. Otherwise, why would she lie?

*

Selena calls mid-morning to say they should be back by teatime.

'What did they reckon is wrong with Ruby?' I ask.

'An infection. Because of her problems they wanted to keep her in. But she's feeling much better. They gave her a strong dose of antibiotics.' The relief in her voice is evident, although she sounds exhausted. In the background I can hear the faint chatter of other people and the clatter of cutlery.

'Thank goodness,' I say happily. 'We were all worried about her.' Evie had been upset when I'd explained that Ruby was in hospital, and asked if she was going to die. I'd downplayed it by telling both girls it was just a check-up. 'Mum said you'd called her earlier. You had her number in the phone I gave you?'

'No.' Her voice sounds echoey. 'I remembered it. Years of calling her, I suppose. She refuses to update her phone.'

*Years of calling her.* How often had they been in touch?

'Do you want me to pick you up from the hospital?' I ask. I can leave Nancy to sort out the rest of the rooms.

She clears her throat. 'Um, no, that's really kind but it's okay. We'll get a taxi.' She says goodbye and hangs up. I stare at the phone in my hand, then replace the receiver. I know I shouldn't let it bother me, it's all so inconsequential in the grand scheme of things, but I can hardly believe Mum and Selena have been in touch all these years. Did Mum feel she couldn't tell me because of my rift with Selena? I glance out of the window to the driveway. It's raining again. I can hear the sheep bleating in the nearby field. I'm in the little office with the 1980s wallpaper and the new leather diary that is depressingly empty. My mind goes back to the dead flowers, and I wonder again who put them there. Is it a threat of some kind? The thought that someone is lurking outside makes me shudder, reminding me to ask Adrian to get some locks for the attic.

I find him in our bedroom, hunched over his laptop. The curtains are still closed and the light is struggling to filter through. The bed is still unmade.

'Adrian,' I say gently, resting my hand on his shoulder so as not to startle him. He looks up, clearly still thinking about the characters and the lives I've awakened him from, and for a moment I feel sad, as though I've lost him. When I first had the idea of moving to the country and starting a guesthouse I had visions of us side by side, running it together. But it's Mum I'm running it with and Adrian hides up here all day, living through a bunch of fictional characters. But then I think of our life in London after his breakdown, all the fear and stress it entailed, and I know which reality I prefer. 'I can see you're writing, but would you mind popping to B&Q at some point to get a lock for the girls' door?'

He groans. 'Can't you go?'

'I don't know exactly what we need.' Adrian is good at DIY, like my father had been, and although I can do lots myself – I'm a dab hand at putting together Ikea furniture – I wouldn't know where to start, drilling locks into doors.

'Okay.' He sighs, running his hand over his beard. It's getting bushier by the day. He looks like he's about to explore the Antarctic. 'I'll go at lunchtime.' He pushes his chair away from the table with his feet.

I tell him about the teenage lovebirds and Janice's tarot cards, and he gives a bark of laughter as I describe the creaking bed. 'Blimey, what a motley crew. I'm glad you told Nancy to clean their room. God knows what you might find. It's bad enough you saw that tarot card in Mystic Meg's.'

I burst out laughing. 'Mystic Meg. I love it! Oh, Adrian. There's enough fodder here for your book.'

I feel good that I've made him laugh. His brown eyes soften as he looks at me. 'I'll come down and help later,' he promises. 'I'll just finish this chapter.'

I kiss the side of his face, my lips brushing his bristly beard. 'It's fine.' But he's already turned away from me, his attention back on the screen.

I want to remind him to get dressed but I stop myself. I'm not his mother. I straighten the bed to the sound of him tapping away at the keyboard.

I'm in the hallway paying Nancy for two hours' work when the doorbell goes. The house is empty apart from us so I wonder if one of the guests has forgotten their key.

When I open it, I'm surprised to see a stranger

standing on the other side. He's around my age, maybe a bit older, and there is something familiar about him that I can't quite place. He has short hair, almost a crew-cut, and is tall with broad shoulders. He's wearing khaki trousers and a North Face waterproof jacket. I'm struck by how big and heavy the rucksack on his back must be. He looks like the kind of man who might run a cadet course.

Nancy sidles past us, saying she'll be back tomorrow for an hour, and I wave her off, distracted by the man standing in front of me.

'Hi, can I help you?' I ask, blinking up at him. It's stopped raining and the sun has come out from behind a cloud, almost blinding me. I have to shield my face with my hand.

'Do you have a room? For one night or two?' he asks. He has a Welsh accent. He's quite handsome, in an Action Man way, with his too-white teeth and 'out-doorsy' tan, but something about his eyes and the way they sweep over me unnerves me.

'I only have a double room, I'm afraid.' I tell him the price, expecting him to refuse.

'It's just me but I'll take it,' he says eagerly, like a dog snatching a treat.

'Oh, that's great. Come in, I'll just need to take some details and then I can show you to your room.'

He follows me into the office. His height and weight are so imposing I feel hemmed into the small room. He's blocking the doorway with his bulk. There is something intimidating about him and I suddenly feel vulnerable at being in the house without Adrian. Maybe it's his stature, or that he doesn't smile. I can feel his eyes on me as I open the desk drawers and I wonder if he's clocking where I keep the spare keys. Thankfully this office has a lock on it. I think of the girls in the garden with Mum. Too far away to hear me if something happened. My hand cups the inhaler in my pocket but for some reason I resist the urge to use it, although I'm short of breath. I don't want to show him any weakness.

He shifts his weight from one foot to the other, then hoists his bag off his back in one swift movement. The action makes me jump, and he smirks. I hide my unease by casually pushing a registration card and pen across the desk. 'Can you fill this in, please? And I'll need to take payment up front if that's okay.'

'No problem, *Kirsty*,' he says, and I look up, startled. The way he utters my name makes me feel as though I should know who he is. He grins, and there is something malevolent in his features as he adds, 'I'm surprised you don't recognize me, but it has been nearly twenty years.'

# 14

Dean Hargreaves. What the hell is he doing here? It can't be a coincidence that he's turned up while Selena's staying. Has she arranged this? Was he the man she met the other night?

'Oh, hi. How are you?' I say, thrown. He's changed a lot since I last saw him. Gone are the grey complexion and the gawkiness. I take the key off the hook, choosing the bedroom furthest away from us. I have duplicates for every room locked in my desk drawer. I hand him the key for Freesia. 'Let me show you to your room.'

He takes it. 'Nah. You're all right. Cheers, though, Kirsty.' He grins, looking me up and down. 'You've hardly changed. I'd know you anywhere.'

I can't help myself. 'You do know that Selena's staying here?'

He contorts his face into an expression of surprise. 'No! She's here? Well, what a coincidence.'

He's lying.

He grins again. I notice a gold tooth just behind the canine. 'Don't look so worried. Always was protective of her where I was concerned, weren't you?' He laughs. 'Now, how do I get to my room?'

I give him a professional smile. 'It's straight up the stairs, first door on the right.'

'Great. Well, see you later.' He gives a weird salute and then, heaving the bag on to his shoulder, he leaves the room, his boot-shod feet heavy on the stairs.

I need someone to talk to. The dead flowers, Selena, Dean . . . I don't want to burden Adrian so I go and find Mum.

She's in the garden with the girls. The lawn is still wet, staining the leather toes of my tan boots. The netting of the trampoline is damp and strewn with cobwebs but Evie and Amelia don't seem to mind as they jump up and down, squealing, the age gap forgotten, their breath like fog. Mum is cleaning out the rabbits, every so often turning to look at the children when they call her to watch a somersault. I wince every time Amelia flips over in the air. I'm terrified she's going to break something.

Mum has a scarf around her neck and a gilet over her smart jumper. She's kneeling on one of those padded gardening mats decorated with rosebuds.

'Bedrooms all sorted?' she asks, as I kneel beside her.

'Yep. Nancy's great. Really efficient. And Selena called. They'll be home this afternoon. Ruby's okay.'

Mum is visibly relieved. 'Thank goodness.'

I hesitate. 'Um. Bit weird, but Dean's turned up, asking for a room.'

She whips around to me, a bag of dirty sawdust in her hand 'Dean?' Is it my imagination or does her face pale? She can't possibly know who I'm talking about. She'd have met him only once or twice.

'Dean Hargreaves. You probably don't remember. He went out with Selena for a bit when they were about eighteen.' He came between us, I want to say, remembering the party, Selena's cutting words, Dean's condescending gaze. But I don't. It's too long ago. It hardly matters any more.

She swallows and turns back to the rabbits. 'Here?' She's trying to sound casual but I can tell something has shaken her.

'Yes. Don't you think it's weird? He says he didn't know Selena was staying but they must have arranged it. I saw her the other night. Outside. With a man. I bet that was him.'

'Why would you assume it was Dean?' she says, and I want to shake her. She's not fooling me. She knows more about this, I can tell. She holds on to the wooden cage for support. Then she stands up and stretches her knees. I know they cause her trouble from time to time and I'm not sure if it's this or the news I've just imparted that's causing the distress she's trying to hide.

'I don't want to sound unfeeling,' I say, 'but I can't have all this drama going on under my roof. This is our opening weekend – and I'm worried about Adrian. I don't want to cause him any stress. You know what his doctors said. It was only last year that he tried . . . that he . . .' I'm trying to erase the image that's stuck in my head of how I found him that day.

Mum's auburn eyebrows come together. 'No. You mustn't bother Adrian with this.'

I take a deep breath of the cold air, trying to compose myself. 'Do you think Dean's here to cause trouble?'

Mum glances towards the girls. Amelia is helping Evie to do a forward roll. They're oblivious to our conversation. Mum's still holding the bag of rabbit droppings and wet sawdust. The cage is empty and I bend down to lay fresh bedding inside.

'I don't know,' she says. She's avoiding my eye.

'If it was him she met in secret the other night, they might have arranged this rendezvous. She could have left her husband for Dean.'

'You can't jump to conclusions. It's probably just a coincidence.' She's staring at the girls, but I can see it in her face. Panic.

'I don't believe it is,' I say. My head is almost inside the cage, muffling my voice as I add, 'And then there's the flowers.' I close the cage and stand up again.

'Flowers?'

'I've found bouquets of dead flowers on our doorstep.'

She blinks but doesn't say anything.

'It looks like they might have come from the churchyard next door, but we've been living here over six weeks now and the first lot arrived the same day as Selena. I can't help but think there's something in that.'

Mum lifts her shoulders, her expression grave. Her eyes go to the two rabbits in the run but she's not really seeing them. She's deep in thought.

'And Nathan's arriving this evening.'

Mum rounds on me, her face stern. 'What's Nathan got to do with it?'

'Nothing.' I back down. I can't tell her he used to have a thing for Selena or that he and Julia aren't getting on that well now they're having trouble conceiving. It would make Mum cross even though she was the one who told me about Nathan's marriage troubles. When Nathan and I do speak, the conversation is stilted. The easy way the four of us had with each other is gone.

Before, they would come up from Cardiff and stay with us in Twickenham, lavishing attention on Amelia and Evie, the perfect aunt and uncle. Nathan and Adrian bonded over their mutual love of Tottenham Hotspur and would sit for hours discussing the game. Then, when Adrian had his breakdown and was admitted to hospital, Nathan became distant. No phone calls, flowers or messages of concern, just silence. My brother has never been very good with emotions or feelings – he must have got that growing up with Mum. The brother-in-law he'd always been so close to had changed, turning into a near-stranger. I might have understood it but I didn't approve. I tried to convince Nathan to get in touch with Adrian, that he – and I – would really appreciate it. I know Adrian missed their football chats. But Nathan never called.

'We can always ask Dean to leave, if he's only come to cause trouble,' says Mum, as she helps me to put the rabbits back into their home.

'You did lock the dining-room door?' I have visions of Dean snooping around the house.

'Of course. Don't worry. It'll be fine.' She says it with finality. Subject closed.

I'm on tenterhooks waiting for Selena to walk through the door. She does so just after four o'clock, carrying Ruby. She's a slip of a thing but, today, Selena looks as though she'll buckle under her weight.

'Here let me help,' I say, taking Ruby in my arms. 'How are you, sweetheart?' I say to her.

She flashes me a beaming smile that makes my heart ache. 'They let me have a lollipop at the hospital,' she says excitedly.

'It was sugar-free,' says Selena, defensively, as she follows me to their room. She manoeuvres herself so that she's in front of me and opens the door. She lets out a little sound of surprise when she sees the beds are made and her tea tray has been replenished. I lay Ruby carefully on her bed. She's still wearing the dressing-gown she left in yesterday, and there's an antiseptic scent about her now, the smell of hospital clinging to her clothes.

'Can I have my book, Mummy?' she asks, and Selena ferrets in her bag. She retrieves a worn paperback, handing it to her daughter.

'She's read this so many times.' She laughs.

I notice that it's one of the *Malory Towers* books. I'd enjoyed them as a child. Evie loves reading – anything magical or mystical – but I'm finding it a struggle to get Amelia to pick up a book. She prefers drawing and is forever doodling in a sketchpad. Selena is shrugging off her coat. I notice dark patches ballooning under the armpits of her thin jumper. 'She's been talking non-stop about your two. Do you think they'd come in and see her?'

'Of course! I'll go and get them.' It will give me a good chance to get Selena on her own and talk to her about Dean. I haven't seen him since he checked in and I have the feeling he's hiding out in his bedroom. As if on cue her phone beeps and she looks towards her dressing-table, then back at me with faint embarrassment. She obviously remembers what she told me last night about it having no charge. I pretend not to notice and leave the room to fetch the girls.

They're in the playroom, watching TV. 'Dad's putting a lock on our bedroom door,' says Amelia, when I walk in. She doesn't look away from the screen.

Evie jumps up. 'Why? Why's he doing that?' She looks worried.

'Just to give you some privacy,' I say, hoping I sound positive.

'It's because Mum's scared that nutters will try and take us in the night,' states Amelia.

Evie's horrified.

'No, it isn't,' I snap, glaring at Amelia, although it goes unnoticed. I bend down to Evie. 'But strangers will be staying here so I think it's best that you keep your door locked at night.'

'I'm scared,' she says, her chin wobbling.

Amelia tuts and rolls her eyes. 'You're scared of your own shadow!'

I take Evie's hand. 'There's nothing to be scared of. Daddy and I are just across the landing.'

'But I won't be able to come and see you at night if I'm locked in our room.'

'You'll have a key, silly,' says Amelia, looking at both of us for the first time.

'Yes. You can keep it by your bed and use it to get out,' I say.

Evie looks at me with her huge eyes. 'I want to go back to the flat. I don't like this house. It's too big and spooky. I hear noises at night. I think it's haunted.'

'It's not haunted,' I say.

'That woman with the dog said so.'

Mystic Meg? What has she been saying? 'Don't listen to her. She's talking nonsense. If there are such things as ghosts I would have seen one. I've been around for a long time.'

She studies me and chews her lip. 'You *are* old,' she concedes.

Amelia turns off the TV and comes to join us. She must be feeling guilty for starting this conversation because she says to Evie, kindly, 'You share a room with me. I'm not going to let anything happen to you, am I?'

I flash her a grateful smile over Evie's head.

'No,' says Evie, in a small voice. 'And I have Lucinda. She's my lucky charm, you know. She'll protect me.'

I don't know where she got that idea. I catch Amelia's eye. We grimace and laugh conspiratorially.

'What?' asks Evie. 'What's funny?'

'Nothing, sweet cheeks,' I say, taking her hand. 'Why don't we go and see Ruby?'

When we get to Selena's room the door is open and Dean is leaning against the jamb. He's still wearing his thick boots. My heart sinks.

'Who's that?' asks Evie, in a loud whisper.

'A friend of Selena's,' I say. 'He's staying here too. In a different room.'

When he sees us approaching, he smiles at me, which throws me a little.

'Everything all right?' I ask, in an effort to remain professional.

He drapes an arm over Selena's shoulders. She looks tiny next to him. 'Great. Oh, and while you're here, would it be okay to have some more coffee? I've used all the sachets.'

Already? He's only been here a few hours.

He lifts his shoulders in what I take to be an apology.

The girls push past us to see Ruby and crowd around her bed.

'Um. Sure, I'll go and get some,' I say. 'I'll be two secs.' I hurry to the kitchen and find the box of sachets in the cupboard. I grab a handful and dash back. I don't want to leave Amelia and Evie with them for too long.

When I get back, Dean is leaning into Selena and whispering something in her ear. She's not smiling.

When he spots me, he moves away from her and opens his hands, as if he's begging, and I tip the sachets into them.

'Thanks.' Then, to Selena, he winks and says, 'And I'll see *you* later.' We watch in silence as he walks down the hallway and rounds the stairs.

Then she turns to me, shamefaced. 'I'm sorry about Dean,' she whispers. 'I didn't know he was going to show up here.'

'What's going on?'

She darts a look at the girls. 'He knows I've left Nigel.'

'But how? You haven't seen him in years.'

She shuffles her feet and studies one of the floor tiles. The tell-tale rash creeps up her neck. Why is she nervous? 'Well . . . I have. When I've been back to Cardiff visiting Mum. And we've kept in touch.'

There's something about this that doesn't ring true. Why would this new adult Selena, who's reinvented herself into a middle-class yummy-mummy, want anything to do with an old boyfriend who's always been a bit of a yob? But maybe that's unfair. Her husband sounds like a brute and Dean has been perfectly polite since he's been here. I can't judge him on what he was like at eighteen. A thought suddenly strikes me. 'Have you been having an affair with him?'

Her head shoots up. 'No, of course not. We're friends. That's all.'

'Then why is he here?'

'Because he says he's in love with me, and wants us to be together.'

I glance anxiously at the girls – particularly Amelia, who has ears like a bat – but they're all huddled in bed, Ruby in the middle, as she proudly recounts her trip in an ambulance. I move closer to Selena, keeping my voice low: 'And you? How do you feel about him?'

She smiles tightly and avoids eye contact as she says simply, 'He's my first love.'

Nathan arrives at teatime and we take over the living room. Luckily all the guests are still out and Dean is upstairs. Selena is with him. I noticed her sneaking up fifteen minutes ago while Ruby was having a nap and she is yet to come down. I think she's lying to me about not knowing Dean was coming and, once again, I'm annoyed that she's bringing her drama into my life.

Nathan is making a fuss of Amelia and Evie, showering them with chocolate, while Julia looks on wistfully. She seems thinner since the last time I saw her. A few years older than me, she's a GP at her local surgery, whip-smart and funny, with dark shoulder-length hair and big chestnut eyes. I'd always admired her. She liked to joke that Nathan, four years her junior, was her toy boy but I always wondered what she saw in him. As much as I love him, Nathan hasn't really grown up. He'll spend hours on his PlayStation 4 after work – he's an accountant for a firm in Cardiff, and hates it. He fell into it not long after leaving university and stayed. His passions are football, beer and FIFA, although a few years ago Julia got him into climbing. It's probably the only exercise he does. But he's funny and kind and adores Julia – as do we all. She's the main breadwinner. I sometimes wonder if not being able to have children is harder on him than her. He had planned to give up his job when the baby came, but after each failed IVF attempt, talk of babies tailed off, and now we're all scared to mention it. It's a wonder we have anything to say to each other with so many subjects off limits.

So, it's heartening to see Julia and Adrian talking about his breakdown. She's sitting next to him on the sofa, looking neat as always in her Boden blouse and jeans.

I can hear his voice, loud and clear, from the other side of the room, and wonder if it's for Nathan's benefit. 'I'm writing and I like to do bits around the house. I helped refurbish it. It's good for me, working with my hands.'

'And the antidepressants? Are they helping?' She has on her GP face.

His answer is considered. 'Yes. After trial and error.'

She flashes him one of her megawatt smiles and I suddenly have an image of her in her consulting room, putting patients at ease. I can imagine that's what attracted Nathan to her. After his traumatic start in life – although he claims not to remember any of it – Julia was a stable, loving influence. And in him she saw vulnerability, someone she could nurture and protect.

Nathan is now rolling around with the girls on the floor. Amelia is climbing on him and Evie is trying to grab his leg. My eyes flicker to Adrian sitting stiffly next to Julia. He's talking to her but I can see that he's watching them out of the corner of his eye, jaw set, face grave. It must be hard for him. Since his breakdown he's lost the connection he used to have with the girls. He tries, but it doesn't seem to come naturally to him any more. I know it worries him. That was another reason for the move, so he could spend more time with his children. Although he seems to have forgotten about that, with all the writing he's doing.

'Evie. Amelia. Leave your uncle alone.'

The girls stop, shocked by Adrian's sharp tone, it's so unusual. Nathan sits up, patting down his dark blond hair. 'They're all right.'

'No. It's too much before bedtime,' insists Adrian, his voice curt.

I have to bite my lip to stop myself saying something as Nathan gets to his feet, dusting down his jeans. There are bits of new carpet fluff stuck to his knees. Amelia's face falls. It was the happiest I'd seen her in ages. I want to intervene but I can't undermine Adrian in front of everyone.

Adrian gets up too. 'Come on,' he says to the girls. 'Let's go and find Nana to say goodnight. It's getting late.'

'It's not fair,' wails Amelia. 'It's half-term tomorrow. We don't have to get up early.'

Adrian ignores her and ushers them from the room.

Nathan looks towards me and shrugs. 'What did I do?'

'It's not you. Adrian's finding his feet with the girls again, that's all.'

Nathan flops down on the sofa next to Julia and rests his head on her shoulder.

'Get off.' She gently pushes him away. 'You're all sweaty.'

Nathan laughs and is about to say something when his eyes go to the doorway and the words die on his lips. I turn to see what he's looking at. Selena is standing there, her eyes locked with his. They're both wearing the same expression: a mixture of horror and . . . something I can't read. I expect her to join us, but she turns away and heads towards her room.

# 15

## *One day before*

Adrian's made a good job of the lock. It took him most of yesterday afternoon to do it, but he didn't even moan that it took him away from his writing. I think he finds it therapeutic to get involved with a task.

Evie keeps the key within reach on her bedside table so that she doesn't wake Amelia if she wants us in the night. We've also got a spare as an extra precaution – Adrian says it's over the top but it makes me feel better. I know Mum will think we're pandering to Evie but I want her to feel secure and safe. It could just be her age – when Amelia was little she hated going upstairs on her own. I'm confident Evie will stop being scared once she's used to living here.

But at three a.m. I'm woken by sniffling coming from across the landing, and know that Evie's crying. I creep to the girls' room with the spare key and gently open the door. 'I'm scared,' she whimpers. I put my finger to my lips so that she knows not to wake Amelia, and, leaving her key beside her bed, I lead her from the room and lock the door behind us. I feel guilty that we've left Amelia alone, although she's oblivious in sleep. I'd prefer to scoop them both up and keep them with me. Safe.

It's still dark when I get up, ready to make ten breakfasts.

We share a bathroom with Mum and the girls so I gather up my wash things and clothes and tiptoe out of the room. Evie, sound asleep, shuffles further into Adrian. He grunts something about his back hurting but instantly falls asleep again. I pause at the bedroom door, looking at my sleeping husband, and wonder if I'm being a walkover. Should I make him get up and help with the breakfasts? If he doesn't want to be sociable he can hide in the kitchen. I worry he spends too much time up here, alone. It can't be good for his mental state. He needs to interact with people.

Halfway down the stairs I stop to look out of the picture window. Adrian took photos of the magnificent view for our website. Beyond the rows of houses there are just fields, hills and mountains as far as the eye can see. The sky is lighter now, with grey angry clouds bunched over the largest mountain. The locals call it the Sugarloaf.

My chest feels tight. I wonder if it's stress. I realize I left my inhaler upstairs so I go down to the Welsh dresser in the living room. I have a few planted around the house. But when I open the drawer it's gone. I look in all the other drawers but there's no sign of it. Puzzled, I run back upstairs for the one I'd left on my bedside table, then down again to the kitchen.

I suddenly remember it's Mum's birthday. I still haven't had the chance to go out and get her something. In London, I would have bought her present and card the week before so it would arrive on her birthday. But I've been so busy – I haven't had a moment to myself since we moved in.

Mum's hunched over a frying-pan, pushing at two fried eggs with a spatula.

'Happy birthday,' I say, going over to her and kissing her cheek.

'Thanks,' she says stiffly, without taking her eyes off the pan.

'I'll, um, give you your present after the breakfast rush is over.' I'm planning to nip out to the gift shop in the village.

She mutters something under her breath. It might have been *thank you* but I'm not sure.

We don't have time to talk after that as all the guests come down for breakfast at the same time. Nathan and Julia are at one table with Amelia and Evie (the only two still in their pyjamas again – I need to talk to them about that: it's not professional to let the girls wander around in their nightwear), the Greysons next to them (the younger boy, Will, keeps throwing Amelia furtive glances), the teenage lovers sit by the window (holding hands under the table) and Janice is sitting with Horace (feeding him titbits of sausage when she thinks nobody is looking).

Selena and Dean are yet to emerge and I wonder if

they've spent the night together. I quickly discount this idea as I can't imagine Selena would leave Ruby alone all night. I wouldn't if I was in her shoes.

When all the guests have been served, I broach the subject of Selena to Mum.

'Did you see her last night? She scarpered as soon as she saw Nathan.'

Mum pours boiling water into a stainless-steel teapot. 'Maybe she feels shy. She hasn't seen him in years.'

'Shy' doesn't sound like Selena.

'Do you know if she keeps in touch with Uncle Owen?' I try to keep my voice light.

'Not that I'm aware of. Can you take this to Janice?' She hands me the teapot and immediately begins filling another, her back to me. Every time I bring up the subject of Selena she clams up. I haven't forgotten how odd she was yesterday when we were cleaning out the rabbits. Selena had said she'd spoken to Mum over the years; that's how she'd remembered her phone number. So she must have talked about her life. Yet Mum tried to make out to me that she knew nothing. It's almost like she's scared of saying the wrong thing.

When I come back into the kitchen, Mum walks straight past me, carrying a tray. I put the frying-pan into the sink to soak and hear cheering and clapping coming from the dining room. I go to see what all the commotion is about to find everyone, even Selena and Ruby (who've just arrived and are forced to sit at the same table as Janice), singing 'Happy Birthday'. Julia stands up and gives Mum a hug and Nathan shyly passes her a present, kissing her cheek. Mum blushes but looks delighted at all the fuss. She unwraps the present and squeals with delight. It's a huge bottle of L'Interdit by Givenchy, her favourite perfume.

When Julia and Nathan have returned to their seats, Selena gets up and steps forwards with an expensive-looking orchid. 'Sorry it's not much.' She gives a self-conscious smile.

'I'm just touched you remembered,' Mum says, embracing her.

I look over at Nathan, who's studying his eggs. Julia smiles politely. It would be a good time for Mum to introduce the two women but she doesn't and Selena slinks back to the table. I notice again the flush to her neck. Julia's eyes flick to Selena and her expression hardens. Then she looks away and carries on eating, but it surprised me. I've never seen Julia anything less than charming.

And then Evie pipes up, loud and clear for everyone to hear. 'Where's our present to Nana?' she says, getting to her feet. 'Mummy! Where's Nana's present?'

I feel all eyes on me expectantly. Julia looks mortified for me while Nathan is smirking and I want to smack him.

'Yes,' says Amelia, flicking her hair off her face (for Will's benefit, no doubt). 'Shall I go and get it?'

'It's – it's upstairs,' I lie. 'I'll get it after breakfast.' And then I disappear to the kitchen to hide.

\*

*For twenty years I've never forgotten her birthday,* I fume, as I walk towards the high street. *And once, just once, I forget and I'll probably never hear the end of it. Whereas perfect Nathan and saintly Selena have made sure to give her something. If it wasn't for everything I've got on my plate with running this place, and sorting out my family, I'd have more time.*

But with each step I take, my anger abates. It's my fault. Nobody else's. I should have been on top of things. She's my mother, for crying out loud. If it wasn't for her we wouldn't have been able to buy and renovate the Old Rectory.

And I'm grateful. I'm grateful. I'm grateful. But sometimes I feel as though I want to scream with all the pressure.

I stop and lean against a tree trunk, gasping for air. I take out my inhaler and breathe in deeply. When I feel better I begin walking again. I'd left in such a hurry I didn't have time to put on a scarf or gloves. There's a dusting of frost on the grass. The trees that line the pavements have started to lose their leaves and look spindly, like little old women.

I pull my hood around my neck. It's so cold, but the sky is that deep wintry blue with the odd hazy cloud and a low-lying mist circling the mountains. As I cross the bridge I glance towards the Seven Stars. In the summer it would be nice to sit outside overlooking the river. Now the tables and chairs are empty, the wood slick with damp, cobwebs clinging to the legs. A few people are clustered outside, smoking. I notice one

139

woman of about my age, trendy mauve hair gathered in a messy ponytail. I recognize her as our neighbour, Lydia Ford – I only know this because when we first moved here one of her letters was delivered to us by mistake. I'd tried to introduce myself, but she'd looked straight through me as though I wasn't there. Nancy's with her. Are they friends? I hurry on, remembering my mission. I need to be quick – there's still so much to do at the house.

The streets have turned to cobbles and I stride past the pharmacist and the café to Dominique's, where I choose an over-priced candle, some This Works bath salts and a printed scarf with little Scottie dogs on it, from the girls.

As I walk back I sense someone following me. But when I turn there's nobody there. I tell myself not to be ridiculous. I'm just unnerved by the quiet.

I'm nearly home when I see Mr Collins slumped against his garden wall. He's clutching his chest and wheezing, his walking stick lying at his feet. There's something about his chunky beige cardigan and skinny frame that remind me of a much older Uncle Owen.

'Are you okay, Mr Collins?' I ask, hurrying to him and picking up his stick. I hand it to him and he leans on it gratefully. He coughs into a handkerchief

'I'm okay, love, just getting over a chest infection. Spontaneous coughing. Made me drop my stick.' He chuckles, bending down to pick up his bag of recycling, then groans.

'Here, let me do that for you,' I say, as he tries to straighten again with some effort. I reach for the bag, then help him to his front door.

'You're so kind,' he says, smiling, as he steps over the threshold.

'Will you be all right?' I feel bad leaving him alone. He looks so frail.

He nods and tries to say something, which starts another fit of coughing. When it's eased he manages, 'Got my son and daughter-in-law staying. Don't worry about me.'

I'm just about to walk away when he grabs my arm. 'You seem like a nice lady,' he adds, surveying me with his watery blue eyes. 'I know a lot of the folk around 'ere aren't happy with you Londoners moving into that big house, but you're all right.'

I stare at him, speechless, for a few seconds. 'I'm – I'm actually from Cardiff originally.' Can't he tell by my accent? I know it's softened over the years but everyone in London can tell I'm Welsh. Except my friend Ingrid, who thought I was from the Midlands when she first met me.

'Dad!' a man's voice calls from inside the house.

Mr Collins grimaces, his eyes twinkling. 'Got to go, but thank you, young lady.' He closes the door before I can say anything else.

Feeling despondent, I let myself out of the gate. I know not everybody's been particularly friendly, but I didn't think us being here was that big a deal.

As I walk the few yards home I sense again that I'm being watched. I spin around to see Lydia Ford, alone in her front garden, staring at me. I give a friendly wave, but she turns away, ignoring me completely.

# 16

I stand outside our bedroom door. It's closed. I've asked Adrian to keep it open. He knows how I feel about it. My tongue seems too big for my mouth. I can hear the reassuring tapping of a keyboard. *It's okay.*

Will I ever be able to open a door without my heart racing? Without the *fear* of what I might find?

Like how I found Adrian.

The image will be fixed in my memory for ever, like a gruesome painting you try to avoid but can't because you have to walk past it every day. I'd thought he was dead. And if I hadn't arrived home when I did, he would have been. I'd left him in bed that morning when I went to do the school run. The sun was streaming through the curtains and he'd been sound asleep. Or so I'd thought. I'd been worried about him for weeks, urging him to go to the doctor. He'd changed: my happy outgoing husband had gone into himself, was constantly irritable and snappy. Where once he'd arrive at the office extra early so he'd be home in time to see the kids before I put them to bed, he'd come home later and later, as though he was avoiding us. When I tried to talk to him about it he refused to be drawn. At first I thought maybe there was someone else. That he didn't love me any more. He became distant. Every time I tried to be affectionate he pushed me away, which was so unusual for Adrian, the demonstrative one of us. When I tried to talk to him about it, he flew into a temper and threw one of the kitchen chairs at a wall, snapping a leg. Deep down I knew it wasn't an affair. Then Julia put a name to it and I forced him to see his GP.

Adrian played it down, of course, not wanting a fuss. The GP suggested counselling.

When I got home from the school run that day, the door to the bedroom had been closed. I hadn't been too worried, more annoyed that he was still in bed. But when I pushed the door open it was hard to budge, as though there was a force behind it.

And then I saw what it was. Adrian had hanged himself with the belt from his dressing-gown.

He said it had been a cry for help. He hadn't intended to kill himself: he'd known I'd come home and find him. But it haunted me. What if I'd popped to Sainsbury's or met a friend for coffee? I'd have lost him.

And now he's happier than he's been in ages, no longer having to do the job he hates. No longer under pressure. And – for the most part – I'm happy to take the burden. To make things as easy for him as possible. Because every day I worry that something will send him over the edge again. And I can't let that happen. I can't lose him.

I push the door open and call the girls. They come

running from their room, Evie clutching that horrible china doll. I don't know why she thinks it's magical. Perhaps because it's old.

'Can you write Nana's card?' I ask them, as I leap on to the bed and frantically start wrapping the presents. The Sellotape keeps sticking to my fingers.

The girls lie on the floor to write the card. Amelia doodles all over the envelope.

Adrian swivels in his chair. There are three dirty mugs on his desk. One has a faint pink lipstick mark on the rim. 'Why didn't you tell me you hadn't bought a present? I could have popped out and got something. I went for a run earlier.'

My head snaps up. 'You went for a run? When Mum and I were rushed off our feet sorting out breakfasts?'

'Sorry. I didn't think.'

*No, you never do.* I swallow the words. I know I'm just feeling stressed because it's all so new. We're still finding our feet. And I'm happy that it's so busy on our opening weekend – even if half of the guests are family.

Amelia takes the present from me, and I gather up the mugs. 'Whose is this?' I ask, lifting up the lipstick-marked one.

He turns and frowns. 'Selena's.'

'Selena's?'

He clears his throat, which he always does when he's stalling for time. 'Yes. Earlier, she came up to check I was okay. I think she might have been looking for you.'

He doesn't meet my eye. Instead he goes back to his laptop and begins tapping at the keys again.

Mum's enthusiasm is lukewarm. 'Thank you. Another candle. It smells divine.' Then she opens the scarf from the girls and exclaims over it, hugging them both to her and proclaiming she loves it.

'Oh,' she calls, as I'm about to walk off, 'Toby Wilson and his girlfriend have checked out. They said they'll put a review on TripAdvisor. I hope it's a good one.'

Later, Nancy turns up and I help her with the bedrooms. She's dealing with the tea tray in Hyacinth and straightening the beds while I hover outside Dean's. I rap on the door and wait a few seconds. When there's no answer I use my spare key.

I don't know what I'm expecting to find in Dean's room, but I'm pleasantly surprised to see it so tidy. The bed is made and his heavy rucksack sits neatly beside the chest of drawers. A jumper is folded on the duvet and a weathered copy of Stephen King's *Pet Cemetery* sits on the bedside table, but otherwise the room is devoid of any personal belongings. I pop my head around the door of the en-suite. His toothbrush and toothpaste are on the side of the basin, as though standing to command. I wipe around the basin and the toilet, even though there isn't much need. *What are you doing here, Dean?*

I'm about to leave the room when I see something in

the pocket of his rucksack. The tip of it catches the light and I edge closer for a better look. It's one of those hunting knives, pointed and sharp-edged with a wooden handle. My mind races as I wonder what he's planning to do with it.

A piercing scream sends chills down my spine. It's blood-curdling and right away I know it's Evie.

I drop my bucket of cleaning products and throw the door open with such force it bangs against the wall. Janice has come out of the room opposite. I'd assumed she'd gone out for the day, to see her sister or to take Horace on one of the many walks or waterfall trails. I dart past her and up the stairs to the attic. Evie is standing in the middle of the landing, sobbing on to Adrian's shoulder, the china doll at her feet.

'What is it?' I say, my heart thumping so hard I can feel it in my throat. *Is it that bloody doll again?*

Adrian glances above our heads. I follow his line of vision and gasp. A noose made from rope has been attached to one of the wooden beams.

'How . . . how did that get there?' I mutter, trying not to show my shock in front of Evie.

He widens his eyes at me, trying to communicate without words. Then he turns to Evie and says, in a soothing voice, 'Someone's having a little joke, that's all.'

'Why?' She wipes her eyes.

I kneel beside her. 'It's like hangman. A silly game. Nothing to be worried about.'

She frowns, tears on her cheeks. 'I came upstairs and it was just hanging there. It's really scary. I thought it was a snake.' Of course. The significance of the rope would be lost on her. She's too young to understand.

'I know, sweetheart. Daddy's going to take it down now, aren't you, Daddy?' I look pointedly at Adrian.

He stands up hurriedly and reaches for the rope that dangles down the other side of the beam. The thought that someone has been up here, in our private space, creeping around, tying nooses, makes me feel sick. But I try not to show it.

Adrian hides the noose behind his back. 'It was just someone messing around,' he says, smiling at Evie.

She looks calmer. Her eyes are still wild, but the tears have stopped. She bends over and picks up her doll.

'Where's Amelia?' I ask.

'She's gone into the village,' says Evie. She hugs the doll closer to her chest.

I feel a burst of anger. 'On her own?' I haven't allowed her to do that yet, even though she's been begging me to let her walk to school by herself now she's in year six.

'No. With Uncle Nathan and Aunty Jools.'

'Ah, okay.'

'You're going to have to let her do it soon,' says Adrian. 'She's eleven. You're a bit over-protective.'

I shake my head, trying to convey that I don't want

to talk about this now. Not in front of Evie. 'I'm just not ready for her to be doing it *yet*.'

Evie scuttles into her bedroom.

'I don't know whose idea of a sick joke this is but I'm not laughing,' hisses Adrian, when Evie is out of ear-shot. 'Who have you told?'

'Nobody,' I reply, hurt that he'd think I'd talk about it as though it's a piece of idle gossip. 'Mum knows, obviously, Nathan and Julia . . .'

'Have you told Selena?'

'Of course I haven't. I wouldn't. I've hardly told anyone so that it has less chance of ever getting back to the girls.' I'd done everything I could to shield them from it.

'Then who would do this?' Adrian shakes the rope at me. 'Who would dare come into our home and do something like this? While I'm in there?' He indicates the bedroom.

'Ade. Calm down.' I take the rope from him. He storms into the bedroom. I follow and watch as he sits on the bed, his head in his hands. I join him and put my arms around him. 'I'll find out who did it,' I say.

He lifts his head, his eyes baggy and bloodshot. How dare someone do this to him? To us? We came here for a new start. We don't need to be reminded of the past.

'Do you think it's the same person who left the flowers a few days ago?' he asks. 'I'd assumed it was just kids messing about. But now . . .'

I can't bring myself to tell him about the second bunch of dead flowers. The calla lilies. My *wedding* flower. 'I don't know,' I admit.

He doesn't have to say it but I know what's he's thinking. Because I'm thinking the same thing. This is personal.

## 17

I leave Adrian upstairs although I know he's on edge and I'm furious that his equilibrium has been interrupted by a sick joke. My mind is racing as I go to find Mum. She's still pottering around in the kitchen.

'Where's Evie?' I can't keep the panic out of my voice.

She turns to me, dishcloth in hand. 'Outside with Selena and Ruby.'

'Selena's here?'

'I've just said she's outside. What's wrong *now*?' The Hughes family aren't allowed to be anything other than level-headed and considered. 'And what's that in your hand?'

I show her the noose and explain what happened. 'Have you told anyone? About Adrian's attempted suicide?' Her face tells me what I want to know. 'Mum!' I cry in exasperation. 'Why?'

'I didn't know it was a secret. I've only told Selena and she'd never do something like that.'

'You do know we haven't told the girls?'

'That's different. They're children. And I'm sure Selena isn't about to tell them.'

That's not the point, and she knows it.

'What else have you told Selena?' I demand. 'She said you've kept in touch over the years. Have you been sitting around gossiping about me and my family?'

'Of course I haven't. And there's no need for hysterics,' she says, infuriating me further.

I open my mouth to reply when Selena wafts in from the garden, smelling of fresh air and bonfire smoke. Her cheeks are as rosy as the apples dropping from our trees and she's smiling to herself. Behind her, I can see that Ruby is in her wheelchair with a rabbit on her lap. There are tyre marks in the grass, and churned-up mud. It must have been an effort for Selena to manoeuvre that chair across the lawn.

Selena looks relaxed. Happy, even. While I'm feeling more stressed out by the hour, the reverse is true for Selena. The only time I've seen her thrown off balance since she arrived is when she saw Nathan again. And, not for the first time, I feel a twinge of envy that she has a better relationship with my mother than I do.

She blows on her hands, which are red and chapped. Despite the low sun, I can see from the frost, which still hasn't melted, that it's cold. Evie's not wearing a coat and I resist the urge to run outside with one.

'Have you had any lunch? Has Ruby had something to eat?' I ask her.

'I brought Selena and Ruby some lunch while I was making it for the girls,' interrupts Mum, before Selena can say anything. 'In their bedroom.' She smiles at Selena indulgently.

Of course she did. Nothing's too much where Selena is concerned.

Selena returns Mum's smile. 'You're spoiling us, Aunty Carol.'

'So what's going on with Dean?' I ask, not wanting to let her off the hook so easily. 'And what's with you and Nathan? There's definitely tension between you. It's like you're avoiding him.'

I can feel, rather than see, Mum glaring at me. I know she'd rather I didn't say anything. She wants to keep the peace. Anything to avoid a row. A scene.

'I don't know what you mean,' says Selena. But her body language has changed: her back is rigid, making her collarbones stick out. She avoids eye contact as she makes her way to the cupboard opposite and takes out a glass, running it under the cold tap. It irks me that she's treating this kitchen as if it's her own. Technically guests aren't allowed in here. I know I'm being immature and petty and I hate myself for it. She is family, after all.

I make an effort to lighten my voice. 'You didn't come in to say hello yesterday, when Nathan arrived. And you stayed away from him at breakfast.'

She leans against the sink and takes a swig of water. I wait for a response. She puts the glass on the worktop. 'I didn't hide. As such. I just felt a bit awkward, I suppose.' Her hand goes to the neckline of her jumper, where her skin has turned red and rashy. 'You're all a family. I felt like an imposter.'

Mum comes bustling over. 'Now you mustn't think like that. You're family too. Isn't she, Kirsty?'

'Of course.' I pause. 'So . . . Dean?'

'Don't be so nosy,' Mum chastises me.

'I'm not being nosy. But someone hung a noose outside our bedroom.' I shake it to emphasize my point and notice Selena balk. 'It's both threatening and personal.'

'And you think it was Dean?' Selena asks.

I look at her squarely. 'I don't know what to think.'

'Dean wouldn't do something like that. Why would he? He knows nothing about what happened with Adrian.'

'He's never liked me,' I say. 'He always thought I was badmouthing him to you.'

She laughs. 'Well, you were.'

'Because he was no good.'

'He's . . . he's changed. He's been in the army. Sorted himself out.' I wonder if she's trying to convince me or herself. She sighs. 'I had what I thought was the perfect life. The big house, the good job, the professional husband. But it wasn't perfect. And now Dean . . .' She stops and glances at Mum. It's almost imperceptible but I'm sure Mum shakes her head.

'What?' I say, looking from one to the other. 'What were you going to say, Selena?'

Selena hangs her head and Mum folds her arms over her chest. Why do I always get the impression they're keeping something from me? Selena referred to herself as an outsider, but in this relationship the outsider is me.

Whatever she was going to say, it's obvious she's now clammed up. The rope feels coarse in my hand. Without saying another word, I throw it on to the worktop and walk out of the room.

I'm relieved when Amelia returns safely from her walk. She bounds into the hallway, Julia and Nathan following, happy now she's expended some energy. She's always been like a dog needing its daily walk. I hug her to me, breathing in her familiar smell, Lush shampoo and cherry lip balm. She laughs and wriggles away.

'She was safe. With us,' says Julia. 'I'm sorry, though. We should have asked you.' She looks concerned. Julia's considerate. Kind. 'I know how you get anxious. I didn't think.'

She knows I get anxious? How?

I wave my hand dismissively. But after finding the noose I can't help but imagine all sorts. I push away the thought that my brother and Julia are keen climbers. They are expert at tying knots in ropes. And Nathan loves a practical joke. I remember the letter he sent Adrian years ago, before we had the girls, pretending to be from an agency who hired ugly 'character' models, insisting they wanted Adrian for his 'unique looks'. There were sillier things too: the clingfilm over the toilet seat when we were kids, the fake finger in my food, the joke-shop dog poo on my bed.

But they were all harmless. This was something else. Even Nathan wouldn't go that far. Would he?

I take Evie into the village to buy some supplies. Amelia, not wanting to go out again, asks to watch TV. I agree, and she trots off to the playroom. I need to get out of the house. It's oppressive being there with Mum, living and working under one roof. I'd been in marketing, working for the same charity for years, until I had Evie, and when I went on maternity leave I found I didn't want to go back. Then Adrian had his breakdown and it seemed the right time to re-evaluate our lives. At least with my previous jobs I could go home at the end of the day and shut it all out. But this is different. I'm living and working in the same place. I have no means of escape, no refuge at the end of the day. Of course I'll adjust eventually. It's just a matter of time.

Evie's running ahead of me, the coat I forced her to wear flapping behind her like a superhero's cape. It's cold, for October, and the pavements are still dusted with frost. I have to keep calling ahead to remind Evie to wait for me. She's in her own little world, talking to her Tinkerbell doll and making it swoop through the air as if it's flying, her breath blooming in front of her. We pass the little butcher's and I pop in for some sausages and bacon. Evie holds her nose. She says the shop makes her feel sick.

She's relieved when we wander into the chemist, which, she says, always smells of fairies. Mrs Gummage glances up at us when we enter. She's in her early seventies with cotton-wool hair and wire-rimmed glasses that always seem about to slip off her long, pointed nose. Evie eyes her with suspicion, as if she suspects her of being a witch. Although I'm in here at least once a week, usually to pick up Adrian's prescriptions, she's never friendly, hardly talking to me if I'm on my own. If I'm with Evie she'll talk to me through her, like now.

'How's things going up at the Big House?' she asks Evie.

'It's haunted,' replies Evie.

'I know,' agrees Mrs Gummage. 'It's always been haunted. Why do you think it's stood empty for so many years?'

I slap Adrian's prescription on the counter. What is she playing at, telling a six-year-old child that her home is haunted?

She ignores me. 'You can tell your mummy it'll be five minutes,' she says to Evie, picking up the prescription without looking at me and passing it through a hatch. The pharmacist takes it. She's young and smiley and calls a greeting to us.

'Evie,' I say later, as we're walking home hand in hand. 'You do know that our house isn't really haunted, don't you?'

She frowns and chews her lip. 'It is, though, Mummy.'

'What makes you say that?'

'The noises. And the things being moved around.'

'What things being moved around?'

'My toys. I put them in one place but then they'll be in another. And Lucinda keeps moving. This morning I found her in Selena's room.'

'It'll be me cleaning your room, I expect.'

She furrows her brow. 'No. You don't move things so that they're in different places.'

'Well, then, it'll be Amelia.'

'It's not Amelia. It's a ghost.'

'Evie, you probably left Lucinda in Selena's room when you visited Ruby.'

She turns to me, her nose screwed up. 'And what about that rope thing this morning?'

'Well, someone put that there as a joke.'

'Who?'

'I . . . well, I don't know . . .'

'Because it was a ghost,' she says, as though I'm very stupid and need it explaining to me.

'Honey, I don't want you to be frightened,' I say, squeezing her little hand gently. 'Ghosts aren't real.'

'I'm not frightened when I'm with you and Amelia.'

'Or Daddy.'

'Sometimes I'm frightened when I'm with Daddy,' she says, and goosebumps break out along my arms.

'Why would you be frightened when you're with Daddy?'

'Because he's possessed. You can see that, can't you, Mummy? He's not the same Daddy any more.'

My heart breaks, and I have to swallow the lump in my throat before I can continue. I stop walking and turn her to face me, bending down so that we're at eye level. 'Evie, darling, Daddy's been ill, that's all. And he's getting better but it will take a while. And he loves you very, very much. He'd never want you to feel afraid of him.'

She looks down at her frog wellies. 'I do still love Daddy,' she concedes, toeing a weed breaking through a crack in the pavement.

'Well, that's good. I'm glad.' I stand up straight again. We continue walking in silence for a bit longer. The pavement stretches in front of us as far as the eye can see.

Eventually, just before we reach our house, I ask her, 'How do you know what possession means, anyway?'

She answers straight away. 'Amelia. She told me Daddy was possessed. She warned me, Mummy. She warned me that I had to be careful.'

Amelia is in the back garden, kicking through crisp brown leaves with Will. As I'm putting the shopping away I keep turning to watch them.

'She's made a friend,' Mum says. 'And she's not the only one. Nathan and Julia are in the front room with Susie and Peter Greyson. I heard Peter say he's a medic too.' Nathan has an innate way of drawing people to him. He has that magnetism, that larger-than-life personality, like Dad.

I drag my gaze away from Amelia and Will to Evie, Ruby and Selena. 'Ruby really loves those rabbits,' I say, closing the fridge.

'She's a sweet little girl,' says Mum, with a wistful look in her eye. 'And Selena is so good with her.'

I want to tell Mum what Evie said on the walk home from the shops. I've been mulling it over ever since we got back. Do I tackle Amelia? She's always been such a daddy's girl. She adores Adrian. That hasn't changed. And, okay, she doesn't sit on his lap any more, or throw her arms around his neck and plant kisses on his cheek, like she used to, but I put that down to her getting older, growing up. She's less affectionate with me too.

So why would she tell her little sister to be careful of the daddy she adores?

# 18

There's a party atmosphere in the house this evening. It doesn't feel like a Monday night. I put it down to the fact that it's Mum's birthday, we have family staying, that all the rooms, bar one, are full and nobody – apart from me and Mum – has to get up for work in the morning.

Evie and Ruby are in Apple Tree having their own little party, although Selena keeps popping in to make sure they're okay. She's already taken the Haribos away from them, and I had to remind Evie that Ruby has to be careful what she eats. Evie looked stricken, probably because her sweets had been taken away rather than because she felt any real concern for Ruby. She seems delighted to have Ruby to herself, and when I look in on them on the way to the kitchen, they're both in Ruby's bed, giggling and watching *Charlie and Lola*.

Selena seems edgy tonight, and I suspect there's more to it than anxiety about Ruby's sweets. She hasn't joined everyone else in the front room and is hovering in the kitchen with Mum. When I walk in to get some glasses they both stop talking and Mum leaves with a bottle of wine to go back to the living room.

Amelia is with the Greyson boys in the playroom on

the Xbox. She's always been more of a tomboy. She used to hang out with boys all the time at her old school until a group of girls began teasing her, accusing her of fancying the boys, which made her self-conscious. It's nice that she's made friends with Will in the privacy of her own home, without worrying what her peers will think.

The rest of the guests are in the living room. I keep leaving to top up drinks and fetch nibbles. Mum's pressed between Susie Greyson and Julia on one of the sofas, necking wine and laughing loudly. Adrian, as far as I'm aware, is still upstairs writing. I make a mental note to go and check on him after refilling the wine glasses.

It's a dark, wet night and the curtains are drawn. The smell of wine and the sound of chatter filter through to me. Even Janice has joined us, her dog on her lap, her cheeks flushed with Chardonnay. The only other guest who isn't here is Dean.

I excuse myself and go upstairs to Adrian. I'm nearly at the top when I see Dean coming out of his room. A grin stretches across his face when he sees me, but it never reaches his eyes. He always makes me feel he despises me. 'All right, Kirsty?' he says. He has his backpack on. Where is he going now in this weather? 'Have you seen Selena?'

I shake my head. 'She was in the kitchen earlier.'

'Isn't that out of bounds for guests?'

'She's family.'

'I've tried her door but she's not answering. It doesn't matter. I'll catch up with her later.' He does that weird salute thing, then stands aside to let me pass and walks down the stairs. I watch him leave through the front door.

Something about him makes my skin crawl. I can't put my finger on it. It's not as though he's rude to me, or aggressive. Maybe it's because I remember what he was like as a teenager. Nobody wanted to mess with Dean Hargreaves back then. And, according to Selena, he's been in the army. He's used to firing guns and channelling his aggression into the skills he'd need to kill the enemy. I'm sure he'd be able to tie a very good noose. My mind goes to the knife I found in his room. What is he *really* doing here?

I continue up to the attic. When I reach the landing, I hear voices coming from our bedroom. The door is ajar and I see Selena leaning against Adrian's desk, her hands clasped around a mug. She's changed into a pretty pink jumper that brightens her complexion and brings out the colour in her cheeks. Adrian's turned to face her so I can't read his expression, but Selena is listening intently, her head to one side.

I push the door open and clear my throat. Selena looks up and Adrian swivels around. Is that panic I notice in his expression? TripAdvisor is open on his laptop.

'So this is where you've both been hiding,' I say, standing behind his chair and peering over his shoulder at the screen. 'Dean was looking for you, Selena. Oh . . . what's this?'

I see 'THE OLD RECTORY' above a photo of our house and an average rating of three stars. My heart sinks. It looks like someone has left our first review.

'It's the teenage lovebirds,' says Adrian.

I scan the review under the headline 'OKAY'.

*Owners friendly if a little overbearing. Felt like we were being watched, and were made to feel quite uncomfortable at times. Couldn't really relax. The owners seemed to know everyone so at breakfast we felt a little out of things. Noisy kids running around the place. There was even a smelly dog. Bed too hard although the decor was modern and our room clean. The area is pretty but there's not much to do unless you like walking. The village is full of old people and hikers. Not quite the romantic break we had in mind.*

Tears spring to my eyes. All our hard work and our first review is bad.

Selena catches my eye and smiles in sympathy. 'It's just one review. I'll write one too. I'm a guest, after all, and I'll give you five stars.'

*Friendly but overbearing.* I can't believe they think we're overbearing. *Kids running around the place.* It's their home. Have we made a mistake in thinking we can run a guesthouse and bring up children too?

'Don't worry about it, sweetheart,' says Adrian, standing up and pulling me into his arms. 'Some people just like to complain.' Over his shoulder I see Selena look down at her feet. 'They should have gone to a hotel if they wanted to be more anonymous.' He pulls away from me. 'And I don't know why they're criticizing the bed. They seemed to get a lot of enjoyment out of it!' He laughs and I slap his arm playfully.

'What's this?' Selena asks, and Adrian fills her in on their sexual exploits while we all walk downstairs.

But as I follow them I want to know why they were in our bedroom together, what they were talking about.

Selena is sitting opposite me in the armchair by the window, her legs crossed, her hands folded around her mug. Her fingernails are bitten down and unvarnished, another thing that's different from how she used to be. Her nails were always long and well cared-for, coated with an array of interchangeable colours that never lasted longer than a few days, although she would always go back to black, her favourite. She is unusually quiet, watching everyone else in the room and quietly sipping her tea – she refused the wine I poured for everyone else. Apart from a polite hello to Nathan and Julia, she's not engaged with them, moving to the seat across the room from Nathan and nearest the door. I can't understand her coldness towards Nathan. Usually Selena can't resist being a bit flirty with any man, and Nathan used to follow her around like a dog when we were growing up. Maybe she feels awkward because she knows he once had a crush on her, although that's not like Selena. She's never been one to shy away from attention.

Janice has turned to talk to Mum so I inch over a bit to hear what Julia and Susie are saying, trying to think of a way to include Selena in the conversation too.

They are discussing their jobs – Susie is a nurse, working in A and E by the sound of it. I glance across at Selena, who seems more and more uncomfortable, her shoulders hunched, as though she's hoping to disappear into the folds of the armchair. She was always such a social butterfly, flitting in and out of different conversations with ease, fluttering around our peer groups at school. I was the awkward one. Now she looks exactly how I used to feel.

When there is a pause in the conversation, I jump in. 'I don't think you've been introduced,' I say. 'This is Selena, my cousin. And these,' I indicate the two women, 'are Susie Greyson and Nathan's wife, Julia.'

A shadow passes over Selena's face when she looks at Julia – it's almost infinitesimal but I notice, although she covers it with a smile. Her neck is turning blotchy and red.

'Lovely to meet you,' says Julia, but there is a coldness behind her normally warm smile. 'Amelia says you have a daughter. She couldn't stop talking about her when we were out today.'

She swallows and nods. 'Yes. Ruby.'

'What a beautiful name.' She angles her body so that she's looking straight at Selena. 'I've heard she's been unwell. How is she now?'

'Julia's a GP,' I interject.

The rash on Selena's neck blooms. 'Oh, right.' There is obvious relief in her voice. 'It's good to know, actually. I'm in a constant state of terror about Ruby's health.'

Julia smiles sympathetically, encouraging Selena to continue. She opens up about Ruby's health issues and I zone out as they talk about digestive tracts and the different procedures Ruby has had. I've never had the stomach for anything medical and admire anyone in that profession. I rang Julia in a state of panic so many times when the girls were younger, terrified that their rashes or temperatures were a sign of something more serious.

I'm asking Susie how she's enjoying the Brecons when, out of the corner of my eye, I see Selena abruptly leap from her chair and dart from the room. Julia is smiling blandly.

'Is everything okay with Selena?' I blurt out, interrupting Susie's tale about seeing the waterfalls yesterday.

Julia frowns. 'I think so. She worries about Ruby. Not surprising, really. That poor little girl. She wanted to check on her.'

I glance towards the door. 'Which reminds me. I need to tell my two to get up to bed.' I stand up. 'I'll be back in a minute.' Before they can say anything further, I hurry from the room just in time to catch Selena before she reaches the bedroom.

'Hold on,' I call, wheezing slightly. I take my inhaler

from the pocket of my jeans and place it in my mouth, pressing the top and taking deep breaths.

Selena stops and waits for me. 'Are you okay?'

I rub my chest. 'Asthma's always worse this time of year. The bonfires, I think.' I shove the inhaler back in my pocket. 'Is everything okay?'

She pulls a puzzled face. 'Yes. Why?'

'I don't know. You just seem . . . distracted.'

She sighs. 'Oh, God, I'm so stressed.' It comes out in a rush, like she's relieved to be finally admitting it.

'Come into the dining room with me a minute.'

She has one hand on the bedroom doorknob, her empty mug in the other. I can hear the girls' laughter coming from inside the room. 'I don't know . . . Ruby really needs her sleep.' I notice a cold sore at the corner of her mouth that's started to crust over.

I want Selena to open up to me. Particularly about Dean. I need to know what's going on there because something doesn't add up. 'Just quickly. It would help if you talked about it.' I take the mug from her. 'I've got some herbal tea.' I try to make it sound enticing.

She laughs. 'Herbal tea! Once it would have been a lager and black. Oh, go on then. Just a quick one.'

She follows me into the kitchen and hops up on to the bar stool. She asks for camomile and I dunk a teabag in a large mug of hot water and hand it to her.

'I just can't sleep at the moment,' she says, taking a sip. 'I go to bed early to be with Ruby but I lie there, staring into the darkness, my mind ticking over.'

I sit next to her and pour myself another glass of wine. 'Are you worrying about Nigel? About Dean?'

'Both,' she admits.

'Have you decided what to do?'

She shakes her head. 'Not completely. I won't go back to Nigel. Not now. I can't. If he finds out about Dean,' she swallows, 'he'd hurt me. And I mean, *really hurt me*.'

'Oh, Selena.'

'He's a nasty man. I should have got out years ago. But Ruby . . .' She pulls at the hem of her jumper. 'I'm not going to lie. I had a nice life with Nigel. Financially. But that's not enough, is it?'

'Of course it's not!' I say, shocked. 'Nothing is worth being treated like shit. Or being used as a punch-bag.' I hesitate. 'Nigel still doesn't know where you are?'

She grimaces. 'No. And he can't find out. He's not the sort of man to take kindly to his wife leaving him.'

'Do you want to be with Dean?'

Her eyes fill with tears. 'I don't know that either. He's pressuring me but I can't jump from one man to another.'

'No. You can't. Do you want to divorce Nigel?'

She nods. *Yes*. And I feel a surge of relief.

'Does Dean have a house? Does he want you to move in with him?'

'That's what he said. But I can't. It wouldn't be fair to Ruby.'

I take a slug of wine. Then, 'Dean's due to check out

tomorrow. He's only paid for two nights. He will go, won't he?'

She picks at the cardboard tag attached to the teabag and, without looking at me, says, 'He won't cause you any trouble. I know you don't like him, but he does love me, you know.'

I'm not sure what else to say. Eventually I ask, 'And Nathan? Is everything okay between the two of you?'

'Nathan?'

'Well, you have been ignoring him . . .'

She laughs. 'I haven't.'

She seems to think the idea is hilarious but I'm not finding it funny. I wasn't imagining the tension between them. 'You've hardly said two words to each other.'

'Probably because this is the first time I've seen him in ages. It just feels a bit odd, that's all.'

I don't believe her. But it's none of my business.

She shuffles in her seat. 'Anyway, enough about me. What about you? Is everything okay with you and Adrian?'

I bristle. 'Me and Adrian? Everything's fine. Why?'

The corners of her mouth turn down and she dunks her teabag. 'No reason. It must be hard, that's all. You've both been through a lot. And I sensed . . .' she hesitates '. . . that you were angry with me earlier.'

I consider this. 'Only because I thought you'd told Dean about Adrian's suicide attempt. Finding that noose was a bit of a shock. On top of the dead flowers.'

She stiffens. 'Dead flowers?'

I explain briefly. 'I haven't told Adrian about the last lot – he doesn't need any added stress.'

Selena has gone quiet, her face deathly white.

'What is it? What's wrong?'

'They're from Nigel. I know it. It's the sort of sick fucking thing he'd do. Oh, God. It means he knows where I am.' Her face is panicked, her eyes round with fear. 'It means he's found me.'

# 19

## *The day*

Selena hardly touches her breakfast. I watch her pick at her scrambled egg while simultaneously fussing over Ruby, and remember our conversation from last night, the fear in her eyes when I mentioned the flowers. Is her husband such a psycho that he would send his estranged wife bouquets of dead flowers as a threat? I imagine him as the villain in that 1990s film *Sleeping with the Enemy* and feel a dart of fear. I knew Selena coming here would mean trouble. But then I look at Ruby. Beautiful, frail Ruby. Today she's back in the wheelchair: last night must have tired her out. I'm struck by another wave of admiration for the way Selena handles it all.

Everybody else has finished breakfast. Adrian, to my surprise, is helping me clear away and Mum sits with Selena and the girls, trying to coax Evie to eat the rest of her toast. It's half-term but the girls are still waking up early.

'I'm sorry I've not been very helpful,' begins Adrian, when we're alone in the kitchen. 'You and your mum have been doing everything since we opened.'

I wonder where this is coming from. 'That's okay.'

He runs his hand over his beard. 'It's not, though, is it?' He moves towards me. 'This is supposed to be our thing.' He takes my hands in his.

I dip my head. 'I know it's not how we imagined it.' I wonder if he would have been any different if it had been just the two of us, distracted by his book, squirrelling himself away upstairs, not wanting to see people.

He shuffles and looks down at our joined hands. He's swapped his usual scruffy attire for smart jeans and a short-sleeved shirt, and he smells of the Tom Ford aftershave I bought him two Christmases ago. 'It was kind of your mum to help us out. Selena made me realize I might have been taking you for granted.'

My head shoots up. 'Selena?'

'Yes. She said—'

I cut across him. 'When was this?'

'Last night. You were in bed with Evie. I'd come down to fetch a glass of water and Selena was in the kitchen . . .'

I drop his hands and he moves towards the dishwasher. I watch as he begins stacking the dirty plates. 'What else did she say?'

His dark eyes bore into mine. 'She thinks a lot of you, you know.'

I'm thrown. 'Right.'

'You don't have to sound so suspicious.'

I pinch the top of my nose with my thumb and forefinger. I have a headache coming on and I hardly slept last night, thinking of Nigel turning up to hurt Selena, or Dean prowling around the house with his hunting knife, getting up to God knows what. Maybe I drank too much wine. 'I'm sorry. I don't mean to.'

He's silent for a few moments. The cutlery clinks as he dumps it in the rack, a baked bean rolls off one of the plates and lands on the back of the dishwasher door. 'She told me about the other bouquet of dead flowers. Did you get more this morning?'

It had been roses again this time, the hints of their original peachy colour still evident underneath the brown. I consider lying. But it must be written all over my face because he sighs, then slams the dishwasher door.

'She shouldn't have told you.'

He closes his eyes as though in pain. When he opens them again they're full of hurt and anger. 'You can't keep things from me. I'm your husband. We're a team.'

'I just didn't want you to get stressed out.'

He holds a hand up. 'I know that.' His voice softens. 'And I love the way you try to take it all on yourself. But that's not good for you.' He walks towards me and pulls me into his arms so that my face is pressed against his chest. I close my eyes and surrender to him. It feels so good to let go for a while, to let someone else take the burden.

He kisses the top of my head. 'I don't want you to think of me as this weak man who can't take any pressure.'

This weak man? Is that how I've seen him since his

breakdown? Someone frangible maybe, someone who is on the mend. But not weak. 'I don't think that. I'm sorry.'

'So, you'll tell me what's worrying you in future?'

I think of his reaction yesterday when he found the noose. 'Of course I will,' I lie.

When I first met Adrian, it was his strength I admired. The way he took charge. He wasn't one of those alpha males who had to shout to be heard. He had a quiet confidence. It was there in the way he led me through crowded streets, always knowing which way to go when I was useless with directions, or in the way he kept his patience when trying to fix my computer or the TV. How he'd listen without judging when I admitted to finding motherhood hard, or when I was filled with fear that something bad would happen to the girls. How honest he'd be if he thought I was being unreasonable about a work situation, or a relationship with a friend.

We'd met in our early twenties when I was a junior in the marketing department of a law firm in Old Street. He was three years older and training to be a lawyer in the same firm. I was impressed with how clever he was. He was like a walking encyclopaedia. He wasn't loud and brash, like some of the others in his team, with their swagger, their booming voices and sexist jokes. I'd find excuses to go into his department just to get a glimpse of the tall man with floppy dark hair and warm eyes. One day, when we were both at the coffee machine

I made him laugh with a caustic joke about the sleazy middle-aged man in Archives who could never meet a woman's eye but stared instead at their chest. I loved his laugh – he'd throw back his head with an actual guffaw. It sent tingles through me. After that he began to seek me out, too, and I started to wonder if the attraction might be mutual. And then he asked me out, a meal and a movie, laughed at my jokes and asked me to talk to him in Welsh. I loved how he thought I was clever and funny, how he would sit back in his chair and assess me, as though I was the most interesting, the most wonderful thing he'd ever seen. I preferred the person I was through his eyes.

Soon we were inseparable, moving in together within three months. I knew some of his background: his Home Counties upbringing, his public-school education and then Exeter University (his parents had been disappointed, he said, when he failed to get into Oxford). He was an only child and his parents were older, his father a professor, his mother an economics lecturer, so the pressure had been heaped upon him. On our first date, he told me he'd wanted to be a writer but his parents wouldn't hear of it. His eyes, the colour of conkers, had lit up when he talked about writing and I remember feeling sad that he had been forced by his parents down a different path. That he'd felt he had no choice but to conform.

He wasn't going to be like that with our children, he

said. He was going to give them the freedom they needed to grow as people.

Maybe I pushed him, too, without realizing it, when I encouraged him to go for that promotion at work so he'd be earning more money, enabling me to give up my job, or when I convinced him to move from our two-bedroom flat in Balham to a three-bedroom house near Twickenham Green, doubling our mortgage. Or when I started to complain that he was working too hard and had less time for me and the girls.

We were all guilty, his parents and me, of piling pressure on that sensitive, creative, clever man. I don't think Adrian is weak. He's stronger than I am in lots of ways. But I am conscious of pushing him too hard.

It's no wonder he eventually snapped.

I catch Selena coming down the stairs. She looks fresher this morning and she's dressed in a black jumpsuit and heels, a slash of bright red lipstick. I wonder if it's for Dean's benefit. She's obviously just been to see him: why else would she be upstairs? Unless she's been chatting to my husband again.

'Hi,' she says. 'I was wondering if I could ask you a favour. I need to pop out – I'm meeting someone at ten. Would you or Carol mind keeping an eye on Ruby while I'm gone? She's still in bed. She seems exhausted today. I shouldn't be too long.'

'Sure,' I say. 'Um . . . can I ask you something?'

She pauses at the bottom of the stairs, her hand on the newel post. 'Yes?'

'Why did you tell Adrian about the dead flowers?'

She raises a perfectly drawn eyebrow. 'But he already knew.'

'Only the first bouquet. I didn't want him to know about the others. I did ask you last night not to say anything.'

Her eyes widen. Her eyelashes are really long and I wonder if she has extensions. 'I don't remember you saying that. But I'm sorry if I spoke out of turn.'

She doesn't sound very sorry but what more can I say? I want to ask what else they talked about, alone in the kitchen, while everybody was in bed. I wonder if she was wearing that nightdress. And then I remember Adrian's words of apology, his acknowledgement that he takes me for granted. He even emptied the dishwasher! Whatever she'd said to him had had the right effect.

'No. That's okay. It's all good.'

She smiles uncertainly and glances at her watch. 'Do I look all right?' she asks, patting down her hair. She seems a bit twitchy, on edge.

'You look lovely,' I say truthfully, although I am not sure about the too-bright lipstick.

She slips on a biker jacket. It's beautiful, dove-grey suede. It must have cost a fair whack. I look down at my own shapeless jumper and skinny jeans. I can't remember the last time I dressed up. That's one of the downsides of working at home, not having an excuse to dress for an office.

'Thank you. I'll see you later,' she calls, as her heels clatter over the tiles and she disappears out of the door.

Mum asks me to pop to the shops to get some more toilet cleaner and bleach. Nancy's upstairs sorting out the rooms and Mum says she'll keep an eye on Ruby and the girls as Selena hasn't returned yet. It's only ten forty-five and I feel like I've done a day's work already. I think wistfully of the laughs we used to have in the office, gossiping over the photocopier or around the water cooler, of Gemma and Katie – I barely keep in contact with them, these days. My work friends were replaced by the mums I met at my local antenatal group when I was pregnant with Amelia, and even they splintered away when Amelia started school and I joined the PTA.

My closest friend in Twickenham is Bex, the mum of one of Amelia's school friends, but we haven't spoken since I moved down here. I keep meaning to call her but it's been so busy. Everyone is so caught up in their own lives. I long to tell Bex about Selena, working with Mum, the bad review and being constantly 'on duty'. But I know I won't. Because I don't want to admit to anyone – even myself – that I might be having second thoughts about it. It sounds so ungrateful. I'm living the dream. My friends were envious when I told them my plans. They promised they'd come and stay. I couldn't wait to show off. I had visions of us all here, drinking and laughing, as if we were at a hen weekend. But it wouldn't be like that. They would be the guests and I would be working.

I shake off my negative thoughts. I'm just tired. It's been a long week and it's only Tuesday.

Just as I'm gathering up my coat and bag I feel a prod to my shoulder blade.

I jump, my hand going to my chest as I spin round. Dean is standing there, the usual grin on his face. 'All right, Kirsty? Can I pay to stay for one more night?'

I consider lying, telling him we have a booking, but then I think of the money. Selena can handle herself, I think, as I take payment, feeling I've sold my soul to the devil. She must have invited him here, after all. 'Just the one night?'

'I think so. I'm hoping that by tomorrow I'll have got what I came for.'

Is he going to stay here until Selena agrees to be with him?

I hand him a receipt and he slinks back upstairs, looking pleased with himself.

Pulling on my coat, I head outside into the rain. It's not as cold today, just damp, the pavements slick, dirty puddles gathering in the concrete ruts, piles of soggy leaves lining the kerb like a rug. I take my time, glad to be out of the house for a bit, breathing in the damp air, my fingers curled around my inhaler in my pocket. Sometimes I wake in the night, gasping for breath, my heart racing.

The mountains seem more oppressive today and I

feel hemmed in by them. They nudge the grey skies, the charcoal clouds circling them like halos.

I'm only halfway to the high street when I see Nathan walking towards me, hands in his pockets, the collar of his coat up against the rain. He has no hood or umbrella and his hair is damp and dishevelled. He looks as though he has the weight of the world on his shoulders. I'm surprised to see him. I'd assumed he and Julia were still in their room. I've been watching them since they arrived to see if I can detect the marriage problems Mum alluded to. And, it's true, they don't seem as close. There have been times that I've seen Julia's smile slip when she thinks nobody's watching. A few times their interactions have seemed forced, like when she pushed him away after he rested his head on her shoulder the other night. She'd looked irritated, although she was trying to cover it with humour.

At first I think he's going to carry on walking right past me but when he spots me he slows to a halt.

'Where's Julia?' I ask.

He digs his hands further into his pockets. 'We're not joined at the hip, you know.' He hasn't shaved, which is unusual for Nathan. He's always been fastidious about facial hair. He openly teases Adrian about his beard and calls him Gandalf.

'Is everything all right?'

He shrugs, his frown deepening. 'Just needed some air.'

'Listen, Nathe, if you ever want to talk . . .'

He shakes his head. 'It's all fine,' he says, the words thrown carelessly over his shoulder as he walks away.

Not talking. It's what we do best in our family.

After purchasing the bleach and toilet cleaner, I pop into the coffee shop and order a cappuccino and a pastry, thinking of my brother and his wife. I wish Nathan would open up to me a bit more. I wish they both would. But I understand why Julia can't – after all, Nathan is my little brother. I know she'd feel awkward admitting there might be problems.

I settle myself in the corner, enjoying the solitude. I feels a bit woozy, a dull ache at the back of my neck – I hope I'm not coming down with a virus.

Apart from an old couple at the table next to me, and the middle-aged woman at the counter, the place is empty.

I get a text message from Sian asking how it's going and if Amelia would like to go over for a playdate with Orla on Friday. I text back eagerly. I'm excited to have contact with someone who isn't linked to the guesthouse and I like Sian. I can see us becoming friends. And I really need a friend right now. I miss Bex and the others more than I'd thought I would.

As I trudge back along the high street, I hear shouting. I turn in the direction it's coming from and see Dean and Selena up ahead, by the bridge. She pushes him away from her and stalks off towards the guesthouse. He follows, calling her name, his cries getting more urgent and aggressive.

'Don't you fucking walk away from me!' he calls after her. 'You'll be sorry! Do you hear me? YOU'LL BE SORRY!'

I need to intervene. I can't let him speak to her like that. But after a few steps he stops following her and turns away. I keep walking towards him, my heart thudding, but he strides past me. I hope he didn't notice me.

## 20

### *The night*

Selena's quiet for the rest of the afternoon. I want to ask her about Dean and their row but I don't have much chance as I'm run off my feet, sorting rooms, answering the phone (much to my delight – I was worried that the TripAdvisor review would put people off), fielding questions from Janice about day trips, and requests from Mr Greyson for recommendations of family-friendly restaurants.

But as I go about my chores I have a prickly feeling at the top of my spine – like you feel when there's someone behind you – and a few times I spin round to find no one there. I had the same sensation yesterday when Lydia Ford was staring at me. Sometimes, when I'm up in the attic, I can hear Evie's wardrobe making the sucking sound it produces when it's opened or closed, but when I go into her room it's empty. I think of Janice – our resident Mystic Meg – her talk of energies and past deaths, and shiver.

I knock on Dean's door. Nancy gave his room the once-over this morning, but I'm armed with teabags as an excuse to see whether he's there.

When there is no answer I let myself in. It looks as

though he hasn't been back since I saw him with Selena earlier. As usual his room is pristine – a contrast to Selena and Ruby's. Again, I wonder what he wants. Why he's here. Is he really hoping Selena will run away with him? Or is there something I'm not seeing?

As I lock Dean's door behind me I hear crying. I stand and listen intently. Yes, someone is definitely crying. Proper, dry, gut-wrenching sobs. It's coming from Julia and Nathan's room. I hover outside their door, debating whether or not to go in. But it's private, and as much as I adore Julia, I don't want to intrude. So I walk away.

Later, when I go into the living room, Nathan is sitting there alone reading a newspaper. He says Julia's not feeling well, leaving me wondering if they've had a row.

'Is she okay?' I blurt out. 'I thought I heard her crying earlier.'

He looks up and irritation flickers across his face. 'No. She's fine. Everything's fine.'

'Nathe . . .' I go to him but he folds the newspaper.

'Not now.' He stands up and runs a hand through his hair.

'If you want to talk . . .'

'You've already said that.'

'I'm worried about the two of you.'

He meets my eye and, for a moment, I think he's going to be honest with me and open up. But instead he says, 'We'll be fine. We always are.'

*

Adrian has taken the girls out to the next town to get more supplies.

'Make sure you hold Evie's hand,' I call from the front door, as they clamber into the car. She has a tendency to wander off if something takes her fancy. It could be anything: a cute puppy, a newborn baby in a pram, a toy. 'And drive carefully.' That awful day from eighteen months ago pops into my mind and I remember the gut-wrenching fear I'd experienced, thinking I'd never see the girls again. No, I can't think of that. That was *before*. Adrian's better now. He'd never do anything like that again.

Mum is in the dining room, giving Ruby her tea – a gluten-free vegetable dish that she made earlier with Selena's help – and I try to get Selena on her own by asking her to help me make coffee in the kitchen.

'What's going on?' I whisper, as I turn on the coffee machine.

She looks nonchalant. 'What do you mean?'

'I saw you with Dean earlier. Arguing.'

She waves a hand dismissively but there are shadows under her eyes. 'It was nothing. Just a lovers' tiff.'

I frown. 'So you are lovers?'

'Not in that sense. We haven't had sex since we've been here, if that's what you mean.'

I raise my eyebrows but I don't say anything.

'You're wondering how long I'm planning on staying, aren't you?' she says, a moment later.

'I . . . No, it's not that. I just want you to be happy.'

Her composure slips and she sinks on to one of the bar stools, putting her head in her hands. 'I don't know what I'm going to do,' she wails. 'I can't go back to Nigel. But I don't want Dean either. I want . . . I always want what I can't have.'

I go over to her and place my hand on her arm. The fabric of her jumpsuit feels silky under my fingers. There's nothing to it. She needs to put a cardigan on. It's always cold in this house. We could really do with double glazing but we can't afford it yet. 'What do you mean?'

She shakes her head. 'It's nothing. I'm just rambling.' She looks up. She has tears in her eyes. 'I've got enough money to rent somewhere for me and Ruby. I've just been . . .' She sighs. 'I just needed a break. Someone to help with Ruby for a bit.' She rubs her face. 'I'm so tired.'

My heart goes out to her. She must be exhausted. And she has no family, apart from us.

'Are you still worried that Nigel's sending the dead flowers?' I want to help her but I don't know what to think of her ex. How someone could do such a thing. He's an enigma to me.

'I'm not sure.' She rubs a hand across her face.

'What attracted you to him?' I ask gently. 'He couldn't have been all bad for you to stay with him. To have a child together.'

'When I first met him I thought he was great. So different from men like Dean. Older, stable, dependable.

He was successful. He had his own house. This huge, double-fronted detached place with Roman blinds in nautical stripes at the windows, which I thought were the height of sophistication, a neat square garden and a double garage on the side. New, boxy and slightly bland. A bit like Nigel himself.' She laughs. 'But bland was good. Bland doesn't have the capacity to hurt you.'

'What changed?'

'It's awful to say it, but the stress of Ruby, I suppose. He was so fastidious, shouting at me if I'd left a Babygro out of place, or a dirty nappy bag on the counter. He wanted that bloody house to look like a show-home. All the time. It's not normal.' She gives a small laugh. 'People need to be able to make a mess in their own homes. Even you, Kirsty!'

I laugh too. If it was anything like her bedroom when we were kids, or her messy room here, I could see where Nigel was coming from. I instantly push the thought away. He was violent. He hurt her. That's never acceptable. 'What can I do to help?' I ask.

'You're doing enough. More than enough. The way I treated you when we were eighteen. I hate myself for it.'

I hug her, which is slightly awkward considering she's still sitting on the stool. 'Don't be silly.' I sit down next to her.

She groans. 'I've been such a fool. But the past has a way of catching up with you, doesn't it?'

And I don't know what it is – maybe it's the way she

says it, or the intensity in her eyes – but I feel foreboding wash over me.

I'm relieved when Adrian returns with the girls. By the look of the McDonald's bags and the milkshake carton that Evie is clutching, I can tell where they've been for tea. Mum eyes the bag disapprovingly.

'I was starting to get worried,' I say, as he dumps two carrier bags of shopping on the counter. I bite my tongue about the junk-food tea. I imagine the girls nagged at him. And it's good for the three of them to spend some time together.

Mum takes the girls to see Ruby while I unpack the shopping. I'm about to ask Adrian to help when I see him drift into the living room where Selena is nursing a coffee. She looks attractive, sexy even, in her slinky outfit. He sits opposite her and they begin chatting, although I can't hear what they're saying.

*I always want what I can't have.*

That night I persuade Adrian to go to bed early. We need some time alone. Away from guests, from the girls, from Mum. And, most importantly, from Selena.

Amelia and Evie are in bed early, too, and are both sound asleep. Evie is curled up with that ugly china doll. I wonder how long she'll stay in her bed before she finds her way into ours.

I instigate sex this time. It was something I never had to do until the depression hit. Since then we're lucky if we make love once every few months. He seems surprised when I start kissing him and, at first, I think he's going to move away, but he doesn't. He pulls me into him and starts kissing me back, passionately, although his beard is scratching my face. I don't protest, trying to stay in the moment, but I can't push thoughts of him and Selena having secret bedroom chats completely out of my head.

Afterwards I fall asleep in his arms, feeling closer to him than I have for a long time.

I'm awoken by a shrill scream. *Something's happened to the girls.* I sit up in bed, my heart racing. The air is still. Silent. Did I dream it? My eyes dart to Adrian's side of the bed. It's empty, the sheet creased and slightly damp, the duvet thrown back as though he left in a hurry. Where is he? My alarm clock shows 5.37a.m. and, through a crack in the curtains, the sky is still dark, the tips of the mountains disappearing into early-morning mist.

I fumble for my dressing-gown, which I'd thrown across the foot of the bed the night before. I pull it around myself as I hurry from the room. Across the landing, the door to the girls' room is closed. I'm just about to go to it when I hear the scream again.

There's no mistaking it this time. It sounds like my mother.

I race down the first flight of stairs, trying to quell my rising panic. My mother isn't the type of woman to scream. I think about the guests ensconced in their rooms, knowing she must have woken them, too, and, despite the circumstances, I worry about upsetting them.

When I reach the top of the second flight of stairs I stop in my tracks. I blink, hoping my eyes are playing tricks on me but the image remains. The hallway below is shrouded in darkness but it looks as though Mum is crouched over a body, its limbs spread-eagled on the refurbished Victorian tiles. I can see the flash of a pale calf, a slim wrist. I can hear Mum groaning.

It doesn't look like a child. The legs are too long.

*It's not one of the girls. Thank God.*

'Mum?'

Her head shoots up at the sound of my voice, her eyes wide with anguish and something else – fear. She holds up her hands as though she's about to pray. They are coated with blood.

# PART TWO
## After

## 21

*Just after*

Mum stands up when she sees me approaching. There is blood on her trousers, on her jumper. Her expression is of utter despair. She'd looked like that before. After Natasha died.

And that's when I see the white nightdress and the arc of blood above a pale blonde head.

My hand flies to my mouth. It's Selena.

Her long limbs are spread-eagled on our restored Victorian tiles, but with one leg bent, her neck at an unnatural angle. Blood is tangled in the strands of her pale hair, and looks too red, unreal somehow, as though the girls have been busy with a paintbrush. I can see her bare foot, the purple polish on her toenails. That foot makes my eyes fill. So vulnerable, so familiar, with the soft fleshy sole and the elongated middle toe. I used to tease her about her middle toe being longer than all the others. She said it meant she was descended from a Roman princess. She was always coming out with stuff like that. It's the sort of thing Evie would say.

I stifle a sob.

'What happened?' I run down the remainder of the stairs, almost slipping in my haste.

Mum stands up, speaking fast. 'I don't know. I heard a sound. Something woke me and I couldn't get back to sleep. So I thought I'd get dressed and make a start. And I found her – I found her like this—' She's sobbing.

There is no pulse. It doesn't matter how many times I push my fingertips into the flesh of her neck, the outcome is still the same.

She's dead.

The horror hits me. My whole body breaks out in a sweat and my arms and legs tingle. Panic sits on my chest, obstructing my airways so that I can't breathe. I reach for my inhaler but realize I've left it upstairs.

*She's dead.*

*I can't breathe.*

Despite telling myself to stay calm, that I don't want to frighten Ruby or the girls, I scream. It's involuntary, a reflex.

Mum's already pulling herself together, wiping the blood from her hands on to her jumper. 'I'm calling nine-nine-nine,' she says, going into the office. I can hear her on the phone. I feel sick.

'They're on their way,' she says, when she returns.

I sink on to the bottom step and wrap my dressing-gown tightly around my legs to stop them shaking. And then a thought hits me. 'Ruby? Where's Ruby?' She can't come out and see her mother like this.

'I'll make sure she's okay.'

I don't want her to go. I don't want to be left alone with Selena's body.

Her eyes are closed. She might have been sleeping if it wasn't for the blood, and her body at that odd angle. She must have fallen. Slipped down the stairs and cracked her head open on the tiles. How else could this have happened?

Mum reappears. 'Ruby's still asleep,' she says. 'We have to be quiet. We can't let the girls see Selena like this.'

'Should we try to move her?'

'No. The ambulance is on its way.'

'I think . . .' I sob '. . . I think she's dead, Mum.'

Mum kneels down and holds Selena's hand. The gesture makes the tears flow even more. 'Yes,' she says gently.

And I wonder how long she's been lying in this draughty hallway, with the muddy wellies and the smelly trainers and the unseen footprints of strangers. If we'd found her sooner we might have been able to save her.

I stand up. Maybe she's still alive. Maybe her breathing is so shallow we can't tell. She could be in a coma. She could be saved. 'I'm going to get Julia,' I cry, racing back up the stairs before Mum can say anything.

I hammer on Julia and Nathan's door. I'm amazed my scream and Mum's cries haven't woken anyone else.

I hear movement behind the door. There's no

197

answer. I knock again and then a little voice whispers, 'Nathan?'

I frown. Why does she think I'm Nathan? 'Julia! It's me, Kirsty. Open up!'

She opens the door in rose-printed pyjamas. From where I'm standing I can see the bed behind her is empty. Where's Nathan? There's no time to ask her as I fill her in on what's happened to Selena as we descend the stairs. She doesn't seem shocked to see Selena lying there: I imagine she's seen a lot worse at the hospital where she used to work before she became a GP.

Julia bends over Selena and feels for her pulse. 'There's a very faint one,' she says, her eyes meeting mine over Selena's prostrate body. 'But it looks as though she sustained a severe head injury in the fall. Have you called an ambulance?'

'Yes, but it's taking a while. Why can't it hurry up?'

As if on cue we hear the knock on the door. I open it to two strapping paramedics who instantly take charge. Julia explains what's happened as they lift Selena on to a stretcher and fasten a plastic mask over her face.

'I'm going with the ambulance,' insists Mum. 'Selena will need someone with her when she comes round. Look after Ruby, won't you?'

'Of course.'

Julia puts her arm round me as we watch the paramedics stretcher Selena into the ambulance, making sure to support her neck, their heavy footsteps crunching over the gravel. Mum climbs in with her, then the doors are slammed and the ambulance races away.

The two of us stand there watching as the ambulance disappears from sight, shivering in our nightwear. Then we close the door.

I turn to Julia. 'Where's Nathan? I know he wasn't in your room.'

Her face pales even more – if that's possible. She wraps her arms around herself. 'I don't know. We had a row last night and he stormed out. I assumed he slept down here.'

The sound of a door opening makes us both turn. Nathan is coming out of the playroom in a crumpled T-shirt and boxer shorts. His hair is standing on end and he's rubbing his eyes. 'What's going on?'

'Did you sleep in there last night?' demands Julia.

'Where else am I going to sleep when you kicked me out?' he snaps.

I go to him and put my hand on his arm. 'Nathe, Selena's had an accident. We found her here,' I point to the bottom of the stairs, 'about fifteen minutes ago.'

He's suddenly wide awake. 'What?'

'She's not in a good way,' adds Julia. Her voice is emotionless. I turn to her, surprised at her tone. There's something about the way she says it that sounds almost *pleased*.

'Did you hear anything?' I add.

He rubs at his stubble, his eyes red-rimmed and sore. 'No. I was out of it. I'd . . . had a few beers last night.'

Julia throws him a withering look and storms back upstairs.

When she's out of earshot, I say, 'What's going on with the two of you? And what were you doing down here?'

'I told you. We had an argument. She kicked me out of the room.'

'And Selena? Did you see her?'

He turns to me, his jaw set. 'Of course I didn't. For fuck's sake. What are you trying to say?'

'I'm . . . I just can't help but think there's something going on between the two of you. The way you are with one another, the rows with Julia . . .'

He clams up. And even though Mum didn't give birth to him, in that instant, with his pursed lips and folded arms, he looks just like her.

I'm just putting the phone down when Adrian walks through the front door.

It's not yet six thirty but I can hear stirrings upstairs.

He stands in the doorway, his hair wet from the rain, sweat patches under the arms of his grey T-shirt. 'What's going on? You look deathly pale.' He sees the blood on my hands and looks alarmed. 'Are you hurt?'

I start crying again and he pulls me to him. 'What is it?' he says, into my hair. 'What's happened?'

Between sobs I tell him everything. 'I've just had a call from the police. We aren't to touch anything. They're coming over. For forensics. Why would they need forensics? It was an accident. She fell down the stairs . . .'

He pulls away, his expression full of shock. 'What? My God. Is she going to be okay?'

'I don't know. Her head . . .' I gulp, trying to push the picture of Selena's dented skull from my mind. 'She was injured badly.'

He wraps me in his arms again. 'Oh, sweetheart, I'm sorry, so sorry.'

'Did you see anything?' I ask. 'When you left to go running?'

He shakes his head vehemently. 'No, of course not. I left about five.'

'Did you see anything before you left?'

He frowns. 'It was dark. But I think I'd have noticed if Selena had been lying at the bottom of the stairs.'

There's something about his defensive tone, and the way his eyes don't quite meet mine, that tells me he's lying.

We're forced to get on with things. We have no choice. We've a business to run. Julia offers to look after Ruby while I shower and dress. The blood runs off my hands turning the water red.

I'm on the landing when Evie wanders out of her room in her nightie. 'What's going on?'

'It's nothing, honey. Go back to bed. It's still early. I'm just going to make breakfast. Can you stay in your room until Daddy or I come to get you?'

'Nana usually fetches us.'

'I know, but Nana's had to pop out.'

She pads back into her room. I know she won't go back to sleep, but hopefully she'll entertain herself for a bit. I pop my head around the door. 'Make sure to lock it while you're in here,' I whisper, expecting to see Amelia still asleep. But she's wide awake, staring into space. 'Moo? Are you okay?'

'W-what's going on?' she asks. 'I heard something. Screaming.'

Her face is drawn and she looks as though she's been crying. 'Darling, there's been an accident. Selena's fallen down the stairs. But Nana's gone with her to the hospital.'

'Will she be okay?' asks Evie, climbing on to my lap.

'I hope so,' I say, putting my arms around them both. 'I really hope so.'

Adrian and I get through breakfast, side by side. I put him on cooking duty while I serve the guests. The Greysons are up early and in their hiking gear. They're going to attempt to climb Pen Y Fan today, according to Susie, although the two boys look thoroughly bored at the prospect. I don't mention the accident and they don't ask. I feel guilty for even thinking it but I worry about our reputation. If they did hear an ambulance they may have assumed it was for Ruby again.

I try to keep my voice light, as though nothing has happened, even though my stomach churns with anxiety. I keep checking my phone but there's still no news from Mum.

The Greysons leave as Janice walks in, Horace under her arm. She's dressed in a bright pink caftan over dove-grey wide-legged trousers.

'I heard a bit of a commotion earlier,' she says, settling herself at the table by the window. She likes to sit at the same one every morning. 'Is everything okay?'

'Um . . .' I scan the room. It's empty apart from us. Nathan has gone to get dressed and Julia is with Ruby. I assume she's telling her about Selena and I'm grateful that she's here.

'Someone's died, haven't they?' she says suddenly.

'No . . . but one of the guests – my cousin, actually . . . Well, she fell.'

'What?' She moves Horace off her lap and on to the next chair. 'The pretty blonde one? Is she okay?'

'We're not sure yet.'

'Oh, I'm sorry, my love. Bless you, you look all shook up.'

She's prevented from saying any more by the arrival of Julia and Ruby, her little face pale and worried.

I help Julia with Ruby's chair. 'Everything okay?'

Julia nods, and says brightly, 'We're just going to have some breakfast, aren't we, Ruby? Until Mummy and Aunty Carol come back. Ruby says she's allowed porridge made with water. And a banana.'

I smile gratefully at Julia and go off to fetch everybody's orders. When Amelia and Evie come down with

Nathan, it's hard to believe that this has actually happened.

I just pray Selena will be okay. That after all the years we have been apart she'll come home soon.

I put the phone down and sit on the bottom step, my throat dry. Tears run down my cheeks, dropping from my chin on to my lap.

'Mummy?' I glance up. Evie stares down at me, her eyes round with wonderment. Amelia is standing behind her, clearly horrified. The only time they ever witness me crying is at the end of a Disney film. Even when Adrian had his breakdown I was careful to hide my emotions from them.

Adrian appears behind them, embracing them protectively.

I concentrate on pulling myself together but I can't get the image of Selena's crumpled body from my mind. I take one of their hands in each of mine. 'Listen. You both have to be really strong, okay? We've just had the news that Selena . . . died.'

I hear the gasp escape Adrian's lips. Evie bursts into tears. Adrian pulls us all into a group hug. Over their heads I notice Nathan standing in the office doorway. He's staring at me with a look of horror on his face, then turns and slams out of the front door.

I'd always thought I'd be practical in a crisis. I dealt with Adrian's suicide attempt and breakdown calmly.

But this, this I can't do. I can't be the one to tell Ruby that her mother is dead. In the end, it's Julia who goes to her room to tell her, Julia who cradles her as she convulses into sobs.

I'm in the playroom comforting Amelia and Evie when Adrian appears. Evie is still crying but Amelia sits stiffly on the sofa, her hands folded in her lap.

'The police are here. We need to keep everyone away from the stairs and hallway if possible. There's a forensics team and a policeman taking pictures.' He grimaces. 'It's all a bit *CSI*.'

I lower my voice so the girls can't hear: 'But there's been no crime,' I whisper.

'I know. It's procedure, I suppose.' He kneels down next to me and, so quietly I can barely hear him, he says, 'Carol rang again. I'm going to pick her up from the hospital. She's in a bit of a state.'

I nod. 'Okay. Thank you for doing that.'

I can't bear the thought of the police here. What will the guests think? I'm going to have to tell them. But it was an accident. It must have been. She tripped, unable to get her balance, and hit her head on the tiles or the skirting board as she fell. The thought sends a shiver through me. It could have happened to the girls. Those original tiles are death traps. If we'd put wooden floor-ing over them – or, better still, carpet – it wouldn't have happened. She might have broken an arm, or her leg, but not smashed her head against such a hard surface. I start to shake.

Adrian puts a hand on my knee to steady it. 'We don't know anything yet,' he says calmly.

'The guests? What will happen to them?'

He squeezes my knee gently, then stands up, flexing his legs. 'The Greysons are still out, thankfully. Janice and Nathan are in the dining room. He must have gone for a walk in the rain – looks like a drowned rat. I said I'll make them a strong coffee, but now that I'm going to get Carol, maybe you could do it. I'd ask Nathan but he's in no fit state.'

'And Dean?'

His expression becomes even more sombre. 'There's no sign of him. I'll see you later.' He kisses the top of my head. I watch him cross the room, thankful he's taking charge. It's like having the old Adrian back. The one who'd steered me through my busy life, like a human road map. Maybe I'd underestimated him. He seems energized.

Evie shuffles away from me and picks up the TV remote, tucking her legs under her. 'Can I put the telly on?' she asks, perkier again at the thought of watching *Sofia the First*. Oh, to be a six-year-old. Amelia is still sitting in the same upright position. She's not moved or spoken. She's just staring at her hands in her lap.

I tell Evie she can watch TV – it'll be a welcome distraction for her. Then I get up, move to the other side of Amelia and pull her into my arms. She's unyielding. It's like hugging a mannequin. 'Amelia, honey, I know we've all had a huge shock but if you want to talk . . .'

She recoils from me as if I've bitten her. 'I'm fine. I don't want to talk about it. Can you just leave it?'

I hold my hands up in surrender. 'Okay. But I'm here if you need me.'

'I just want to watch TV,' she mutters, her eyes trained on the screen. My heart breaks for her. For both of them. I want to shield them from the bad things that happen. From death. But here it is, turning up unannounced on our doorstep.

I can feel tears threatening again when I think of Selena. Why had she been upstairs when her bedroom is down here? Had she been meeting Dean? Or someone else?

## 22

I tell the girls I need to see to the guests and reluctantly leave them in the playroom. As soon as I step into the hallway I'm collared by a uniformed policeman who looks to be in his early twenties. He introduces himself as PC Avebury. Behind him I can see a forensics team and the photographer that Adrian mentioned. He's kneeling down and taking snaps of the blood on the tiles.

'Are you the owner of this guesthouse?' he asks me.

'One of them. Yes.'

'We need to look through the victim's room.'

The victim? Why refer to her like that? Do they suspect something?

I show them to her room. Ruby is asleep on her bed and Julia sits beside her, looking morose. I explain why we're here and she scoops up Ruby, who stirs and opens her eyes, then leans her head against Julia's shoulder. 'You can take her into the playroom, if you want,' I say. 'The girls are in there watching TV.'

She nods and smiles sadly.

PC Avebury turns to me. 'Thank you,' he says. 'We'll let you know when we've finished. Can I ask what Mrs Perry was wearing yesterday?'

I point to a pile of clothes in the corner. 'She was wearing that jumpsuit,' I say.

'Okay. Thanks. We'll let you know when we've finished.'

I leave them to it and go to the dining room to make coffee.

Nathan is in the dining room when I enter. He jumps up when he sees me.

'The police are here?' he says. He looks wired, like he's drunk too much coffee.

I nod and explain what they're doing.

'Will they ask us questions?'

'I don't know, Nathe,' I say irritably. I'm tired and upset and I haven't got the energy for Nathan's odd behaviour.

'You can't tell them I was sleeping downstairs. It'll look weird.'

'No, it won't.'

'Please. Don't say anything. I'm not asking you to lie, just not to say anything.' He looks so stricken that I find myself agreeing. But it's not until I'm making a cup of tea that I ask myself what Nathan's so afraid of.

I'm in the kitchen when Adrian returns an hour later, Mum holding on to his arm as though her life depends on it. The police won't let them through the front door, so they have to come through the back.

I envelop her when she steps over the threshold and,

to my surprise, she returns my hug, her hair brushing my cheek. She smells of disinfectant and something I can't quite place. Hospital wards and death.

'I can't believe she's gone,' she whispers, her voice croaky and full of tears.

'Me neither,' I say, my eyes filling again.

I lead her into the dining room. Nathan is still sitting alone at one of the tables, with a mug in front of him. He stands up when he sees us, his expression mirroring hers. He goes and fetches us some tea. Mum asks after Ruby and I reassure her that she's with Julia, Amelia and Evie in the playroom, watching TV.

'I need to go and see Ruby,' Mum says, as she sits down.

'Have this first,' urges Nathan, who's arrived with a tea tray. He passes her a mug. 'You look like you need it.'

Mum sips her tea in silence. There is a large bloodstain on the front of her jumper. She notices me looking and brushes at it self-consciously. 'I need to change before I see Ruby.' Her face crumples. 'That poor child . . .'

I swallow the lump in my throat.

'Why are the police here?' Mum asks.

'It's just procedure,' says Adrian, by my shoulder.

'What do you think happened?' asks Nathan. He's clutching his mug so tightly his knuckles have turned white.

'She must have slipped.' If I say it enough, it must be true. But I can't help the niggling suspicion that the police think there's more to it.

Adrian turns to me. 'Have you seen Dean this morning?'

'No.' I glance at the clock on the wall. It's only eleven but it feels much later. Nancy will be here soon. We need to clean the rooms, although what I'd like to do is curl up in a ball and cry.

'She died on the way to hospital,' Mum blurts out. She takes off her glasses and wipes under her eyes, which look small, like a mole's. 'I held her hand as she passed.'

I squeeze her shoulder. 'Oh, Mum.'

We fall silent listening to the clock ticking on the wall and the rain drumming on the windows in the kitchen.

I'm making more coffee when I see a man standing at the bi-fold doors. I jump and put my hand to my chest.

I peel back one of the doors. 'Can I help you?' I ask, wondering if he's looking for a room. Maybe the police told him to come to the back.

'Are you the proprietor of this establishment?' he asks. He has a sour face and is in his late fifties, with steel-grey hair and the sort of rectangular black glasses that Ronnie Kray used to wear. The rain beats down on his head, flattening his hair and splattering his glasses, but it's like he doesn't notice, or care. He's wearing a long grey overcoat over a suit that looks like it needs pressing.

'Yes. I'm Kirsty Whitehouse.'

It's then I see he's holding up a badge. 'I'm Detective Sergeant Middleton from South Wales Police CID. Can I have a word?'

A detective?

'Come in,' I say, stepping aside to allow him into the kitchen.

He looks around without saying a word. He reaches inside his coat, which is marked with dark patches of rain, and takes out a notebook. 'I understand there was an incident here earlier this morning involving a Selena Perry.' It's not a question.

'Yes. That's right. She's my cousin.'

'And that she fell from a flight of stairs?' His voice is monotone.

'Yes. I found her. Well, actually, my mother found her. Her cries woke me.'

He scribbles all this down without speaking. Then he lifts his head and blinks at me. 'Can I speak to your mother?'

'Of course. Please come through.'

I lead him into the dining room. Mum sits at the table with Nathan. Adrian has left. I hope he's seeing to the girls. I know they have Julia with them but they need a parent. It must be so confusing and upsetting for them.

I make the introductions, and when Nathan notices I'm empty handed, he gets up to make more tea. He almost runs to the kitchen.

DS Middleton takes a seat opposite Mum and rests his notebook on the table.

'Can you tell me what happened, please, Mrs Hughes?'

Mum nods. She still looks shaken. I wish she'd changed her jumper. I can't bear seeing Selena's blood.

'I woke up early. I can't be certain if someone woke me. I think I heard something. A noise. A banging, like a door closing. I lay in bed for a bit but I couldn't get back to sleep so thought I'd get up.'

'And what time was this?' asks the detective.

'About five thirty. I got dressed and came downstairs. And that's when . . . that's when I saw something at the bottom of the stairs. It was Selena.'

'And what was she like when you found her?'

'Very still. I thought she was dead. I didn't know what to do. I cried out. The next thing I knew, Kirsty,' she inclines her head in my direction, 'comes down. 'Then Kirsty ran back upstairs and got my daughter-in-law, Julia. She's a doctor. Anyway, she came and assessed her and said she was still breathing.'

DS Middleton frowns. 'When did you call the ambulance?'

Mum scratches her neck. 'I think it was before Julia came down.' She looks to me for confirmation and I nod. 'Yes. It was before.'

'And you told the operator you thought Selena was dead?'

Mum nods. 'Well, yes. Because I thought she was. And then Julia said she felt a pulse.'

'And you think she slipped and fell?' DS Middleton pauses from his notes and looks up.

Mum looks puzzled. 'Yes. Of course. What other explanation could there be?'

Nathan returns with a pot of tea. He offers to pour some for Middleton, who nods a yes.

'And where is her husband?' he continues, in that same droning voice.

'They're estranged . . . She said she left him because he was violent.'

'In what way?'

Mum looks at me. 'Well, I – I don't know. Selena never told me.'

'But she did tell me,' I pipe up.

DS Middleton turns to me and I sidle into the seat next to Mum. 'She didn't go into details.' I remember the look on her face when I told her about the dead flowers. I explain it all to DS Middleton. 'She thought the flowers were from him. A threat. And that he had found her. But it was obvious she was terrified of him.'

He averts his eyes to scribble in his little black book.

Mum leans forwards, her face earnest. 'You do think it was an accident, don't you?'

'We can't rule anything out at this stage.' He changes tack suddenly, like a car swerving at the last minute to take a different road. 'I understand this is a guesthouse.'

'Yes,' I say.

'I might need to come back and speak to everyone who was here. It depends, of course.'

I'm not sure what it depends on and I don't like to ask. I just want him out of the house.

I wrap my arms around myself. I'm so cold. I wonder if I'm going into shock.

*What will this do for the business?* It's a selfish thought and I instantly hate myself for it. Just then Susie Greyson walks into the room led by an exasperated-looking PC Avebury. 'We're trying to keep the scene clean,' he says, almost pushing her into the room and closing the door behind her.

She stares at us all in bewilderment. 'What's going on? I only came back because I had a headache. There're police everywhere.'

DS Middleton stands up. He's going. Thank goodness.

Nathan offers Susie a seat next to him and she sinks into it, eyeing the detective warily.

'A family liaison officer will be with you shortly,' says DS Middleton. I must look perplexed because he adds, 'Because of Selena Perry's daughter. And we're going to have to contact Mr Perry. He's the child's father, after all.'

'You're going to contact Nigel?' I cry. 'He's violent. She was scared of him – Ruby can't go back to him.'

'Kirsty.' Mum's voice is a warning. I glare at her. Why is she trying to stop me talking about it?

DS Middleton's expression remains impassive.

As I'm showing him to the door I spot Janice hovering in the garden, Horace under her arm, his little legs wiggling.

She ignores the detective and he walks away without saying goodbye.

Janice says, 'Oh, my love. I had to take Horace out

for a walk. I wasn't allowed to come back through the front door. The police have just told me what's happened. I'm so sorry.'

I let her into the kitchen. She puts Horace on the floor and I try not to grimace. We're not supposed to have dogs in the kitchen, according to Environmental Health. His paws are filthy, and I ferret in the drawers trying to find a towel so that she can dry him. I hand her one. 'You said this place has a bad energy,' I mumble. 'Maybe you're right.'

She smiles regretfully, and takes the towel. She rubs Horace vigorously. He seems to be enjoying it. Then she stands up, her face serious. 'She was murdered, dear. You know that, don't you?'

'It was an accident,' I say again, annoyed that I have to keep repeating it. None of it feels real. I keep expecting Selena to walk through the door and tell me that this was all just one big joke. A game.

Janice picks up Horace, still wrapped in the towel, and I lead her out of the kitchen and into the dining room. Mum, Susie and Nathan have been joined by Adrian, Julia and the girls. She's still wearing the bloodstained jumper and I realize she's not been allowed upstairs to change. Susie has her head in her hands. I offer to bring her some paracetamol and she nods gratefully.

Adrian follows me to the kitchen. 'Sweetheart,' he says, as I reach up to one of the cupboards to retrieve the pills, 'how are you holding up?'

I grab the packet and sigh, turning to face him. 'The

house already feels too empty without her.' He pulls me into his arms and, I can't help it, I cry against his chest. 'I feel like I've let her down. In so many ways.'

He strokes the hair back from my face. 'You gave her a place to stay when she needed it. A refuge.'

I look up at him. 'Yeah . . . reluctantly.'

'At first, maybe. But you made amends. And you healed a seventeen-year rift.'

We're interrupted by Nathan. He clears his throat. 'Thought you should know. The police have said we're allowed in the hallway now and upstairs. But they're still in Selena's room. Mum's gone to get changed and Susie's gone to bed.'

I hold up the paracetamol. 'I'll take this up to her. She didn't bring any with her.'

I leave the room, Adrian following me. When we're on the stairs I turn to him. 'Where are you going?' I hope he's not planning to shut himself away to write again. Not now. The girls need him and so do I.

'We should check Dean's room.' He holds up a spare key. 'I haven't seen him all day. He was supposed to check out at ten and it's nearly two.'

'Let me just give these to Susie.' I knock on her door. When there's no answer, I call to her.

'Thanks, but I've found some in my suitcase,' she calls back. She sounds groggy, so I leave her to it, slipping the packet into the back pocket of my jeans.

I head to Dean's room. Adrian's already turning the key and the door swings open.

The room is empty. I walk in slowly, as though expecting Dean to be hiding down the side of the bed or in the wardrobe. I scan the room. The bed has been made but his rucksack has gone. I pop my head around the door to the bathroom. His toothbrush and toothpaste are no longer sitting by the sink. I open the mirrored cabinet but it's empty.

'Kirsty!' Adrian calls from the bedroom.

I dart into the room to see him holding up a key. 'I found it on the dressing-table,' he says.

I take it from him. 'He left it here? He skulked out without saying he was leaving? How strange.' I pause. 'And when did he go? Before Selena fell . . . or after?'

# 23

When Adrian and I return downstairs Mum is coming out of Ruby's room. She's changed her clothes but still looks dishevelled, her hair, usually lacquered to within an inch of its life, all over the place. Her smart blouse and navy M&S trousers are creased and she looks as though she's been crying. She tells me the police and the forensics team have left. 'Ssh. Ruby's cried herself to sleep. She's distraught, as you can imagine.'

I peer over Mum's shoulder. Ruby is curled in the foetal position, her face resting on her hands, her long lashes creating shadows on her cheeks. I want to weep for her. 'It's just so awful.'

Mum touches my shoulder. 'I know,' she says softly. 'I'm going to stay with her tonight.'

'She needs some food,' I whisper. 'Look at her. She's so thin and pale. We've all been too distracted and we've missed lunch.' Not that I have an appetite, but it's nearly three o'clock.

'If she wakes up hungry I'll bring her into the dining room and we can give her something. Although . . .' she pauses, looking panicked, '. . . I don't know what she *can* eat.'

'She'll know,' I say, sounding more confident than I feel. 'She can tell us what she's allowed.'

'She's only seven,' Mum says. And then she bites her lip and I can tell she's stifling tears. Before today I can't remember the last time I saw her cry.

'I'm sorry, Mum,' I say. I mean for another loss in our family. First Natasha, then Dad and now Selena. Three Hugheses.

She must think I'm apologizing for something else, though, as she says, softly 'All those wasted years.' She shakes her head sadly. 'All that time lost being angry with Selena. What was the point?' I get the impression she's not talking about me.

I try to keep busy. Adrian is preparing food for the girls without being asked, and Mum is with Ruby. Julia and Nathan must have gone out. Nancy is upstairs, cleaning rooms.

I can't stop thinking about Dean. Why didn't he check out? And when did he leave? I clean his room anyway, ready for the next guest.

I'm just wiping down the bathroom tiles when Nancy pops her head around the door. 'There's someone here to see you,' she says. 'The police.' Her eyes shine with excitement. 'What's going on?'

The police? Here again? They've only just left.

'There was an accident this morning. My cousin fell down the stairs and died,' I explain.

Her hand flies to her mouth and her eyes look like

they're about to pop out of her head. In that moment she reminds me of Horace and I feel guilty for such an inappropriate thought. 'Oh, my God!'

'Can you take over?' I thrust the bleach and cloth into her hand and head downstairs without waiting for an answer.

DS Middleton is standing in the hallway. He has someone with him. An attractive woman in her early thirties with clear green eyes, freckles and long red hair tied up in a bun. She looks sombre, slightly intimidating, until a smile lights her face, making her look warmer, approachable. He introduces her as DC Rachel Banner, our family liaison officer. 'I'll leave you in DC Banner's capable hands,' he says. 'I'll be in touch.'

I watch as he strides out of the front door – his legs are so long, he seems to be wearing stilts. Then I turn to DC Banner.

She smiles again. Her skin is so pale that I can see the blue veins mapped out on her eyelids. 'Please, call me Rachel.'

I try to return her smile but I can't. I don't feel like I could ever smile again.

'Can I speak to you and your immediate family? In private?'

'Sure. Please go through to the kitchen.' I indicate the way, then round up Mum and Adrian. Mum is reluctant to leave Ruby but I tell her it's important and she finally agrees because Ruby is still sleeping.

I put the kettle on and make tea. Rachel takes hers

gratefully. I notice her nails are short and painted a pale pink. I think of Selena and her toenails and my eyes well up again.

Rachel notices. 'I'm so sorry for your loss,' she says. 'I'm here to offer you support, particularly if the police decide there will be an investigation into Selena's death. I've been trained to assist with practical matters and to help you liaise with the media.'

Media? Why would Selena's death be newsworthy?

'And I have a logbook, which I'll use to record our conversations,' she continues. 'This is to help you and to remind me to do anything in the future for you.' She blushes slightly as she comes to the end of her speech. It sounds pat, like she's said it many times before.

I nod mutely. Mum sips her tea and Adrian looks confused. He clears his throat. 'So, you're here to support us?'

'For how long?' asks Mum.

'For as long as it takes.'

'And Ruby?' I ask. 'Selena has a daughter.'

'As you're family, and she's comfortable here, she can stay with you tonight. But custody would usually go to her next of kin, which I expect is her father. We're still trying to contact him. Neighbours have said he's often away on business.' Rachel puts her cup down. 'We will make sure Ruby's needs are met. Please don't worry about that. I understand she's ill?'

'Yes,' I say. 'Crohn's disease, among lots of other things.'

She pulls a sympathetic expression and adds softly, 'I can also put you in touch with any bereavement charities.'

Mum scoffs. 'We don't need anything like that. Thank you all the same.' Mum doesn't believe in counselling. She didn't have any when Natasha died, although I think she would have benefited. And so would I.

Rachel ferrets inside her blazer and retrieves a card. 'I'll be back here tomorrow with more information, but if you need anything in the meantime, this is my number.'

Adrian shows Rachel out, leaving me and Mum to stare at each other over the rims of our mugs.

'I still can't believe this is happening,' she says eventually. Her face is haggard, her cheeks hollow, her eyes lined and red-rimmed.

I inhale deeply. My chest feels tight. 'Me neither. They can't really think her death is suspicious, can they?'

I remember Dean and his hurried departure. I should have told the police about him. The way he ran off without saying anything, the row I overheard them having in the street. My stomach twists.

'No. Of course not. It's just procedure,' insists Mum.

How many times have we said that to each other since the police arrived?

After a few minutes I go to see the girls. Evie is still glued to the television and Amelia is drawing, her A4 art pad resting on her knees. I haven't the heart to turn the television off, although I'd never normally let them sit watching it all day. But I'm hoping it's taking Evie's mind off what's happened to Selena.

I sit between the girls and lean over to see what Amelia's drawing. She has such a talent for art. I'm not sure where she gets it from as neither Adrian nor I can draw, although Selena was always creative. She used to sell her drawings of Garfield in the playground, they were so good. When Amelia sees me trying to look she moves away and pulls the cover over so I can't see what she's sketching. She's never normally so secretive. She usually can't wait to show me her doodles.

She stands up with the pad under her arm. 'I'm going upstairs,' she says, looking at me as though all of this is my fault. I know she can be surly, especially since we moved here, but things were getting better and she'd seemed happier over the last few weeks. It's like she's regressed since Selena was found. But I know that's to be expected.

I stand up and switch off the television. Evie cries out and jumps up, shouting, 'I was watching that!'

'You've been watching it for hours.' I hold out my hand to her. 'Come on, why don't we go and see Ruby?'

She looks as though she's about to have a tantrum. Her brows furrow and her lip trembles. Then she takes my hand. 'Will Ruby have to go and live with her dad now?' she says, as we walk out of the room.

I think of all the negative things Selena had said about Nigel. 'I don't know, honey.'

I leave Evie with Mum and Ruby and head up to the attic to find Amelia. I need to try to talk to her.

She's sitting on the edge of her bed, flicking through a Top Model colouring book.

'Moo,' I begin, sitting beside her. She doesn't answer or even acknowledge that I'm there, but I continue anyway. 'I had a chat with Evie about Dad. She said you'd told her he was possessed. What did you mean by that?'

She shrugs.

'Amelia . . .' I press.

She throws the colouring book to the floor and sighs. 'Just that he's different now. Like he's another person.'

I uncross my legs. 'Okay. Do you mean because of his illness?'

'My friends in London said he was crazy.' She stares down at her hands in her lap.

I take a deep breath, trying to figure out how best to deal with this. 'He's not crazy. He has depression. It's an illness that affects your brain. But he's on medication now and he's getting better.'

'He scared me that time in the car.' She's still not meeting my eye.

I brush her long dark hair away from her face. 'I know. But he'd never do anything like that again. He loves you. You can trust him. He's still the same daddy.'

She turns to me then, narrowing the brown eyes that are so like her father's. 'I don't know who to trust.' And before I can reply she jumps up and flounces out of the room.

# 24

## *One day after*

Rachel is at the door by eight the next morning. I can tell by the nervous energy she's trying to hide behind a professional demeanour that she has something important to tell us.

Adrian lets her in. He's still in the T-shirt and checked trousers he slept in. The girls are in bed and Mum hasn't surfaced yet with Ruby.

Rachel steps over the threshold, bringing with her a gust of cold air. She rubs her hands together. I notice that her fingers are bright red. Her fashionable wool coat doesn't look warm enough to keep out that bracing wind. She needs gloves. There are no dead flowers on the doorstep this morning and I wonder if they'll stop now that Selena is gone. I think again of Nigel. Was he sending them? Had Selena been right to fear that he'd found her?

'Come in,' urges Adrian. 'Can I get you a coffee?'

'That would be lovely. Thank you. The traffic was bad this morning.'

'Where have you come from?' I ask politely.

'Bridgend. Headquarters are there, and I live just outside. I feel like I've been in the car for hours.'

We troop after Adrian through the empty dining room to the kitchen. I've only just begun cooking breakfast. It feels wrong to carry on working, and if it was just us, Nathan and Julia I wouldn't bother, but Janice is still here and the Greysons, so I have to be professional even though it's the last thing I feel like doing. Apart from Susie, who stayed in her room, I haven't seen the Greysons since Selena died, and I was beginning to worry that we'd have to send for the mountain rescue team because they'd got lost somewhere in the Brecons. Thankfully I heard them arrive back late last night. Nobody else has come down for breakfast yet.

I go to the frying-pan and flip over the eggs. One has burned in my absence so I scoop it out and throw it into the bin. Adrian switches on the coffee machine and waits for it to heat up.

'I'm sorry to have to tell you this,' says Rachel, her face serious, 'but the police – we – are treating Selena's death as suspicious.'

I prod another egg so hard that I end up breaking it. The yolk oozes out and settles at the edge of the frying-pan. 'Suspicious?'

'I'm afraid so.'

'What makes them think that?' blurts out Adrian. 'I mean, it was an accident. It must have been!'

I reach over and take his hand, squeezing it gently, trying to communicate for him to stay calm but he moves away from me and shoves a capsule into the coffee machine with more force than is needed.

Rachel continues, 'The way she landed, it's . . .' I can see that she's trying to find a way to explain in layman's terms. 'Put it this way. If it had been an accident, if Selena had stumbled or caught the hem of her night-gown, she'd roll or tumble down the stairs. As a result, injuries aren't usually fatal. I know that's not always the case,' she acknowledges, when Adrian opens his mouth to object, 'but usually it wouldn't be a head injury. When someone is pushed, though, they would be standing, their body in an erect position at the top of the stairs, which means they would have taken off into the air, causing a greater impact when landing.'

Adrian clears his throat. 'So, just to be clear. You're saying that Selena was pushed?'

Rachel nods. 'Yes.'

I grip the handle of the spatula so tightly it digs into my palm. 'So she was murdered?' Janice was right. *How did she know?* I can't believe that 'the spirits' told her, even though I'm sure that's how she'd explain it. She must have been attention-seeking, unless she was involved somehow, but I can't imagine that. Although I wouldn't have imagined Selena was murdered either.

'I'm sorry. I know this must be a shock. There will be an investigation. And I will be here.'

It suddenly occurs to me. 'Did the police suspect this yesterday? Is that why the forensics team were here and that detective?' I ask. They'd deliberately kept us in the dark.

'We had to cover every eventuality,' she says non-committally.

We fall silent. The only sound to be heard is the coffee machine as it spews hot liquid into a mug. Adrian hands it to Rachel and she takes it gratefully, wrapping her hands around it as she gulps it back. She must have a Teflon mouth. I watch her carefully, noting the diamond studs at her ears, the silk scarf around her neck. Her hair has been scooped into a chignon and a few tendrils escape around her face. How are we supposed to trust her? She won't have our best interests at heart. She'll be here watching and waiting, hoping someone will slip up. I think of Adrian. He was lying to me yesterday, I could tell. Does he know more about Selena's death than he's letting on? Did he see something? Or do something? I won't let my mind go there. I can't. I trust him, of course I do. Yet I felt he wasn't being completely honest with me.

Rachel might not be on our side per se but she'll be on Selena's. She'll have *her* best interests at heart.

I've always been a stickler for the rules. Adrian teases me about it – and so did Selena. *Before.* I've never parked on a double yellow line, or had a parking ticket. I stick to the speed limit. Once, when Adrian and I first met, we found a wallet stuffed full of twenty-pound notes. Adrian wanted to keep it – we were broke, we could have done with the money, which amounted to about three hundred pounds – but I insisted we gave it in to our local police station. I even went through a phase when I wanted to join the force. It was only the thought of having to confront dead bodies that put me off.

Rachel places her mug on the counter and I scoop another dud egg out of the frying-pan. I can't concentrate. Adrian, who notices, gently removes the spatula from my hand and takes over. He's come into his own since Selena's death. He's like he was before his breakdown.

'We need to talk to all the guests,' she says. 'When would be a good time? The sooner the better, obviously.'

I have to tell her about Dean. 'They'll all be down for breakfast soon,' I say, sitting at the island next to her.

'Right. Good. I'll wait until they come down, then. For more extensive interviews I'll need to call DS Middleton. But for preliminary questions . . .' She lets her words hang in the air while she drinks more of her coffee. She can't fool me. I know she's trying to lull us into a false sense of security by trying to make out she's on our side, that she's the good cop to Middleton's bad. But she's not our friend. I must remember that.

'So, Kirsty,' she turns to me, 'I know your movements that morning but, Mr Whitehouse . . .' She turns to my husband. He's taken the frying-pan off the heat. The eggs are cooked to perfection.

'Please,' he says, 'call me Adrian.'

'Of course. Adrian, where were you when your wife found Selena?'

He stands with his back to the sink, his legs crossed at the ankles. I know he's trying to give the impression of nonchalance but it doesn't fool me. I can tell by the tension in his shoulders, the way his hand picks at a non-existent spot on his upper arm that he's feeling uncomfortable. 'I was out running.' It comes out in a rush.

'And what time was that?'

'I think it was about five when I set off.'

'And do you normally make a habit of going running at that time?'

He's never gone out running *that* early before, I want to say. But I don't. I can't.

His eyes flicker to me and then back to Rachel. 'Um. No. Not every day. Sometimes I'll go about six thirty, or in the afternoon. Or late morning. It depends how I feel. But I'd woken early and couldn't get back to sleep.'

'And did you see or hear anything when you left?'

His fingers dig deeper into his skin. I can see the impressions of his nails. I can tell Rachel is watching this too. What is she thinking?

He shakes his head. 'No. Everything was quiet.'

'And Selena wasn't lying on the floor when you left?'

His face burns. 'You think I'd just leave a woman to die and go off for a run? Of course she wasn't there when I left!'

I try to communicate to him through my eyes to calm down. Why does he sound so defensive?

Rachel's silent for a moment as she scribbles everything down. I glare at him and shake my head.

When she's finished writing she looks up at Adrian and adds, in a gentler tone, 'It's okay. I need to ask these questions and I know some are difficult.' Adrian nods. 'We're still trying to get hold of Ruby's father, Nigel Perry,' she continues.

Now is the time to tell her about Dean. Rachel's face is serious as I recount everything. 'I saw them arguing the day before. He was screaming at her,' I finish.

Adrian raises his eyebrows in surprise. Another thing I hadn't told him. After I've finished describing what happened, Rachel's eyes narrow and she leans forwards. 'Okay. And you never saw him at all after Selena was found?'

'That's right.'

She takes out her notebook and begins writing down what I've just told her. 'But Selena thought the dead flowers were from her estranged husband? Not Dean?'

I nod.

It must have been Dean who killed Selena. Maybe she refused to go away with him and in anger he pushed her, then did a runner. I always knew he was bad news. If I'd refused him a room this would never have happened. Selena would still be alive. Why didn't I go with my instincts and turn him away? I close my eyes. *Oh, Selena, I'm so sorry.*

\*

Rachel sits quietly at a table in a corner of the dining room. If you didn't know better you'd think she was just another customer waiting for breakfast. I suddenly feel sorry for the guests about to walk in unaware. I wonder how she'll do it. I hope she's tactful. I don't want to offend any guests, particularly Peter Greyson. He appears prickly at the best of times, with his unsmiling face and his upright posture. I've heard him barking orders at his wife and kids as though they're in his regiment, not members of his family.

Julia comes down first with Amelia and Evie. There is no sign of my brother. They sit morosely at the table by the window, ignoring Rachel. They're dressed and look particularly sombre in dark colours, although Evie still manages to clash in a navy-and-red-striped top and purple flowered leggings.

I go over to them. 'Thank you,' I say to Julia, 'for sorting out the girls.'

'I can sort myself out,' snaps Amelia. 'I'm not a baby.'

I bite back a sigh. 'I know, honey. I just mean that you had Aunty Julia to supervise you while Dad and I were downstairs.'

Julia reaches out and touches my arm. 'How are you?' she asks, holding my gaze.

'Muddling through. Where's Nathan?'

Julia's smile fades. 'In bed. He hardly slept last night.'

'I don't think any of us did,' I say sadly. The girls ended up in our bed last night. We sat up and watched TV – a family romcom to try to take our minds off the horror of the day – until the girls fell asleep. Then Adrian held me as I cried silent tears into the pillow, the TV screen turned to mute, flashing at the corner of my vision.

Julia averts her eyes. They're puffy. What is going on between her and my brother? I wish she'd open up to me about it, but I know she won't.

'Also,' I lean in closer to Julia, 'I hope it's okay to ask, but would you mind taking a look at Ruby later? She has all these health issues and I'm worried we're totally unprepared. They're still trying to get hold of her dad.'

'Sure,' says Julia, meeting my gaze again. 'But I won't know her medical history. You'll have to set up a meeting with your GP about that at some point. They'll be able to access Ruby's records. Selena . . .' she grimaces as if she's swallowed something sharp '. . . she told me a bit, the other night, about Ruby's issues. Mainly allergies, growth problems as a result of Crohn's. She also said something about ME.'

'That's what she told me. I've never had to deal with anything like this before, thank goodness. I'm worried.'

'We're all here to help you,' she says, smiling kindly. 'Excuse me.'

I turn. Rachel is standing behind me. I make the introductions, then usher the girls out of the room. I don't want them to know that Selena was killed. It would freak them out, especially Evie, who's still convinced the house is haunted.

I hear Julia's sharp intake of breath after Rachel's

spoken and assume she's just told her that Selena was murdered. I don't hear what else she says, although I'm sure all of the guests' answers will be the same. *They were asleep. They heard nothing.*

Except someone must know *something.* I think of the noose we found. Was it put there by the person who killed Selena? And had it been a threat aimed at her?

Rachel spends about an hour going from guest to guest, notebook poised. Mr Greyson, as predicted, looks as though he should have smoke coming out of his ears, like in one of Evie's cartoons. I hear him mutter something about 'impertinence'.

When Rachel's finished she comes into the kitchen. Amelia and Evie are eating toast at the island.

'Right. I've nearly finished speaking to everyone,' she says.

'What are you doing about Dean? Surely he's a suspect,' I ask.

'That's a matter for my DS, I'm afraid. I'm passing everything on to him. I just want to have a word with your mother, Kirsty. Where can I find her?'

'She's looking after Ruby,' I say. I direct her to Apple Tree.

When she's out of earshot Evie asks, 'What's a suspect?'

Amelia doesn't say anything, just picks at the corner of her toast.

'Um, well, it's someone who might have committed – *done,*' I clarify, 'something bad.'

'Has Dean done something bad?'

'I don't know, honey. Right,' I say, wanting to change the subject. I clap my hands together. 'Anyone want any Nutella with their toast?'

I'm placing the toast on the table when the dining-room door opens and Mum walks in with Ruby. She's not wearing her leg braces, although she seems unsteady on her feet, like a puppy walking for the first time.

'Ruby!' Evie comes bounding out of the kitchen and rushes over to her, flinging her arms around her waist and almost knocking her off balance.

'Careful,' warns Mum, holding on to Ruby's arm. Ruby returns the hug, her little face pinched with grief. I want to wrap her in my arms and keep her safe. I glance up at Mum, who's wearing the same expression as Ruby.

'Can I have a word in private?' Mum says to me, inclining her head towards the door. I help Ruby to the table so that she's sitting beside Evie.

'You go,' says Julia. 'I'll help Ruby with breakfast, don't worry.' She flashes me a tired smile. It doesn't brighten her face like it usually would.

'Thank you,' I say, and follow Mum out of the room.

We go into her room. It needs airing. I throw open the windows while Mum sits on the edge of the bed she slept in last night. The bed that had been Selena's. My cousin's red suitcase is still by the wardrobe, open, with some of Ruby's jumpers on top. Selena's clothes must be underneath, still ironed and folded neatly, never to be worn by her again. I wonder what they'll do with the nightdress she was wearing when she died. I move towards the dressing-table and idly pick up a brush. Selena's fine blonde hairs are interwoven in the bristles. I put it down again, my heart heavy. I go to the wardrobe and open it. Selena's grey suede jacket hangs next to Ruby's pink padded coat. I remember she was wearing it the day she died. I'd told the police about her jumpsuit, but I forgot to give them this. I touch the sleeve. *What happened, Selena? Did you leave Ruby here and spend the night with Dean? Did he push you?*

I look towards the window and out over the garden to the mountains. Is he there somewhere? Lurking? Waiting? The landscape I've always loved becomes sinister.

Mum clears her throat. I close the wardrobe door and turn to face her.

She speaks first. 'Rachel's told you that Ruby can stay with us until they contact her dad?'

'Yes. What else did she say?'

Mum shrugs. 'They wanted to know the sequence of events leading up to me finding Selena. Timings, alibis . . . you know.'

'Will they make Nigel take Ruby home?'

Mum's brow furrows and she removes her glasses to rub her eyes. 'I expect so. He's her dad.'

'Even though he's violent!' I feel incensed. How can Mum be so – so *casual* about it when she knows Selena was running away from him?

'Kirsty . . .'

'What? Don't tell me we can't get involved or that it's none of our business. We owe it to Selena. To Ruby.'

'It's in the hands of the police.' She stands up. 'Anyway, I'd better get back to Ruby.'

I can't let this go. I stand up too and we walk out of the room together. I'm just about to follow her into the dining room to continue the conversation when I hear a commotion by the front door. Adrian is talking to the Greysons, his arms folded. Peter Greyson's tone is threatening. He's standing too close to my husband and gesticulating, something about wanting a refund.

I join them. 'Everything okay?' I ask.

Mr Greyson whips around to face me. 'No, it isn't. We're on holiday and we've just been *interrogated* by a policewoman, only for her to tell us somebody was murdered here yesterday morning.' He has a booming voice that instantly grates, although I can see his point. 'We've paid until Saturday. But I want to leave today. And I want a refund.'

Adrian glances at me and raises an eyebrow. I give a nod in reply, suddenly overcome with exhaustion. 'I understand. I'm sorry for any inconvenience,' I say. As I'm about to head upstairs, Susie stops me.

'I'm sorry about your cousin,' she says.

'Thank you,' I reply. I guess we won't be seeing them again. I can just imagine their review on TripAdvisor. *Great B&B, lovely location, but holiday ruined by dead body in the hallway* as though Selena was nothing more than a corpse, not a mother, a daughter, a cousin. Not someone who was loved and who'll be missed.

On the landing I pass Nancy carrying a tea tray. She stops when she sees me. 'It's the talk of the village,' she says, her eyes lighting up. 'People are saying this house is cursed.'

Not her too. It's bad enough having one Mystic Meg under this roof. I can't cope with another.

'Yes,' she continues relentlessly, shifting her weight from one leg to the other. 'Your cousin isn't the first to meet her end here. A woman who lived here in the 1950s hanged herself.' She inclines her head towards the attic. 'Right up there.' I can't hide my disbelief and she adds, 'Look it up if you don't believe me. They say her ghost haunts this place.' Her gaze is unwavering, almost challenging. 'Bad luck, don't you think?'

# 25

After lunch I drive the girls, Mum and Ruby to the local library in the next town, leaving Adrian to hold the fort.

I hope the outing will be a welcome distraction, for them and for me. The house is claustrophobic. The hills and mountains, once my sanctuary, now feel like a prison, and all I can think about is that Dean must be out there somewhere, hiding. Even Hywelphilly seems too small. Adrian said that when he went for a run earlier he was accosted by some local bloke wanting to know why we had the police here yesterday. According to Adrian, the man had seemed almost gleeful when he asked if we were having 'trouble'. Nancy's right, we are the talk of the village, and the likes of Lydia Ford and Mrs Gummage hated us from the start. I dread having to walk to the chemist or the newsagent's in case we're stared at or, worse, people start asking questions. What must Kath and Derek think? I shake myself. I sound like my mother. Going further afield is just what we need.

Evie has been begging me to take her to the library all week, and although Amelia isn't bothered, the promise of Starbucks afterwards persuades her. She says the hot chocolate at the café in the high street 'tastes like plastic'.

Our car isn't big enough for the wheelchair, and it didn't feel right to take Selena's, so we half carry, half walk Ruby into the building. She refused to wear her leg braces and we didn't want to upset her by insisting. She's – understandably – still very subdued, only wanting to engage with Evie and Amelia. She sits now on one of the orange floor cushions, watching through large grey eyes, so like Selena's, as my daughters riffle through the books, taking out the ones they think she'll enjoy. Amelia holds up a hardback with two cats on the front to show her. When Ruby nods, she trots over to her and they curl up, legs tucked under them, to read it together. The sight brings tears to my eyes and I have to look away so they don't notice.

I leave Mum in charge and wander off towards the computers. They're set up on desks pushed together to make a hexagonal shape.

After Nancy told me about the woman who'd killed herself in our attic, I'd logged on to my laptop and searched the internet, but there was nothing about the history of our house. On the drive over here it occurred to me that the library might have newspaper archives. I'd like to look up the history of our house. Not that I think we're cursed, whatever Nancy and Janice say, but it might take my mind off Selena for five minutes.

I ask one of the librarians, a studious-looking young man who happens to be passing. He's pushing a trolley with so many books on it they look like they could topple over at any second. He has a nametag fastened to the pocket of his checked shirt. *Tom.* He leaves his trolley by the counter and guides me over to one of the computers; it's a little more dated than the others. I sit down and he leans over me to type in a password.

'We only have the local newspapers here,' he says, his eyes narrowing as he taps at the keys. He has the same thick accent as Nancy.

'That's fine. I'm only after local stuff. How far do they date back?'

He pulls a face, considering. 'Hmm. To the early 1900s? How far back do you want to go?'

I have no real idea. Nancy said something about it happening at the beginning of the 1950s. 'Maybe from 1950 onwards,' I offer.

He shows me what to do, then leaves me to get on with it. It's a laborious task, scrolling through news-paper after newspaper. Just as I'm wondering if it ever happened at all, or if Nancy was just listening to idle gossip, a headline jumps out at me.

## WOMAN FOUND HANGED AFTER SHAMEFUL CONVICTION

The newspaper is dated Tuesday, 3 March 1953. My stomach gives a little flurry as I scan the article, sud-denly apprehensive about what I'm going to find out.

*A woman found hanged in her home was driven to despair after the shameful arrest and imprisonment of her husband, an inquest heard.*

*Violet Brown, 32, became isolated after her husband, Albert, 37, was arrested for Gross Indecency last year. His subsequent 22-month prison sentence meant that Mrs Brown found it increasingly difficult to run the boarding-house at 1, Church Lane, which she owned with her husband, eventually running into financial problems.*

*Mrs Brown was found by her older sister, Margot Burton, on the morning of 20 November 1952.*

*Giving evidence, Mrs Burton said that on the day in question she had 'popped' over to see her sister and, when there was no answer, she became concerned. 'The door was open so I went inside to look for her. She hardly went out by this stage as she was getting more and more out of sorts, so I knew she would have to be in the house somewhere. It had been days since I last saw her, and Mary from the local shop said she hadn't been in to pay her shopping bill for ages. I found her upstairs in the attic. It was obvious she had been dead for a while and there was nothing I could have done to save her. She was such a proud woman. We would have helped her if we'd known. I think the shame was too much for her.'*

*Coroner William Woodley recorded Mrs Brown's death as suicide. He said: 'Although she didn't leave a note, it is most probable, due to her husband's incarceration and subsequent money worries, that Violet Brown intended to take her own life.'*

I stare at the screen, shocked and saddened to think that these events had taken place in our home, and of the similarity between Mrs Burton finding her sister and that terrible day when I'd found Adrian. Thankfully, I'd been able to save him.

'What are you doing?'

Mum's voice makes me jump and I whip around to face her. She's standing with the three girls in front of her. Evie comes towards me, her little face alight, holding up a book about Claude the dog to show me, and I prod desperately at the keys, not wanting her to see the words on the screen.

I stand up quickly, my back to the computer, and usher them towards the desk.

'We've got our books,' Evie says happily. I notice even Amelia has a book in her hand. Something about a Geek Girl. I hang back as they go to the counter to check out their haul, Ruby holding on to Amelia for support.

'What were you looking up on the computer?' hisses Mum.

'The history of our house. Nancy said something to me earlier and it piqued my interest.' I recount what I've just read.

Mum glances at me and purses her lips. She has that disapproving look on her face again.

'What?'

She folds her arms across her chest. 'I don't understand why you care about the history of the house.

We've got enough on our plates after what's happened to Selena, and you're het up about something that happened to people over sixty years ago – people we never even met.'

I frown at her. 'What are you trying to say? That I'm not sad Selena is dead? Of course I am. It's terrible. It's . . .' I lower my voice so the girls can't hear '. . . it's fucking dreadful. Okay? And it terrifies me to think that she was murdered. That a *murderer* was in our house. With *my* children. How do you think that makes me feel? I've put my children at risk. My job is to protect them! And for you to insinuate that I don't care just because – for twenty minutes – I was concentrating on something else . . .'

'You don't have to swear,' she replies coldly.

'And you don't have to be so bloody critical all the time,' I snap back.

We eyeball each other. Amelia notices when she comes back: she glances from me to Mum and sighs. 'What's wrong now?'

The *now* doesn't pass me by.

'Nothing,' I say hurriedly, trying to keep my voice light. 'Let's go and get a hot chocolate.'

Amelia and Evie link arms with Ruby as we walk to the car, Mum behind them, making sure Ruby doesn't fall.

At the café, Mum and I both sip our lattes in silence while the girls spoon off cream and marshmallows from their hot chocolates. Ruby, who is allergic to dairy, has a soya alternative with no chocolate or marshmallows. I didn't want the girls to have marshmallows either, worried that it wouldn't be fair to Ruby, but Ruby said she didn't mind. 'I've never tasted them, anyway,' she said, smiling up at me, 'so I don't know what I'm missing.'

I take out my phone, scanning my most recent photos. There's one of Selena with the three children, and my heart contracts. I look up just in time to see Evie feeding Ruby a spoon loaded with cream and marshmallows.

'What are you doing?' I shout, grabbing the spoon from Evie. It clatters to the floor, making the other customers look at us. But it's too late: Ruby has swallowed the sugar and dairy concoction. Amelia gasps, realizing what her little sister has just done.

Ruby bursts into tears. 'I'm sorry for eating it,' she cries. 'I just wanted to taste it.'

Evie looks mortified, her cheeks burning. 'I'm sorry, Mummy,' she says, her bottom lip wobbling.

'For goodness' sake,' snaps Mum. 'That was a really stupid thing to do, Evie.'

Tears stream down Evie's face.

'It's okay,' I say to Evie. And then to Ruby, 'It was just a little bit. Don't worry, Ruby darling.'

On the way home the girls are chatting in the back. I've never heard Ruby talk so much. She sounds just like any other little girl her age. I keep an eye on her, terrified that she'll have a reaction to the cream and marshmallows but, as yet, she seems fine.

Mum carries Ruby into the house. The little girl looks exhausted after our day trip, probably not helped by all of us constantly asking if she feels okay.

I notice the girls' downcast expressions as they watch Mum take Ruby to her room, and I guess they might be feeling a little jealous of the time Nana is spending with her. I used to feel the same way about Selena sometimes, especially as I was the one Mum always told off if she caught us up to mischief. But now, with an adult's perspective, I know it was because Selena had a hard home life and Mum was trying to protect her. I've no doubt that she loved Selena and, to her, Selena was a second daughter. I've made my peace with that. I even understand it.

'Nana still loves you both, so much,' I say to them, as we stand in the hallway. 'Ruby just needs a lot of attention right now.'

'Oh, we know that, Mum,' says Amelia.

'We understand,' insists Evie, and I pull them both to me and kiss their foreheads.

'You're both so special, you know that?'

'Aw, Mum.' Amelia pulls away from me, but she's smiling.

'Are you going to your room to read?' I ask, indicating the books in their arms. Evie looks at the staircase uncertainly, fear in her eyes. 'Daddy's up there, I expect,' I say. Even Amelia seems hesitant. I can never tell them about Violet Brown. If they find out that she died in this house – in the attic where we all sleep – then Evie for one will never go upstairs again.

'Or they could come and play a board game with me and Aunty Julia?' says a booming voice. I look to see Nathan standing in the living-room doorway, his eyes brightening at the sight of the girls. He's wearing a long-sleeved navy T-shirt with a crease down the middle and hasn't shaved today. Maybe he's following Adrian's example and growing a beard.

'Yay!' squeals Evie, rushing to him. They head into the living room and Amelia follows.

I wonder if there have been any bookings in my absence. The phone has been silent since Saturday.

There is no sign of the family liaison officer and I'm relieved. Having her here is unsettling because I know she's always watching, waiting, listening. It's like I have a CCTV camera installed in my home. I look down at the Victorian tiles, thinking of Selena.

My chest feels tight, which is happening more and more frequently. I know stress can make my asthma worse. I reach into the pocket of my coat and take out my inhaler. I put it to my mouth and pump but nothing comes out. I hear shouts of laughter from the living room and feel glad that Nathan and Julia are here. I hope they stay until Saturday as planned and don't hot-foot it like the Greysons. We can't afford for them to go, really. Especially now we've had to give the Greysons a refund.

I find Adrian in our bedroom – as I knew I would – hunched over his laptop. The curtains are still closed but at least the duvet has been straightened. He looks up when I enter, a film of distraction over his eyes. I sit down on the bed to talk to him, and although he swivels his chair around so he can hear what I'm saying, I know his mind is readjusting to normal life from its immersion in his book.

'How are you getting on?'

He shrugs. He has dark shadows under his eyes and his beard needs trimming. 'Halfway through. This is the first time today I've had a chance to get stuck in.'

'When can I read it?'

He laughs. 'Not yet.'

'And how've things been here? Where's Rachel?'

He groans. 'It's hard work having her around. Anyway, she's left for the day but she'll be back tomorrow. She's managed to contact Nigel to inform him about Selena. I expect he'll want to come and see Ruby. The police need to find out where he was when Selena died and who Selena met up with the day before.'

Why hadn't I asked who she was meeting? How did Adrian know about it? Did she tell him? They spent quite a bit of time having cosy chats. I wonder again what they talked about when they were alone. Was there an attraction between them? *I always want what I can't have.* I push away my doubts. 'What else?'

'She wanted to know about Selena's parents. The police have her mum's address but they wanted to speak to her dad too.'

My chest feels even tighter when I think of Uncle Owen. 'They were estranged.' There's so much I haven't told him. About Selena's eighteenth-birthday party and her lies.

'They've found her mum but still can't get hold of the dad.'

'Mum might know. She kept in touch with him.'

I take out my phone and scroll to the photo I took earlier in the library. I show it to Adrian. 'Nancy mentioned something so I looked it up,' I say. He takes the phone and reads.

'Blimey,' he says, when he's finished, handing me the phone. 'That's tragic.'

I put the phone back in my pocket. I'm still wearing my coat. I inhale deeply and rub my chest. Adrian notices. 'Are you all right? Is it your asthma?'

'My inhaler's run out. I have another here.' I get up and fumble around in my top drawer. It's usually tucked down the side of my underwear. I rummage around, relieved when I find it. And that's when I see the note. It's small and folded into four. I pick it up, puzzled, and unfold it. For a second I wonder if it's a little love note from Adrian. We used to leave them for each other all over the house when we were first living together. Adrian would write me poems, sometimes funny, sometimes romantic. Even if we only reminded each other to get milk we'd declare how much we loved each other at the end, signing off with hearts and kisses and nicknames, But that faded away after we had the children, and now our notes have turned to perfunctory texts.

My heart feels like it's being squeezed when I see the note isn't addressed to me but to Selena.

# 26

I scan the words. The writing is messy and it ends abruptly with no name at the bottom.

*Selena,* I read. *Talk to me. I can't bear not knowing where I stand with you. You promised me. I know too much, remember? I know about your dad.*

'Adrian!'

He turns in alarm, his mouth open. 'What? What is it?' He stands up and hurries over to me, knocking his hip against the bed frame.

I thrust the note at his chest. 'Read this.'

He takes it from me, confusion flitting across his face. 'What is it?'

'It was in my drawer.'

He hands it back to me. 'Who do you think it's from?'

I glance at him. Could it be from him and he'd hidden it, forgetting about it because of what happened to Selena? I can't tell if the writing is his.

'I – I don't know.' I frown as it suddenly dawns on me. 'Why is it in my underwear drawer?' Did Selena put it there? But why? 'We're going to have to give it to Rachel.'

'Yep.'

'*I know too much* sounds threatening, doesn't it?'

Adrian moves away from me and back to his desk. 'We don't know anything.'

I sink on to the bed, overcome with a mixture of sadness and anger. Could it be from Dean? But, if so, how did it find its way into my bedroom? The only person who's here during the day is Adrian. 'Why couldn't Selena have been honest for once in her fucking life?' I cry, surprising myself and startling Adrian. 'We could have helped her.'

He sighs and swivels his chair round to face me. 'She sounds like she was a complex person. I got the impression that she was lonely.'

'You don't know the half of it.'

'Then tell me,' he says gently.

So I do. It's a relief to speak the words I've kept to myself for so many years, and they tumble out on top of each other. I can see that Adrian is trying to keep up with my garbled account of what happened on her eighteenth. When I've finished he doesn't say anything, just looks at me with those big brown eyes.

Eventually he says, 'You didn't believe her when she said her dad was abusing her?'

I stand up. I pull the curtains open and look out over the garden. The sun is low in the sky, highlighting the brown leaves scattered across the lawn, and the bare trees looking on, almost forlornly. The hills and mountains look bleak and threatening. My back is to him when I say, 'She was always making up stuff. She was

253

drunk. I thought she wanted to hurt me because she knew how much I loved Uncle Owen.'

'Kirsty ...' he begins, and stops as if thinking carefully about his next words. 'Did you ever tell anybody, just in case it *was* true?'

I feel a burst of anger and whirl round to face him. 'But it wasn't true. I knew that. She was always lying. *Always.* About everything. I couldn't believe a word that came out of her mouth half the time!'

His eyes search my face. 'Even something like that?'

I hang my head. 'I know how it sounds, but you didn't know Uncle Owen. He was gentle. Kind. *My dad's brother.* I didn't believe her.'

'And now?'

I think of the letter. *I know about your dad.* How would Adrian know anything about Uncle Owen? Unless she'd told him during one of their little chats. 'She admitted she lied. Here, the other night. She said she'd been a foolish kid, wanting attention.'

He crosses his legs, his jaw set. 'What if one of our girls came to you and told you something like that? Would you believe them?'

I gasp. 'Of course! That's different. It's hard to explain. You didn't know Selena. Not properly. You didn't grow up with her. You don't know what she was really like. I thought, when she came back, that she'd changed. But now this.' I shake the note at him. 'She was still lying. I could always read her. The way she was with Dean. She was hiding something.'

Adrian turns his chair away from me. 'I've got to get on,' he says. 'Like you say, I didn't really know Selena.'

'But you're judging me!' I cry. 'I can tell. It's written all over you face!'

He takes a deep breath. 'No. I'm not. You're judging yourself.'

I'm just about to walk out the room when I remember my conversation with Evie. 'Evie said something about you the other day.'

His head shoots up. 'Me?'

'She told me that Amelia had said to be careful of you. That you were possessed.'

He runs his hand over his beard. It's getting out of control. I wish he'd shave it off. 'Possessed?'

'She implied they were scared of you. It worried me at first. But then I thought about it and realized she was referring to your breakdown, how different you were afterwards. And it *was* like you were possessed, for a while. I could see what she meant.'

His brown eyes look sad and I feel guilty. 'What are you trying to say?'

'I'm trying to say that out of context it sounds odd. Something to worry about. But, given your breakdown, it makes sense why they would feel that way. It's the same with Selena. If it had been anyone else telling me their dad had abused them, then *of course* I would have taken it seriously. I would have alerted someone. But it was Selena.'

He turns back to his laptop. 'You've made your point.'

'I didn't do anything wrong,' I mumble, as I close the door behind me, wondering if I'm trying to convince Adrian, or myself.

I'm going to have to give the note to the police. It sits like a bomb in my pocket, waiting to explode. *I know too much, remember. I know about your dad.* I can't get that line out of my head. I think of the night I saw Selena with a man in the driveway. Was it Dean? Was that when he first found her? Why didn't she just tell me? I would never have given him a room if she'd warned me.

*I know about your dad.*

I'll give Rachel the note tomorrow. They're already looking for Dean. They might have found him by now. And it's nearly teatime. Soon it will get dark. The clocks go back this weekend.

I'm in the kitchen, dithering, not sure what I'm doing. I can almost feel the note in my pocket, as if it's on fire, burning my skin. I switch the kettle on. I'll defrost a chicken. Make everyone a meal. Even Janice, if she wants one. She's the only real guest here now. Nobody will want to come and stay when they hear about Selena. It's bound to be on the news. Maybe it already has been. I suddenly think of Violet Brown, who lived here all those years ago, unable to do anything as her livelihood floundered and died. Maybe this place *is* cursed.

I turn the dial on the oven. My hand is shaking. Delayed shock? I can't get the note out of my head. I need to speak to Mum. She saw Selena over the years and is in touch with Uncle Owen. She might know.

I'm about to go and find her when I notice Julia hovering by the kitchen door. She gives me a half-smile. 'Can I come in?'

'Of course,' I say. 'Is everything okay?'

'Yes. Nathan's with the girls.' She comes into the room. She looks attractive in a fitted blouse and indigo straight-legged jeans. She's not trendy, not like Selena was, with her tight skinny jeans and her All Saints' jumpers. Julia has more of a classic look. 'I've just been to see Carol and Ruby. I wanted to check her over, after what you said at breakfast.'

'Thank you. How is she?'

'She's sad and she understands her mummy is in Heaven,' I feel tears at my eyes and blink them away, 'but she hasn't raged or played up. Although she has cried a lot, according to Carol.'

'And physically?'

'Like I said earlier, I don't know her history. I think you should register her so that they can collate her notes from the GP where she lived with Selena. Maybe Selena's husband could also help. He must have notes and medical letters. Referrals. That kind of thing. But, if I'm honest, she looked a bit malnourished to me.'

'That's understandable, though, isn't it? With her allergies and Crohn's and everything?'

Julia hesitates. 'Yes, in a way. But she's had Crohn's and allergies for a long time. She would have been

257

referred to a dietician. With Crohn's there are flare-ups. She might not suffer all the time.' That would make sense, considering she's had no adverse reaction to the cream and marshmallows Evie gave her. 'And she might be naturally skinny anyway – you said Selena was as a kid, but there are signs of recent dehydration . . .'

'Well, she was blue-lighted into hospital the other night. She had a fit.'

Julia looks grave. 'Did Selena say what caused it?'

I think back. 'I'm sure she said it was a virus.'

'It would be really useful to have her notes. Can you give me the name of your GP? I'll sort something out. We need her records as a matter of urgency. If I can find out who her dietician is, he or she could give me her diet sheet. At least then we'd know exactly what we're dealing with.'

'That would be great, thank you.' I flash her a grateful smile.

'Listen,' she says, lowering her voice. 'I just want to say I'm so sorry.'

I assume she means Selena. 'It's been a shock to us all. Reunited after all these years just to lose her again.'

She looks embarrassed. 'I meant about what happened last year. You know, with Adrian. How we weren't there for you.' She reaches out and touches my shoulder. 'I was going through so much with the failed IVF. My mind was all over the place. It was taking a toll on our relationship. Nathan and I . . . Well, we almost split up over it.'

I pause, thrown. They almost split up? I couldn't bear to lose Julia. She makes Nathan nicer, not so annoying. She keeps him in line, stops him becoming that geeky, thoughtless man I know he can be. Not because he's unkind but because he doesn't think. He'd never remember Mum's birthday – or mine, or the girls' – if it wasn't for Julia. If it wasn't for Julia I doubt I'd hear from Nathan for months at a time. Don't get me wrong, Julia's not a saint. She's steely – as a GP she has to be. She's had to deal with some horrific situations in her job. And when she gets something into her head she can be stubborn. She badgered Nathan about going for counselling when they first met. She felt he had hang-ups about his biological mother giving him away, even though Nathan insisted he didn't. She didn't give up until Nathan finally agreed. And, even though she's invariably polite, I can always tell if she doesn't like someone.

Like Selena.

Maybe she'd felt threatened by her. Maybe she'd noticed the tension between her and Nathan. Whatever it was, I know she'd never tell me. I'm sure she's fond of me, but she'll always see me as Nathan's sister first and foremost.

'I'm so sorry,' I say, after a beat of silence. 'I knew there were problems, but I didn't realize it was that bad.'

She shakes her head. 'It's all okay now. We're getting there.'

There's something she's not telling me. Is it about

the morning Selena died? Nathan was in the playroom, which is right next to the stairs. I know he was sleeping off a hangover but I'm surprised he didn't hear Selena fall. And he was so weird afterwards, asking me to keep it from the police that he wasn't with Julia.

'You know you can tell me anything,' I say.

'He's your brother.'

'Yes. And even though I love him I know what an idiot he can be at times.'

We're interrupted by the sounds of children playing and I look towards the bi-fold doors. Mum is in the garden with Amelia, Evie and Ruby. Evie is running around with a princess costume on and Amelia is sitting with the rabbits on her lap. But it's Ruby I can't tear my eyes away from: she's trying to run after Evie in her leg braces. And then she flops to the grass and begins to undo them, slipping them off. I jump from my seat. Julia, who is also watching, gets up too.

'What is she doing?' she asks.

Mum notices and rushes over to Ruby, but she's up from the ground and walking unaided. She's unsteady at first but then gains confidence, her strides lengthening as she gradually becomes more sure-footed.

'Look at her,' I say in wonderment. Maybe the fresh air and the mountains are good for her. 'She seems fine walking on her own.'

Julia's also watching, her face in profile, her eyes narrowed.

For the first time I wonder if Selena was too ready

with the leg braces and the wheelchair. She was being over-protective – though I understand that. I'd probably be the same.

'Evie's obviously good for her,' observes Julia, as we continue to watch Ruby. She's trying to run now, with Mum close behind. And then Ruby and Evie flop on to the damp grass together, giggling. 'Being with other children will help her grow stronger.'

We return to our stools. 'Sorry, Julia. What were you going to say?'

'It's nothing. Please don't worry. Everything's fine.'

She gives me a reassuring smile but I don't believe her. And it flashes through my mind that Julia was alone in her room when Selena was pushed, and has no alibi. Just like Nathan.

I bump into Mum in the hallway. She looks frazzled.

'Where's Ruby now?'

She fiddles with the wedding and engagement rings on her finger: a plain gold band, beneath a single emerald between two small diamonds. When Dad died she told me she'd never take them off. 'They were getting cold outside so now she's with Amelia, Evie and Nathan in the front room. They're playing Connect 4.'

I fill her in on what Julia said about contacting the GP regarding Ruby's medical records.

Mum's whole body relaxes in relief. 'Thank God,' she says. 'I've been so worried about doing something wrong and giving her food that could harm her.'

'There's something else.' I touch the pocket of my jeans where the note is. 'I need to talk to you. About Uncle Owen.'

Mum stands up straighter and her voice takes on a wary tone. 'What about him?'

I incline my head towards the playroom. 'In there,' I say.

Her lips have gone thin, in annoyance or disapproval.

She follows me into the room. The TV has been left on pause, Scooby Doo, frozen, pulling a silly face. I reach for the remote and turn it off. 'Can you close the door?' I ask her.

She sighs theatrically but does as I ask.

Without a word, I retrieve the note and hand it to her. Puzzled, she takes it from me and begins to read.

I watch her carefully. 'It sounds like whoever sent it was blackmailing her,' I say.

*I know about your dad.*

I expect Mum to brush me off, or purse her lips and tell me it means nothing. But she doesn't. Instead her face drains of colour and she slumps on to the sofa.

'I'm going to have to show it to the police,' I add. 'I don't know how it got into my drawer. A cry for help from Selena, perhaps.' I don't voice the deep-seated fear that Adrian might have written it.

Mum places a hand on her heart. Her reaction is worrying me. 'Are you feeling okay?' I'm suddenly afraid she might be having a heart attack.

She doesn't reply. Instead she stares at the note, as if hoping she's misread the words. Her hands begin to shake.

'Mum?'

When she looks at me her face is filled with such fear that anxiety blooms in my stomach. 'What does this person know about Uncle Owen?' I urge, fear making my voice harder than I intend.

She takes her glasses off and rubs at the corner of her left eye.

What is she not telling me? 'The police will want to speak to Uncle Owen. I told them you keep in touch with him. Have they contacted you yet?' I can feel my anger rising at her resistance to talking. 'For God's sake, Mum! This is serious. You can't keep protecting Selena. She's dead now. Somebody killed her and the police will want to talk to her dad!'

'They won't find him.' Her voice is so quiet it takes me a few seconds to register what she said.

'What do you mean?' The anxiety travels to my chest and I reach for my inhaler. 'I thought you were in touch with him.'

She looks up at me. 'I've not been in touch with him.' And then she surprises me by crumpling the note into a ball. 'And you can never show this to the police.'

I take a puff of my inhaler. I've never seen Mum like this. She's usually so together, so capable. I perch next to her. 'Mum, you're scaring me.'

She pushes her glasses back on. I notice a tear seep

out of her eye, travel down her cheek and disappear into her jawline. I'm mesmerized by it. Before Selena died I can't remember the last time I saw Mum cry. Definitely not since I've been an adult. She would get a bit teary around Christmas, and Natasha's birthday, just a few seconds when her eyes would smart and her voice would thicken, but just as quickly she would compose herself, making me doubt it had happened at all. 'I never wanted to involve you. Once I tell you this, it will sit with you for ever. You'll be complicit. I never wanted to put that on you.'

My stomach tightens. 'What is it?'

She sighs and squeezes the note with her fist. 'The police won't find Owen because he died back in 2001.' She blinks at me.

'What?' I'm so shocked it comes out louder than I intended. Mum winces. 'How do you know?'

She doesn't miss a beat. 'Because Selena killed him.'

# 27

There is a shocked silence, just the faint hum of the Sky box and the wind rattling the window panes. I stare at her, my mouth hanging open. I feel sick. I must have misheard her. I can't believe that Selena killed Uncle Owen. I wonder if this is due to the stress of the last two days – she's confused, she has to be.

Her voice is detached as she says, 'I know it's a shock. I wanted you never to find out.'

I feel like I'm on a ship, dizzy, off balance. I have to hold on to the arm of the sofa to steady myself. 'Selena killed Uncle Owen? She *killed* him?'

'She said it was self-defence and that Uncle Owen had been abusing her. She was pregnant, she said, with his baby.'

No. No. No. No. This is all wrong. All wrong. She was lying about Uncle Owen. She told me.

'She made it up!' I cry.

'Of course she made it up,' she snaps, much to my surprise. I was expecting her to shout at me and accuse me of being despicable for not believing Selena. She continues, 'I found that out later. But at the time she made me believe it.'

My mind is whirling. 'So you knew? All this time you knew she'd lied? But you always seemed so – so fond of her. You said she was like another daughter.'

Mum closes her eyes and breathes in deeply. When she opens them again, she says, 'I wanted to protect you. All of you. And I felt responsible, in some ways, for how she'd turned out. Her mother,' she practically spits the word, 'damaged that poor girl. She was a monster. Owen's only crime was that he was too soft. He stood back and did nothing. The bruises, they were from Aunt Bess. Your dad and I, well, we tried to protect Selena. We tried to persuade Owen to get Bess help. And I think he did try, but he was ineffectual at the end of the day.'

Oh, God. I sink on to the sofa next to her. My legs feel weak. 'What on earth happened? How do you know Selena killed Uncle Owen?'

'She came to me. Not long after you'd left for university. It must have been the October. She told me everything. How she'd argued with her dad, how she'd pushed him and he'd hit his head on the fireplace. Bess was out somewhere on a drinking binge and Dean helped her bury the body.'

*I know too much.* So Dean must have sent the note. 'Where?'

'She refused to tell me. I think it must have been out in the woods somewhere. At first she tried to make out that Owen had left her mother. I believed her at first, although I thought it was odd that he didn't come and say goodbye to me. Then, after he'd been dead a week, she came to me and admitted the truth.'

I frown. 'But why? Why did she tell you? She could have kept it from you.'

'Because she was pregnant.'

'Who was the father?'

Mum clenches her fists in her lap. 'That's the thing. She told me it was Owen and that he had raped her. She made me believe she'd killed him in self-defence.'

I groan. 'Oh, God, Mum . . .'

I feel as if everything that's happened in the last two days isn't real. I watched a film once, years ago with Adrian, where the main character was experiencing very realistic lucid dreams, which started to become nightmares. That's what this feels like. I lower my voice, shooting a glance at the door. 'I think we need to go for a walk.' I check my watch. It's gone five thirty. I hadn't got round to putting the chicken in the oven. 'We can't risk somebody overhearing us.'

Mum agrees and gets to her feet slowly, pocketing the now-crumpled note. It's like she's aged ten years in the last ten minutes.

I go to find Adrian. He's still at his desk. I pop my head around the bedroom door and ask him to put the chicken on, disappearing from view before he can answer or ask me any questions.

It's drizzling, a fine rain that falls softly on our hair and coats as we walk. It's not quite dark yet, that strange ethereal time between night and day. The sky is one thick smoky-grey cloud. The clocks go back on Saturday. This time next week it will be dark by now. I inch my scarf further up my chin. The damp air hurts my chest. Mum is walking beside me. We are aimless, our boots thudding on the pavement as we take a right over the bridge that crosses the River Usk to the high street. There is nobody around. The shops are shut, the nearby park empty. Even the Seven Stars looks desolate on this wet Thursday evening. It's impossible to see the tops of the mountains, shrouded in a heavy mist.

We stop on the bridge. We are completely alone. 'Tell me everything,' I urge.

Mum holds on to the railings for support. Her hands look shrivelled in the cold, the veins protruding. I thought I knew her but she's constantly surprising me. She's so strait-laced, so proper. And yet she's telling me she's concealed a crime for the last twenty years.

'Tell me. From the beginning, Mum.'

She takes a deep breath, closes her eyes and presses her fingers into the sockets as though trying to erase the memory. 'Like I said, you were at Durham and Nathan had just started sixth form. It was late. Nathan was out with his friends and Selena came to me in a dreadful state. She said she was pregnant and wanted an abortion. I tried to persuade her to contact Owen for help – he'd been gone about a week at this point. She broke down and admitted the truth about Owen, that he didn't leave but was, in actual fact, dead, that she'd killed him in self-defence and Dean helped her bury the body. She told me that Owen had been sexually abusing her. I promised I'd keep her secret and I'd pay for the abortion. We had an appointment all set up for the next week. But as I was driving her to the clinic she told me she wanted to keep the baby.' Mum shakes her head. 'I couldn't believe my ears. I told her not to be so stupid, that the baby was the result of abuse, of incest, that it could be born with a disorder. I went on and on about it until she screamed at me. I'll never forget her words. "The baby's not my father's! I lied! I lied about the abuse, okay? The baby's Dean's."'

'Oh, Mum.' I feel sad to think she'd been so utterly taken in by Selena. What a hideous lie to tell. And just so she could take advantage of my mother's love for her.

'I could hardly look at her on the drive home. She admitted she'd felt resentful towards her father for not protecting her from Bess. But she hadn't meant to kill him. It was just a row that got out of hand. An accident. She'd wanted to go to the police, she said, but Dean persuaded her not to. He told her they'd never believe her.'

She takes a deep breath and grips the railings tightly. The water looks dark and perilous in this light.

'So what happened to the baby?' It couldn't have been Ruby. The child would be at least sixteen by now.

I'm holding my breath. In the distance I see two men staggering out of the pub. They walk off in the opposite direction but we wait until they've rounded the bend, following the route of the river.

When they've gone, she says, 'She had a miscarriage. A month later.'

'And Dean?'

'As far as I was aware, she never saw him again. Until recently.'

'And you promised never to tell anyone the truth about Uncle Owen?'

She nods. Her face is drawn. 'I felt I owed her that much. I felt guilty, you see, for not stopping Bess treating her so badly. I couldn't see her go to prison. So I kept tabs on her over the years. I was worried about her state of mind. Then, nearly eight years ago, she rang me to tell me she was pregnant, and that she had met the man she wanted to marry.'

'Nigel?'

'I assume so. I was relieved. I hoped she'd have a conventional life. No more drama. No more lies.'

It's dark now, the mountains just black shapes in the background. Everything looks more sinister in this light. All this talk of murder has given me the creeps. I just want to get back to the guesthouse. The kids and Adrian will be wondering where we are. 'Perhaps we should go back?' I say. She agrees and we begin walking. I take her arm. I keep imagining Dean watching us from somewhere in the shadows and quicken my steps. Mum follows suit. 'Did you ever think Selena would crack?' I ask. 'Tell someone what really happened?'

Mum blows on her hands. 'Sometimes. But we never talked about it. And after a while it was like it had never happened. We told everyone Owen had moved away and we almost managed to convince ourselves. Then Selena left Cardiff.'

'Did she ever say why she and I didn't keep in touch?'

Mum shakes her head. 'No. I tried to find out but she wouldn't tell me. Anyway, I wanted to keep you out of it.' In the distance – in the direction of the mountains – I hear the shriek of a fox and a shiver runs through me.

We pick up pace so that we're almost running. 'I know it's a lot to take in,' she says, her heels clipping the pavement. 'But you can never tell the police. Do you understand? And we must destroy that note.'

'I think you already have,' I say, remembering it balled-up in her pocket. I'm seized by a wave of fear so intense I stop walking. 'What if they find out that Owen hasn't been seen in twenty years? Will Dean say something?'

'He helped bury the body. He's hardly going to say anything, is he?' she says. The rain has eased but it's left her usually neat hair a big auburn frizz around her head. 'I don't know. I don't know what to do. Dean might have killed her but if we show the police the note they might start looking into what happened to Owen.'

'So what if they do? They can't touch you, Mum. You didn't do anything wrong.'

'I did, though,' she says, in a small voice. 'I kept her secret. I protected her. I helped her conceal a murder.'

And now Selena is dead and unable to tell anyone what my mother did for her all those years ago.

## 28

## *Two days after*

The next morning Rachel arrives bright and early, her red hair tied back in a loose bun, her green eyes boring into me as I push a mug of strong black coffee across the worktop to her. Animal eyes. I always get the sense she knows more than she's letting on and is just watching and waiting for one of us to trip up. She shrugs out of her wool coat and bundles it up, shoving it on top of her bag by her feet.

'It's lovely and warm in here,' she says. The smell of bacon lingers in the air, making me feel nauseous. I can't quite meet her stare, worried that she'll be able to see right through me into the maze of lies and secrets I'm keeping locked within me, like one of Amelia's diaries. I hardly slept last night for trying to picture Selena and Dean heaving Uncle Owen's body into his old banger. Where had they buried him? Did they dig a hole in the ground? Had it been cold? Raining? Had Selena been crying or too shocked to speak? Had they felt sick, repulsed? Relieved that it was all over?

Adrian enters the kitchen carrying an empty tray. He acknowledges Rachel but doesn't stop. Instead he goes to the plates I've already prepared with eggs and toast. He's perspiring around his hairline and wipes his forehead with the back of his hand before carrying the plates out of the room.

Adrian got up early to help me today so that Mum can spend some time with Ruby, but the goodwill he showed over the last two days has dwindled this morning. He's baggy-eyed and lacking enthusiasm, and I know it's because he wants to bury himself away with his book. He's realizing, as I have this past week, that running a guesthouse is harder work than we imagined. And that's before one of our guests decided to murder another.

Mum didn't join us for dinner last night but Ruby did. We were all amazed to see her devouring the chicken, roast potatoes and peas put in front of her. She ate more than either Evie or Amelia. My gaze kept flicking to Julia, trying to convey my terror that the food would make Ruby ill, but Julia responded by nodding encouragingly. I know I'll feel better when we speak to a dietician. Julia said that Mum had tried to find some kind of diet sheet for Ruby among her things, but there was nothing. Julia tried to get it out of Ruby but she just rattled off all the things she wasn't allowed to eat as though she'd been made to learn them by heart.

While we were getting ready for bed last night I suggested to Adrian we should keep the note addressed to Selena away from the police for now. He didn't understand why, of course, and I couldn't tell him. Would I ever be able to? I wish I'd remained oblivious. He had frowned, and something I couldn't read passed across his face, but he agreed. He trusts me, I thought, with sorrow. He admitted to me once, after we had been together a few years, that one of the things he most admired about me was that I was honest. *Straight* was the word he used. Trustworthy. Solid. I'd liked that he saw me in that way. And it was accurate. I was honest. I *am* honest. Selena called me a goody-goody when we were kids. A square. And that was a fair assessment. I've always tried to do the right thing.

But dobbing Mum into the police, watching her go to prison because she covered up a crime to protect someone she loved? How can that be the right thing?

Rachel clicks her tongue against her teeth, pulling me back into the present. 'How's everything going with Ruby?'

'Fine,' I say. 'Well, as fine as can be expected. She seems a plucky little thing underneath it all.'

'It's often my experience that children bounce back quickly. Even after something as horrendous as this.' She smiles reassuringly. 'Ruby's still too young to fully understand.'

'She must miss her mother, though,' I say sadly. 'Selena was Ruby's primary carer. She was home-schooled for a bit and they had an occasional tutor. Also she was in hospital a lot.' I pause. Dean was also in my thoughts last night. I kept imagining him outside on our driveway with a bunch of dead flowers. I just wish the police would hurry up and catch him. Where is he? Is he still in the area, hiding out somewhere in the Brecons? With his army training, he's used to being resourceful.

As soon as I opened the door to Rachel this morning, that was the first thing I'd asked. Had they found Dean? She'd looked disappointed when she admitted they hadn't. She assured me they were still looking for him, though, and that finding him was a 'priority'.

She leans towards me now. She's wearing a necklace with a cross attached and it swings forward. She tugs at it gently, running the fine silver chain through her fingers. 'We managed to speak to Nigel on the phone. He's travelling down to see us today.'

'Here?' I ask in alarm. 'Does that mean he's going to take Ruby back with him? Selena said he was violent. I told DS Middleton.' *Selena said a lot of things*, a little voice in my head tells me. *Who knows what's true?*

'We'll know more after we've spoken to him,' she says.

'Did he say where he was the day Selena was pushed? I know it's unlikely he would have come here and killed her, unless she gave him a key. But she did meet up with someone the day before she died.'

Rachel holds up a hand to stop me. 'Just let us do our job,' she says firmly.

I can hear the clatter of cutlery and the faint murmur of voices, the odd bark of laughter that could be

Adrian's. She turns her attention back to me and lowers her voice. 'There's something else too. When the police took Selena's handbag and phone, we found something that might imply she was being threatened. Possibly blackmailed. Did you know anything about this? Did Selena say anything?'

I rearrange my face to look shocked. 'No! She said nothing. Who was blackmailing her?'

She narrows her eyes. Does she suspect I'm lying? 'I'm afraid we can't divulge that right now. But there are several lines of enquiry we're exploring.'

'Why would someone want to blackmail her?' I say, almost to myself, testing her to see if she knows about Uncle Owen.

But if she knows more she doesn't show it. As if realizing she's said too much, she stands up, her shoulders stiffening, and pushes away her now-empty mug. 'I'll hang around for a bit. I'd like to have a chat with Nathan and Julia, if that's okay?'

Why does she need to speak to them again? I tell myself it can't be anything serious or DS Middleton would have returned. She reaches inside her suit jacket and pulls out her little black police book. 'It was on the news last night. Just a very short segment, confirming that a woman was found dead here. But you might have the press trying to get hold of you. If I'm here when they call, you can direct them to me, okay? Otherwise please don't speak to them.'

I nod.

'Thank you for the coffee,' she says, and smiles. I wonder if she's married, or living with someone. If so, does she tell her partner/husband/wife what she really thinks happened to Selena? I know she's keeping a lot of things back from us. She's here to support us, I understand that, but she's a police officer.

Nancy hovers by the front door with her coat still on and a tote bag hitched over her shoulder. She looks startled when she sees Rachel walking into the front room with her police identification tagged on to the pocket of her jacket.

'Why are the police here again?' she whispers, when Rachel is out of earshot. She's still standing by the door as if afraid to come any closer.

'They're investigating Selena's death. They think she might have been pushed down the stairs.'

Her black-rimmed eyes widen. 'Murdered? Really?'

'Yes. The police are taking it seriously, as you'd expect.'

She bites her lip. She has an iridescent pink lipstick on and some of it comes off on her tooth.

'You can come in,' I say pointedly, noticing she hasn't moved an inch. 'Would you mind just giving the rooms a general sweep around? Apart from the ones that are empty.'

'Not getting any bookings, then?' She looks almost gleeful.

'Unfortunately not.'

'Not good for business, is it, a murder? This place is cursed, I'm telling you.'

I'm surprised by her glibness. I walk away without answering.

Later, when Mum is in the playroom watching TV with the girls, I take the spare key and let myself into Apple Tree. Mum has made the beds and pulled back the curtains. Ruby's wheelchair has been folded up and propped next to the dressing-table. Her leg braces lie on top of it, discarded, like the broken body parts of a doll. Everything is neat and tidy. I wouldn't expect anything less of my mother. I'm in here because I remembered seeing Selena's suede jacket hanging up in the wardrobe, and it suddenly occurred to me while I was wiping worktops in the kitchen, that I should have checked the pockets. I'd forgotten to tell the police about it, although I only saw her wearing it once, the day before she died. It's a long shot, but there might be some clue as to who she was meeting.

I pull open the wardrobe door, relieved when I see it there. I'd half wondered if Mum might have removed it. I pull it from the hanger and bury my face in the soft fabric. It smells of Selena's perfume and I close my eyes. It's like she's back in the room with me. I rummage in the pockets. They're deep, filled with bits of crap. Which was so like Selena. She never emptied her pockets – when she was a kid, they were stuffed with sweet wrappers, bits of tissue and other junk. I empty the contents on to the bed and I'm surprised when something hard falls out with a thud. It's a mobile phone, the one I gave her the night Ruby was taken into hospital. I'd forgotten about it. I'm not really expecting to see anything so I'm surprised when a conversation thread pops up from an unrecognizable number. I scroll through it. It looks as though she messaged this person the day Ruby was admitted to hospital.

Selena: Don't try to find me.

*She's my daughter.*

Selena: You know she's not.

*I need to see you.*

Selena: It's over. Leave me alone.

*I'm worried about what you're doing to her.*

Selena: I'm protecting her.

*I still love you. I don't understand why you left me. Is it because of the letter?*

There's no reply and no more messages. She must have forgotten to delete them. Or she was planning to before she gave the phone back to me. I slip it into my pocket and sift through the rest of the rubbish, smiling to myself when I see a lollipop stick, the end still sticky and red, a piece of used chewing gum wrapped in a tissue, a few copper coins, a crumpled receipt. I pick up the receipt, expecting it to hold some clue as to where Selena went that morning but it's dated six months ago. I'm about to give up and throw the whole lot into the bin when I see something scribbled on the back of a small piece of card. I pick it up. It looks like it's been torn from a cigarette packet, and someone has etched a mobile number on to it in blue biro.

I stare at it, my heart racing. I'm good with numbers. I only have to look at them a few times to commit them to memory. And I recognize this one straight away.

Because it's Nathan's.

# 29

Nathan is alone in the back garden. I can see him through the kitchen window. He's toeing the hard ground with his boot. He has his back to me but I can tell he's having a sneaky fag because every now and then a plume of smoke trails over his head and dissipates in the cold damp air. He's wearing a ribbed navy jumper with jeans. He must be freezing.

This is the ideal opportunity to speak to him alone. I finger the card in the back pocket of my jeans.

I grab my coat and take him out a cup of tea. 'Julia will have your bollocks if she sees you're out here smoking,' I joke, handing him the mug.

He starts. 'Christ, Kirsty, you nearly gave me a heart attack! I thought you were Julia,' but he takes the mug of tea gratefully. He's like me with tea and coffee: we can consume ten cups a day easily. We get it from Mum.

He flicks the cigarette to the ground and grinds it into the mud with his foot. We stand in silence as we sip our tea. There is so much I want to say to him. I long to confide in him about Selena, about Mum and Uncle Owen, but I can't. It would be selfish, offloading on to him. He'd be buried under it all. And he's got enough on his plate with his recent marriage troubles.

We used to be close. Only two school years apart, we'd spend hours playing together, me with my dolls and him with his Action Man (until he'd ruin the game with his Action Man trying to 'kill' one of my Barbies). Even at university we kept in touch – he visited me in Durham, and when he started at Manchester, I'd spend the weekend with him. It's only in the last few years that we've grown apart, not helped by our own private conflicts: Adrian's breakdown and Julia's miscarriages. I miss the easy way we used to have with each other.

He'd asked me once about Selena. We were both living in London, me in a flatshare and on the first rung of the marketing ladder, and him briefly while he worked dead-end jobs and tried to figure out what he wanted to do with his life. We'd met up for a drink in our favourite bar – more of an old men's pub, really, but it was near to where I was living in Whitechapel. He'd graduated from university the year before so it must have been about thirteen years ago.

'Why don't you keep in touch with Selena?' he'd asked over a pint.

As much as I loved Nathan he was quite self-involved so I was surprised he'd noticed that Selena and I were estranged. I had shrugged it off, tried to make light of it. 'You know how it is,' I said, toying with my pint glass. 'Keeping in touch with friends back home is hard work.'

He'd frowned then. 'But you're not friends. You're cousins. She's family.'

'I know that. But she's changed. We've ... Well, we've just grown apart. Have you seen her? Has she said something?'

'Not exactly. I mean, yes, I've seen her. I bumped into her in Manchester the other weekend.'

'Manchester?'

'She's living there now. I was visiting some uni mates. We grabbed a quick drink. She told me Uncle Owen's left and Aunt Bess still goes on benders. She wanted a new start away from Cardiff.'

'And did she mention me?' I was worried she'd have told him about our fight, her accusation, my reaction.

'Only to ask after you. She said she hadn't seen you since you left for uni.'

I'd made regretful noises and vague promises to get in touch with her that I had no intention of keeping, and Nathan left it at that.

Not long after, he moved back to Cardiff, met Julia, eventually married her, and never mentioned Selena again.

'How are you doing?' I say now, stamping my feet against the cold.

He lifts his shoulders. 'It's a shock. I never knew Selena would be here when Mum suggested we came to stay. I thought something weird went down between the two of you years ago and that you'd lost touch.'

'Mum,' I say simply.

He raises his eyebrows. 'Ah, Mum. Meddling again.'

I laugh, my breath blooming in front of me. 'Yep.

She was the one who invited her here, despite my better judgement.' I realize it sounds harsh now, under the circumstances. 'Although I'm glad I got to see her and that we made up.' A lump has formed in my throat and I'm unable to say any more.

Nathan grips his mug and his face crumples. If I didn't know better I'd think he was on the verge of tears. 'Nathe?' I touch his arm, bracing myself to bring up the subject of why his number was among Selena's things. 'Is everything okay?' I reach into my back pocket and hand him the piece of card. 'I found this in Selena's coat. It's your number.'

He takes it. His hand is trembling.

'Nathe?'

He hands me back the card. 'Yes, it's my number.'

'What's going on?' I ask. 'Why did she have it? I thought you'd lost touch years ago.'

He shakes his head and his dark blond hair flops into his face. It reminds me of how he used to be as a boy. I often wondered what went on in his head and whether he could remember his first few years with his biological mother. Sometimes, when he played up, I worried that those eighteen months of neglect had damaged him more than any of us realized. 'I've really messed things up,' he says, his voice hoarse.

'What do you mean?'

'I've done something stupid. Really, really stupid.'

I'm seized by fear. I think of the morning Selena lay unconscious at the foot of the stairs and Nathan's plea not to tell the police he was sleeping on his own just feet away from where she was found. 'What have you done?'

'I'm going to have to tell Julia. It'll all come out. It's going . . .' his voice catches and he composes himself '. . . it's going to ruin us. And I love her. I love her so much.'

It's as though I'm travelling in a runaway car, knowing it's about to crash but bracing myself for the impact. 'What have you done?' I repeat, even though I know the answer.

'I slept with Selena,' he says.

I exhale.

'It was my friend's stag night in Cardiff. We bumped into each other. I was drunk and so was she. It was just that one night. It was a mistake. We both knew it. She went back to Manchester and I never saw her again . . . until the other day.'

'How long ago?' I try to calculate when he moved back to Cardiff, when he met Julia.

'Before I was married. But I was living with Julia. It was a stupid, reckless, selfish thing to do. My feelings for Selena were confused. I thought I loved her, until I slept with her and then I knew it wasn't love. It was just infatuation. Julia's the one I love.'

'How many years ago?'

He finally meets my eye, his expression distraught. 'About nine months before Ruby was born.'

# 30

I can't stop myself. I punch Nathan's upper arm really hard. 'How could you?' I cry. 'How could you do that to Julia?'

He swears under his breath and rubs the spot where I punched him. 'That hurt.'

'Selena never said Nigel wasn't Ruby's father. Does he know?'

'I don't know what she's said to him. I've only recently found out myself. She told me. The day before she died.'

She could have been lying. Selena lied about everything.

'That's why you gave her your number? So you could arrange your little rendezvous?' I should have twigged before. I knew Selena had gone to meet someone and I'd bumped into Nathan coming back from the village that day. That explains why she'd behaved so strangely around him.

He hangs his head. 'She wanted to meet,' he mumbles to his shoes.

'Have you told the police?'

His head shoots up. 'Not yet. That liaison officer was

probing this morning but then she got a call and rushed off. Anyway, I wanted to tell Julia first.'

'You've had two days!'

'It's not easy! Don't be judgemental. We're not all bloody perfect like you!'

'Oh, fuck off!' I'm hurt. Especially as I know that I'm anything but perfect.

I stand my ground, although I want to storm off, the silence yawning between us. Nathan lights another cigarette and inhales deeply. I move away slightly. Smoke isn't good for my asthma.

'We met in the park,' he says. 'I'd told Julia I wanted some time alone.'

I groan. 'This is a bloody mess.'

He takes another drag. 'We weren't together long. Just enough time for Selena to tell me about Ruby. It made sense. The dates matched. She said . . .' his voice breaks '. . . she said she'd heard that Julia was finding it hard to get pregnant. She wanted me to know I was a father.' I can't help but think that was selfish of Selena. One-upmanship on Julia?

I take a deep breath. Although I'm standing a few feet away from Nathan I can still smell the smoke and I cough. Nathan notices. 'I'm sorry.' He stamps out the cigarette. 'She said the ball was in my court. And then she left. I walked around for a bit by myself and then headed back to the guesthouse. That's when I saw you.'

'Was Selena there when you came in?'

'I'm not sure. I didn't see her. I went upstairs when I

got back. Julia was cross with me and we argued . . . I still haven't admitted to the police that I was asleep in the playroom when Selena died.'

'Oh, Nathan,' I sigh, 'why not?'

'I don't know. Julia said . . . We agreed it would be better not to say anything.' He groans. 'We only ever spent one night together.'

'It only takes one bloody night,' I say, through clenched teeth. It begins to rain lightly and I shiver, pulling my coat tighter around my body. I scrunch up the card with Nathan's number on it and put it into my coat pocket. Hiding more evidence. I'm already protecting Mum, now Nathan and Julia too. I feel weighed down by it all.

I have a sudden thought. I turn to him. 'Does Mum know?'

He balks. 'I hope not! Can you imagine?' He still hasn't shaved and he rubs at his stubble. 'Unless . . .' he pulls a face as though he's swallowed something unpleasant '. . . unless Selena told her. Do you think she would?'

'I think if Mum knew Ruby was her grandchild she would have told me,' I say. Although that isn't necessarily true. It's obvious now that Mum can keep her own secrets. Maybe that was why she invited Nathan here in the first place, so that Selena could tell him. It makes sense. 'Did she suggest that you and Julia come to stay? Or was it your idea?'

'It was hers, of course. And then, because it was her birthday, we thought it would be a good idea.'

'Then maybe Mum did know.' She was the one person Selena didn't lie to, it seems.

He groans. 'I'm going to have to tell her, aren't I?'

'Julia?'

He nods.

'Of course you are.' I don't want to ask the next question but I have to. Because something doesn't add up. Why hasn't he told the truth to the police about where he was sleeping when Selena died? Was it because he wanted an alibi? It's inching its way up my throat and I choke it out. 'Did you push Selena down the stairs?'

He jumps away from me as if I've shot at him. '*What?* Of *course* not. Is that what you really think?'

'I don't know what to think. Maybe you bumped into her as you were going back to your room. You could have rowed at the top of the stairs. Maybe you didn't want her to tell Julia the truth.'

'I can't believe you think I could do something like that!'

'It might have been an accident. A spur-of-the-moment thing. Nathe?' I look around to check we're still alone. 'You can tell me.' Although if he did suddenly confess what would I do with that information? Hide it along with everything else?

Before I can say more we're interrupted by Mum striding across the lawn, looking more formidable than usual. Sian and Orla trail behind her. Damn it. I'd forgotten about the playdate.

'Here she is. The Wicked Witch of the West,' Nathan mumbles.

Usually I'd laugh. But not today. I'm still furious with him.

I greet Sian and Orla enthusiastically, steering them into the house. I round up Amelia, who's upstairs doodling in her art book. She looks sullen until she sees Orla and then she jumps up from her bed. It's the most excitement I've seen from her in days. Evie is in the corner of her bedroom playing with her teddies and the china doll. She hardly looks up when we enter.

Amelia loops arms with Orla and Sian says she'll have her back by six. As she's leaving, she pauses at the door. 'I'm so sorry to hear about your cousin.'

It must be all over the village, although Selena hasn't been named on the news.

'Thank you.'

She gives me a hug, enveloping me in the smell of her freshly washed hair. 'I hope everything else is okay. The girls? The business?'

I long to tell her everything, this woman I hardly know. 'When the girls are back at school, shall we go for a coffee?' I say instead.

She smiles kindly. 'I'd love that.'

I watch them drive away, my heart twisting. I hate Amelia being in a car without me. I worry about accidents but Sian seems sensible. It's there, all the time, the underlying fear that the girls will be taken away from me. Just like Natasha was taken away from Mum. From all of us.

*They live on the other side of the village,* I think, trying to convince myself that she'll be fine but I can't help texting Sian half an hour later on the pretence of forgetting the pick-up arrangements but really to check if they've arrived safely. Sian doesn't text back straight away, and as I clear the kitchen, I'm trying to vanquish visions of crumpled metal and ambulances. Eventually, ten minutes later, she reiterates that she'll be bringing Amelia home at six.

I can still see Nathan in the garden with Mum. They look like they're having a heart-to-heart, heads bent together, ignoring the rain.

I'm stacking the dishwasher when Ruby wanders in, startling me. I'm still not used to her walking around. When Selena was alive, Ruby was handled with kid gloves. I wonder again what will happen to her. Nathan needs to tell the police that he's Ruby's real father. It might prevent Nigel taking her home with him. I don't want him near that little girl if he's violent.

'Hi, Aunty Kirsty,' she says, smiling shyly. She has her favourite fluffy mouse tucked under one arm. I notice that one of her front teeth is missing. 'Can I go upstairs and play with Evie?'

I glance at her legs. She hasn't worn the braces since she took them off in the garden. When she arrived on Friday she'd been frail, in a wheelchair. Now – much to everyone's surprise – she's walking about, even if it is a little shakily. 'Of course, but are you strong enough to climb the stairs?'

She sticks out her chin stubbornly, reminding me of Selena. 'Yes. If I'm careful. Mummy would never let me try. She said it was too dangerous if I fell. She didn't like me walking.' Her eyes fill with tears. Selena had been over-protective, like me. Natasha's death must have had an impact on her too. It's understandable. I'd be the same if my daughters had Ruby's problems.

'Oh, sweetheart, I'll help you,' I say, rushing to her. I want to wrap her in my arms. She holds my hand as she leads me to the stairs. I stand behind her, like I used to with Amelia and Evie when they were toddlers, as she slowly climbs. It takes her a while, and she seems a bit out of breath when we reach the top, but she's smiling broadly, showing her gappy teeth. Her strides are more secure as she crosses the landing. She seems to know straight away which door is Evie's and pushes it open eagerly. Evie squeals in surprise to see us and jumps up from her circle of stuffed animals.

'You have a visitor,' I say, stroking Ruby's long, fine hair. Her little chest is rising and falling rapidly and I experience the frisson of terror I have when I'm worried about Evie or Amelia. 'Will you look after Ruby for a minute, honey? I just want to ask Aunty Julia a quick question.'

Evie takes Ruby's hand and leads her into the middle of the room. I'm just about to leave when I see Amelia's art pad in the middle of her bed. Almost without thinking I pick it up and flick through it. I stop at the most recent one. It's a sketch of a ghost chasing a girl. It's bleak and heavily shaded. I'm impressed but there's something disturbing about it. I put it back where I found it.

I poke my head around our bedroom door to see Adrian immersed in his novel. He's hardly spoken to me since yesterday, and I fear the chasm between us is widening since Selena's death. For a while I felt closer to him as he helped me with the breakfasts and seemed to take more interest in the running of the guesthouse. Now it seems he's retreated into himself again. And I don't understand why. He doesn't look up when I ask him to listen out for the girls, just grunts in response.

I race down the stairs, noticing that Nancy has disappeared and didn't ask for her money on the way out. I find Julia in the front room. She's sitting alone on the sofa with papers on her lap. She's frowning as she reads but looks up when I enter. 'Are you okay?'

I get my inhaler out. 'Sorry,' I say, after I've taken a few puffs. I fill her in on Ruby. 'I'm wondering if she has asthma. She seemed really wheezy after walking up the stairs. It could be lack of fitness but . . .'

She gathers the papers from her lap and puts them into a bag that's beside her on the sofa. 'I've got my doctor's bag upstairs. I can check. Have you registered her with a GP yet?'

'Yes. I spoke to someone this morning. Early. I need to go in and fill out some forms.'

'When you do, I'd like to come with you, if that's okay.' She frowns, her brown eyes flitting to her bag, then back to me. 'I've just been looking over Ruby's notes. There're a few anomalies.'

'Anomalies?'

'Not in what I've read but in what Selena told me. She said Ruby has Crohn's, right?'

I remember our conversation that first morning. 'Yes. Crohn's. Allergies to dairy and wheat. And growth problems. She also said she thinks she might have ME.'

'Umm,' Julia says, biting her lip. 'That's what she told me. Here, the night before she died.'

I don't understand what Julia's getting at. 'What does it say in her records?'

'Well, that's the thing. Ruby's had a lot of procedures. Some of them pretty hard core. She's been in hospital a lot. She's been tested numerous times for Crohn's, once when she was just four years old, then again when she was five and also earlier this year.'

'Why so many times?'

'Because each time it seems that Selena was insistent that's what Ruby had.'

'And?'

Julia shakes her head, her face serious. 'Each test was negative.'

I think of Ruby's small, undernourished body. Her pale face. Her weak limbs. Her fatigue. 'So, what are you saying? That Ruby's not really ill? Because it's obvious that she is. The second night she was here she had to be rushed to hospital. She had a seizure and a fever. Selena wasn't overreacting.' I feel defensive on Selena's behalf.

'I don't know,' replies Julia, her brown eyes so dark I can't see the pupils. She stands for a few seconds and chews a thumbnail. She swallows, as if worried about what she's going to say next. 'It's rare and I've never seen a case. I've only read about it. And I'm not sure if this is what's going on here. Maybe there are other reasons why Ruby is so unwell. But the things that Selena said and the notes I have here, they don't fit.'

'I don't understand what you're trying to say.'

'Ruby was born with a few issues. She was jaundiced, and she had breathing problems and an allergy to dairy as a baby. And she's had many blood tests and invasive procedures in the last few years and they've found nothing. She's no longer allergic to dairy, according to recent tests. And she tested negative for Crohn's three times. Having a wheelchair and leg braces when, it seems to me, there isn't any need, the food that she can now miraculously eat, even though Selena told you her diet was so limited . . .' She gives me a considered stare as if weighing up whether to be completely honest. Then, 'Have you ever heard of factitious disorder in others?'

'I don't think so.'

'You might know it by its former name. Munchausen syndrome by proxy.'

## 31

I stare at Julia, open-mouthed. I can't talk for a few moments. 'Now, wait a minute,' I say eventually, when I've found my voice again. 'Selena was no angel, I'm the first to admit that, but what you're suggesting would mean Selena was deliberately making Ruby sick, wouldn't it?'

'Munchausen syndrome by proxy is a psychological condition where a person pretends someone vulnerable in their care is sick, needing operations and procedures, when they don't,' says Julia, in her GP voice. 'They do it for attention. It could have started when Ruby was a baby and it was picked up that she was allergic to dairy. Selena might have basked in the attention the staff were giving her . . .'

'But that's – that's child abuse!' I splutter.

Julia nods gravely. 'It's a huge accusation to make. I know that. And I'm sorry, I really am. But we have to consider the possibility that Ruby may not be ill at all.'

'There's no proof of that!' I protest. 'I mean, Ruby's obviously ill. The doctors just haven't found the cause yet.'

Julia sighs, the sound echoing around the living room. 'I've thought of all of that. But she told you that

Ruby had Crohn's. Why tell you that when the tests suggest otherwise?'

'I . . .' I think of pretty little Ruby with her elfin face and skinny limbs. I can't believe Selena would do that to her daughter. She loved her. She wanted to protect her. Just like I want to protect my girls. That was why she'd left Nigel. She'd been worried that he was going to hurt Ruby.

Julia comes over to me and rubs my arm affectionately. 'I know it's a lot to take in. And I'm not saying it's definite. It's . . .' she hesitates '. . . it's a really awful thought. Let's just keep an eye on Ruby. That's what I'm saying. I'll go and get my medical bag and I'll listen to her chest to see about the asthma. Okay?'

I smile gratefully and she moves past me out of the room.

I go to the window and look out over the mountains. Usually when I see the Brecons in the distance I remember Dean and the recurring thought that plagues me: he could be living up there waiting for his moment to come back and hurt us. But now all I can think about is Ruby. A flash of red catches my eye. Nancy is across the street, just opposite from the church, in her scarlet mac. She's with our neighbour Lydia Ford, their arms linked as they shelter under Nancy's umbrella. They're talking to someone. I peer closer. My vision is obscured by the rivulets of rain snaking down the glass but it looks like Janice. Yes, it's definitely Janice. She's also holding an umbrella, hers in a garish floral fabric, and she has

Horace cradled under her arm, one of his little legs sticking out at an angle. Do they know each other? They seem to be engaged in deep conversation, not the passing small-talk of a guest and a cleaner. Before I can think any more about it Janice breaks away from Nancy and Lydia and heads back towards the house, a determined look on her face as she struggles with her umbrella, which is being buffeted by the wind.

I turn away, thoughts of Janice and Nancy flying straight out of my mind. All I can think about is what Julia's just told me.

Munchausen syndrome by proxy. I don't know much about it, only what I've seen in the newspapers. I remember reading about a case years ago when a mother pretended her child was terminally ill. But that was for money. I'm sure of it. She'd shaved his head and pretended he had cancer so she could go on a holiday of a lifetime. Selena hadn't done anything like that. I turn back to the window and grip the sill. My palms are sweating. I can't believe Selena would purposely cause her child pain by making out she was ill when she wasn't. All the procedures that Ruby's had, the operations, the hospital stays. As if Selena would make her go through all that if she was healthy. She would have had to be extremely mentally disturbed and, okay, she had her issues but she couldn't have done more for Ruby. She came across as a loving, attentive mother. No, Julia's got it wrong. I can't let her think that about Selena. It would sully her memory. *But she murdered her own father,* a little voice inside my head insists. *Is it really that much of a stretch to imagine she could harm her daughter too?*

I make an effort to pull myself together. There are real things to worry about, like Nathan being Ruby's father and Julia knowing nothing about it. I feel hot and flustered.

I head into the hallway just in time to see Janice bursting through the door, wrestling with her umbrella. I notice one of the spokes has broken and hangs limply, like a snapped finger. 'Ah, hello, dear,' she says, when she sees me. She throws the umbrella on to the step outside and closes the door. 'How are things?'

'Okay. Considering. Listen, I just want to say I'm so sorry for everything that's been happening here . . .' I pull an apologetic face '. . . I know it must have ruined your stay.' *Please write a positive review on TripAdvisor.*

We'd had one from the Greysons last night under the headline *Dire.* I couldn't bring myself to read the rest.

She waves a hand. 'Not at all. I've loved staying here. I grew up around here, you know.'

I remember she said she was visiting her sister. 'Your sister lives in this village?'

'Yes. Clara Gummage. She runs the little pharmacist in the high street. I've just spent the morning with her. When I leave on Saturday I probably won't see her for another year. She can't really afford to travel over to me.'

Mrs Gummage is Janice's sister? They couldn't be more different. Mrs Gummage looks like she's biting down on something nasty half the time and Janice is so chatty.

Janice plonks Horace at her feet. 'Goodness, he's so heavy. He's getting fat.'

That's an understatement. I force back a chuckle.

She heads towards the stairs, Horace at her heels. 'You know . . .' she says, turning to survey me, one hand on the banister. She has that unnerving look in her eye again, the one she gets before she starts spouting off about energies and murders. Sure enough, '. . . there's still a bad energy about this place. You must be careful, dear,' she says. 'Those mountains and hills . . .'

I try to hide my annoyance.

She closes her eyes. 'Bad things have happened here. And there is more to come.'

'Stop it!' I blurt out.

She opens her eyes in surprise. 'Pardon?'

'I said stop it. I can't hear this kind of talk, Janice. I'm sorry. I have two children to think about. And Ruby, who's just lost her mother. I don't want to hear it.'

She steps back down from the stairs and comes closer. I can smell the rain on her. 'I'm sorry, dear, but it's got to be said. This place isn't good. It has a history. A bad history. Everybody who's lived here has had a terrible life. Over the last thirty years it's been empty more than it's been occupied. And there's a reason for that.'

'So what do you think I should do?' I'm humouring her, but now I want to know what she's trying to say.

She lifts her shoulders. She has on a brown coat over her favoured caftan and thick tights. 'If you want my honest opinion, I don't think you'll find happiness here, in this house. It's cursed. I know you don't believe me, and that's fine. But I'm telling you.'

I fold my arms across my chest. I spot a tea stain on my jumper. 'Well, thanks for that.'

She steps even closer so that I can see the fine hairs above her top lip. She touches my hand softly. 'I like you. And your family. You're good people. But I know the history of this house. Not just going back to Violet Brown but after that. I grew up here, remember? As kids we were terrified of this place. Right creepy it was. By the church and all. Derelict for years. Nobody would touch it with a barge pole. But I doubt the estate agents told you all that when you looked around it, did they?'

She moves away from me and scoops up Horace. 'Going to have a nap now. I'm sorry to scare you, my dear. Your face – you look petrified. I'd feel dreadful, though, if something else happened here. You might think I'm just a bit batty, or that the whole psychic thing is mumbo-jumbo, but you need to know the truth. This place is cursed.'

I watch her walking up the stairs. Janice is obviously trying to unsettle me. But I can't figure out why.

Adrian isn't at his desk. His laptop is closed and a stack of A4 paper is in a pile by the side, face down so that I can't see the words. I wonder if he's gone for a run. There is a photograph of me and the girls on his desk, taken when we first moved here, near one of the waterfalls. I have my arms around both of them and we're all smiling, our faces lightly tanned, me and Evie blonde and wild beside Amelia's chic dark looks. I wonder how Amelia is getting on at her playdate. I miss them both when they're not with me – I'm used to seeing more of them now we've moved here.

The bed is unmade and the curtains are still shut, even though it's nearly lunchtime, so I draw the curtains and tug down the sides of the duvet, smoothing the middle. Tidying, always tidying. If I'm busy I don't have to think.

I hear someone clear their throat and jump. Julia is standing in the doorway. She doesn't step into the room and seems almost embarrassed, as if she's walked in on Adrian and me naked in bed.

'I checked on Ruby,' she says. 'I think she might have asthma.'

'I wonder why it wasn't picked up before. She's been in and out of hospitals so . . .' I trail off. 'What?' I ask, when I see Julia's about to speak.

'It could be caused by stress. After everything.'

I'm not sure if she's referring to Selena's death or the suspected Munchausen syndrome by proxy. I don't reply.

'I'm going to write a prescription for an inhaler. But

you need to speak to your own GP as soon as possible.' She sounds stern and I get a flash of what she must be like at work. I feel a wave of love towards her when I think about what I know. And what she doesn't.

We fall silent when we hear Nathan's voice on the stairs and I feel a punch of anxiety to my gut, as if I'm about to go into an exam. She smiles. Trusting, lovely Julia, about to walk into the lion's den. I give her a quick but firm hug.

'What's that for?' She laughs when we pull apart.

'Just thank you.'

'Oh, you,' she says, blushing as she moves away. She gives me another dazzling smile and disappears down the stairs. I stare at the spot where she was standing, as if the energy of her is still there, and I'm overcome with sadness. I'm feeling emotional not just about Julia but about Selena. And Ruby. And all of it.

I take a deep breath and reach for my inhaler, patting my pockets, but I must have left it downstairs. I open the window instead, letting in some of the damp air. A sudden gust blows the curtain away from the window-sill and I hurriedly close it again. But a page of A4 has fluttered to the carpet. Adrian will be cross if I mess up his manuscript – if that's what it is. I rush over to the page and pick it up. When I read what he's written a feeling of dread creeps slowly around my insides, turning them to ice. Frantically I rummage through the other pages. There're about twenty altogether. I was expecting to see part of his novel, sentences and scenes that mean nothing to me. Instead there's just one word typed over and over and over again. Line after line of it filling the page and filling my head.

Selena.

## 32

I stare at the pages in front of me, confusion and shock tussling for supremacy, and my hand starts to tremble. I think of Adrian, hunched over his laptop, punching away at the keys. I thought he was up here creating something, an outlet for his mind after all the turmoil of his illness. But he wasn't. Instead he was thinking of Selena. Why? A thought so awful enters my head that I try to bat it away but it refuses to budge. It's like when Nathan and I used to dare each other to say 'Candyman' from that horror movie, in front of the mirror. I was too scared to voice it, terrified it would unleash an evil spirit like in the film, but I couldn't stop the word going round and round inside my head, like numbers in a lottery ball spinner. Is that what it's been like for Adrian, his infatuation with Selena making him unable to think of anything else? So that in despair he was forced to write her name over and over again?

I think of the times when I'd come up here and seen Selena standing by his desk.

Where is Adrian now? I frantically scan the room as if expecting him to materialize in front of me. I shove the papers back on to the desk. They're all messed up now, no longer in a neat pile. I dart across the landing to Evie's room. She and Ruby are playing with the Sylvanian Family on the carpet. The china doll sits on the mantelpiece, staring at me with its one glassy eye.

'Evie, honey, have you seen Daddy?' I try to keep the panic out of my voice.

Both little heads turn towards me, each girl with a fox character in her hands. 'No,' says Evie, turning back to her game.

'Call me if you need me to help Ruby down the stairs. Don't try and walk down on your own, okay?' I say to her.

'Yes,' they chorus, but I'm not sure they heard.

I dart around the house, like a superhero in a cartoon. I never knew I could run so fast. The house seems empty. There's no sign of Nathan, Julia or Mum. I'm grabbing my mobile from the charger in the kitchen to ring Adrian when I notice I have a missed call and a voicemail. It's from Sian. I ring back without listening to the message, hoping everything is okay.

'Sian?'

'Kirsty. Hi. Is Amelia okay?'

I feel a white-hot panic. 'Amelia? What do you mean? She's with you?' The phone crackles and I move to the front of the house where there's better reception, my legs weak.

'Adrian just came to pick her up. I left you a voicemail. She's not feeling well and wanted to go home.'

'How long ago?'

'About ten minutes. I left a message for you and then

I tried Adrian's phone. You're both on the school contact list.'

Ten minutes. I instantly feel guilty that I missed Sian's call. I should have had my mobile on me. I normally do. 'Thank you. Sorry. I'll . . . We must arrange that coffee soon.'

'Definitely. I hope Amelia's okay.'

I abort the call, puzzled. Amelia was looking forward to seeing Orla. It's not like her to want to come home. Straight away I ring Adrian's mobile. Orla lives a few streets away: they should be home by now.

I think of the pile of papers upstairs with Selena's name on it. Is Adrian heading for another breakdown? Evie's words come back to haunt me. Should they be scared of him? They both think he's possessed. And then the memory of another time, before his attempted suicide, hits me. I begin to shake. It can't be happening again. Can it? He's better now . . .

I begin pacing, my phone in my hand. I ring Adrian's number again. And again. And again. And again. Eventually, when he still fails to pick up, I throw the phone on to the sofa in frustration. *Where the fuck is he?*

Oh, God. Something's happened to them. I just know it. I clutch at my throat, rushing to the window every time I hear a car. Where has he taken her? And then I realize. Our car is on the driveway. Did Adrian walk over to pick her up? My face is hot with panic. I can't concentrate on anything else, my eyes trained on the window. Eventually – and it can't be more than five minutes later – Adrian rounds the corner, holding Amelia's hand, and she's chatting away to him animatedly. The relief is immense. It floods my body, relaxing me instantly as though I've been given a sedative.

'Thank God!' I cry, when I open the door. Adrian's face darkens, his expression guarded. I run to Amelia and hug her. Her face is cold. She stands there, arms at her side, while I cuddle her to me. 'I've been so worried.'

'She's just got a bit of a tummy-ache,' says Adrian, clearly puzzled. 'No need to overreact.'

'Why didn't you take the car?'

'I was out on a run when I got the call so I just headed straight for Sian's house.' I can see that he's wearing his running gear.

Amelia pulls away from me. 'I'm going to lie down for a bit,' she says.

'Amelia? Honey? What's wrong?'

'I don't want to talk about it,' she says, stomping up the stairs.

'But—' I move towards her but Adrian takes my arm.

'Leave it, love.'

Reluctantly I watch her go. Then I turn to Adrian. 'Why didn't you pick up your phone?'

In reply he ferrets in the pocket of his tracksuit bottoms. 'Six missed calls. Bit excessive, don't you think?'

'I was worried.'

'But why?'

'I thought something might have happened. You left without telling anybody where you were going.'

'I told Nancy when she was here earlier that I was going for a run.'

'Oh. Right. Well, she didn't tell me. She disappeared without collecting her wages.'

'I gave them to her.' He takes off his fleece and hangs it over the banister. I immediately take it off again and fold it over my arm.

'Oh. Right,' I say again, momentarily distracted. And then I remember. 'You'd printed out something. I thought it was your manuscript. But it wasn't.'

Adrian looks surprised. 'What? I've not printed anything.'

'I'll show you.' I'm trying to remain calm, feeling foolish for my panicky missed calls earlier. I walk up the stairs. He kicks his trainers off and follows me.

When we reach our room, he runs over to his desk and gathers up the papers. Then I notice the light on the printer flashing. There is more paper in the tray. I pick them up, dismayed to see they say the same thing. *Selena*.

I thrust the pages at him. 'What's going on?'

His eyes scan the pages and he doesn't speak. Instead a pulse throbs at his jaw.

Oh, God. He's going to admit it, isn't he? He's going to tell me he was in love with Selena.

I wait, my heart pounding. I'm holding my breath. The world seems to stop. Will I remember this afterwards, this pivotal moment in my life? Will I think of it in the Before and After?

I know things could be better between us. But I've tried, I've really tried, to mend our relationship. To get things back to how they were. Maybe that's the problem: I wanted him to be like he was before his breakdown, but it's altered him and I need to love him for who he is now. And I do. I do. I don't want to lose him.

He lifts his head, his brow furrowed. 'I don't know. Honestly, I didn't do this.'

I'm thrown. I wasn't expecting him to say that. 'What do you mean?' Is he in such a bad way that he's forgotten? I assess him. No, he seems calm, stable, nothing like he was in the days before his breakdown.

He tidies up the papers so they're in a pile and clicks on his laptop. I peer over his shoulder. There, on the screen, is one page full of 'Selena'. But when he scrolls up to the previous pages, there is his novel. He goes to the print set-up and I can see that someone has arranged for just that page to print thirty times.

He turns to me and his eyes are intense, desperate. 'I didn't write this.'

I exhale in relief. He's telling the truth. Thank God.

He twists back to the computer and I squeeze his shoulder. 'I'm sorry for thinking you did.'

He sighs and sits down heavily on his office chair. 'Are you always going to doubt me? Because of what happened?'

*Because of what happened.*

I slump to the floor. 'I thought I'd never see them again.'

His voice is thick with emotion. 'You don't know how sorry I am. That I put them at risk like that.'

Two weeks before he'd tried to take his own life, Adrian had picked up the girls from school. It was unusual that he was home in time: he never normally finished work until at least six. But unbeknown to me he'd walked out of his job. He hadn't been thinking straight and drove them into the centre of London. I'd been desperately trying to get hold of him, wondering why they hadn't come home. It had been two hours and I was on the verge of calling the police when he eventually answered my call. I'll never forget his voice and how panicked he'd sounded to find himself driving past Buckingham Palace. It was like he'd just woken up, he said.

He sounds resigned and a bit sad. I kneel at his feet. I have to be honest with him. 'There's always going to be a part of me that will wonder if it could happen again. Your behaviour was irrational . . . and scary.'

'I know. I'm so sorry.'

'You need to make things right with Amelia about it. She, in particular, is finding it hard to trust you.'

'You're right. I'll talk to her. Put her mind at rest. We used to be so close.'

I fight back tears. 'My biggest fear is something happening to you or the girls.'

He leans forwards and grasps both my hands in his.

'Please don't take this the wrong way because I know I've made things worse after what happened in the car. But I think you should see someone too. Because . . .' he hesitates and continues gently '. . . of your over-protectiveness with the girls. It stems from what happened to your sister.'

I can't help it. A tear runs down my cheek. I know he's right. I grew up witnessing Mum's pain and seeing that someone you love can be torn from your life, suddenly and cruelly. The possibility of it happening to me terrifies me every day.

His voice is tender as he says, 'We all worry about our kids. But your worry has become something else. You can't control what happens to them. Or me. And I'm so sorry, my love, that I put you through more pain last year.' There are tears in his eyes too.

And now Selena. More death. More pain. More fear.

'You seemed to have a soft spot for Selena,' I say, as I stand up. 'Did you have feelings for her?'

He laughs. 'Seriously? We got on well and I felt sorry for her, I suppose, but I never thought of her as anything other than a friend.'

I rest my head against his chest, his T-shirt slightly damp against my cheek.

'Mummy?'

I lift my head to see Evie standing in the doorway, her eyes flitting to us both with concern. I step away, smoothing my hair and trying to compose myself. 'Are you okay, honey?' I sense Adrian behind me.

'Can you help Ruby down the stairs? We want to play with the wabbits now and Amelia's being grumpy.'

'Sure.' I catch Adrian's eye. He gives me a tiny, reassuring smile. And in that moment I feel closer to him than I have done since his breakdown. We've finally been honest with one another.

He goes over to his desk and gathers up the sheets of paper. 'Evie?' he asks, almost nonchalantly. 'Have you been messing with my computer?'

She raises just one of her eyebrows. Evie's always had very expressive eyebrows: they seem to have a life of their own. 'No. I've been playing with Ruby in my bedroom.'

I sense she's telling the truth. I can't imagine Evie touching the laptop. She's not interested in computers and wouldn't know where to start. I doubt Ruby knows much about technology either. Not with her background and being home-schooled. Julia's accusation flits through my mind and I push it away. I'm still not ready to accept it.

I move towards Evie. 'Have you seen anybody come or go out of this room today?'

'Apart from you and Daddy?'

'Yes.'

She chews her lip. 'Um, Nana.'

'Nana?'

She frowns. 'I think she was looking for Daddy. Oh, and the cleaner lady.'

'Nancy?'

'Yes. Can you help Ruby now?' she asks, bored with the conversation. Ruby's head appears over Evie's shoulder and I wonder how long she's been standing there.

'Of course.' I turn back to Adrian. He has the wedge of paper pressed against his chest. We don't say anything but communicate with our eyes, both having the same thought: what would Nancy be doing in our bedroom? She's not supposed to clean up here. I employed her purely to help with the guest bedrooms. I reach up and kiss him. He's surprised so doesn't react at first. But then I feel him kiss me back. There is so much conveyed in that small, quick kiss: apology, love, desire.

I help Ruby down the stairs with Evie close behind, then instruct them to put their coats on and watch them stride across the lawn to the hutches, their little feet making prints in the dewy grass. Ruby seems to be walking just fine. No different from Evie. Such a contrast to how she was when she arrived nearly a week ago.

*Munchausen syndrome by proxy*. I'm not going to think it.

Adrian joins me in the kitchen. He's still carrying the papers. 'I think we need to talk to the family liaison officer about this,' he says gravely. Considering the note and the phone number I'm still keeping away from the police, it feels a relief to be able to be honest about something.

I tear my eyes away from the girls and try to concentrate on what Adrian's saying. 'Shouldn't we ask Nancy about it first when she comes here tomorrow? We can't just accuse her of something like this.'

He shakes his head. 'You're right. It seems such a peculiar thing to do. Why would she?'

'Rachel will be back tomorrow. We can show her these after we've spoken to Nancy.' I indicate the wodge of paper.

He opens the kitchen drawer where we keep odd bits and pieces and crams it in. Usually I'd admonish him for his untidiness, but not today. Not when we seem to have reached some understanding. He closes the drawer. I try not to smile when I see it won't quite shut.

He agrees but he looks cagey, unnerved.

'Ade? What is it?'

He shuffles. 'I wasn't going to tell you. I didn't want you to worry. But we can't do that any more. We have to be completely honest with each other from now on. About everything . . .'

My scalp prickles. 'Go on,' I say.

'This morning, on the way out for my run, I found some more dead flowers. On the doorstep. Like before. And this time there was a card.' His hand dips into the pocket in his tracksuit bottoms to extract it.

I take it from him. The once-white card is faded to a tobacco-stained yellow and the writing that was there originally is barely decipherable. But written on top of it, crudely in black biro, are the words 'IT'S NOT OVER.'

## 33

## *Three days after*

The wind whistling outside the window is keeping me awake. Adrian is snoring beside me. Evie, as yet, is still in her own bed. I'm bracing myself for her to wake up crying. And maybe that's why I can't sleep. But I know it's more than that. It's that Dean is still out there somewhere. I need to tell Rachel about the latest bouquet when she arrives in the morning. The Brecons I've always loved so much now feel like a threat. They are harbouring a fugitive.

And it's not just Dean. It's Julia and Nathan. It's my mum and Ruby. It's Amelia and her sulkiness. It's Nancy, who might have tampered with Adrian's computer. It's knowing that someone who was – *or still is* – staying here killed Selena.

I reach for my phone on the bedside table. It's only one thirty. There's no point lying here tossing and turning. I decide to get up. I drag my dressing-gown from the foot of the bed, put it on and go downstairs. I pass Nathan and Julia's room and Janice's, my heart falling at the thought of all those empty rooms waiting for new guests who might never come, now there's been yet another scandal here.

I shudder when I think of Violet Brown hanging from the rafters in the place where we now sleep. So much tragedy has happened here. Will we be forced to move? But where to? We can't afford to return to London.

When I reach the kitchen I'm surprised to see the light on. My heart skitters. I immediately think of Dean. *Don't be so ridiculous*, I tell myself. Gingerly, I push the door open. Mum and Nathan are sitting at the breakfast bar, their faces solemn, a half-empty bottle of wine in front of them.

They turn to look at me when I come in.

'What's going on?' I ask.

Nathan looks stricken. He's still fully dressed, although Mum's in her nightie, which makes me think he hasn't been up to bed yet.

I switch the kettle on. I can't face wine. 'I take it you've told Julia,' I say, as I unwrap a mint and camomile teabag and add it to my mug.

Nathan drops his head into his hands and groans.

'Yes, he's told her,' says Mum, rubbing his back as though he's six years old.

'And? Does she know about Ruby?'

'He's told her everything.' Mum shoots me daggers but I ignore her.

Nathan lifts his head. His eyes are red-rimmed. He pours himself more wine and gulps it back.

The kettle boils. I pour the water over my teabag and join them at the island. I deliberately sit at Nathan's other side so that he's between Mum and me.

'Nathe?'

He puts his glass down. It's empty. He sighs, long, deep and full of regret. 'She knows about Ruby,' he says. 'It's upsetting, as you can imagine. Especially as Julia can't stay pregnant.'

'Where is she now?'

'She's in bed. She doesn't want me to join her so Mum's given me a key to Freesia.'

*Dean's room.* I want to ask more – like will Julia forgive him. But it would be insensitive. And I'm not sure I'm ready to hear him tell me that Julia wants a divorce.

'So you knew about this too, then?' Mum says, her voice clipped, accusatory. She's talking to me: she uses a different tone, with an edge there never is for Nathan.

'I suppose you're going to say that this is my fault too, aren't you?' I reply, without looking at her.

Nathan pushes back his stool. 'I'm going to bed.' He's a bit unsteady on his feet.

Mum and I speak at the same time. 'Will you be okay?' I ask.

'Shall I help you to your room?' she says.

Irritation passes across Nathan's face, like a storm cloud. 'I'm fine. I just want to be on my own.' He staggers from the room and we hear his heavy footsteps on the stairs.

Mum and I sit in silence, staring at the open door. Eventually Mum stands up. I notice her wine glass is also empty. She pulls her rose velour dressing-gown firmly around her waist. She's lost a bit of weight, and seems small and frail in her nightwear.

'You knew,' I say, 'about Nathan being Ruby's father.'

Mum doesn't answer but her face says it all.

'Selena told you?'

'She did. But not until recently.' She rubs at her eyes. 'The thing is, Selena scared me. She was so unpredictable. It was easy to see she was damaged from Aunt Bess's abuse.' She lowers her voice. 'She killed her own father, for goodness' sake! She was a time bomb waiting to explode. I thought if she came here I could talk some sense into her. I wanted to persuade her to go back to Nigel. He gave her the security she craved – she needed.'

'But he was violent towards her?'

Mum groans. 'No, he wasn't. She lied about that too, just as she lied about everything else.'

'How do you know?'

Mum takes a sip of wine. 'Because she told me. She could never lie to me. Not for long, anyway. He was a big softy, apparently. That's why I didn't say anything to the police or advise them against asking him to come and get Ruby. He knew he wasn't Ruby's father but he didn't care. He loved them both anyway. No, she left him because of a letter.'

'A letter?'

My mind races and I think of my spare phone, which I found in Selena's coat. I tell Mum about the conversation I'd read. 'He mentions the letter. It must have been Nigel she was contacting. What sort of letter?'

'She didn't say.' She replaces her wine glass. 'It sounds like it was something to do with Ruby. It caused a big row. I think Ruby overheard some of it, according to Selena. Anyway, that's why she left.'

I consider telling her Julia's suspicions about Ruby's health but decide against it. She looks exhausted.

She stands up. 'Right, I'm off to bed.' She bites her lip. 'I hope Nathan's okay. He's not strong like you. He's fragile. Those first years of his life, who knows what impact they had on him emotionally?'

It's Saturday. Julia and Nathan are supposed to check out today, as is Janice. Not that we have any more bookings. The one we had for tonight has cancelled stating illness. I can't help but think it's due to the negative reviews.

The only people who have come down for breakfast are the girls, Ruby and Janice. I'm tired. Evie woke in the night and came into our room. This morning, though, she'd seemed amazed to find herself in our bed and said she couldn't remember getting there. It's become second nature – she does it nearly every night. On the odd night she doesn't come into our bed it feels like a little triumph, the one shining jewel among rocks.

I'm still worried about Amelia, though. She picks at her breakfast while Evie devours her toast, and Ruby eats so quickly it's as though she's terrified her eggs will be taken away.

I'm bringing Janice her pot of tea when Nathan

comes into the room. He has dark smudges under his eyes and still hasn't shaved. He looks crumpled and worn down. He sits on a table behind the girls, with a good view, I notice, of Ruby. She's sitting next to Evie and they're giggling together. Every now and then Amelia rolls her eyes. Nathan is staring at Ruby as if he's unable to believe she's actually his. But now I can see the resemblance: the pointed chin, the dark blonde hair, the Hughes nose (which would have come from Selena), the dimple just above a full mouth. It's uncanny. Why didn't I notice it before?

Mum herds the girls away when they've finished and started messing about. I'm surprised to see how happy Ruby seems. To look at her you wouldn't think she'd lost her mother only three days earlier.

When Mum and the girls have left the room, I pull out a chair opposite Nathan and sit down. I lean across the table so that Janice can't hear. 'Are you okay?'

'I still can't believe she's mine. I mean, I know she is, but I just . . .'

I rest my hand on top of his. 'I know.'

'I don't think Julia will ever forgive me. She won't speak to me. Will you have a word with her?' His eyes are so desperate, so sad, that I find myself saying yes. 'Selena said she was sick,' he continues. 'She's so thin. And – and small for her age?'

I squeeze his hand and lean in closer so that our noses are almost touching, but I can't risk Janice hearing. 'Julia was looking into Ruby's medical history. She thinks that Selena was maybe . . .' I fumble for the right words '. . . exaggerating Ruby's illness.'

He lifts his chin a fraction and I know I have his full attention. 'What? Like Munchausen syndrome by proxy?'

I nod.

He makes a noise through his teeth. 'Shit. She wouldn't do that, would she?'

I take my hand away. 'I thought the same initially, but since Selena's death, Ruby is steadier on her feet. She can walk without leg braces and a wheelchair. She's eating things that Selena said were bad for her. She's got a healthy appetite, in fact. She's just wolfed down two eggs and toast. Julia said there is no evidence of any allergies to wheat, dairy or anything else.' The idea makes me feel queasy but I have to face the possibility that Julia is right. I can't disbelieve something just because it sounds unpleasant, sick even.

'But that's child abuse.' He slumps back in his chair. 'Fucking hell. I can't take all this in right now.'

Janice swivels around in her chair. 'Everything okay?'

I mouth an apology to Nathan. I shouldn't have blurted it out like that. I get up, go over to Janice and plaster a smile on my face. 'All good. More tea?'

Adrian is with Rachel and DS Middleton in the front room when I walk in. They are midway through a conversation about the most recent delivery of dead flowers. I notice Rachel's holding a wedge of papers in her hand. Adrian must have got them from the kitchen drawer while I was with Nathan. We were supposed to ask Nancy about it before we said anything to the police. We'd agreed.

DS Middleton's face is grave as he listens to Adrian. I sit next to him on the sofa. A united front.

When he's finished speaking DS Middleton clears his throat. 'What time are you expecting the cleaner?'

I look at my watch. 'In the next ten minutes or so.'

'Great. I think we need to talk to her. Find out if she had anything to do with the papers. But the dead flowers and the note, are you saying you think they're from Dean?'

'Who else would send them?' I ask. 'You still haven't caught him?'

DS Middleton shakes his head regretfully. 'No. But we're doing everything we can. There's something else too. We've managed to notify Selena's mother about her daughter's death. There's no sign of her father, though. Do you know where,' he consults his notebook, 'a Mr Owen Hughes now resides?'

I glance at Adrian. He knows nothing about what really happened and I can never tell him. It'll be a secret that will always lie between us, which makes me sad. Especially after our recent vow to be honest with each other from here on in.

'I haven't seen Uncle Owen in years,' I say truthfully. 'The last I heard he'd walked out on Selena and Aunt Bess . . .' I pretend to think '. . . over fifteen years ago.'

'Didn't you say your mother kept in touch with him?'

I swallow. 'Er . . . I thought she did but when I asked her about it she said she didn't. That she hasn't heard from him in years either.' I'm babbling. I do that when I'm lying.

He scribbles something in his book. 'Right. Okay. I don't know if Rachel told you, but we found some letters in Selena's bag. They're from Dean and they allude to a secret he shared with her. He wanted money.'

So the letter I found was from Dean. Why had Selena put it in my drawer? Did she suspect he was going to kill her and wanted evidence for me to find?

Had he been in love with her? She'd said he wanted to run away with her. Was that another of her lies?

I gulp. 'No. I have no idea.'

Silence hovers between us. I maintain eye contact. I can't be the first to look away or it might show I'm guilty.

I almost breathe a sigh of relief when he says, 'Okay. Let's wait for Nancy to turn up so we can find out more about this.' He indicates the papers which Rachel has given him.

I smile in response, still unnerved by having to lie to two police officers. I was the sort of child at school who felt instantly guilty when the teacher accused someone in the class of misbehaving, even if it wasn't me (which it never was: Selena was right – I had been a square).

Adrian offers to make Rachel and DS Middleton a cup of tea and I glance out of the window to the mountains, the mist obscuring the summits like icing on a cake. My chest tightens. They still haven't caught Dean. How can he be near enough to plant dead flowers and threatening cards but far enough away that the police can't find him?

## 34

Nancy stares at the four of us, her mouth open in mock horror. She's a terrible actress. I can tell straight away she's lying.

And so can the police: DS Middleton and Rachel sit up straighter and Rachel crosses her legs. A pose that tells me she means business. 'You were seen, Nancy,' she says simply.

It's enough to make Nancy cave. Her eyes droop at the corners in dismay. She picks at a loose thread on her leggings. I'm staring at her in shock, wondering why she'd go to such lengths to type Selena's name over and over again on Adrian's computer and print it out numerous times. Does that mean she had something to do with Selena's death?

'It wasn't my idea,' she cries, 'but we were so pissed off. We just wanted to make them see.'

*We?*

I can feel the blood draining from my face. She's going to admit it. But it doesn't add up. Dean killed Selena. It has to have been him. He was blackmailing her and probably threatening her. And now he's run off.

Adrian's beside me on the sofa. He takes my hand and we exchange quick, worried glances.

'Nancy?'

A voice in the doorway makes us all look up. Janice is standing there with Horace in her arms. I remember seeing her and Nancy talking – was it only yesterday?

Nancy stands up, looking desperate. She's got to be in her mid-forties but there's something childlike about her. Sian told me she still lives at home with her mother and has never married or had children. 'Aunty Janice!' she wails.

*Aunty Janice!*

'What's going on?' My gaze whips from Nancy to Janice. 'She's your niece?'

I can tell that Janice is gripped by indecision as she hovers in the hallway. Rachel stands up too. 'I think you should come in and have a chat with us,' she says, her voice formal. DS Middleton doesn't move.

Janice scuttles in and joins Nancy on the opposite sofa. I notice that she clutches the younger woman's hand tightly, as if they're both on a ship that's about to sink.

'I want to know what the hell is going on,' says Adrian. His voice is full of command and authority. He's the old Adrian, lawyer Adrian, who would bark orders on the phone.

'It was me,' says Nancy, before breaking down in sobs. Janice pats her back.

'You killed Selena?' I say, my legs feeling weak. 'But why?'

She shakes her head. Her tears are black-streaked

with eyeliner. 'No. I don't know anything about that. I wrote the note on Adrian's computer. It was me that did the noose. Put the dead flowers on your doorstep. Moved your inhaler.' She sniffs loudly, the sound reverberating around the room. She hid my inhaler? So it was she who had taken it out of the dresser that time.

DS Middleton stands up. 'I think we might have to carry on with this down at the station.'

I don't want them to leave. I need to know more. I stand up too. 'But why?' I blurt out. 'Why?'

Janice's usual jolly face has paled, making the spot of blusher on each cheek stand out. 'It was my fault too. I helped Nancy with the noose. We were doing it for my sister. For Nancy's mum.'

'Who's Nancy's mum?' I ask.

'Clara Gummage. From the pharmacy,' replies Janice.

Of course.

'But why would she want you and Nancy to do this kind of stuff?'

'We don't want you here,' cries Nancy, spittle flying out of her mouth. 'Nobody wants you here.'

'You mean Lydia?'

'She's got nothing to do with it,' insists Nancy, glaring at me.

'You're friends. And she's made it clear she can't stand us. Is that down to you?'

She crosses her arms across her chest but doesn't answer.

I turn to Janice, my voice pleading. 'Please, what's going on?'

'This place should have been my mother's. Not yours,' blurts out Nancy.

'What?' I look at Rachel, who is furiously noting down the conversation.

'We never meant no harm,' says Janice, quickly, clearly trying to dig herself out of the mess she's made, as it hits her she could get into serious trouble. 'I like you, Kirsty. And you, Adrian. You have a lovely family. It wasn't personal.'

Adrian is staring at them as though they've both sprouted an extra head. 'Not personal?' he splutters. 'I'd say that noose was very personal.'

'Violet Brown was my aunt,' says Janice. 'She hanged herself here, in the early 1950s.'

'I'm sorry to hear that,' I say. 'But I still don't understand . . .'

DS Middleton clears his throat impatiently. 'You both need to be formally interviewed,' he says. 'Come on.'

Janice and Nancy stand up and follow him from the room. Nancy is still crying, although Janice is more composed. Only the slight trembling of her hands gives her away.

I watch from the doorway as they troop to the car after DS Middleton. Rachel brings up the rear. They make a motley crew: Nancy with her shiny leggings and dyed black hair scraped into an eyebrow-lifting topknot, and Janice resplendent in another tent-like frock. She holds Horace under one arm, his eyes bulging.

My head is spinning. I don't understand what any of this has to do with Selena.

Two hours later Rachel phones. She tells me that Nancy and Janice have admitted under caution to the dead flowers, the accompanying note and the noose.

'Why?' I ask.

'They felt your house should have stayed in their family,' she says. 'They had some naïve idea about trying to scare you into selling up. They had wanted to buy it back and, apparently, because it had been standing empty for years, they thought they had a chance to get it cheap.'

I swallow. 'Right. So the dead flowers – none of it is anything to do with Selena?'

'That's right. Do you want to press charges?'

I sigh. 'No.' I don't want the police to be distracted by this. They need to find Dean. He might not have sent the flowers, but I'm still convinced he killed Selena.

Janice returns a few hours later. She's full of contrition as she packs up her things, stuffing her caftans into a suitcase. Horace sits in the middle of the bed, watching her with big, mournful eyes. 'Thank you,' she says, for the third time. 'I'm so grateful that you're not going to press charges.'

'Did the police question you about Selena?'

'Yes. But I honestly didn't have anything to do with her death – you've got to believe me.'

I do, but I'm not going to tell her so. Let her sweat a bit. I'm still shocked and disgusted by what she's done. Just because I don't want the police to press charges it doesn't mean I'm not furious. I just want them to be looking for Dean.

'Where will you go?' I ask.

'I'll see if the pub can put me up for a bit, then go home.'

'Are you really psychic?' I don't know why I ask. It's not as though I ever seriously believed her.

She pauses and turns to survey me. Her eyes are sad. 'I'm sorry.'

It had sounded so out there, so Mystic Meg, that of course it had been an act. I don't know why I didn't see through it sooner. It was just another scare tactic, like Mrs Gummage trying to convince Evie we had a ghost.

Without saying anything further I leave the room, letting the heavy fire door bang closed behind me.

I stand outside Janice's room, my heart racing.

'Are you all right, love?'

I start. Adrian is behind me. I didn't hear him come up the stairs. 'I'm fine. Would you mind keeping an eye on Janice? Make sure she leaves the premises and hands over her key? She's in there, packing.' I incline my head.

'Sure. I'll wait here.'

'Thanks. I'm going to knock on Julia's door to make sure she's okay.'

I start to walk off but Adrian grabs my hand. 'What about you? How are *you* doing?'

'I'm fine.'

He squeezes my fingers gently, and I smile before I walk away, aware that his eyes are on me. I stop outside Julia's door. When I turn back, Adrian is ushering Janice down the stairs, her suitcase in one hand, his jaw set. His eyes meet mine and he pulls a silly face behind Janice's back. I can't help but laugh. 'You wally,' I mouth.

I rap on Julia's door. There's no answer. I call her name through the wood. I wonder if she's somewhere with Nathan, talking through everything. I do hope so.

I glance out of the picture window. It's raining again and the sky has darkened so that it looks a lot later than three o'clock. I'm about to retreat when the door is wrestled open and Julia is standing there. She looks dreadful. Her usual pristine bob is a mess, her Liberty-print long-sleeved T-shirt is dishevelled and her eyes are red and puffy.

'Oh, Julia, I'm so sorry,' I say.

Without speaking, she opens the door wider and I follow her into the room.

The bed is unmade. Perhaps she fell asleep in her clothes.

She slumps against the headboard. 'Did you know?'

'I only found out yesterday, like you. I had no idea

before that. Nathan is devastated and deeply sorry. It only happened once.'

She holds up her hand to stop me. 'I don't want to talk about it.'

'I understand.'

She closes her eyes and I'm not sure what to do: comfort her or leave her in peace? I decide to sit down beside her. She doesn't say anything for a few minutes and when she does her voice cracks: 'He's got a child. Part of me is jealous that she's not mine.'

I rub her forearm in response. She inches her weight further into the middle of the bed so that I can sit beside her, legs stretched out, our shoulders touching as we lean against the headboard.

'I want a child so desperately,' she says eventually. 'And Ruby's been through so much . . . Look at this.' She gets up and grabs her laptop from the oak dressing-table. 'I found a blog of Selena's. Did you know that for the last few years she's been documenting Ruby's *abuse*?'

I flinch. The word sounds so harsh. Yet if what Julia is saying is true, that's exactly what it was.

She joins me on the bed and places the laptop on my legs. 'Look.'

I pull it further up my thighs. The page in front of me is pink and red, with rubies and diamonds cascading down the screen, like raindrops. The title reads 'PRECIOUS RUBY' and there is a small square photograph in the corner of the screen of Ruby in a hospital bed wired up to a drip, clutching her mouse. My heart contracts. The words make for sickening reading. If you didn't know any better, you'd think it was the blog of a caring mother, desperately worried about her child. You'd think it was about her frustration and her desire to make sure the doctors found out why her daughter was so ill. But now, in light of Julia's theory, it's disturbing. Bile rises in my throat, and I push the computer away, unable to read any more. 'Do you really think it's true?'

Julia is kneeling beside me on the bed. 'I'm looking at this without bias, I promise,' she says gently. 'I'm angry at what Selena and Nathan did. But I don't blame her. He was the one in a relationship. All of this, though, it's the classic symptoms. Numerous operations but nothing wrong. Ruby's symptoms worsening at home yet miraculously disappearing in hospital. The fact she moved Ruby to so many different GP surgeries.' She gulps. 'I'm sorry.'

'What do we do now?' I whisper.

'We need to tell the police,' she says, 'because her blog might be the reason she was killed. She had a lot of followers. What if one of them got obsessed? Or grasped what she was up to?'

I think of the guests who came and went this week: the teenage lovebirds, Janice, Dean. Then my mind turns to the Greysons. Weren't they in the medical field? I'm sure Susie said she worked at a hospital. Did she say she was a nurse? Had she ever treated Ruby and suspected what Selena was up to?

I'm just clutching at anything. But the truth remains: I don't know who to trust.

'And what about Ruby?' I whisper.

Julia rubs at her eyes. She's wearing no make-up. 'She's the most important person in all of this. We must protect her,' she says. 'At all costs.'

## 35

I leave Julia to rest but I can't forget Selena's blog, those words and that photo of Ruby in a hospital bed. How could a mother do that to her child? I'd rather die than see my daughters hurt or in pain. I can't connect this Selena to the one I knew, who seemed so protective of Ruby. There's still a huge part of me that can't believe Selena would do it and I'm still hoping that Julia's got it wrong.

I'm heading downstairs when I see Adrian standing in the doorway talking to a man I don't recognize. He's in his early fifties with grey hair and blue eyes. His face is long and thin, with a sharp nose and a large mole on one cheek. Adrian steps back to allow him in. Maybe he's a guest who wants a room for the night. Or the weekend. I bristle with anticipation and excitement. This house already had a reputation, which has only been cemented by the events of this week. If things don't pick up soon we'll struggle to pay our mortgage . . .

I stop when I reach the bottom step. Adrian's closing the door behind him and ushering the man into the living room. He glances at me over the man's head and pulls a face, as if the gas man had turned up unexpectedly to do a reading, or a parking attendant was on the prowl and we had only moments to dash back to our car. This man isn't a guest.

I follow Adrian into the front room. It's empty, apart from the three of us. We stand in the middle, uncomfortable, on edge. Adrian's acting a bit skittish around him, talking in the fake jovial way he does when he's nervous. Is this man a detective? No, he can't be. He seems too passive somehow.

I step forward and introduce myself, thrusting out a hand. He takes it and pumps it up and down a few times. His feels hot and slightly sweaty.

'Pleased to meet you,' he says. He has a soft Mancunian accent. 'I'm Nigel Perry.'

Nigel Perry. Nigel.

*Selena's husband.*

There's something vulnerable about him. He's tall and skinny, his grey suit hanging off him, the jacket slightly too short in the arms. Or maybe it's the pain behind his pale blue eyes: they burn with it.

'Please sit down. Adrian will get you some tea.'

Adrian looks glad to have an excuse to leave the room.

I take a seat opposite Nigel. He's nothing like I expected. Hearing Selena talk about him, I'd imagined a large, stocky man with an aggressive stance and a loud voice. Instead he seems mild-mannered and placid. Mum told me Selena had lied about Nigel being violent. This man doesn't look as though he has it in him. But I know, better than most, that appearances can be

338

deceiving, as they were with Selena. Child abusers don't look a certain way and neither do violent spouses.

'Have you come from Cheshire?' I ask.

'I drove down last night. I'm staying at the pub in the village. I didn't think it appropriate to stay here.' He smiles shyly.

'I'm sorry. About Selena,' I say.

'The police asked me a lot of questions. But I want to assure you that I didn't kill her. I have an alibi. She left me. But I loved her.'

'I know you couldn't have killed her,' I say. It was somebody who was in the house. 'And I believe you loved her.' Even though she probably lied to you over and over and over again.

Adrian comes in with a tray of mugs. Outside I see that it's got dark. I wonder if Mum's put the dinner on. Ruby. Is Nigel here to take her home even though he's not her biological father? My heart starts to pound and I reach for my inhaler. It's not in my pocket. I must have left it upstairs. I take a deep breath instead, trying to quell the panic and the tightness in my chest. Questions are layered in my mind. I don't know which to ask Nigel first.

Adrian hands him a mug. 'I didn't know if you took sugar,' he says apologetically.

'No sugar.' Nigel takes the mug. I notice his hand is trembling as he lifts it to his lips.

Adrian places mine on the coffee-table but I barely acknowledge it. All I can think about is the man sitting opposite me. I notice he's wearing smart lace-up shoes.

They look expensive. Selena would have liked that. She had a thing about men's shoes. She said it showed the type of man they were. If trainers were scuffed and messy it meant the man wearing them hadn't grown up. If they wore good-quality leather shoes that were polished to a shine, they were dependable and classy. I thought that was a load of crap.

I go straight for the jugular. 'I found some text messages that Selena sent you from my spare phone,' I say. 'In them you say something about a letter. What did you argue about that last night? Why did Selena leave?'

Nigel winces at my direct question. He clears his throat. 'It's – it's awkward now that she's no longer with us. You have to understand that I loved her. And Ruby. She's not my biological daughter, I always knew that, but Selena tried to make me believe she was. I'm not stupid. I knew she was already pregnant when we met. But I led her to believe I thought the baby was mine. And I loved Ruby like she was my own. However, over the years, Selena slipped away from me. I understood why. All her time was taken up looking after a chronically ill child. But lately . . . lately I've begun to wonder if she was playing up Ruby's illness.'

I don't say anything but I can see Adrian sit up straighter. 'What do you mean?' he says.

A faint blush crawls up his neck. 'She made out Ruby needed a wheelchair. It puzzled me as there was nothing wrong with the way Ruby walked. But she did get tired at times so I let it go. But when we were out and Selena

340

got attention she seemed to revel in it.' He coughs. Adrian and I wait for him to continue. 'I had my suspicions but nothing concrete, until I read a letter she'd left on the sideboard from the NHS to say that Ruby's recent allergy tests were negative. When I challenged her about it she denied it all. She said Ruby was ill and that I was jealous of the time she spent with her.' He looks stricken. 'And it's partly true. I did sometimes feel jealous.'

'What are you saying? That Selena made up Ruby's illness?' asks Adrian, in disbelief. He turns to me with a can-you-believe-this-guy look on his face. Noble and kind, Adrian looks for the good in everyone.

'My sister-in-law is a GP. She suspects the same,' I say to Nigel. Adrian's head whips round and he stares at me, his mouth hanging open.

Nigel gazes at the mug in his hands. 'Ruby heard us rowing. It was awful. We hardly argued normally, but Selena was in a right state. She accused me of calling her a liar. She was very indignant, of course. I tried to back down – after all, I didn't know what I was talking about. It was only suspicions I had. But she told me she was leaving me. I begged her . . .' His composure melts and he stops talking. I can see why she chose him. He adored her – that much is obvious. She'd told me he worked away a lot. He's not her usual type but he obviously has money so would have offered her the security she craved. She probably walked all over him. I expect this was the only time he ever questioned her mothering skills. And she couldn't bear it, so she left him.

'Would it . . . would it be possible to see Ruby?' he says, his eyes finding mine.

I experience a flicker of contempt for him. He could have stopped Ruby's abuse if he hadn't been so weak. Or so blinded by love for Selena. That child suffered and he did nothing to stop it.

'How many operations did Ruby have?' I say, my voice cold.

He looks from me to Adrian in panic. 'Um, I'm not sure exactly. I wasn't there a lot of the time. She had a number of hospital admissions. I'd say at least three or four operations . . .'

The room spins and I have to close my eyes. I feel like I'm on a fairground ride. When I open them again Adrian is leading Nigel from the room. When Adrian reaches the door, he regards me. His eyes are accusing. *You knew,* they say. *You knew and you didn't tell me.*

I wait five minutes before getting up to join them. I can barely trust myself to speak to Nigel. I hear laughter from the dining room. They're all in there: Mum, Amelia, Evie, Nathan, Ruby, and now Adrian and Nigel. Adrian is standing awkwardly by the door, surveying the scene, clearly disconcerted. Nigel has joined the others at the table and Ruby is sitting on his lap, her arms around his neck. She seems delighted to see him. Nathan looks on jealously. There is no sign of Julia. Ruby is chatting away to Nigel, about the rabbits and playing dolls with Evie.

'Am I going home with you, Daddy?' she asks, her huge eyes searching his face. He blushes.

'I have an unavoidable business trip next week.' He looks at me hopefully. 'I was wondering if you could stay with Aunty Kirsty, just until we sort everything out.'

Mum answers for me. 'Of course Ruby can stay here. For as long as she needs,' she says to Nigel.

I wonder if Selena had made a will. And what about Nathan? Now he knows he's her real father, will he want custody?

Evie looks delighted and claps excitedly. 'It's like having a twin,' she says, throwing an arm around Ruby's neck. I look towards Nathan. Someone should tell Nigel who Ruby's real father is. Will Ruby's case have to go to the family court? Or will Nathan automatically get custody? Or Mum? She is Ruby's grandmother, after all.

'Are you happy to stay here?' Nigel asks Ruby gently, and we all wait for her response. Evie and Amelia watch her with interest, their forkfuls of food paused before their mouths.

'I like it here,' she says. 'But I'll miss you and the Barn.'

'I'll come and see you again after my business trip. Okay?'

She nods eagerly.

'And you look so well, my petal,' adds Nigel.

'I feel well,' she says. 'I don't need my wheelchair or

my leg braces.' Nigel meets my eye over the top of Ruby's head and I nod in acknowledgement.

There is no mistake, much though I wish there was. The proof is right here, before our eyes. Ruby's regaining her health because there was never anything wrong with her. Selena was making her ill.

I'm with Mum clearing up in the kitchen. She had a heart-to-heart with Nigel over dinner, and I wonder if he's told her about Selena and the Munchausen syndrome by proxy?

She's loading the dishwasher and I'm wiping down the worktops when Evie comes running in. 'Mummy!' she cries. 'The wabbits. They're still in their run. They need to go back into their hutch otherwise the foxes will get them.'

'Can't it wait five minutes, honey? I've nearly finished here.'

Mum tuts. 'Don't worry, my lovely. Nana will do it.'

'No,' I say to Evie firmly, irritated with Mum for interfering. I was only going to be five minutes. Would things ever change between us? 'I'll do it. Don't worry. The rabbits will be fine.' I kiss her soft cheek and go into the garden. It's cold and dark, the light from the kitchen illuminating only the patio. I should have fetched my coat but I was making a point to Mum and didn't have time to go rooting around in the understairs cupboard. If I had, she'd be the one out here doing this. I stride across the lawn. The frost has already begun to set in and the grass crunches under my feet. I walk blindly into the darkness. As I approach I can just make out the rabbits in the distance, cuddled up in the corner of their run, and feel bad for forgetting to put them in. Usually Amelia would do it but she's seemed so distracted since she came back from Orla's. Every time I vow to talk to her about it, something comes up. I feel as if I've neglected her since Selena's death. I wish she'd talk to me about what's bothering her. She told me she doesn't know who to trust. Why would she say that?

I take my phone from my back pocket and use my torch to light the way.

I reach the run. It's under the tree and the rope swing knocks against my head as I bend down. I lift the rabbits out, and bundle first Mrs Whiskerson, then Princess into their hutch, shutting the door firmly.

I'm about to stand up again when I hear a crunch behind me. I instantly freeze. Before I can react, I feel a hand on my shoulder and I'm wrenched to my feet. I cry out but a hand is pressed firmly over my mouth. I struggle, and kick someone – I don't know who. Strong arms have grabbed me and the smell of unwashed flesh and damp clothes fills my nostrils, making me gag.

'All right, Kirsty,' says a familiar voice in my ear.

## 36

Dean.

The realization makes me struggle even more, but he has me firmly in his grip, one arm across my chest, the other clamped around my shoulders, hand over my mouth. 'Don't do anything stupid,' he hisses. He has me pinned so tightly against him that I can feel his erection prodding into my back. I'm repulsed – he's getting a kick out of this. He slowly turns us both round so that I'm facing the house. I can just see Mum in the kitchen – she seems very far away, no more than a silhouette.

'Now,' he says, 'if I take my hand away, you promise not to scream?' His voice is gruff and he sounds a little out of breath.

I nod vigorously. I pray that the children stay in the house. I can't bear the thought of them coming out to find me. I'm no match for Dean. He's nearly a foot taller and twice as strong. If he's going to hurt anyone, I'd rather it be me.

He removes his hand from my mouth but he still has his arms around me.

'I've been waiting a long time to get you on your own,' he says.

'W-what do you want?' My throat is so dry, and my

breathing so ragged, I'm surprised I can get the words out.

'I want you to tell the fucking rozzers that I had nothing to do with Selena's death. Then I'll leave you and your family alone.'

'But why would they listen to me?'

He grabs me tighter – I'm worried he'll break my ribs. 'They'll listen to you.'

'They've found your letters,' I splutter. 'They know you were blackmailing her.'

'I didn't fucking kill her,' he growls. 'She was already like that when I found her.'

I'm tempted to tell him I don't believe him but that would be stupid. I need to play along if I'm to get out of this unscathed.

'I've seen that police officer skulking around. That pretty redhead. You can tell her.'

'Okay. I will. I will.'

'I needed money. I'm in debt. But she wasn't playing ball. She wasn't stupid.'

I keep quiet. I don't want to say anything antagonistic. But he must take my silence for rebellion because, in one quick move, he's turned me round, grabbed me by the throat and pushed me against the shed so hard that I'm winded. 'Please,' I squeak.

Then something glints in the faint moonlight and I see that he has a knife. 'I'd love to cut you up so bad,' he says, his mouth pulled into the familiar snarl, his flinty eyes narrowed. 'I've always hated you.'

I want to tell him I've always thought him a nasty piece of work, but I can't breathe.

'You tell the police I had nothing to do with Selena's death. I don't care what you say. Make it up. Convince them. I'll be watching you. And those daughters of yours. You wouldn't want anything to happen to their pretty little faces, now, would you?'

I hate him so much that I could cheerfully plunge that knife into his heart. He presses his fingers deeper into my windpipe. 'Are you fucking listening?'

'Yes,' I rasp. 'I'll convince the police. Please, let me go.'

He releases me and I slump to the ground, trembling all over. He bends down and I scrunch myself into the foetal position. He touches my cheek with the point of the knife and runs the tip along my skin, as though he's doing nothing more than drawing a line on paper. It hurts and I cry out.

'Remember what I said. I'll be watching you. All of you.'

I put a hand to my cheek. There is blood on my finger. I think about screaming loud enough for my next-door neighbour, Mr Collins, or my family to hear but decide against it. If they hear me they'll come running, and then what? Dean will feel cornered. He'll attack them. I can't risk that. 'Okay, please, I'll do what you say,' I whimper. My chest feels so tight that I can hardly breathe. 'Asthma,' I tell him, as I sit up and reach into the pockets of my jeans. Then I remember I left my inhaler in the bedroom. Panic makes my airways close even further and I clutch my chest. Dean grins: sinister, disturbing, full of menace. He stands back and watches me gasping for breath on the ground. Then he does that weird salute and turns on his heel, as if he's on parade. I watch in disbelief as he jumps over the wall that separates our garden from the graveyard, then everything goes black.

Someone is shining a light in my eyes. 'Kirsty. Can you hear me? You've had an asthma attack. But you're okay now.' A paramedic is leaning over me. She says something to the man next to her who's also wearing a fluorescent jacket. I'm shivering uncontrollably. I have an oxygen mask over my face and I take deep, grateful breaths. Someone has thrown a blanket over my shoulders and I pull it around me. I can't get warm.

'Can you stand up?' asks the paramedic.

I nod. 'I think so.'

It's then that I notice Mum and Adrian hovering uncertainly to the side of me.

'Thank goodness,' says Mum, and Adrian wraps his arms around me, helping me to my feet. I'm feeling desperate. I need to tell them about Dean, before he gets away.

I pull the mask away from my face despite the words of protest from the paramedics. 'It's Dean,' I say to Adrian, between gasps. 'He was here. He grabbed me. He cut my face – he ran off. You need to tell the police.'

'What?'

'Dean. Here. Call the police,' I rasp, before the male paramedic – a young guy with very short hair – forces the mask back over my face. They lead me towards the house, as if I'm old and infirm. Adrian has broken away from us and is speaking urgently into his mobile. I hope it's not too late.

I'm on the sofa tucked up in one of our spare duvets, Amelia and Evie on either side of me. I'm so happy to see them that I can't stop hugging them. Amelia, for once, isn't trying to get away but burrows into me. I feel calmer now, my breathing more even. The paramedics wanted to take me to the hospital but I refused to go. They could see that their suggestion was upsetting me so they gave me a stronger steroid inhaler and made me promise to go straight to A and E if my breathing got worse. In normal circumstances, I would have done exactly as they'd asked and gone to hospital but I can't leave the girls here, knowing Dean is out there some-where. Luckily the cut to my cheek wasn't deep so they've just put a big padded plaster over it. I'm told it looks worse than it is.

Mum is fussing. She's brought me a cup of tea and is perched opposite, urging me to drink it. 'It has sugar in it,' she says. 'For the shock.'

Adrian sits with Ruby on the other sofa. I notice Nigel has disappeared. He must have felt a bit out of place while the drama was unfolding.

Ruby is watching me with wide, round eyes. She looks petrified.

'It's okay,' I say to her. 'I'm okay now.'

'You collapsed,' she says matter-of-factly.

I pull a funny face to cheer her up. 'It was my fault. Silly me. I forgot my inhaler.'

She chews her bottom lip. She has more colour in her cheeks now, but she's still painfully thin. My girls are like whippets too, especially Amelia, who seems to have had a growth spurt. It's more than just being thin, though – Ruby has that sickly pallor. Wan, I think it's called. Although over the last day or so I've noticed more colour in her cheeks.

'I thought the ambulance was for me,' she says, biting her nails.

I'm not surprised. The poor child has seen more than her fair share of ambulances and hospitals. 'Not for you, honey,' I say, 'not any more. You're getting better now. Don't you feel better?'

'You certainly look better,' adds Adrian, smiling at her encouragingly.

'I do,' she says seriously. 'But Mummy said I'll be ill for ever.'

'Sometimes mummies are wrong,' I say gently. 'Aunty Julia is a doctor and she says you're getting better.'

Ruby hugs her toy mouse to her and I can see that Selena's name has evoked a painful memory. 'No more ambulances?'

'Hopefully not,' I say, and see her relax. I catch Mum's eye. If I didn't know better I'd say her eyes were smarting with tears. But it must be my imagination, or a trick of the light, as she stands up, suddenly officious again. 'Right, girls, let's go upstairs and have a bath. How would you all like to sleep in the same room tonight? Like a giant sleepover?'

'In our bedroom?' asks Evie.

'Yes. We'll find a spare bed for Ruby. Now that she's staying for a while we can all move into the attic, don't you think, Kirsty?'

I smile at Mum gratefully.

Adrian told me Mum had found me. She'd gone looking for me when I didn't return to the house. She'd called the ambulance and sat cradling me in her lap until it arrived.

Now she touches the duvet over my knee, tenderness on her face. She doesn't say anything. She doesn't have to.

She ushers the girls out, although Amelia looks back a few times, as though checking I'm still in one piece. I smile at her. 'I'll be up to say goodnight soon,' I promise.

When they've gone, Adrian sits beside me and takes my hand. 'The police should be here soon.'

'They're taking their time,' I say, glancing at the clock on the mantelpiece. 'It's been over half an hour since you called them. I'm worried.'

'He's not going to risk coming back tonight,' says

Adrian, tucking the duvet closer around me. 'It's nice being the one to look after you, for a change.'

I fight the urge to bat him away, then decide it doesn't mean I'm weak if I give in to it for a few minutes. So I rest my head on his shoulder and admit to him how scared I was.

'I want to fucking kill him!' he says, into my hair.

I move away from him and laugh gently. The thought of Adrian hurting anyone is absurd. He's never been in a fight in his life. Even at school he'd managed to talk his way out of conflict. Not because he has the gift of the gab – he doesn't – but because he's a natural peace-maker. He's never had any violent tendencies – before or after his breakdown.

There's a soft rapping on the front door and I stiffen, imagining that Dean has come back to kill us all.

'It'll be the police,' says Adrian, getting up. 'Don't worry.'

My heart is pounding as he leaves the room. I can just about see him as he opens the door. He steps aside to let Rachel in. She's beaming, her red hair almost bronze under the overhead light. With her porcelain skin, she resembles a beautiful statue.

'It's great news,' she says, beaming widely. 'We've caught Dean.'

## 37

I feel an overwhelming sense of relief. The threat that has been hanging over me – over us – all week has gone. I don't think I'd realized, until now, how on edge I've been feeling, with Dean up in those mountains, watching us, biding his time, like a predator, until he was ready to pounce. Hopefully the police will charge him and we can get on with our lives as best we can.

I'm alone in the living room. I've sent Adrian to ask if Nathan's okay. I haven't seen him or Julia for hours. I'm not even sure they're in the house. I feel drained after everything that's happened and my eyelids are heavy . . .

I must have fallen asleep because when I open my eyes Julia is sitting beside me.

'I'm so sorry I wasn't here,' she says, clasping my hands in hers. They feel cold and her cheeks are ruddy, as if she's just come in from a brisk walk. 'Your mum has just told me what happened.'

'Where were you?'

She looks sheepish. 'Out. With Nathan. We decided to go for a stroll around the village. We've talked . . .'

'And?'

'It's going to be a long road ahead. I don't know if I'll

ever be able to forgive him. But we have Ruby to think about. She needs a mother and a father now. I don't know how it's all going to work – if Nathan will even get custody of her – but he's her real father and he wants to get to know her. She has no idea yet that he's her dad. We can't rush it but . . .'

I squeeze her hand. 'I'm so pleased.'

'Ruby's been through so much.'

'She knew, I think,' I say, 'about what Selena was doing. That she wasn't as ill as her mother made out.'

Julia frowns. 'How do you know?'

'Because Nigel – Selena's husband – turned up earlier. I think Ruby overheard part of their row.' I fill her in on what he said. As I'm talking, Julia's face turns a strange colour and she looks as though she's about to faint. 'Julia?' I say, concerned.

'Oh, God.' She groans, putting her head in her hands.

'What? What is it?' I'm half standing up, the duvet gathered under my armpits, ready to call someone.

She indicates for me to sit down, so I do. I wait for her to say more.

She collects herself and straightens, a look of resolve in her eyes. 'It's nothing. Really. I've not eaten. I'm just feeling a bit faint, that's all.'

'Okay,' I say, although I don't believe her. When I spoke about Ruby and Nigel something seemed to occur to her. But I can't press her on it. She's already closing up.

Maybe it's something to do with the Munchausen syndrome by proxy. 'Ruby's health definitely seems to be improving. Do you still think it was all fabricated? Ruby's illness, I mean?'

She nods. 'I really do. Selena has had a traumatic past. Your mum told me about her upbringing and how she was treated by her own mother. Maybe she was getting the attention she felt she deserved through Ruby. I don't know.'

I remember how she'd looked at Evie in the garden that day, with something close to hatred. Was it because Evie was getting the attention she felt she and Ruby deserved? I suppose I'll never know.

'It's just so sad,' I say, my eyes filling with tears at the thought of Ruby being subjected to that. And then I remember something. 'Before you and Nathan arrived, Selena woke me in the middle of the night. She said Ruby was fitting. But when the paramedics arrived she was fine. She woke me and Adrian saying her phone had died. When they were at the hospital I found her phone. It was partly charged.'

'She wanted the attention from you and Adrian. That's why she called you before she phoned for the ambulance. For the drama. I doubt Ruby even had a seizure. She probably had a temperature that would have gone down with Calpol.'

'I tried to give her some Calpol but she walked away,' I say, remembering. 'Now I know why.'

We stare at each other in silence. Eventually Julia

says, 'Ruby will never have to go through that again. At least something good has come out of Selena's death.'

The next morning Mum accompanies Nathan, Julia and Ruby to the park. I know they're planning to tell her the truth about who her dad is. I watch them troop out of the house with a heavy heart. Ruby's already been through so much.

'You'd better tell the girls,' says Adrian, watching me.

'She's my niece,' I say, as it hits me for the first time.

I go upstairs to find Amelia and Evie. I still feel slightly breathless but I have my inhaler with me. Evie is playing with her teddies in the corner of her bedroom and Amelia is lying on the bed with her diary resting on her knees. Her expression is dark. She's never been a smiley child, but over the last few days she seems almost shrouded in misery. I sit beside her on the bed and see the words 'I HAVE A SECRET' in large letters before she whips away the diary, snapping it shut.

'What do you want?' she barks.

I wonder whether to mention what I've just read. I decide on another tack. 'Honey, is everything okay? You've not been yourself for days.'

She scowls. 'Duh, not surprising when someone has died here.'

I ignore the smart-alec comment. 'Is that all it is? Why did you come back early from Orla's house?'

She sticks out her lower lip. In that moment she

reminds me of Evie, despite the difference in their colouring. 'She was asking too many questions about Selena. It was upsetting me.'

I stroke her hair. 'You've been amazing with Ruby. I'm proud of you,' I say.

She shrugs me off.

'Amelia? Please talk to me.'

She glances at Evie and, without a word, stands up and leaves the room. Evie is oblivious, talking in a high-pitched voice to her teddies. I follow, wondering where Amelia has flounced off to.

She's sitting at the top of the stairs with her head in her hands, staring towards the picture window on the floor below. The view is hazy, the mountains obscured by mist again. I resist the urge to rush over to her. I join her on the steps. 'Budge up,' I say, bumping her with my hip. She moves over. We sit in silence for a while and then she surprises me by burying her face in my armpit. I smooth back her hair. 'Oh, honey, what is it?'

She's not crying but I can tell she's distressed. I cuddle her to me without speaking, hoping she'll open up. I don't want to say anything that will make her bolt. Eventually she pulls away. 'Moo?' I look into her eyes. 'Please tell me what's going on. Is it Selena or is there something else?' She's wearing a hoody in a cobalt blue that's too big for her and looks so young and vulnerable that I just want to hug her to me.

She sniffs but there are no tears. Her face is white, strained. 'It's Ruby.'

My stomach clenches. 'Ruby?'

'Before Selena died, I saw her. Up here.'

I blink at her. 'Up here?'

'Yes. I got up to go to the loo and saw her. Sitting on the landing in her pyjamas. It was like she was waiting for something.'

Or someone. It sounds like Selena had been with Dean that night – even if they'd met up just for her to tell him to get lost. Maybe Ruby woke up, saw that Selena wasn't there, and panicked.

'Okay.'

'When she saw me, she put her fingers to her lips. I didn't know what to do but when I came out of the toilet she'd gone.' The blue vein near her eye is prominent, like it always is when she's tired or stressed. 'I didn't understand how she could get up here when she was supposed to be so ill.'

I play with her fingers, unfolding them from my hand. She has glittery blue varnish on her nails. I wonder where she got it from. I can't remember buying it for her. Maybe she did it at Orla's.

'I don't think Ruby is as sick as we first thought. Selena was . . . making it up.' I hate having to tell her something so awful.

'Making it up? Why?'

'It's a long story. And something we won't ever be able to fully understand.'

'So that's why Ruby could get up here. I thought it had something to do with Aunty Julia.'

'Aunty Julia? What do you mean?'

'When I came out of the toilet Aunty Julia was on the landing. Down there.' She points to the floor below, where the guest bedrooms are. 'She and Selena were hissing at each other. I could tell they were trying to be quiet. I couldn't hear what they were saying but Aunty Julia looked really angry.'

I feel a cold lurch of dread. 'Arguing? What time was it?'

She looks unsure. 'I don't know. It was still dark. But not long afterwards I heard your screams.' She looks doubtful. 'Am I in trouble?'

I pat her knee. 'No, of course not.'

She picks at the nail varnish on her fingers. 'When I got back into bed I saw Ruby sitting on our floor playing with Evie's toys and that china doll. I told her to go back to her room. It was so weird. I thought I was dreaming.'

I remember Evie telling me that her things were being moved about. Not a ghost, just Ruby sneaking upstairs to play.

'And where was Evie?'

'She was asleep. Fast asleep.'

For once she hadn't come into our room.

'I whispered at Ruby to go. I felt bad, but I wanted to go back to sleep,' she says. 'I saw Ruby leave and then I must have dropped off.'

My heart sinks when I think of Julia. What was she arguing with Selena about at that time of the morning?

Did she already know that Nathan was Ruby's real father? Did she push Selena in a fit of anger? Of jealousy? But that can't be right. Julia wouldn't do that. Would she? Julia is sensible, level-headed. She's not prone to emotional outbursts. She thinks with her head, not her heart. Nevertheless, I feel unnerved by Amelia's words.

My mind is reeling. I don't know what to think. 'Did you . . . did you say anything to the police or Rachel about this?'

She hesitates. 'Well . . . no. Rachel asked where I was but I said me and Evie were in bed, which was true.'

I squeeze her hand. 'Yes. It's okay. But, honey, why didn't you say before?'

'I didn't want to get Ruby or Julia into trouble. I thought you'd be cross with Ruby if you knew she wasn't really ill and . . . I was worried it might have been her.'

'What do you mean?'

'Who pushed Selena.'

I frown. Is that what she's been worried about this whole time? That Ruby killed Selena? The idea is ludicrous. 'Oh, honey, Ruby wouldn't have done that. What makes you say it?'

'Because she lied. About where she was. She never told anyone that she was upstairs.'

'She's only seven. She would have been worried about getting into trouble, that's all. She probably wanted to see where her mother was. Selena shouldn't have left her.' If only she'd stayed in her own bed that night instead of wandering around meeting Dean, if that's what she'd been doing. I frown. But Dean was blackmailing her. They weren't lovers, like I'd first thought, so she probably hadn't been with him. So where had she been? What really happened in those early hours before she was found at the bottom of the stairs?

Amelia adds, 'And Ruby gave me a letter she'd found. It was written to Selena. It sounded a bit threatening and I didn't know what to do with it. Ruby told me I couldn't show it to anyone as she'd get into trouble for reading it. So I hid it in your drawer.'

So that's how the note had got there.

'Thank you for being honest, Moo. You can always tell me anything, okay?'

She stands up. 'Can I go now?' she says. She doesn't look like a child who's just unburdened herself, and I worry that there is still something on her mind. Something else she's keeping from me.

# 38

I survey Julia over lunch.

Ruby is chattering away to her – she's a different child from the one who arrived with Selena. Julia says something to make her laugh and she gives a proper giggle. Mum is fussing around them, a role she excels in, dishing out cheese and ham sandwiches. She's happy – she's humming a little tune to herself. Nathan, Amelia and Evie sit opposite Julia and Ruby, and my brother is watching his daughter with pure pleasure. The scene before me should fill me with delight but I feel only dread. I don't want to believe it, of course I don't, but it swills around my head, like coffee beans in a grinder: *Did Julia already know that Nathan was Ruby's father? And, if so, did she kill Selena so she could have all of this?*

Selena was abusing her daughter. She wasn't the woman I'd thought she was. She was despicable. Twisted. Sick. Quite frankly, Ruby's better off without her. Yet my feelings for Selena can't just be erased. She was part of my childhood. She deserved to be punished, yes, but not to die. She needed professional help. Julia makes people better, she helps them. She's not a killer. Is she?

'Earth to Kirsty.'

I jolt, realizing that someone's talking to me. It's Nathan. He's grinning at me inanely.

'Mum's on a totally different planet,' deadpans Amelia.

'Sorry. I was miles away.'

'Dreaming of Ryan Gosling again?' teases Julia.

I try to smile back at her but it's more of a grimace. I need to talk to her. I can't just let this go. But if she admits it, do I hand her over to the police? Sensible, honest Kirsty, who's always tried to do the right thing, to abide by the law. I'm already keeping Mum's huge secret, and that's one thing. Mum didn't kill Uncle Owen. She helped shield Selena. But if Julia did push Selena down the stairs . . .

Julia gets up and comes over to me. 'Are you okay?' she asks gently, touching my arm.

'I need to speak to you. Alone,' I say, through clenched teeth. Her eyes widen in surprise but she addresses Nathan in what Amelia calls the fake-happy voice, telling him we'll be back shortly.

We go into the living room. Adrian is still out on his run and I hope he doesn't come back and interrupt us.

'What's this about?' she asks. 'You seem cross.'

'There's no easy way to ask this. But please be honest with me. Did you push Selena down the stairs?'

She's staring at me as though I've just metamorph-osed into an animal. Her obvious shock almost makes me want to laugh. Under other circumstances I would have. But I'm terrified of her reply. I'm holding my breath.

'No. Of course not. Why do you ask that?'

She sounds genuine.

'Amelia heard you arguing with Selena. Just before she died.'

Julia's eyebrows almost disappear into her hair. 'I wasn't arguing with her. She was getting agitated with me. She kept asking me about the symptoms of ME and I said I thought Ruby didn't have it. Then she turned nasty, said something about how she'd met up with Nathan earlier, but I shut the door in her face, not wanting to listen to her any longer. I thought she was acting oddly, to be honest. But now, with the Munch-ausen syndrome by proxy, it makes sense. She wanted me to validate that her daughter was ill.'

'What? She asked you all this at five thirty in the morning?'

Julia looks down at her feet. My God, she's lying.

She pushes her hair off her face. 'I didn't kill her,' she mumbles.

'Then what happened?'

She looks towards the door, as though worried we'll be overheard. 'I went downstairs to see where Nathan was. We'd rowed, as you know. I found him asleep on the sofa in the playroom. I was going back up when I saw Selena come out of her room. I'd woken her, she said. Then she started asking me about ME but I was angry with her. I knew, you see. I've known for years that she and Nathan slept together.'

'*What?*'

'I found out at the time. Nathan isn't very good at deception. I didn't realize who Selena was then, of course. I just thought she was some floozy he'd met when he was visiting his friends. I found text messages and read what he said about it being a one-night stand. So I decided not to say anything. I knew what we had was worth something. And then I came here and saw the way they were with each other and I knew. I mean, Selena isn't a common name.'

She knew. All this time and she'd said nothing.

I obviously don't know Julia as well as I'd thought.

I go to the sofa and sit down. I'm exhausted. She joins me. 'Are you okay?'

'I'm fine, just in shock. Carry on.'

'I told Selena I knew about her and Nathan. I was pissed off and angry and I stalked off upstairs. She followed me. She came into my room, we argued. She told me about Ruby. I was furious as that was something I'd never guessed. She told me she'd already informed Nathan. I shouted at her to get out. We argued a bit more. And then I closed the door on her. I went back to bed and burst into tears. That's honestly what happened, I promise.'

'Did you tell the police?' I ask, even though I know the answer. She had a motive. If she'd told the police the truth they would have whisked her down to the station.

She looks ashamed. 'No . . . There's something else.' She lifts her eyes to mine. 'When I closed the door on Selena I saw something in the attic. It was Ruby. I didn't give it much thought. But when you said Ruby had overheard Selena and Nigel arguing and knew the truth about her illness, well, that's when I realized . . .'

'What?'

She sighs. 'More wondered, I suppose. Kirsty, the last person to see Selena alive was Ruby.'

Is Julia just saying this to deflect suspicion from herself? But then I remember what Amelia told me. Ruby had been upstairs just before Selena was pushed.

I grab my inhaler and take three puffs. 'Have you told the police any of this?'

Julia shakes her head. 'No.'

I suppose she couldn't, or her argument with Selena might have come out. 'But Ruby wouldn't have harmed Selena. She's just a little girl. It was Dean. He's a violent, nasty thug. It was him.'

She leans towards me and lowers her voice. 'Did anyone see Dean that morning?'

I think back. It's all a blur now. All I can remember is finding Selena's body, the fear and horror that came afterwards. I'm hot with panic and fumble with the neckline of my jumper. 'I don't know. I don't think so.'

Nobody suspected Ruby because everyone assumed she was in her room, asleep. Too ill and weak to climb stairs. But she was there. And she might have been vengeful and angry.

'She's a clever girl,' says Julia, out of the blue. 'She would have known what Selena was doing. Maybe even before she overheard her argument with Nigel. But Selena didn't feed her properly. She made her weak. If Ruby hadn't put two and two together before, it wouldn't have taken her long once she was staying here. Especially if Selena made out she'd had that seizure when she must have known she hadn't.'

I move towards the window and stare out into the dank sky. The trees bend and stretch in the wind, like they're doing an aerobics class. Adrian will be home any second. And I'm sure we'll hear from Rachel soon. If not today, then tomorrow. They can only hold Dean so long without charging him. She'd let me know either way, I'm sure. And if they charged Dean, based on what happened to me, coupled with the blackmail, then he'll hopefully be sent to prison. But he could be innocent of Selena's death. Maybe he was telling me the truth last night. His attack might have been a desperate attempt to clear his name. He told me he'd seen her lying there that morning but had run off without helping her. If he had stopped to help, he might have been able to save her.

'What do we do?' says Julia. I turn to her. She looks devastated. Her eyes are pleading. But I don't know what to believe. She'd argued with Selena and she'd lied about it.

'We do nothing,' I say simply. 'Ruby's been through enough. She's already lost so much of her life, thanks to Selena.'

More secrets and lies. I, always such a follower of rules, am now withholding vital information from the police.

Julia nods. 'But she could have killed. How will I ever know?'

'You and Nathan just need to love her,' I say. 'If she did push Selena it would have been a moment of desperation after years of abuse.' The abused fighting back: how can that be wrong? Yet I'd judged Selena for doing so after Aunt Bess's abuse.

I close my eyes, rubbing my temples. I don't know what to believe any more.

# 39

### *Four days after*

Nathan and Julia decide to stay on for another few days. Rachel has advised them to get a solicitor who specializes in family law. She doesn't think there will be a problem as Nigel is happy to state he believes Ruby should be with her biological father, supported by us. He was never around much anyway, thanks to his job. That was how Selena was able to get away with the abuse for such a long time. I'm sure Nigel loves Ruby in his own way. He just doesn't want to have to be responsible for her full time.

Dean's been arrested and Ruby is gaining strength by the day. If she did push Selena, I don't believe it would have been a deliberate act but a moment of madness. I guess none of us will ever really know what took place at the top of the stairs that day. There are still moments when I doubt Julia. After all, she had a motive and she had been arguing with Selena. But it's Amelia who worries me most. She should be happier now she's spoken to me about her fears, but nothing has changed. She still seems morose, spending hours in her room sketching or writing in her diary. *I'VE GOT A SECRET.*

Sometimes, at breakfast or lunch, she glances at Evie and Ruby with something akin to distrust on her face. I wonder if she's jealous of the close bond they've formed. They talk as though they're much more than cousins. Like sisters. *Twins*. It's how Selena and I used to act, all those years ago.

After breakfast I find Amelia in her bedroom. The lack of guests means there's not much to do. I don't even know if I'll advertise for another cleaner. I need to see if business picks up first. I try not to think about what we'll do if it doesn't.

The wind is rattling the window panes and from here I can see the mountains through the rain and mist. I don't want to leave, despite all that's happened here. I'm hoping the Brecons will start to feel like a haven again.

Amelia is lying on her bed, the art pad resting on her knees as she scribbles away. At the bottom, horizontal to her and Evie's beds, is the futon we made up for Ruby. I switch the light on, making a comment about straining her eyes in the darkness. She doesn't look up but carries on sketching, the pencil flying across the paper as she shades in an area of hair.

I sit on the edge of her bed and stroke the duvet cover. It has butterflies and birds all over it, pretty but not too girly. 'Moo,' I begin, wondering what I'm going to say. 'I'm still worried about you.'

'I'm fine,' she says, her eyes still on the page. She's drawing a girl in the style of Manga. It's impressive. But the drawing is dark and angry. Punky. I remember the drawing I saw the other day of a young girl running away from a ghost. Why won't she draw happy things?

'You're clearly not fine,' I persist. 'Is it because you've got to go back to school tomorrow?' I know it's more than that.

She shakes her head. 'No. School's fine, I suppose.'

'I thought you hated it.'

'It's okay.' She doesn't lift the pencil from the page and the tip scratches as it makes contact.

I watch her, wondering what else to say. 'Are you happy with Ruby staying with us for a while?' She doesn't say anything. 'Moo?'

She turns to me, her pencil poised above the page. Her large eyes, so like Adrian's, are sad. 'I'm fine about it. I like Ruby.'

'Then what is it? Because I know there's something. Something is worrying you and you're never going to be happy unless you tell me what it is.'

She sighs, and I think she's going to turn away from me, but suddenly she closes her book and puts down her pencil. 'You wouldn't believe me even if I told you. Sometimes I think I must have dreamed it.'

'What? What do you think you saw?'

She closes her eyes and balls her hands into fists, pressing them into her eye sockets. It's how she used to cry as a little girl and I put my hand on her shoulder. 'Sweets?'

Her shoulders shudder. 'I don't want to get Evie into trouble. She doesn't know.'

I brush her hair back from her face. 'What doesn't she know?'

She takes her hands away from her face. But without looking at me she whispers, 'That she killed Selena.'

My scalp prickles. 'What do you mean?'

She sobs. 'I saw what happened. After Ruby left and I went back to bed I think I fell asleep. But then I heard a noise. I sat up and saw that Evie wasn't in bed.'

My heart starts to thud. 'Okay.'

'I know she sometimes goes into your room. And I thought I'd come in too. The door was open, and I realized I must have forgotten to lock it again after I went to the toilet. I was worried that someone – that someone had taken her . . .'

Oh, Amelia. She hasn't been immune to my fears and now I've made them her own. I hate myself for causing her anxiety. Adrian's right. I need to curb this over-protectiveness before I damage the girls.

'. . . so I got up and saw her on the landing below. I think she was sleepwalking again. Like she did that time before. I was worried she was going to fall so I went after her. And then I saw Selena coming out of Julia's room and she startled Evie. I heard Evie mumble something about a ghost and she pushed Selena.' Tears seep out of her eyes. 'She didn't mean to. She thought Selena was a ghost. And she did look like a ghost, Mummy, in that long white gown. And Evie was asleep. She didn't know what she'd done. And it was so spooky.' Her tears are flowing fast now. 'Evie had this weird glazy look on her face. I saw Selena topple over and Evie just walked back upstairs, really calmly. I ran over to her and I could tell she was asleep. And you always said,' she sniffs, 'you said never to wake up Evie if she's sleepwalking, remember? So I led her back to bed. And I was too scared to do anything so I just went back to my own bed and kept my eyes closed really tightly, hoping it was a nightmare. And then I heard you get up. I thought you'd see Selena and get help and Selena would be okay. I never thought . . .' She's sobbing now. 'I never thought she'd die.'

I feel like I might be sick. 'Oh, God,' I say. I pull my sobbing child into my arms and hold her as she cries. She's been carrying the weight of this around with her all week. 'It's okay,' I say, even if it's not. 'It will be okay, it's just an accident.'

'So it wasn't Dean,' she says. 'He was telling the truth.'

Dean. He might not have killed Selena but he's still guilty of a lot else: nearly killing me, blackmailing Selena, helping her bury Uncle Owen. And I realize, much to my surprise, that I'm happy to let Dean take the rap for this. Because the alternative would hurt Evie.

'Listen to me,' I say, grasping her hands. 'It was an accident, okay? Evie wouldn't have done it on purpose. She was sleepwalking and she saw Selena and thought she was a ghost. You know how over-imaginative Evie is? Dean is a bad man. He's done a lot of bad things. We can't tell Evie about this, okay?' I feel terrible asking her to keep such a secret. But what would happen if

I told the police? Would they take Evie away from us? They may think she has mental health issues. They may not believe that it was an accident. And then Evie would never be allowed to forget what she did. I can't let that happen.

All these years I've been afraid of someone hurting the girls, yet one of them has taken a life.

'Don't carry the burden of this, honey,' I say sternly. 'You've told me now. Let me take it from you. Evie must never know. I don't know what it would do to her.'

Amelia sniffs and rubs her sleeve across her eyes. 'Okay.'

'We have to try to move on now. Selena wasn't the person we thought she was. She made out that Ruby was sick when she wasn't. She was a bad mother. Okay?'

'So Evie's done Ruby a favour?' she asks, her face brightening.

I cringe inwardly. It sounds awful to put it like that. But, in a way, she's right. 'Yes, she saved Ruby, really. And we must be thankful for that.'

# 40

*Five months later*

It's two days into the Easter holidays and we have a full house for the first time since half-term. It's not been easy: the bookings dried up after Selena's murder, but then Dean was arrested, and charged, and slowly people started staying here again. Luckily, Selena's murder only warranted a small piece in the national newspapers: a domestic killing isn't that rare nowadays, according to Rachel. If it had been a stranger attack or a serial killer, that would have been different. Yet I've no doubt that the real truth would have grabbed headlines.

It's been a steep learning curve, particularly for my relationship with Mum. Having to live and work together hasn't been easy. We've never talked about Selena or Uncle Owen. It's as though she's put them in a box in her mind somewhere, taped up and stored away. Some things never change, and Mum has always found it hard to talk about feelings. But she only has to look at Ruby to see exactly what went on. Even she can't fail to notice just how much Ruby's changed since Selena's death. It's obvious to everyone now that Ruby doesn't have Crohn's, ME or any food allergy. The only thing she suffers from is mild asthma. I don't like to think too much about what Selena did to that poor child to make her so ill. Julia had some ideas, and once mentioned deliberate starvation, but I sensed she was too sickened to go into details. I've read up about Munchausen syndrome by proxy now and it's a condition I'll never understand. It goes against every instinct I have as a mother.

It's lovely to see how much Ruby has blossomed: she's put on weight, goes to her local school, and seems content living with Nathan and Julia in Cardiff. They come and stay often. Julia rings me once a week with an update. Things haven't been all plain sailing, of course. The adjustment for Ruby has been difficult and sometimes she acts up. Despite everything, she misses Selena.

Dean is still awaiting trial. He denies the charge, protesting his innocence. What he did to me has undermined his defence, though. The prosecution will no doubt use the attack on me as proof that Dean has violent tendencies.

Sometimes I feel guilty knowing he'll probably go down for a murder he didn't commit. But I'm a mother. My children come first, before anything. And it's not like Evie did it in cold blood. She's just a little girl.

Sometimes it hits me how similar I am to Selena. She was as ruthless in how she went about persuading everyone Ruby was ill as I am in guarding my daughter's innocence. I've learned a lot about myself since Selena died. I've discovered I'm not so law-abiding after all.

Amelia seems happier at school and is finally making friends. She has a nice little group, and they all live locally. I'm trying to pluck up the courage to let her walk to school with them. She hardly mentions her London friends.

Even the locals have started to accept us. Mrs Gummage speaks directly to me when I go into the chemist now, instead of through Evie (although there's never been an apology from her or Nancy), and the other day Lydia waved at me from her front garden.

The only people who know what really happened to Selena are Adrian, Amelia and me.

Julia still believes that Ruby pushed her mother down the stairs and I've never corrected her. It doesn't escape me how willing I am to threaten Julia's relationship with her adoptive daughter in order to protect my own with Evie.

Adrian was shocked when I told him about Evie. He said he'd had his suspicions that it had been Julia. When he'd gone out for his run that morning, he'd seen Julia go into the playroom. That must have been when she was checking on Nathan. That's why he'd been so defensive: he'd thought he was protecting her. He's still hiding things and so am I.

Evie goes about her life in ignorance of her crime, her wonderful imagination intact. I'd hate her to know the truth. She was upset when Ruby left: she's got it into her head that they're twins despite the year's difference in their ages. But they're coming to stay next week and she's so excited.

There have been a few issues with Evie since Selena died.

She's become even more obsessed with the china doll she calls Lucinda. She takes it everywhere with her and won't go to bed without it. I was hoping it was just a phase but, so far, there are no signs of it waning. I've wondered a lot about where it came from. Was it from Violet Brown's day? Or after? Another of the house's secrets, and I doubt I'll ever get to the bottom of it.

Her flights of fancy that I've always loved have taken a slightly darker turn. Last week she upset Amelia by saying Ruby was her real sister, not her. And then the other day I heard her trying to convince Amelia that she could understand animals like Dr Dolittle. It had sent chills through me because she had sounded just like Selena.

I'm in the kitchen. The sun is shining and the birds are singing. It's at times like this that I'm so thankful we moved to the country. The bi-fold doors are open and I can see Evie from where I'm wiping down worktops. Amelia is on the trampoline and Evie has Princess on her lap. She's grooming the rabbit with a comb.

I hear a scream. It's Evie. The rabbit is on the floor, hopping away, and she's holding her hand. 'Princess bit me,' she sobs. 'She bit me.'

I run over to her and examine her hand. It's just a

little nip. 'It's because you're being too rough with her,' I say.

'Stupid rabbit,' she hisses, stamping her foot. 'I don't want her any more. I hate her!' She throws down the comb and storms into the house.

I pick up Princess, glancing over to Amelia. She catches my eye. 'I thought she could speak to animals,' she says drily.

I can't bring myself to laugh. These days, Evie's either quiet and withdrawn, whispering to that horrible doll, or she's overreacting and having tantrums.

I return Princess to her hutch. 'Evie's acting a bit oddly. Have you noticed?'

Amelia stops bouncing, chewing her lip. 'She's always been a bit odd.'

I flash Amelia a reassuring smile and she continues jumping up and down, the trampoline squeaking rhythmically. I don't want to worry her.

I walk back into the house, my heart heavy. Evie used to love animals. She was so gentle and kind. Lately there have been times when I wonder if Evie pushed Selena on purpose. That, desperate for Ruby to stay, she'd do anything to make it happen. Perhaps Ruby admitted to Evie that her mother was making her ill. I'm wondering if I should take Evie to see a counsellor. Maybe she does remember what she did to Selena. Perhaps it's sitting there in her little brain, ready to explode, and it's coming out in her behaviour.

No. She's not capable of that. She's just a little girl. It

was an accident. I know that, really. Evie's *nothing* like Selena. So what if she's a bit fanciful at times? She's only seven.

And even if Evie did mean to push Selena, I'd keep her secret. Of course I would.

Because my daughters are my world and I'd do anything – *anything* – to protect them.

# Do Not Disturb
## Reading Group Questions

1. How do you think the author used the landscape of Wales to convey the mood of the characters in the story?

2. In what ways do you think Adrian's illness affected his relationship with Kirsty? If she had been more open with him about her fears, do you think it might have changed the outcome of the story?

3. Selena and Kirsty are both mothers, but how do their roles as parents differ? Why do you think this is?

4. Who did you think was responsible for the strange incidents in the guesthouse? Do you believe that a house can be haunted by its past?

5. To what extent do you believe a person's upbringing determines their future? How does this shape your opinion of Selena?

6. Do you think Evie was really sleepwalking? Does this make her responsible on some level, or not?

Discuss whether Kirsty was justified in hiding this information from the police.

7. Kirsty, Adrian and Amelia are the only people who know what Evie did. How do you think this will affect their relationship with her?

8. Do you think Julia will ever be able to accept Ruby as her daughter, knowing what she does about her parentage? How do you think her struggles with fertility might affect her view of the situation?

9. Do you think anyone was punished unfairly at the end of the novel – or not enough? Did you believe Nigel was guilty of Selena's accusations?

10. Kirsty says that 'my daughters are my world and I'd do anything – *anything* – to protect them'. How far would you go to protect your loved ones? Can this motive excuse any action?

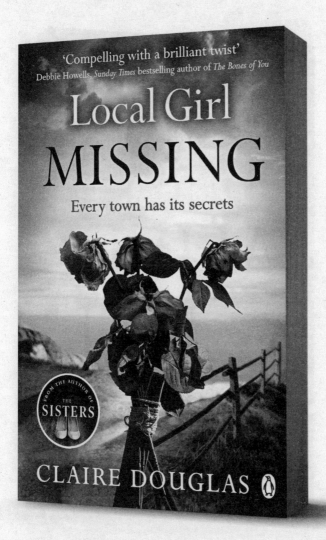

Available now

THE *SUNDAY TIMES* BESTSELLER

FROM THE AUTHOR OF
Local Girl
MISSING

Last Seen
ALIVE

CLAIRE
DOUGLAS

'Thrillingly tense and twisty'
B A Paris